Erica Munro lives on the Black Isle in the Highlands of Scotland.

Also by Erica Munro

Guilty Feet

DATING GAMES

Erica Munro

PIATKUS

Visit the Piatkus website!

Piatkus publishes a wide range of bestselling fiction and
non-fiction, including books on health, mind body & spirit, sex,
self-help, cookery, biography and the paranormal.

If you want to:
- read descriptions of our popular titles
- buy our books over the Internet
- take advantage of our special offers
- enter our monthly competition
- learn more about your favourite Piatkus authors

VISIT OUR WEBSITE AT: **www.piatkus.co.uk**

Copyright © Erica Munro 2005

First published in Great Britain in 2005 by
Judy Piatkus (Publishers) Ltd of
5 Windmill Street, London W1T 2JA
email: info@piatkus.co.uk

Reprinted 2005

The moral right of the author has been asserted

A catalogue record for this book is available from the British Library

ISBN 0 7499 3574 X

Set in Palatino by Palimpsest Book Production Limited,
Polmont, Stirlingshire

Printed and bound in Great Britain by
Mackays Ltd, Chatham, Kent

Acknowledgements

Grateful thanks, as always, to the entire family, for encouragement, support, and precious time. Thanks to Alison Martin for her legal advice, and to the kind lady in Hobbs on the King's Road, for the London input. Huge thanks to Jenny Brown, my agent, and to Gillian Green, my editor at Piatkus.

To Miles

Chapter One

Restaurateur. It became our special word.

Walking into the Maltings Bar charity quiz night I realised immediately that I was horribly overdressed. Oh, but it can't ever really be a mistake to be *over*dressed, can it? *Under*dressed, now there's a *faux pas* not worth making, and *badly* dressed, well, that's unforgivable. It's also not good to be *tartily* dressed, especially at my age (thirty-six), but *over*dressed? Surely not? Wrong, wrong, wrong! All around me, huddled in groups of six all over the hot, smoky pub, were jeans, fleeces and rugby shirts as far as the eye could see – and that was just the women. I was wearing – well, how best to describe it? Think Monsoon at Christmas time. Think lilac, embroidery and sheer, glossy tights. Think crystal drop earrings and shoes with spike heels which strictly speaking ought to be reserved for the bedroom. Oh God. But Iris and Lisa were waving madly from the corner so I took a deep breath, moulded a smile on to my scarlet face, minced over, and sat down. Iris's boyfriend Pete and Lisa's husband Martin budged up so I could join them on the red velvet bench behind the table.

'My my, Anna, you look great!' enthused Iris, fondling the hem of my slippy little skirt. 'This new?'

I put my head in my hands. 'I thought this was going

1

to be a smart do! I thought a *charity* quiz night would be formal! Can we leave now, please?'

'Don't be daft,' Lisa spluttered, 'we're in it to win it, aren't we? Or at least, if there's going to be a prize for the best turned-out team . . .'

'Shut up.' I looked around the room, which was your standard, horse-brasses and widescreen-telly-in-the-corner affair. Apart from the tables of teams, a fat yellow Labrador sat beside the bar being fed crisps by his owner, and an old woman wearing a padded bodywarmer and an eyepatch muttered to herself as she swigged a lurid green alcopop straight from the bottle. 'Aren't we one short? Don't we need six in a team?' I decided I'd rather have the dog than the old lady, if it turned out we had to pressgang another body into joining us.

Pete cleared his throat shiftily. 'Um, yes, I've got a mate from work who should be here any minute.' He turned his attention awkwardly back to his pint and Iris and Lisa nudged each other and giggled.

'Oh yes?' Something about their body language made me smell a rat.

'What's his name again – Jack, isn't it?' said Iris, furrowing her brow prettily and trying to look like she hadn't known the name perfectly well all along. Cottoning on, I faked an exaggerated yawn.

'That's right, Jack Anderson,' put in Pete. 'He's a senior construction engineer and . . .'

'A builder, then?' I cut in, snippily. 'Single, I suppose?'
'Erm, yes, but . . .'

'Just checking.' I glowered at Iris and Lisa, who smiled right back at me and shrugged.

Here we go again. Ever since I had moved back up here from Glasgow, these two had been waging a covert and possibly illegal campaign to set me up. Well, it flipping well wasn't going to work. Oh no sir.

2

'Here he is now,' said Pete, waving at the figure who had just walked in and was weaving his way through the crowd towards our table. Tall, with very short light brown hair, wearing an open-necked shirt, jeans, and a jacket, he appeared at first glance to be . . . well, unfortunately for my steely resolve, he appeared at first glance to be the best-looking man in the place by about a thousand miles, tastier even than the gin and tonic Martin had just placed in front of me and for which I was gagging. Tasty enough, even, to earn the benefit of the doubt over the Rupert Bear scarf which was wrapped around his neck. And as he reached our table and Pete made the introductions, I looked into the friendliest, brownest eyes I'd ever seen apart from those of Lassie the Dog, and realised that staying on my high horse all night was going to be something of a tall order. Pete commenced a round of introductions.

'And this is Anna Morris,' he finished, presenting me to him with a wave of his hand.

'Hi, Anna.'

'Hello, Jack. Nice to meet you.' Mmm. *Extremely nice to meet you, in fact! And nice to see that those white teeth of yours are just a little bit crooked, as well* . . . Martin ducked off to buy him a pint, as Tom Harrison, the pub landlord, came round all the tables handing out blank answer sheets.

'Could you chalk your team name and table number up on the board over there?' he asked, before moving on to the next table, who, as Pete whispered to me, were the legendary Rulebenders. Of the dozen or so teams crowded into the Maltings, the Rulebenders were obviously the hotties to be watching out for.

'Budge up a bit, Anna, so's Jack can get a seat,' ordered Iris. I budged up, but not too much. God, but he was warm.

'Oh, shit, look! It's the Dirty Beasts!' exclaimed Pete,

pointing towards a team of middle-aged men in the middle of the room who were rapt in a serious huddle around their table.

'The who?'

'The Dirty Beasts! Haven't you heard of them? They're practically professionals! They hunt out quizzes all over the north, and usually win them by about a thousand points – it's their little *hobby*.'

'What, being quizzy anoraks?' hissed Lisa, who possessed a bit of a competitive streak.

'Bastards!' Iris growled, looking daggers at their table. 'Don't much like the look of yours,' she went on, indicating the one on the left who was shaped like a spinning top and was engrossed in doing probey things to an electronic personal organiser with a stylus.

'No, no, that's the Bastards over there,' Martin put in, indicating a rough-looking crew of stubbly men downing pints next to the bar. One of them caught my eye and winked. I winked right back, and we grinned at one another. I giggled. 'Let's see, who else have we got . . . see them over there? That's the Wunch of Bankers from the Union Bank – they take it pretty seriously too. And just behind them is Universally Challenged from the council – God, all the big guns are out tonight!'

'Do we have a team name?' asked Jack. He had a nice voice, too.

'Not yet,' Martin replied. 'I thought we'd wait until we were all together so that we could decide on one.'

'Sounds like it's got to be something pretty filthy,' observed Lisa. 'That's it! How about "The Filthy Mingers"?'

I shuddered. 'Definitely not.' Jack nodded in agreement, which I liked. Not being thought of as a Filthy Minger was a Very Good Start.

'OK, let's see,' said Iris, 'there are six of us, we've all got nothing whatsoever in common work-wise, three male,

4

three female, we're sitting in a corner, we've probably got a wide spread of knowledge . . .'

'The Wide Spreaders?' suggested Martin, returning with Jack's drink. Lisa whacked him on the arm. 'OK then, perhaps not.'

'Sad Losers?' said Pete, glugging his pint as though it would self-destruct if he didn't polish it off in five seconds flat.

'Or the *Bad* Losers?' put in Jack.

We pondered.

'Well, that's certainly true of most of us, isn't it?' said Lisa.

So the Bad Losers we became. Pete jumped up to chalk the name on the board, just below Underage Six from the Senior High School, as Tom Harrison grabbed the microphone, which let out a shriek of protest, and began.

'Ladies and gentlemen, welcome to the quiz! Let's make a start – have you all got a drink?'

'Mine's a pint, thanks!' shouted the winking Bastard, to raucous laughter from his team.

'OK, the first category is sport! Ready?' Judging by the *yesss!* that hissed round the room, this was the category everyone had been looking forward to the most. 'First question. In what sport would you perform a "snatch"?'

A dirty giggle went round the room as someone muttered "the leisure centre car park!" and Tom Harrison had to call the room to order. I squirmed, glancing sideways, and Jack's quiet smile travelled straight through me.

'Falconry?' suggested Iris, whose strengths really leaned more towards celebrity break-ups and wine. But the lads had confidently written weightlifting and were poised for the next question.

'In what sport would you be expected to draw your stone to the house?'

'Fencing?' Iris again.

'Curling, definitely,' said Jack. 'I've tried it – brilliant game.'

'Isn't it a bit cold, though?' I asked, flirtily.

'A bit, but, hey, I could handle it,' he replied, equally flirtily. Why didn't I know before now that pub quizzes could be so much fun?

'In what sport would you find "chukkas"?'

'*That* must be falconry!' exclaimed Iris. 'Isn't that the noise they make?'

'Iris, darling, could you possibly keep your powder dry until we get to a category you actually know something about?' asked Lisa, tenderly.

'Do you really think there'll be one on handbags?' Iris replied. I smiled at her. She was playing up to the lads, that investment analyst was.

'Which football team is known as "The Bairns"?'

The answer zipped round the room like a firework. *Falkirk!* Then an even louder *shhhh!* was followed by more laughter.

'Could you say that a bit louder, please? There must be some folk in the Caledonian Bar along the road who didn't quite catch it . . . OK, next question, what's the nickname of the Australian freestyle Olympic swimmer who has size seventeen feet?'

'Well, I don't know the answer, but I *would* like to meet him – wonder if he can cook, as well?' mused Iris, wistfully twirling a strand of hair. 'Big feet . . .'

But I knew it – 'Wasn't it "The Thorpedo"?' Lisa offered me her hand and we exchanged high-fives.

'So it was!' said Jack. 'Well done!' He was sitting so close to me that our thighs were pressed together, which was an altogether not unpleasant sensation. I cursed my lilac dress and wished I was wearing something cool and funky, like Lisa, who was in a Fat Face sweatshirt and combats. Or Iris, in her petrol-blue Crew Clothing rugby shirt and baseball cap. I wondered how I'd manage to get the chance to explain to Jack that the girly, cocktail-party-escapee look wasn't one I worked all the time. But then, I realised, sometimes you have to make your own chances.

'I didn't have time to change after a cocktail party,' I lied in a whisper, turning bright pink in the process.

He turned round towards me a little, looked at me all over, and smiled. 'I'm glad to hear it.'

'How many beans make five?' Actually, that wasn't the next question, but it may as well have been. 'How many players are there in a five-a-side football team?' could have been the next, but probably wasn't. The next was something about the World Cup, and the one after that was on cricket. Or golf, or something. The last one in the category was also, most definitely, a question about sport. We were flirting! But wait a minute – *pray, just who was this handsome stranger?* And why the heck was I coming over all peculiar over a man I'd only just been introduced to? And on a fitted-up, blind-date type of situation, as well? There was something faintly pathetic about that, wasn't there? A little needle of self-preservation kicked in, and my mind started roaming over various possible complications of the psycho/married/computer-porn-addict variety. What if he lives with his mother and eats chicken nuggets? And I hadn't heard him laugh yet – maybe he laughs like a throttled goat? There again, another part of said mind, far, far away from the self-preservation needle, was already wondering how good a kisser he was. Probably excellent, judging by those tight, firm lips. I was phobic about big wet lips, thanks to an eighteen-year-old called Conrad . . . oh, yuckers, some other time.

Martin got up to get another round of drinks in as the answer sheets were collected up.

'Think we got most of those,' said Pete, and we nodded smugly. 'Shame that's my best category out of the way –

it'll be downhill from now on – unless handbags come up, of course. What about you, Anna, what subjects are you hoping for?'

I hadn't bothered to move along a bit, even though Martin's departure to the bar had given us a bit more space. 'Um, books, maybe? Capital cities? Dunno, really.'

'You never know, Anna,' put in Iris, 'maybe there'll be a round on property prices in the Highlands!' She turned to face Jack. 'Anna's an estate agent, Jack, and a very high-class one, at that! She runs the show round at Blakemore Properties in Union Street – you must know Blakemore Properties? That fancy office that only deals with the expensive stuff on the market?' I glowered at her, wondering if she was going to manage to slip my entire CV into the conversation. *Single, one daughter aged eight, riverside apartment, solvent, nice car, hobbies include going to the gym, hillwalking, shopping, being kind to old people . . .*

'Really? Yes, I know of Blakemore Properties. Sounds impressive,' replied Jack. 'Bet you get the inside track on all the best places to buy up here, then?'

He didn't recoil in horror at the phrase 'estate agent'! This was . . . still nice. And promising. 'Well, sometimes, I suppose,' I replied. 'Why, are you looking?' Never missing a trick was one of my professional strengths.

'I might be.'

'OK,' boomed Tom Harrison above the chatter, 'the next round is on Flags of the World!' A huge groan went round the room. 'I'm going to hold up some pictures of flags, and you have to write down the names of the countries they represent. Ready? Here's the first one.' The flag was two horizontal stripes, red at the top and white at the bottom.

'Poland!' whispered Pete confidently, writing it down. We looked at him, impressed, as Iris rubbed his arm proudly.

'OK, next, this one!' Tom Harrison proceeded to turn the picture upside down, so it became white at the top and red at the bottom.

'Oh, shit. *That's* Poland.'

'So what's the first one, then?' asked Lisa.

'Try Hungary,' suggested Iris.

'Probably one of those Russian jobs,' muttered Martin. We ended up writing Poland for both.

Japan was easy, although we nearly got caught out with Belgium, having to take a team vote on whether it might in fact be France. Jack got New Zealand, fighting down a strenuous argument from Lisa that it was Australia. Something to do with the number of stars. And Pete knew Brazil.

'Check out the Dirty Beasts,' hissed Pete. 'They swot up this sort of thing all the time.' We all looked round. The Dirty Beasts were looking deadly serious, pens poised, waiting for the next flag and looking round the room at the other teams, most of whom appeared to be in the middle of furious debates.

'OK, last one!' Tom Harrison held up the last picture. It was horizontal stripes of black, white and green, with a red triangle cutting through the left hand side, and a white star. My heart lurched.

'That's Jordan,' I said, quietly.

'Oh . . . !' exclaimed Lisa, and she and Iris turned to stare at me.

'Sure?' asked Pete.

'Completely,' I replied.

By the end of the round, having been flummoxed by assorted stripes and sickles on questions three to six, we reckoned we'd be lucky to have got about four right. A short interval was announced, and Iris stood up and grabbed her bag.

'*Ladies*, ladies!'

Jack got up to let me out and Lisa and I followed Iris obediently to the loos.

'Well?' Lisa gushed excitedly, once we were safely inside. 'What do you think? Isn't he yummy?'

'Pete never told me he was gorgeous! Well, not in so many words. "A good bloke" was how he put it,' remarked Iris, shaking her head.

'"Good bloke" must be boy-speak for "he's gorgeous but I'm not gay enough to say so", I suspect. Well, Anna?'

'Look, you two,' I began, 'how many times have I told you that I don't want to be set up with anyone? It's so embarrassing! But . . .'

'Yes?' they chorused.

'Having said that, he seems . . . nice . . .'

'Whoo-hoo! Result!' Iris and Lisa high-fived in glee.

I turned to examine my face in the mirror. My lipgloss had worn off, but there was still way too much make-up clinging to my face for a pub quiz night. I cursed myself for dressing like such a fool. 'Where's the catch, though, Iris? Men like that don't just get to be on the loose, do they?' There's *always* a catch at my age. Issues. Baggage. Complications, all that stuff.

'This one does, according to Pete. Pete doesn't think he's been out with anyone for ages.'

'Has he ever been married? Kids?' I asked.

'Don't know.'

'Hmmm, maybe he's a commitment-phobe?' pondered Lisa.

'So what?' I replied. 'Who needs *commitment!* I've only just met the guy!'

'Just a wee shag or two, perhaps?' put in Iris. 'God, what's so great about commitment?' For a moment she looked a little wistful. She and Pete had been together since school. They even went to the same hairdresser.

'But you like him, yes?' added Lisa.

'Um, yes, I think so,' I replied, reversing into a cubicle and closing the door. Then, as an afterthought, I called out, 'Did Pete tip him off about me before he came?'

'Not telling,' Iris called back from the neighbouring cubicle.

'Ah. That'll be a "yes", then.'

'Yes, well, I suppose that would be a "yes". Yes.'

We returned to our table just as round three was getting under way. Jack stood up so I could squeeze back into the tiny little space between his thigh and Pete's. More drinks had appeared.

'Round three, ladies and gentlemen – geography! OK, question one, name the capital of the Canadian state of British Columbia!'

'Vancouver,' said Martin.

'No, it's Victoria,' corrected Jack. 'I've been there.'

'Is it nice?' I asked.

'Very nice. I'll tell you about it later, if you like.'

'That would be nice.' God, everything was nice, tonight, wasn't it?

'Question two, name the deepest loch in Scotland.'

And so on, round the world, until the final question of the round.

'By what name is the city of Stalingrad now known?'

'Volgograd,' answered Lisa, firmly.

'Sure?' asked Martin.

'Totally. I've just been reading about a McDonalds outlet opening up there.'

'Not in *Hello!* magazine, by any chance?' sneered Pete.

'*Financial Times*, actually,' Lisa replied. 'Cheeky git.'

'Oops, sorry,' said Pete, making a backing-off gesture with his hands. The barmaid collected the answer sheets as the noise in the room grew louder. Martin and Pete headed off to the gents and Jack bent his face a little closer towards mine.

11

'So, do you like being an estate agent?'

I thought about my reply for a moment or two. 'Well, yes I do, actually. I love poking round people's houses; sometimes we get some really gorgeous ones to handle. And I really love the feeling when a sale goes through successfully. Usually it's a win-win situation all round. Plus, the market's so volatile these days, you never know what each day's going to bring.'

'Mmm, I can see that. What about the downsides? It can't all be fun, can it?'

'The downsides? Let's see, now.' Downsides? In *estate agency*? If only that had been an accumulator quiz question! 'Houses that won't sell. Estate agent jokes. Oh, rush jobs. And advertising deadlines. Sellers with unrealistic expectations. Buyers who disappear.' By now I was counting them off on my fingers. 'Scary dogs. Working on Saturday mornings. People who complain we haven't properly earned our fee if we manage to sell a house in a day . . .'

Jack was laughing by now. 'Not much, then? And you can truly say you like your job?'

'Well, yes, I can, I think.'

'So do you dread Mondays?'

'Who wouldn't rather stay in bed?' I countered, grinning at him as he raised his eyebrows sexily. That was it – I realised I wanted him and there was going to be nothing he could do about it. I could bind his wrists with his stupid Rupert scarf . . .

'Fair comment.' He had moved on to whisky and as he drained the last of it from his glass he threw his arm across the back of the bench, kind of round my shoulders, in a way . . .

'What about you? You're an engineer, is that right?'

'Yup. I've been up here for eight months, working with Pete for the Lomax Construction Group. And yes, I like my job, too.'

12

'Are you one of those blokes who swans around building sites with a walkie-talkie, wearing a safety helmet and tie, then?'

He nodded. 'Correct. Although sometimes I put other clothing on as well, depends how cold it is.'

'Nice image,' I said, appreciatively. 'Thank you for that.'

'My pleasure.'

'Ladies and gentlemen!' Tom Harrison's voice crashed into our flirt-a-thon. 'With two rounds to go, the scores are as follows: currently trailing in last place with twelve points, we have Alfie's All-stars! Take a bow, gents!' The team rose from the far corner, punching the air proudly, to cheers and the sound of the Bastards' impromptu rendition of 'Why were they born so beautiful?' until they were shushed by the rest of the room.

'And moving up to the top of the table, in second place, on twenty points, we have the Bad Losers!'

'Eek, that's us!' squealed Lisa.

'And, I have to say, it's getting a bit exciting this evening, as, in joint first place on twenty-four, give it up for the Dirty Beasts' (mucho booing) 'and . . . .the Bastards!'

The roar was deafening, as the Dirty Beasts stayed firmly in their seats, poised and focused for the finish, and the Bastards stood up and milked the applause for all it was worth. Once again, I caught the eye of the one who'd winked at me earlier, and he bowed ostentatiously in my direction. After the applause died away, we settled down for the final two rounds.

'Remember, guys,' began Pete, 'it's not about the winning, or the taking part . . .'

'*It's the money!*' chorused Martin, Lisa, Iris and Jack. I giggled, in a left-out-a-bit, snorty way.

'OK then, the second last round this evening will be pop music of the eighties!'

'What the . . .' Underage Six groaned and a couple of

13

them threw their beer mats at Tom Harrison. I felt a surge of optimism. Here was a subject right up my street! 'Settle down, please, for question one. Which eighties pop group had a hit with "We are Detective"?'

So easy! 'The Thompson Twins!' I hissed, triumphantly, and Iris, Lisa and I began a tuneless version of the chorus.

'Question two, name both members of The Proclaimers.'

'Charlie and Craig Reid.' That was me again.

'Question three. Name the female members of the Human League.'

'Joanne Catherall and Susanne Suley.' Yup, me.

'I'm sure Christian names would have been enough,' grumped Pete, writing the answer down.

'Question four, in which song will you hear the line, "Ain't you heard of the starving millions"?'

'Specials. "Too Much Too Young".'

'Name the band fronted by Clare Grogan.'

'Altered Images.'

'What girl band had a hit with "Really Saying Something"?'

'Bananarama.'

'Which song prevented Ultravox's "Vienna" . . .'

'Joe Dolce, "Shaddap yo Face".'

'. . . getting to number one?'

'Which movie legend appeared on one of Adam Ant's . . .'

'Diana Dors.'

'. . . videos?'

All me.

'Who was the female vocalist on Meatloaf's *Bat out of Hell* album?'

'Ellen Foley.'

Oooh! That was Jack.

'Sorry, were you about to say that?' he asked, with just a hint of cheekiness in his voice.

'I didn't know that one, actually.'

'No!' said Martin. 'You're fired!'

'What nationality was the pop group A-Ha?'

'Norwegian.' I looked round the team. Pete was pretending to be asleep. 'Sorry, am I boring you?'

'Yes!' replied Lisa. 'Your pop music knowledge is verging on the worrying.'

'Final question. Complete the song title: "John Wayne is . . ."'

The others looked at me wearily. I hesitated.

'Dead?' offered Iris.

'Come on, girl, you know you must have sung it in the shower,' murmured Jack. 'I know I did.'

I looked at him and smiled. 'OK then, all together . . .'

'*Big Leggy!*' we chorused.

'Big what?' said Pete, incredulously.

'Leggy!' I repeated. 'Hayzee Fantayzee! Shall I sing it for you?'

'No!' everyone shouted.

'Excuse me?' a deep voice called out from the middle of the room, and one of the Dirty Beasts, a tall, balding man who, like the spinning top man, was large enough to be concealing his Apple Mac under his shirt, stood up. 'We'd thought this was going to be a *proper* quiz! Those questions were ridiculous! We'd like to complain formally and insist that that round be discounted from the final score.'

'Oh, sit down,' shouted a blonde woman in the Rulebenders team beside us. 'You're such a bad loser, Brian.'

'No, that's us!' squeaked Lisa.

Anyway, Tom Harrison ignored the request and, to cheers and jeers from the rest of the room, the Dirty Beasts rose from their table and walked out.

'Oh, dear,' said Iris.

'What are you doing later on?' Jack whispered, taking me by surprise, as I was still watching the last Dirty Beast depart the pub.

'Sorry? Oh! Getting back home and going to bed, obviously.'

I felt him hesitate, taking in my words, before he spoke again. 'I guess you've had a busy night, what with your cocktail party, and all, haven't you?'

'Um, that's right . . .'

'OK, ladies and gentlemen, after that unscheduled interruption, let's get on with the final round – it's all to play for!' Tom Harrison was such an old pro. 'Eyes down, for ten questions on general knowledge!'

'Who's general knowledge?' giggled Iris, who was a bit drunk by this time.

'Falconry expert from the Middle Ages,' hissed Pete. 'Concentrate, everyone!'

The questions rattled on. Nothing came up on handbags, but we knew who wrote *Tess of the D'Urbervilles*, Jack knew the one about the inventor of the internal combustion engine, Iris knew the name of the Japanese Stock Exchange, Martin, a history boffin, got the tricky one about James the Sixth, Lisa knew that tahini was made with sesame seeds, but none of us had a clue who designed the Clifton Suspension Bridge, or the name of the Shadow Secretary of State for Transport. We had a guess about how many millions made up a trillion, and argued about the name of the third man on the moon before writing down 'Baby Clanger'.

'OK, last question, folks! Here it comes. Spell *restaurateur*.'

'That's an easy one,' I said. '*Restaurant*, with *eur* at the end.' Pete nodded and began writing it down.

'No, there's no "n" in the middle,' said Jack, confidently, jabbing his finger at the page. We all looked sceptically towards him.

16

'What?' said Lisa.

'Yes, there is!' I exclaimed.

'No, there isn't. Trust me, I'm an engineer.'

'No way! Tom Harrison definitely pronounced it with an "n"!' *Restauranteur!* Trust *me*, I'm an estate agent!'

The men all sniggered.

'Well, res-ta-ra-teur does sound a bit strange,' said Pete.

'I'm telling you,' insisted Jack, 'it's a trick one! You say *restauranteur*, but you spell it *restaurateur!*'

The rest of us were still doubtful. 'Vote?' suggested Iris. 'Who's for the "n" in the middle?' Everyone's hand went up apart from Jack's. 'Sorry Jack, but we're going with *restauranteur*.' Pete finished writing the word just as the answer sheet was whipped away, and Jack just shrugged and went to get another round of drinks.

'There will be a short interval while the final scores are added up. Please take the opportunity to get some more refreshment from the bar.'

'I told you, mine's a pint!' yelled the Winking One.

Watching Jack order the round, I felt my insides go funny. Something odd was going on. I'd come out to a quiz night with nothing more complicated on my mind than having a laugh with my friends, albeit a more formal laugh than events had turned out, and now, here I was, lusting over the man with whom I had been covertly set up by my friends. It was so juvenile! Was I desperate? True, it had been two and a half years since I'd ended my last relationship, which had been with a football-mad actuary from Newcastle called Michael and which had lasted all of five months before we finally admitted to each other that we were bored stiff, but I'd been having such a good time being without a man and just being a mum to Miranda, that finding a new one hadn't really entered my head. Besides, turning round the Blakemore office in Inverness had taken up every ounce of my reserves – apart

17

from my precious times with Miranda, I felt I had nothing left to give anyone.

I'd been out for the odd lunch and drink with various business associates and acquaintances, and although one or two of them could quite plainly have ended up in the sack I just hadn't wanted to know, and it had been a relief, a *joy*, even, to bid them goodnight and return home by myself. There had been no spark with anyone for ages – *years*, really. In fact only recently I'd been congratulating myself on the fact that I must be graduating on to some new, mature phase of early middle age, comfortable with myself, my sometimes thrilling youth fading gently to grey (Visage – great song), and rolling softly into a future which may, or may not, include a new man in my life.

And, if it did happen to include a man, then just who would he be? Well, I sort of fancied the idea of dark suits, greying temples, cocktails, theatres – the whole elegant, chiffon-wrap, hand-kissing, grown-up thing. I was looking forward to buying drapey, crêpey dark clothes – no, not clothes – *pieces* from the likes of Jean Muir, and to investing in handbags with tortoiseshell on the clasp, to striding around John Lewis buying trimmings for cushions and being taken seriously by the staff, to deciding upon a chic hairdo and having it tended weekly by some dear girl, instead of my current ponytail and scarf arrangement. Yes, I'd thought I was moving into a new, *sorted* phase. Well, perhaps I had been, earlier on today, but right now I was admiring the pert backside of an engineer in jeans who knew his Meatloaf, and hoping desperately that he fancied me, too. God, before you know it, I'll be *texting* the guy!

'Anna?' Lisa's voice jerked me back to reality. 'Coo-ee!' She leaned over Pete and whispered, 'You're checking out his arse, my friend. What do you think – marks out of ten?'

'No, I'm not!' I shot back. Then, 'Probably about a nine.'

Tom Harrison stepped up to the mike. 'OK, we have a winner.' We all sat to attention, stupidly nervous as, thanks to my encyclopaedic knowledge of eighties pop gleaned in my teens from *Top of the Pops* and the Bible (aka *Smash Hits* magazine), we knew we'd done pretty well. That tiny plastic shield, the first prize – the only prize, by the looks of things – had our names on it already.

'I shall announce the results in reverse order.' Tom reached behind the bar and produced a wooden spoon with a red ribbon tied around the top. 'In last place, having notched up a magnificent zero points in the music round, we have Underage Six!'

'We weren't even fucking born when that eighties shite was around!' shouted one of the lads at the table.

'Lucky you!' came a voice from far back in the room.

None of the team wanted to stand up to receive the wooden spoon so Tom Harrison walked over and presented it to the prettiest girl at the table, grabbing himself a kiss in the process. Then he returned to the mike and checked his list.

'In third place, with thirty-six points, it's the Rulebenders! Well done!' There were cheers all round the table next to us, as we applauded and waited to hear who'd come second. The tension was unbearable.

'In second place, and may I say only a single point separated this team from the winners, we have . . . wait for it . . .'

Pete grabbed Iris, Lisa put her hand on Martin's knee, and Jack grabbed my hand as we tensed to hear . . . no, wait a minute, JACK GRABBED MY HAND! It wasn't clammy, it wasn't papery, it was just . . . nice.

'It's those Bad Losers! Hope you're not going to live up to your name tonight, folks!'

'Second!' breathed Iris. 'So who on earth . . .'

'*Restaurateur*,' murmured Jack, softly. 'Our Waterloo.'

He let go of my hand at this point, but when his eyes met mine, he was smiling.

'And tonight's winners, scoring a magnificent thirty-nine points . . .' he gestured to the worldly-looking barmaid. 'Enid, a drum roll if you please?'

'Ham roll, do you, Tom?' she deadpanned.

'Get on with it!' someone shouted from the back.

'It's the Bastards! Well done, lads! Step right up to claim your prize!'

A huge roar went round the room as the One who Winked went up to claim the little plastic shield. He held it aloft, to whoops from his teammates, and shouted, 'Now can I get that pint, Tom?' before returning to his seat.

Pete got up and went over to talk to Tom.

'Well, well,' said Martin, scratching his head. 'Those Bastards must have at least matched your eighties pop knowledge, Anna – who would have thought it?'

'Oh, we're everywhere, you know. It's a sort of cult thing. You can't tell just by looking at someone whether they still harbour Duran Duran fantasies or not.'

'A bit like being a Trekkie, then?' asked Jack.

What did he say? I whipped around to look at him in panic. *The catch! Was he into* Star Trek? *Could it have been any worse?*

'You . . . you're not, are you?' I hissed, brazenly running the tip of my finger around his ear for Spockish mutations.

'Well, I dabble. I'm not proud of it, Anna.'

'I see. Well, thank you for being honest, at least.'

'Could you find it in yourself to just accept me as I am?'

'I . . . I'll need some time.'

'I understand.'

If I'd been a winker I would have winked, but winking isn't really my thing, unlike the triumphant Bastard, who'd managed another one at me just a few moments earlier.

Pete returned at that moment, and edged his way back into his seat.

'Jack was right,' he said, gloomily. 'It is restau-RA-sodding-teur. Sorry, mate.'

Jack shrugged. 'You know I'm not one to say "I told you so", but . . .'

'You just did anyway. Thanks.'

I checked my watch. It was half past ten, and even though Jack's thigh was still pressed thrillingly up against mine, I was anxious to get back to Miranda, and to let my mother, who was babysitting, get home.

'More drinks?' asked Iris, reaching for her purse.

'Not for me, thanks, I'd better be getting home. Thanks, you lot, it's been really nice.' Standing up, I fumbled for my coat. Jack stood too, and helped me into it. I didn't dare look at Iris or Lisa, as I knew they'd be watching with glee.

'Want me to call you a cab?' he asked.

'A cab? Oh, no thanks, I only live a little way along the river. It'll only take a few minutes to walk.'

'Going so soon, gorgeous?' leered the winker.

'I'll come with you,' said Jack, firmly, glowering at the man.

'There's no need . . .' I began, before realising that that wasn't at all what I wanted to say. 'Well, if you wouldn't mind, that would be great. Thanks.'

'My pleasure. Goodnight all, thanks for a great evening.' He pulled on his jacket then leaned down towards Pete and hissed 'Rest-au-RA-teur!' before steering me, gently yet firmly, towards the exit.

Outside the air was decidedly chilly and I pulled my coat tightly around myself and shivered.

'It's this way,' I said, indicating the road that led along the riverbank, and cursing the tight little clippy noises my

21

high heels made on the pavement. It was late April, and the trees which lined the way were rustling in the nippy breeze which always flew down the river from the hills to the west. Ropes of lights were hung from tree to tree and above us, the castle which dominated the town was illuminated in eerie green. For a while neither of us said anything; I was concentrating on not letting my heels make any of those slapperish, scrapey noises, and Jack, his hands in his pockets, seemed preoccupied as well.

'So, where do you live, then?' I asked, eventually.

'Spencer Road, near the theatre,' he replied. 'I'm just renting, at the moment.'

'Where were you before you came here?' He had an unplaceable English accent, with undertones, or possibly overtones of Scots, I couldn't tell.

'Edinburgh, most recently, but I'm originally from Gloucestershire. I moved to Edinburgh for a complete change of scene, then I began to realise that the Highlands were pretty special, so I got the Lomax Group to transfer me up here last year.'

'Ah. So no family then?'

'No.'

'Ah.'

'I understand you've got a little girl, isn't that right?'

I smiled at the thought of her. 'That's right. Miranda. She's nearly nine, though – not so little any more! She's brilliant.'

Jack nodded, but said nothing. It occurred to me that there wasn't much a guy could say when he was being told about someone's little girl, without sounding shifty – and then I despised myself for having such random, unfair thoughts in the first place. Must be hard being a guy. Har har har. Whatever – I tilted my head towards the apartment block on the other side of the road. 'Here we are, this is mine.'

We'd stopped in front of Fyrish House, where big, shiny cars, mine included, cluttered the parking bays, banks of gently lit rosebeds rustled in welcome, soft lighting bled through the curtains and expensive blinds of the windows above and Andy, the concierge, was peering out from behind his desk to make sure I was all right.

'You live *here*?' he asked. 'Wow, estate agency must be the way to go round here!' Then he added, quietly, 'This is one of my favourite buildings in the town. It's a brilliant piece of design, and a fantastic location – right on the river!'

'Couldn't have put it better myself,' I smiled. 'Ever considered a career change?'

We stood, facing each other, as I rummaged as elegantly as I could for my key. Andy bent his head and pretended to go back to his newspaper.

'Well, thanks for walking me home,' I said, trying, but failing, to look him in the eye.

'No problem. Er . . .'

'Yes?' This was it. It had to be.

'Got your key, then?'

My heart plummeted. 'Yes, I've got it.'

'Great.'

'Well, goodnight, Jack.' I turned towards the door, making a horrendous, high-heeled scraping sound as I did so.

'Goodnight, take care.'

I reached the door and spoke softly to the lock. 'You too.'

'Anna?'

'Yes?' I turned back to face him.

'I understand the *restaurateur* at Potters runs a rather good operation these days . . .'

Hurray! I raised my eyebrows, primly. 'Do you, now? I'd heard that, as well. They had a change of *restauranteur*

23

recently, didn't they?' I piled as much emphasis on the middle 'n' as I could.

He grinned. 'Will you come with me some time to try it out?'

I had no desire whatsoever to play hard to get – that sort of stuff was for kids. Probably.

'I'd love to.'

'I'll phone you at your office, if that's OK?'

'Yes, that's OK. Goodnight, Jack.'

'Goodnight, Anna.'

Andy looked up from his paper as I clipped across the marble floor to the cream-carpeted stairs. 'That seemed to go well,' he said, thoughtfully, as I passed.

'Yes, I thought so too. 'Night, Andy.'

'Goodnight.'

Chapter Two

The next morning was Sunday, and, after some thrilling dreams involving a certain Jack Anderson, in uniform, at the controls of a very large plane, I wandered through to the sitting room shortly after nine to find Biddy, Miranda's long-haired miniature dachshund, still asleep in her basket by the fire, pretty much where I'd left her the previous night; after I'd shared a pot of tea with mum before she went home.

My mother was longing for me to find a man. To *settle down,* that disturbing phrase she'd used once or twice and which always made me think of a big old mama partridge snuggling smugly on to feather-cosseted eggs and never bothering to get up again. It annoyed me, too, that she couldn't just be proud of the amount of settling down I'd managed to achieve *without* a man around the place. In her eyes, I think, my family unit was incomplete, but more than that, she imagined me to be lonely – only I wasn't. Nope, no way, not ever. How could I miss what I'd never experienced for myself? I mean, Michael and I had never lived together – we just hadn't wanted to. My role models ought to have been my parents, who coexisted in a grownup state of companionship which was for ever, in my mind, destined for the generation above my own, and although I was grateful for the happy stability that their partnership had afforded me and my brother as we were growing up, nonetheless I held within the deeper, immoveable departments of my brain a reasonably secure belief that Miranda and I already possessed everything we required. I had full-on human contact all day, every day at work, and in the evenings, I had Miranda. My child, my job, my responsibilities – my very reasons to get up in the morning were already in place, and Miranda and I, or so I believed, were happy. *Happy.*

That's not to say I didn't want a man, though, because I *did*, kind of. Sometimes I yearned for grown-up snuggles, for pillow-talk, for a man's waist to trail my fingers around as we passed each other in the kitchen, preparing supper, or breakfast, or any old thing. And sex! Yes, absolutely – *I suppose* – but after such a long time, well, the idea of it, the intricate intimacies, the organisation, the consequences, the explanations to Miranda, all crowded around to make the prospect inordinately *difficult*, even a bit ho-hum, like fancying taking up skiing but managing fine without ever bothering. So hit-and-miss, as well. Plus (and this had to be an important factor), I hadn't really fancied anyone for ages; not a living soul. The Highlands just hadn't yielded up a man who'd managed to cram himself into the available areas of my psyche so I made do with, well, the things that single people make do with when they are alone in bed. So far Miranda had never asked why my bedside cabinet was always locked, and even if she did, I'd never tell.

I hadn't explained any of that to mum last night. I'd just mentioned, as casually as possible, that I'd been walked home by a vaguely promising man who had asked me to dinner. And after an Oscar-winning display on her part of pretending to be only mildly interested, she'd departed, moments afterwards, berating me a little for not bringing him upstairs so she could take an early look at him (although she did acknowledge the preposterousness of how that meeting might have gone) and practically sprinting towards her car so that she could get home and give dad the good news.

Anyway, sinking on to the sofa to plan the day, I didn't hear Miranda shambling sleepily in, looking like a baby owl as she rubbed her eyes and peered at me through a curtain of tousled hair.

'Morning, mum – what time is it?'

'Hiya, sweetie!' I glanced at the clock on the DVD player. 'It's five to nine. You're up early for a Sunday!'

Miranda looked aghast. 'Five to nine? Oh no! Flora's mum's picking me up at nine – we're off to the wildlife park!'

'You're what?' I exclaimed. 'You didn't . . .' Then I stopped myself. Oh yes, she did. I'd known for about a fortnight that she was going to spend the day at Flora's house – it had just slipped my preoccupied mind. I shot to my feet. 'Go and get dressed – quickly! I'll get you some breakfast.'

Two minutes later, Miranda was dressed and gobbling down jammy toast at my silver granite breakfast bar. The door buzzer went, and as I checked the TV link to the ground floor, expecting to find Patricia, Flora's mum, instead I groaned inwardly as the ratty face of her dad, Roy Howarth, loomed bulbously out at me.

'Oh, hi, Roy, come on up,' I said, faking chirpiness before remembering that I was wearing my tight green satin pyjamas and silk tartan robe. Shit – Howarth'd love that, oily git. He'd propositioned me last year outside the school seventies fundraiser disco, of all places, where my 'Anna from Abba' boots and long blonde wig had clearly ticked most, if not all, of his fantasy boxes. Such a missed opportunity, then, that his black PVC Alvin Stardust cat suit, fake sideburns and huge silver rings had failed to have the same effect on me. Actually, I don't know if he'd truly

27

propositioned me or not – I'd just stepped outside to check in with the babysitter on my mobile, and he'd sort of slithered up behind me and gurgled something like 'warraboutabittayknowluvvlyfancyyousexxxy . . . ' before spinning round on an invisible axis and lurching back indoors towards the gents – or the boys, given that we were outside Miranda's school hall. But, wannabe seducer though he undoubtedly was I forgave him that one as he'd never done it before, he'd been howling drunk at the time, and, on the 'once is never, twice is always' principle, he hadn't done it since. However, I did occasionally get the impression he secretly thought himself to be the answer to my single-gal frustrations, and that all I needed to do was to reach out and tug his chain.

Despite this shortcoming, however, he was a great dad, devoted to Flora's happiness, and I knew Miranda would have a great day.

I opened the door a tiny crack when I heard his footsteps on the landing outside.

'Miranda's just coming, Roy, I'm afraid she slept in.' He was trying to peer around the door. 'Sorry about this, I'm afraid I'm not dressed.'

'Ah.' He added an inflexion in the middle of the 'ah' that managed to make it sound dirty.

'How's Patricia?' Best to mention his wife at the earliest stage possible.

'Pat? She's fine, thanks – in the car with Flora.' He was still trying to look round the door. Fortunately Miranda whirled up to me for her goodbye cuddle. I pressed twenty pounds into her hand and held her close for a moment.

'Sorry, Roy, we won't be a second.'

'Nae bother!'

I told her to be good. I told her to be polite. I told her to be careful. And after she'd gone skipping down the steps, with Roy's ringing assurances that they'd have her

28

back by four, I told myself to get a grip, and suck up the feeling of melancholy which crept up from my slippers now that I knew I'd have to get through Sunday – my only whole day off – without her.

Miranda was my pride and joy. Often I couldn't take my eyes off her – even if she *hadn't* been beautiful I would have thought her the most beautiful girl in the world. But she was, though. Tall, clever, with dark eyes, a sparkly, inquisitive nature, shiny, almost black straight hair and her father's olive skin – she was full of fun, yet was developing a fledgling maturity which I sometimes thought was leaving me behind.

She was the unplanned result of a tipsy night of passion, when I was away in London on a course. It was as simple as that. Yet, not simple at all – I guess these things rarely are.

It wasn't long after I joined Blakemore Properties, starting out in their Glasgow office, when I was sent on a week-long intensive property accounting course, based in an elegant five-star hotel right smack bang in the middle of London – Knightsbridge, no less. I remember being blown away by the city, and by the hotel in particular, its opulence, the marble, the chauffeur-driven limousines which swished up to the entrance, teased out urbane rich folks, then swished away again, the fact that when I rang for an aspirin it arrived on a silver platter . . . the whole shebang just, just *caught* me.

Anyway, the course was a killer, utterly mind-frying, held in those opulent five-star surroundings to cushion its impact, presumably, and at the end of the second exhausting day, I'd retreated into the gilt and damask Palmwood Lounge on the first floor, to order myself a nice pot of tea. My head was swimming after a particularly dry lecture on stamp duty, covering everything from its history to its future, its inside leg measurements and its taste in girls, so I needed to find somewhere quiet to get my notes into some kind of order before the entire point of the lecture slipped into hopelessly confused uselessness. I knew that if I went up to my room I'd just slip between the linen sheets of the king-size bed and fall instantly asleep, so the Palmwood Lounge, with its tinkly piano and blousy chandelier, seemed just the place to regroup for a spell, before taking myself up to my bedroom, to wallow in the bath and get dressed for dinner.

But as the waiter arrived from the kitchens, bearing aloft my tea tray, a very tall young man burst noisily into the lounge, wearing sunglasses and barking into a tiny silver mobile phone, his expensive-looking raincoat billowing dramatically out behind him. He was looking at the ground and making emphatic downward gestures with his free hand, so he didn't notice the approach of the waiter and slammed headlong into him, sending waiter, tea tray and contents flying to the four corners of the room.

Barely an apology did the young exec (or oaf, as you will) proffer to the bewildered and shaken-up waiter. I remember yelping in shock, then rushing over to help pick up the bits of debris. 'Sorry, mate!' was all that was heard from phone-man as he beat a hasty retreat to the cocktail bar beyond, still engrossed in his call.

A few minutes later, after order was restored and a fresh tea tray produced by a fresh waiter, I had settled back to try to compose myself and make some sense of my notes and handouts. Then, from the sofa next to mine, I was gently interrupted by a soft, low voice.

'Madam, may I ask if you are all right? I think you have suffered quite a shock, have you not?'

Thus did I meet Omar, the handsome, no, make that the *beautiful*, Jordanian businessman who was quite simply the most charming man I have ever met, before or since, who was to sweep me off my feet for the rest of the week and who, on our final night in London, after champagne and oysters, shared my bed.

Funny how much less arduous the course became from that moment on, how I miraculously managed to carve out time in the course schedule for our picnic in Kew Gardens, our opera trip to Covent Garden, that San Lorenzo dinner, those cocktails . . . I may have lost Blakemore brownie points by not brown-nosing with the course organisers in the hotel bar each evening, but I gained a *Pretty Woman*-style week of fun, company and conversation with a wonderful gentleman – and I wasn't even a leggy hooker, nor was he in town to break up a few worthy factories and throw salt of t'earth family men on the scrap heap for profit, either.

And on our last night together? Make no mistake about it; it was me who seduced him, oh, yes. Champagne (too much), one oyster (Omar had ordered two dozen of them but believe me, one was too much), perfume (too much), kissing (too much) and then, instigated mainly by me, a frenzied sex session on top of my decadent linen sheets (too, *too* much!).

Omar's return to Jordan and mine to Glasgow was taken for granted by both of us – he had told me during the course of our time together that he was expected to marry a nice Jordanian woman, and the sooner the better – in fact, I had often wondered during that week whether perhaps he had a wife at home already, but I instinctively knew not to press the point directly; after all, we were just enjoying each other's company temporarily, weren't we? Where exactly was the harm? Besides, my work in Glasgow was just starting to take off and become exciting for me, and frankly, the thought of a long-term overseas entanglement just seemed too complicated and scary for words, so, even though we had had a truly magical time, somehow

31

I was quite happy, after our wonderful last night together, to bid him farewell with no promises, no future dates planned – only a phone number to tuck away and sigh, *'what if . . . ?'* over. The whole week was all so other-worldly, in a way, that it was almost a relief to return to humdrum British people and punchy Glasgow life.

Whatever, drunken bonk, if you will, magical night of soon-to-be-ended romance, possibly, dangerous un-protected sex – *definitely*, but I discovered soon after-wards that I was pregnant, and nine months later I had Miranda, all on my own. You know I said things are rarely simple? I think one day, though not yet, I shall admit to the knowledge that I *wanted* things to turn out precisely as they had. I mean, I hadn't planned to get pregnant, but I most definitely *was* in control of my own mind when we'd gone to bed, so I guess saying that the pregnancy was an 'accident' would've been akin to walking backwards on to a motorway in the dark and being 'accidentally' run over.

But what of that phone number? The one I tucked away to sigh *'what if . . . ?'* over? When I was about five months' pregnant, I dialled it, and broke the news to Omar. I made it very clear that I didn't want anything from him but I just felt he had a right to know. That he could visit in future if he wanted to – or not. That I was sorry, but wasn't sorry, all at the same time.

And his silence on the other end of the line was long, and troubled. Eventually he simply said that he was sorry too, and although it was a relief not to hear him shout, or slam the phone down, or deny anything, somewhere a little part of me – the baby, perhaps – hurt that he didn't promise to come straight to me. It would have been im-possible, of course – I was still sure that a long-distance relationship wasn't for me, but it would've been nice, lovely, even, to have been asked!

About a month after that, I received a letter from him. Here's what it said:

Dear Anna

I found your details in the telephone directory, and when I rang the number and heard your voice on the machine, I knew I had found you, although I did not leave a message. Forgive the intrusion.

I am glad you told me your news, and glad that you are happy. For this, I am thankful. I will not visit, and I hope you will understand why. It would be too hard – for me, and for you. But you have a part of me, and always will – I treasure that honour. Please accept a gift for the child, from me. I would like only to have the small happiness of knowing that you and the child will not struggle. I am here if you need me, but hope and pray that you will understand my anguished wish not to see you or the child. It tears my heart to write this, but, as I have said, it would be too hard.
Your friend,
Omar

Attached to the letter was a banker's order for one million pounds.

You know, I cashed that cheque. Did I mention that he was loaded? Really, it was too much money NOT to cash – somehow, sending back that amount of money wouldn't have been fair on my baby, would it? Which raises the interesting question – if he'd sent me a tenth of that amount, or even a hundredth – would that have been an affront to my dignity, and would I have returned it to him with a flourish, saying 'I can manage on my own, you impertinent bounder?' A thousandth of that amount – yes, that would definitely have been torn up ... oh, I don't know. *It was a million pounds, for heaven's sake!*

No, only when you're standing in your kitchen, in your dressing gown, needing the loo, queasy, dreading getting dressed because your clothes are too tight for you, holding an unexpected fortune in your hands, can you begin to imagine how you'll react. After the shock had worn off, I made a cup of hot Ribena (the only hot drink I could stomach without throwing up), sat down with a notepad and pen, and weighed up the pros and cons of accepting the money. Ultimately, after many jottings, scribblings-out and pen-chewings, I came to realise that my main fears had nothing whatsoever to do with the rights and wrongs of accepting the money, but everything to do with my vague, frightened thoughts that in accepting, he would have some kind of hold over the baby and would appear from nowhere one night and kidnap the child, or take me to court and win him or her away from me . . . but then I realised that not only was this unlikely in the extreme, the fact of my accepting the money, with apparently no conditions attached, would have no bearing on that scenario whatsoever, would it?

And I *wanted* it. I figured out the padded, comfortable lifestyle I'd be able to afford for myself and my baby, the work options, all the help with childcare I'd be able to afford, and knew, quite simply, that if I had a whole lot of money, the chances were that my baby would have a happier childhood than if I did not. OK, perhaps that was an unsound conclusion, but try reaching a different one when you're pregnant, without a partner, and holding a million pounds in your hands. If Omar was to be taken at his word, then he was a moderately decent man who was sorry and concerned, and who had the means to make things easier for me and my – *his* – child. So I did. I decreed that the moral high ground was to be placed on the side of trust (mine for him), and responsibility (his for his baby), rather than ethics (my tearing up the money) and pride.

And so, I took the money. I just put it in the bank without explaining myself to a living soul. *Not a soul.* Well, apart from telling mum and dad that the baby's father had made some provision for its comfortable upbringing – I mean, if I'd let them know the amount I know they would have panicked and leaped to the conclusion that I had been bought off, or something – after all, they didn't know Omar, nor would they, so how on earth could they reach any other conclusion? *And why, in that case, had I?*

Whatever, it was important to me that my parents should know I was financially OK. *Financially bloody loaded* would have been a more accurate description, but then, there are some things a girl never reveals to her folks.

Anyway, a year or so later I began to invest the money in riverside warehouse apartments in Glasgow and thus, within six years, I'd doubled it.

Still, it hadn't been easy, having a baby alone. But then, from the moment I held Miranda after her birth I knew for certain that I couldn't live without her, a feeling which only intensified as the years went by, and I did often wonder whether having a father around would have made life all that much easier – I mean, night feeds? I'd have done these myself. Work? Well, giving up would never have been an option, it just wasn't in my nature. Moving to Jordan? When I wasn't in love (and neither, patently, was he)?

Mum and dad had been terrific, after the initial trauma of learning that I was pregnant had worn off, but from the outset it was abundantly clear to all of us that the child was to be my absolute responsibility, even though they adored her and looked after her for me whenever I asked.

I did tell them everything about Omar, every single detail, apart from the quantity of zeros on his money order. And once they were convinced (A) that he wasn't a shady

35

stalking nutter-type, (B) that he was out of the country and (C) that he'd promised in writing to leave us alone, I saw them, over time, relax into the situation, although the spectre of their granddaughter's unknown father hung over them for years – I could sense it, and it made me sad.

I built my working life around her, thanks to skilled negotiations with considerate employers at Blakemore in Glasgow, and together, Miranda and I grew up. I enrolled her in a brilliant day nursery (I could easily have afforded a nanny but the idea was just too intrusive for my tiny family) and she thrived under its care. Later, when she started school, I mixed childcare with working long into the night at home so that I could be around for her as much as possible – it was knackering but hey, the job gave me too much of a kick to squander the chances Blakemore gave me.

Then, two years ago, I'd been offered the opportunity to manage the new branch of Blakemore which was opening up in Inverness, my home town, so I took the chance to say farewell to the big city, to leave at last the cooling embers of my relationship with Michael, and come home.

Meanwhile, back in the present, I shuffled back through from the sitting room to the kitchen in my pyjamas and began to make coffee. My mind swung itself back to the previous night. Jack Anderson. *Restaurateur*. That long, warm thigh against mine. Should I tell Miranda about him, when she came home? Probably not. *Definitely* not. Good grief, we'd only just met!

It was a beautiful day outside, and as I finished my coffee and toast, Biddy came snuffling through, sat down, and stared at me expectantly.

'OK, madam, let's go for a walk.' That was me talking, not her.

It was an ideal day to go for a proper, long walk, rather than the usual run round the Ness Islands in the middle of the river to which Biddy was accustomed, so I dressed warmly, loaded anoraks, leads, drinks, dog and poo-bags into the car, wished Miranda was with me, and set off.

Biddy lay regally on the front seat as I drove out of town, down the side of the Beauly Firth, then off up the single track road which led seventeen miles into the heart of Glen Seilagan. I knew this road well; it was my favourite place in the world: ancient, tranquil and stuffed with memories, mine and countless others'. You could be anyone you wanted up here, a tragic heroine, a farmer's daughter, an intrepid explorer, Britney Spears, and there was rarely a soul to stop you. I just loved it. I'd come here often as a child, on picnics and camping expeditions with the family – in fact it was our childhood adventures in this very glen which had inspired my brother Alasdair to become an outdoor sports instructor, which led him to New Zealand, where he now taught mountaineering and abseiling.

As you travel further up the glen the landscape plays a trick on you – you think as the trees and rhododendrons thin out that you are about to emerge on to a wide open plateau, but in a seamless sleight of hand, the hills on either side overtake the trees just as the woodland throws up its hands in defeat and thins out to heather and peat, and soon steep valley sides are pressing in on you, daring you to go further, while whispering to you to go back. The bold are rewarded not far from the end of the road by a narrow stalker's trail which takes you round the side of Ben Seilagan to the Falls of Broom, which you usually get all to yourself. It's my idea of heaven.

I parked the car in the wide lay-by at the foot of the stalkers' path. Biddy jumped out, wagging her tail enthusiastically, and shot off ahead of me, turning back every few moments to urge me to hurry up. Swiftly I pulled my walking boots from the back of the car, laced them on, and followed. It was much chillier up here, so I walked briskly up the narrow, stony path, zipping my down-padded anorak and wrapping my cream wool scarf over the top of my head and around my neck. The biting wind from the west was making my ears throb, so I quickened my pace.

The stalker's path to the Falls was in a hanging valley, leading off the side of the main glen, a brooding vestige of its glacial past. The path was lined with heather with the occasional hardy little birch tree and countless gigantic, lichen-clad boulders, brought down by that old glacier and simply dumped with the sort of carelessness which these days would have earned it a fine. But there they had remained, for thousands of years, littering the way like immoveable sculpture, punctuation marks in the story of the glen. To my left was the stream which flowed back down the valley from the Falls, to link up with the river on the main valley floor. Too big to be called a burn, too small to be a river in its own right, dancing over small rocks and round big ones, it was as busy as Biddy. Then the ground sloped up steeply on either side, and although the path had seemed endless to me when we'd picnicked up here in my childhood, it was only about fifteen minutes before I could faintly hear the roar of the waterfall.

Biddy was on the trail of something, her long body with its silky caramel coat writhing intently through the heather as she pursued a bird, or a rabbit, maybe even a pine marten, or possibly nothing at all, but she was obviously in her element, just like me. She still kept whipping round to check up on me and bark, looking for all the world like she was saying *Thanks! thanks! thanks!* or possibly *'Don't turn back yet, for God's sake!'*

And then, there it was. The valley sides, which had been

38

becoming progressively rockier and more claustrophobic the higher I went, finally gave up the struggle and joined together at the top into a cavernous basin with majestic, sheer sides, over the top of which tumbled the Falls of Broom. I stood at the bottom, at the sides of the deep, black pool which Alasdair and I called the Lagoon and which we'd swum in during the endless, hot days of our summer holidays. Miranda and I sometimes swam here too – this was the place where she first learned to float on her back without armbands. Looking at the Lagoon now, black and icy, it was hard to believe we were ever so daft, although Biddy snuffled and splashed around the edge as happily as Miranda did, and as happily as Alasdair and I had done all those years ago.

The Falls were as impressive as I'd ever seen them – it had been a very wet early spring and the water which hurled itself off the top was almost brown, the colour of the peat in the earth.

Jack Anderson. Cool name! You don't get many grown-up Jacks around here – lots of little boys, but precious few men. He'd sort of accompanied me on the walk up here. I'd imagined him first in the car with me, then following me up the path, marvelling at the beauty and isolation of the Falls and trading witty, flirty conversation, and I wondered if, after our yet-to-be-scheduled dinner date, I would ask him up here. That was a bit of a major thought, though – sort of like sharing a secret with someone. He'd have to *earn* that invitation, and it thrilled me to imagine how he might go about doing just that.

I sat on a rock and Biddy bounded over, shaking herself violently and showering me with water.

'Aargh, you little monster!' I shouted. 'I'm cold enough already!'

Miranda had wanted a dog for ages, and I'd finally given in two years ago on her seventh birthday, when we'd gone together and picked Biddy out from a litter of four of the most adorable puppies we'd ever seen. Biddy had stood out from the others as she'd rushed straight over to Miranda and jumped up and down repeatedly, all four of her tiny legs leaving the ground, so it was love at first sight.

That reminded me. Miranda's birthday. In just a few weeks' time she'd be *nine*! Her party was agreed upon – all she wanted to do was have a birthday tea and a sleepover at Flora's, which was fine, but I still had her present to buy. She wanted a mobile phone, as most of the other children in her class had them – apparently they spent their breaks texting each other all around the playground instead of running around playing healthy games, so I wasn't keen. But what do you do if your daughter feels left out? I'd spent my childhood being the only one without Kickers, the only one without a hula hoop, the only one without pierced ears, and I knew it felt horrible. Besides, mobile phones were safety devices for young people, weren't they? You can talk yourself into anything if you feel like it.

By now I was freezing, so I called Biddy and we struck a brisk pace back down the path, her tiny legs taking about forty midget paces to each one of mine.

Back in the car, I started the engine up, but instead of turning for home, carried on up the road towards the very end of the glen. Like the smaller valley, here the steep, bare sides gradually close in on you but instead of ending with the flourish of a waterfall, you turn a corner, past a rocky bluff, and come face to face with a little loch, outstandingly pretty and unspoilt, with a small island in the centre which, ludicrously for its barren surroundings, overflows with tall trees.

Mrs Ferguson's cottage sits on its own at the head of the loch, the only building for miles. It had a thatched roof until as recently as the seventies – replacing it had been one of the last things Mr Ferguson had done before he died. The old lady had lived alone there ever since and now, in her eighties, she peered out of her sitting-room window on hearing my car, and appeared at the door a few seconds after.

'Come in, come in!' she cried as I got out. 'Cold day, isn't it? But seasonal, for all that . . . hello, doggy, you'll have to come in too, won't you?'

Biddy and I accepted the invitation happily, and followed Mrs Ferguson inside.

'Sit you down, I'll put on the kettle. You'll take a cup of tea, or something stronger?' Her voice was brittle with old age, but her Highland hospitality was timeless and legendary; she was a sort of honorary granny to Miranda and me.

A coal fire glowed encouragingly from the hearth, and as I followed her indoors and made myself at home on her scratchy red sofa with its slightly discoloured linen arm protectors, Biddy shook herself again and lay down on the rug. Glancing at the rug, I spotted countless burn-marks where sparks from the fire had fizzled and died, and I realised that Mrs Ferguson could be getting to be a danger to herself, all alone here in Ben View Cottage, miles from help. Concern flooded through me, gleaming like the brass ornaments on the mantelpiece, as I accepted her offer of tea.

Bird-like, with paper-thin skin beneath which her old blue veins protruded, Mrs Ferguson had sparse white hair which formed a tightly permed helmet above her watery pale blue eyes. Old lady personified, really. She disappeared into the kitchen, soft-footed on the mercifully faded swirly carpet, her slippers worn through at the toes. The carpet was lifting a little at the doorway and I saw another terrible accident waiting to happen – worn

41

slippers, worn carpet – calamity, surely? Fractured hips are the curse of the elderly, and there wasn't a pick on Mrs Ferguson to gird her against a spell in hospital – if indeed she were ever to be found . . . and the housecoat! I remembered it from my childhood visits – nylon the likes of which hasn't been seen in the shops for forty years! Brown and yellow flowers! I tell you, one spark from that fire and Mrs Ferguson would go up like a Catherine wheel on Bonfire Night.

'Can I give you a hand?' I called through, as the rattling of crockery grew more frenzied from the kitchen. There was no answer. I wondered whether Mrs Ferguson might be hard of hearing as well and hurried through the passageway (for narrow, dark halls covered with brown linoleum, exposed wiring, raincoats on hooks and abandoned wheeled shoppers have got to be *passageways*, rather than *halls*, haven't they?) to the kitchen.

Hmmm. Anna the estate agent kicked in. An old gas cooker, stainless steel sink, ancient cupboards high and low, with sliding doors thick with green gloss paint, and round holes instead of handles. Circa 1950, as a rough estimate. G-Plan? Or perhaps the late Mr Ferguson's own work? Mrs Ferguson was rummaging through the high cupboard beside the window (with a perfect view of the loch), going through a stack of ancient biscuit tins and pulling out a baking of scones and an unopened packet of gypsy creams. She jumped when she noticed me and almost dropped the rusty gold tin in her hands. Horrified, I lunged towards her.

'Go through and sit you down,' she scolded, waving me away. 'I'll just spread a scone. Make yourself comfortable.'

'Oh, no food for me, thanks, I've just . . .' In fact, I've just realised I'm starving.

'Wheesht you! Can't be having tea without a scone!'

I returned to the sitting room and stood at the window,

peering through a forest of potted geraniums on the sill, down the track which led to the loch and the real world. In the distance, Ben Seilagan strutted its stuff against the skyline, jagged and forbidding. A rush of longing overtook me, and I had to drag my eyes away and sit down. Some of the tiles on the fire surround were cracked, making the dismal little fireplace feature even more desperate and horrible. Might the original stone hearth still sleep behind this monstrosity? It was a thrilling thought.

Mmm. Four elderly power points. TV aerial socket. Horrible aluminium secondary glazing on the inside of the house, which at least kept the old sash windows intact but which whispered *'Replace me, I won't struggle!'*

Not much of a gardener, not that much of note manages to grow in the acidic moorland soil anyway, Mrs Ferguson seemed to prefer her flowers indoors – they festooned the wallpaper, the unlined curtains and the thin pictures on the walls, and the heavy, green scent of the geraniums filled the hot indoor air.

She returned unsteadily, carrying a tray on which were placed china cups and saucers, a small milk jug made of roughly cut glass, a chipped sugar basin sprinkled with hard brown nuggets of previously dripped tea, a brown earthenware teapot under a bobbly knitted tea cosy in purple and yellow stripes, and an enormous plate of jammy scones.

'You'll manage a wee something,' she said, taking my hand and squeezing it. 'There's nothing of you! You young girls are always watching your weight!' Then she disappeared back towards the kitchen, muttering something about gypsy creams.

Highland hospitality, eh? A dying art. Ask anyone what it means to them and you'll get some interesting replies. Some think it's all about whisky and bad food. Or ceilidhs, nylon sheets and accordions round the fire. Is it, though?

Is it bloody hell. Put simply, Highland hospitality is about control and supply. The control is on the part of the visitors – what time they arrive, and what time they leave. And the supply is by the hosts, of a seat by the fire, refreshment to order, conversation, and time, time, time, as much as the visitors need. Heart bypass operations have been missed for this. Everything else waits. No, there are no exceptions, *everything else waits*. That's the main thing. And it's about being prepared for visitors, not having them prepare something for you. There's nothing in the least bit hospitable about expecting your guests to pitch up bearing something to eat. A cake of soap, maybe, or a hankie in a box, yes, I've heard of things like that doing the rounds up north for years on end and never being opened, but with those items it's the *thought* that counts, not any concerns about bringing something you might get to eat a bit of. In fact I'd stuffed a little tartan notepad in my anorak pocket as I'd left home, and was planning to hand it over to Mrs Ferguson just as soon as she sat down.

But anyway, next time you get invited round to someone's house and are told to bring a contribution to the catering, by all means cook your socks off, watch whatever you've been told to make seep on to your car upholstery on the way over, hand it over to the hostess who's gone to all that *immense* amount of bother of hoovering and putting a fresh toilet roll in the loo, and stuff, and ask yourself on the way back home as you cradle your own personal bit of washing-up, is that little glow in my tummy the warm satisfaction of having contributed to some enchanted evening, or is it a niggling ember of fury that you have in fact just spent an evening dancing to some lazy cow's tune? *Hospitality my arse.*

'I've just done a boiling,' Mrs Ferguson said, a little shyly, returning from the kitchen and handing me a warm, ruby, speckled jar of raspberry jam, snug under its tight

44

cap of wax paper and Cellophane. 'The last of the rasps from the freezer.'

'Oh! That's far too kind! Thank you! I mean, I'd love a scone, but I couldn't possibly take one of your jars ...'

'Not at all,' she urged, shaking her head. 'There's always far too much for just myself. That wee lassie of yours will enjoy it, what age is she again?'

'Miranda? She's going to be nine next week – I can't believe it! And yes, she loves jam. Thank you very much.' I placed the jar carefully into my bag, knowing with a little surge of pride that Miranda would scribble a thank-you note on her Powerpuff Girls stationery without being asked, and fished out the notepad.

'Em, I've brought you this,' I faltered, thrusting the notepad towards her as she sat in the armchair opposite. 'Thought it'd be useful for shopping lists and the like ...'

She looked charmed, as she accepted the gift. 'Yes indeed, thank you, pet. What a fancy cover is on it!'

'Shall I pour?' I went on.

'Certainly, if you like it weak. Watch the spout for dribbles.'

We settled back to catch up on each other's lives. I devoured three scones like a greedy pig, urged on by Mrs Ferguson, who insisted that she'd be making more later on anyway. She told me about her arthritis, her sons and their families in England whom she rarely saw, the approach of the midgie and tourist season which cast a shadow on her summer with their different irritations, and I told her all about Miranda, our last holiday in Majorca and my job.

'And have you not managed to find yourself a nice young man yet?' she chuckled. 'The good thing about getting to my age is you can ask what you like!'

What the heck. Coyly, I told her a little bit about the previous night, about my erstwhile quiz teammate who

45

hadn't so much as even fixed a date for our date yet, but whose presence was already filling up a large portion of my head, and she listened intently, nodding in approval.

'He sounds very nice,' she said, when I'd done. 'See he looks after you well, now. A woman your age has no business sleeping on her own!' Her eyes twinkled mischievously.

'You're quite right, it's a scandal!' I laughed.

We sat in contented silence for a while, then Mrs Ferguson said, 'My sons have started telling me I should be moving to a sheltered house in Inverness, you know.'

'Really?' I looked at her in surprise. Her gentle face was cast downwards, and she was staring intently at the flowers on her housecoat. 'Leave Ben View Cottage? Do you want to?'

She shook her head. 'No, but I may have to, sooner rather than later. The boys say they don't want me staying here another winter – the bad weather was why they couldn't come up at Christmas.'

'Oh.' Last winter had been one of the mildest there'd been up here for twenty years. Miranda and I had eaten breakfast outside on our balcony on Christmas morning. 'That's a shame. I didn't know you were on your own at Christmas.'

'Well, Dougal did ask if I wanted to go to Florida with his family, but what would I be doing there? You wouldn't catch me on an aeroplane, anyway. And James's house just doesn't have the space for an extra body at such a busy time – you know how expensive houses are in London these days.'

'But this has been your home for . . . how long?'

'Fifty-five years, almost. But it is getting hard to keep going, I must say.'

'Oh!' I suddenly remembered something. *Cedar Park!*

'What is it, dear?'

46

'Well, this may be completely the wrong thing to say . . .'

'But you might as well say it! Go on,' she urged, 'spit it out!'

'My firm's been handling the sale of a new development of retirement apartments by the river in Inverness, just about a mile from my place – they've been beautifully finished, actually, we're very proud of them. They've been built on one of the last pieces of available land by the river in the whole town. There's twenty-four-hour assistance, lovely kitchens, a grocery service, door intercoms, a garden . . .' I tailed off. Had that just been the most insensitive thing in the world to say at this moment? 'Mrs Ferguson, I really hope I haven't offended you, and I can't believe I'm even telling you this when you've only just started thinking about moving, but . . .'

'But what?' she smiled.

'There's only one left.' My face was flame-hot, and it was nothing to do with the fire. I had managed to horrify myself that I had done what was to all intents and purposes a sales pitch on her when she was so vulnerable, but the bare fact of the matter was that everything I had said was true, and that there was no other sheltered development approaching anything like the quality of Cedar Park, or in anything like as good a location, to be found anywhere else in town. And if Mrs Ferguson was going to leave Ben View Cottage, whether by her own free will or not, I realised that I wanted her to be going to the nicest surroundings possible.

'Well, that's very interesting.' She smiled kindly at me. 'Thank you, pet, I'll think about it.'

I left Mrs Ferguson a short time later, feeling strangely excited, and wondering why.

Chapter Three

'Morning Anna – good weekend?' Rod, my assistant, had got in before me again, and was going through the mail. 'Oakdene Lodge has fallen through, we've got a cheeky git chancing his arse with a stupid offer for Cromlieford Castle, seventeen requests for Glassfield Estate brochures, a bill from the *North Courier*, an invitation to Young's Insurance Services' silver anniversary party and a free paperweight from Rentfromus.com.'

'Wonderful.' Rod was lithe and funny – one of those rangy, sinewy, outdoor types who spent his salary on epic holidays trekking in Nepal, hiking in Canada, tramping in New Zealand and bushwalking in Australia, but as far as I was aware, when he was in this country, he just went for *walks* like the rest of us. Friendly and smart – you could trust him with your life.

'Can I have it?'

'What?'

'The paperweight. It's a little snowstorm with a wobbly naked woman inside.' Rod had even put the coffee on. 'Shaking a pair of maracas.'

'Course you can.'

'It's the most vulgar thing I've ever set eyes on,' sniffed Monica Izzard, my second-in-command, from behind her desk at the front of the office. Monica had lost out to me for the manager's job, and had never forgiven me, what

48

with her fifteen years' experience, her millions of contacts, her *God-but-I'm-posh* telephone manner and her acrylic nails, and Rod thought that she had since entered into a sinister pact with the devil to make us all pay for her having been passed over. She was horrible to the rest of the staff – shy Katy who handled the accounts, indispensable Rod and Geraldine at the reception desk, and she daily trod a fine line between the upper hand and the official warning. The others called her the Monitor Lizard. Actually, so did I.

Blakemore Properties is a good place to work, all things considered. It's warm, it's full of funky furniture and it's really close to Marks & Spencer for those essential lunchtime tights and sandwiches. Located on the nice side of Union Street, between Gray's Antiques and the aforementioned Young's Insurance Services, we tend to look a little down upon the Krayzee Phone Shop, Kenny's Kameraz and Tartan Daze (where I'd picked up Mrs Ferguson's notebook) opposite.

When I'd arrived our window was just like every other estate agency in town, covered with spot-lit, laminated A4 photos of our clients' houses, tasty nuggets of enticing information typed underneath:

> *Spacious eat-in breakfasting kitchen*
> *Spacious lounge*
> *Spacious master bedroom with four-piece*
> *en-suite in 'pampas'*
> *Spacious family bathroom with low-level*
> *WC and bidet*
> *Spacious double garage with up-and-over door*
> *Spacious UPVC conservatory*

All that sort of stuff. '*The shite*,' as we called it. I loathed the clinical lists, the fact that all the agencies in town were basically the same, and the dreariness of managing an office whose reputation turned on the quality of its clichés and the efficiency of its photocopying. How many times can you say 'eclectic' to describe chaos? So, one of my conditions in accepting the Inverness job was that I had to have a free rein with regard to the office layout – and call it what you will, but our market share had increased by 20 per cent since I trashed the old look.

You see, just like Martin Luther King, I had a dream. A dream that one day, estate agents would rise up and face up to the true meaning of the insults: 'We hold these truths to be self-evident: that estate agents have a reputation roughly on a par with people who do unnatural things to farm animals.' I had a dream that one day, in estate agencies all over Britain, agents and their clients would be able to sit down together and the clients would not be thinking: *This slimy shyster is out to cream as much commission as he can off me by subjecting me to a horrible hard-sell patter and dishing out selling schedules full of meaningless bollocks.'* I had a dream that one day even the Highlands, a strong, self-contained region, sweltering with the exertion of its property market finally catching up with the rest of the country, would be transformed into a place where the process of finding a new home would lead the country in integrity, new direction and *care*. I had a dream that my estate agency in Inverness would one day be recognised in a town where it would not be judged by the brash standards of its competitors but by the content of its individually tailored marketing plans, its complimentary coffee and biscuits, its *out-there* window art and its fundamental credo: *'How can we do it better?'* I had a dream.

I'm particularly proud of our window display this month – it's a frosted glass dining table, laid with silver cutlery, crystal and white linen napkins with a centrepiece of orchids, lilies and Solomon's seal, and instead of placemats, lying flat on the table are framed photographs of the six houses we're currently pushing the hardest. Place-cards in silver holders give the locations of each one, but no more – people buying at this end of the market can add on or knock down at will if the look of the place and its location are right so they don't give a stuff how many bedrooms it's got. The wrought-iron dining chairs have cranberry silk cushions which match the richly swagged curtains, and on the walls to either side, framed in natural oak, is the single word: *Home*. I've cut a deal with Carlton's Luxury Furnishings up in the retail park that I can borrow what I like so long as it's returned unscathed, and we tell anyone who admires it where we got it from.

Last month's bathroom display had been altogether more of a challenge, but the ingenious way Rod managed to electronically get the pages to turn on the brochure being read by the pipe-smoking tailor's dummy in the bubble bath had earned us a colour picture in the local paper, where I'd managed to slide in the following promotional gem: *'We love innovation here at Blakemore, and our clients seem to have the flair to respond to that – it's only one of the many reasons why our market share has increased dramatically over the past twelve months!'*

It's something I grew to feel strongly about over the years, as I crashed into people's houses in Glasgow with my voice recorder and my electronic tape measure, while the owners stood back quietly and watched me measure up. I found that as I stalked from room to room burbling on about fire surrounds, picture rails and cornices, I was simultaneously performing an act of depersonalisation, which over time began to leave me cold. I felt like a vulture picking over an old antelope while the rest of the herd looks on dolefully. But still, the trouble was, despite all that I *loved* the job! I loved houses, the excitement of launching a new place on the market, the vagaries of the

51

whole system, the buzz of being a player, the thrill of persuasion, not to mention the deep satisfaction of achieving a good sale. So eventually I realised that if I was going to stay happily in the property business, I'd have to reinvent the process from the sellers' point of view. I began to work on the 'Home' concept, which, I realised, was almost too obvious to pay any attention to, resulting in nobody paying any attention to it. Does that make sense? It did to me at the time. I began to spend far longer talking to the sellers than measuring up, asking them things like what they felt were the strong points of their home, and what, apart from a nice fat cheque, they hoped to get from their move. Often the answers were surprising, but more often than not, someone, usually the woman, would say, 'I hope someone nice buys it.'

It's to the credit of the Blakemore Properties board that they agreed to give me a shot at it. The Inverness branch had been struggling, partly because of a sluggish market in the previous few years, but I think the board recognised that the lack of a distinctive image was muddying it up with the other agencies in town. I told them that people who genuinely wanted to buy a house would never linger for long over the minutiae of a window display; they'd come right on in to make sure they were seeing the full range. And I'd been proved right. Sales figures climbed, large homeowners – as in owners with big houses rather than fat people who owned homes, came to us first and we swiftly nailed that coveted 'Oh, you're using *Blakemore*, are you? Oh my!' reputation. Without wishing to sound in the least bit bigheaded, I was showing not just Inverness but the entire world that with estate agency, there *was* another way. Oops, bigheaded it is, then. It was intoxicating. How could I have got that across to Jack Anderson last night when he'd asked me about my job, without sounding like some kind of odd, cultish, estate-agent fanatic? The man would have run a mile . . .

'You free, Anna?' Rod called over. 'There's a phone call for you. Personal.'

'What?' At nine twenty-seven on the Monday morning? Flipping heck! I'd have put money on him not phoning until the afternoon at the earliest, to avoid accusations of being over-keen, uncool or perhaps just plain desperate. *Wa-hay, though, I'd conjured him up by mere power of thought!* OK, girl, deep breath, don't sit down – people always sound more businesslike standing up – don't squeak . . .

'Helleeeaugh?' came out so deeply and throatily that Rod and Geraldine looked up in surprise. I even gave myself a bit of a scare, to be honest.

'Hello? Anna, is that you?'

I jumped. 'Oh! Mrs Ferguson!' I deflated like a bouncy castle at the end of a party, sinking into my chair, before straightening up again and pulling myself together. 'How are you today? Thanks again for the tea and scones yesterday.'

'Oh, it was no bother. Listen here, I've been speaking to my son about what you said, and I think I'd like to go ahead and let you sell my house so I can take that flat.'

Wow. If only all my transactions could be that easy. 'Pardon?' And what a crying shame it felt so darned *wrong!* 'But Mrs Ferguson, you haven't even *seen* Cedar Park yet!'

'I know. But that doesn't really matter.'

'Or asked how much it is!'

'I know. But I'll manage.'

I was thinking hard, fighting a sensation of panic which was creeping around my insides. Just what precisely had I started? And how long would it take for me to be splashed all over the local paper: *Evil estate agent hoodwinks elderly widow! Busty estate agent Anna Morris etc. etc.*

'Mrs Ferguson . . .'

'It's all right, Anna, I haven't been on the sherry, if that's what you're thinking!'

'As if!' I retorted. But then, hang on, though, perhaps it *wasn't* so darned wrong? Perhaps it really did make practical sense, all things considered? Perhaps Mrs Ferguson could leave the home she loved and make the solitary transition to town centre apartment-style living as seamlessly as a pair of Marks & Spencer knicker-line-removing pants? 'Listen,' I said eventually, 'you'll have to at least have a look round first, won't you? To see what you think? Tell you what, how about I reserve the flat for you until you can get in to Inverness to see it – you could speak to your sons, to see if they want to travel up and come with you to check the place out – would that be OK?'

She hesitated. I could hear her soft breath on the line. 'But I don't know when they might be able to come up . . .'

'No problem. Take as long as you like.' Boy, was that the first and last time I ever planned to use that line. Empathic and revolutionary I may be, but if you sliced me in half you'd still see nothing but *'estate agent'* written all the way through.

When she spoke again I could hear that she'd relaxed. 'Well, that would be very nice of you . . .'

'It's the least I can do, honestly.' So it was. But the whole conversation still made me feel unaccountably shifty. 'I do so hope you don't feel under pressure to do something you're not ready for, just because I told you there was only one apartment left, Mrs Ferguson.'

Another pause. Then, 'There's some things you're never ready for, Anna, but we all have to face up to reality at some time.'

We said our farewells and I stared for a long time at the silent receiver, imagining Mrs Ferguson, standing in her draughty passageway by the front door, speaking into the old-fashioned, wall-mounted phone, and no doubt returning unsteadily to her fireside, with a heavy heart. Would her lovely views of the loch and the mountains be a comfort or a torment to her today?

Unaccountably shifty. *Unaccountably* shifty. Why was I feeling unaccountably shifty? Unaccountable shiftiness occurs when you do something that makes you feel unaccountably shifty, doesn't it? And what *had* I done, mmm? Only listened to an old lady's dilemma and stepped in with a possible solution, that's what. After all, Ben View Cottage was becoming too much for her, she'd said as much herself, hadn't she? Ben View Cottage was remote, draughty and downright dangerous for an old lady living all on her own. Ben View Cottage was chock-a-block with out-of-date utilities and hazards for the elderly. Ben View Cottage was about to lose its post bus service. Ben View Cottage sat right in the middle of my favourite place in the whole world. Ben View Cottage would be the most exciting renovation project the free world had ever seen. Ben View Cottage was going to be a gorgeous weekend retreat for Miranda and me. *Ah, that was it.* Unaccountably shifty just shifted, unaccountably, up a gear.

'Rod,' I called over. 'Put that bloody snowstorm down and stick a "reserved" sign on the last Cedar Park flat, will you, please?'

Rod looked puzzled. 'Cedar Park? Thought we weren't allowed to reserve them – cash deposit up front or piss off, isn't that what . . .'

'Well, we are now.'

The Monitor Lizard was listening. 'Bending the rules, are we, Anna? I've got a couple of people on the books interested in that flat – no, wait – or might that be three? Hang on, I'll just get the file.' Oh, bugger. I watched her guiltily as she stood up and went in search of the file. She was as thin as a whip, and her straw-blonde hair was sticking rigidly to its coiffured, chignony, chic, *magnifique-madame* thing that it always did, only today it was show-casing scary new auburn streaks. Rod was always threatening to sidle up behind her and ruffle it violently, shouting *'Diggadiggadiggadigga, let your hair down, missus!'* but we both knew he'd pay dearly for his fun after-wards in severed bollocks. Her suit today was emerald green – same style as always, pencil skirt and short, fitted jacket with gold buttons. Rumour had it she only had one actual suit, but in proper reptilian fashion it changed colour each morning, according to her mood. Her earrings were of the tennis-ball sized, pearl clip-on variety, but at least they balanced out her long, sharp nose. She also had exceptionally large nostrils.

I waited like a penitent schoolgirl as she leafed through the file. 'Yes, here we are, three definite interests, two of several weeks' standing, and one from last Friday. Would you like to see?' An acrylic fingernail tapped the page.

It's times like this, I find, when the phrase *'Remember who's the boss here'* counts for very little indeed. Monica was fifty-six years old, and for the past year had been living with a wealthy elderly widower in his eight-bedroomed Georgian farmhouse on the shores of the Beauly Firth, and in my book that alone calls for a large measure of grudging respect.

'Go on, then.' I took the file and returned to my desk. Hmm. This was tricky. Normally I was a bit of a stickler for doing things by the book – the last person who tried to work a flanker by whispering to me that he'd add 10 per cent to the highest offer we received for one of our forestry plantations, in order that he could secure it for himself, had received a stern letter from me, which I had copied to the rest of my staff *and* to head office, so full of righteous high dudgeon and words to the wise about 'this type of conduct' and 'upholding the system' and 'the integrity of Blakemore Properties' that you'd have sworn I'd been beamed down from Heaven on a celestial tide of indignation specially to write it, and then beamed straight back up again.

There was only one thing to do, and it had to be done in private. I stood up and strode with as much bravado as I could muster into the interview room (only we call it the 'meeting lounge'), where I closed the door behind me and proceeded to make the first of three awful, awkward calls to the people on the list, explaining that there had been a mix-up for which I took full responsibility, but that unfortunately the last Cedar Park apartment was now gone, and could I interest them in one of our future prestige developments . . .

It was excruciating, but I did it, and when I eventually replaced the receiver at the end of the third call, I was reasonably confident that not one of the three was going to take us to court, or go howling to the press. I had my suspicions that the first one of them wouldn't have been able to come up with the cash in any event, the second even expressed a mild interest in an apartment elsewhere and the third, the one who only came on to the scene on Friday, just said sadly that she'd known it was too good to be true, but what's for you won't go by you and this obviously wasn't for her . . . anyway, to say I felt like shit would be flattering to feelings of shit. I'd have loved to have felt like shit just then, it would have been so much more pleasant than the wormy, slimy grubbiness which overtook me as I returned to the main office and silently handed the file back to Monica, who glanced at the notes I'd made, said nothing, and put it away.

Geraldine had a bad cold, and spent the morning coughing and spluttering all over clients, her phones, her desk, us, the window display – everything, in fact, but she flatly refused to go home to bed. 'It's duthig! Just a dorbal code! Baybe I'll have a Lebsip and a bug of tea, though.' The phone rang again and she picked it up. 'Blakebore Properties, good bordig?' Monica shuddered dramatically as Geraldine let rip another almighty sniff. 'Doh probleb. Bay I ask who's speakig?' Then she turned to me. 'Bister Addersod for you, says it's a persodal batter.'

Rod raised his eyebrows and shook his naked-lady snowstorm suggestively, which I ignored in my haste to grab the phone on my desk, once germy Geraldine had put the call through to my extension.

'Jack. Good morning.' I was still in recovery from the earlier worminess, so my voice was brisk and not at all sexually intriguing. In fact, if sexually intriguing has a direct opposite (lumpish? clunkish? brisk?), then that's how my voice probably sounded just then.

'Anna? You sound busy.' It was startling to hear his voice on the crackly line. Startling, and terribly exciting. Children must feel this way when Santa Claus rings them up.

'Oh, as ever. You on a mobile?'

'Yup, reception's not so good here, I'm underneath the Kessock Bridge checking out a pontoon for some work we're about to start. But yes, before you ask, I *have* got clothes on today.'

I smiled. 'Nothing was further from my mind, Mr Anderson.'

'Ah. That's a shame.' I heard the smile in his voice, too. 'So how are you?'

'Not too bad – em, just wondering if you were still on for coming out for dinner some night?'

Monica Izzard, Rod, Katy and Geraldine had all stopped what they were doing and were brazenly watching my pinkening face. I wonder what vibes I was giving off to show I was talking to a potential hot date? I mean, I hadn't dropped my hip, or twirled my hair, or giggled, or said 'Oh, you, you're terrible, you are, you know you are – *yes you are!*' or anything like that . . .

'I'm looking forward to it.' Rod and Geraldine high-fived in glee.

'I've taken the liberty of reserving a table for Friday night at Potters, but if that's not OK . . .'

Friday night? *Four days away?* Couldn't he have been just a *tad* more desperate than that, please?

I hesitated as Jack continued, 'I'd love to have made it before then, but I'm going to be away at a conference in Aberdeen all the rest of this week.'

Phew! Joy. Relief. Anguish. Trepidation. Delight. Excitement. Realisation of requirement to say something aloud before suspicion of having been cut off creeps up on caller.

'Conference, eh?'

'Yes, why?'

'Not a *Star Trek* convention, by any scary chance?'

He laughed. Do you know, he really did have the nicest laugh – especially as he was applying it to one of my home-made quips. 'No, definitely not one of those.'

'That's OK, then.'

'Star *Wars*, actually.'

'*What?*'

'Kidding.'

'Ah. Funny.'

'So?'

'Yes?'

'Friday?'

'Great.'

'Great! Eight o'clock be OK? I'll pick you up.'

You already did. 'That'd be nice. Thanks, Jack, I'm looking forward to it.' Oops, said that already. Bugger!

'Me too.'

'Enjoy the conference – oh, and Jack?'

'Yes?'

'May the Force be with you.'

'And with you also, Your Highness. Goodbye, Anna.'

'Bye.'

Katy, Geraldine and Rod, arranged together around Geraldine's reception desk like a trio of over-keen drama school brats, were wearing the stupidest grins I'd ever seen. You could almost hear the introduction to 'Summer Lovin'' from *Grease* kicking off in the background – *Bomp-adomp-adomp-adompadomp* . . . it was only the Monitor Lizard who had returned to being straight-faced, and had resumed primly glueing photographs of a kennel block on to a piece of card, her nostrils even more huge with distaste than I'd ever seen them before.

'He sounded probisig,' ventured Geraldine.

'Well?' said Rod. 'Anna, if you don't tell us what that was all about we shall be forced to fabricate the details for ourselves.'

'You wouldn't dare!'

'Oh yes we would!' they choroused.

'We usually do anyway,' added Katy, whose blistering honesty had got her the accounts job in the first place. Geraldine whacked her on the arm. Rod was smiling at me. Honestly, if that dear boy hadn't been nine years younger than I was . . .

'OK, then . . .' I began.

'Don't biss adythig out, Adda,' prompted Geraldine.

'His name is . . .'

'Jack Anderson!' they chimed in again. 'We know!' Monica Izzard's head shot up at the mention of his name, but then she swiftly turned her attention back towards her glueing when she realised that we had all spotted her interest.

'Yes, thank you, ladies and gentlemen of the chorus. His name is Jack Anderson, and he works for . . .'

60

'Lomax Construction Group,' put in Monica, without looking up from her kennel.

'Lomax . . . Monica! Do you know him?' I looked at her in astonishment.

Now either Monica Izzard is a very good actress, or else her scheming deviousness reaches depths never before plumbed by the normal mortal mind, for she managed to look at each one of us, take a deep breath, appear a trifle bored and yet slyly knowing all in one twitch of her nose, to look above it all and yet to manage to convey knowing troubledness WHILE STILL GLUEING HER FUCKING KENNEL TO ITS FUCKING CARD ALL AT THE SAME TIME!

'Come on, Monica, spill!' prompted Rod.

'Well,' Monica began, 'the name does seem a bit familiar. I'm sure I've spoken to a Jack Anderson' (the very sound of his name was giving me unprofessional shivers by this point) 'recently . . .'

'Did he ask you out, too?' asked Geraldine. Rod mimed pulling a pin out of a hand grenade, lobbing it and covering his ears, as we all tensed to see what Monica would say next.

'Hardly,' she began. 'I can't really remember much about the conversations, to be honest, they seemed so . . .' (looking in my direction) '*inconsequential* at the time . . .' God but that woman was a bloody, fucking, flesh-eating, patronising bitch, wasn't she?

'Come on, Monica!' burst out Katy, to surprised glances all round. 'Um, if you think it's OK to give out personal information . . .'

Monica sniffed. 'Oh, I don't think it was *personal*. Heavens, I wouldn't be saying *anything* to you if it was!' She smiled at her professional little home-run. I realised quite calmly that I was harbouring an urge to rip her throat out with my teeth, chop it up into little pieces, sauté it in

61

butter, throw on some chopped parsley and lemon juice and serve it up in our dining-room window display, with a nice Chianti. How *could* Monica Izzard spoil my moment! Did she bloody hell know a Jack Anderson! Not *my* Jack Anderson, anyway!

'Monica,' I began, 'if there's something you feel I should know, then I'd appreciate it if you'd just speak up? Please?'

That got her. Glowering, she raised herself up from her glueing to face us. 'Well, I think I've spoken to a Jack Anderson recently, but I can't quite seem to remember what it was about. OK? It's a common enough name, isn't it?'

'Absolutely. Common as muck,' I sighed.

'But Anna, I take it you're going to be going out with him?' put in Rod.

Again, a feeling of intense . . . what? OK. A feeling of goddarn lust surged through the bits covered up by my suit.

'Yes, Rod, we're going to Potters on Friday night.'

'Friday?' exclaimed Katy. 'Couldn't he . . .'

'He's off on a course this week,' I cut in.

'Ah. That's OK then. Friday's *ages*!'

'Potters? This Friday? I'll be seeing you there, then!' said Rod, winking.

'You'll be what?' shot out untrammelled from my over-stimulated gob.

'Har, gotcha!'

'Get back to work, you,' I said, feeling for my metaphorical reins, picking them up, and hollering 'hiyyyaaaarghh!' to my team. Even Monica got going with her glue pen with a bit more zeal, and I set to trying to care why the hell Oakdene Lodge had fallen through.

Chapter Four

So, then, what's the best way to approach an old lady and ask her if you can do a private deal to buy her house? Notwithstanding the minor fact that you are her trusted friend who in all probability sowed the seed in her mind that she really ought to get cracking and flog the place without delay? And then chucking in the issue of your being an estate agent, to boot? Isn't it a bit like, well, *mugging*?

My sitting room is a far cry from the brown tiled fireplace and worn carpet of Ben View Cottage. To hell with wooden floors, I say – who wants to sprawl on planks? I've filled the room with warm, spice colours, like saffron and cinnamon – and no, it's not bloody terracotta, OK? It's *cinnamon*, and the warm, pale-ochre wool carpet is matched by sheer drops of raw silk curtains, both at the bay window to the back which overlooks a hardy cluster of Old Scots pines, and the balcony doors to the front, which overlook the river, the park on the other side and, in the far distance beyond the rooftops of the other side of town, the hills surrounding Glen Seilagan. It's a miraculous spot for a town-centre apartment – but that's what you pay good money for, I guess. I'd paid cash for the place with Omar's money, my conscience crystal-clear – after all, wasn't this Miranda's home, too? To say nothing of the fact that it's a cracker of an investment – I reckon it's already worth 40 per cent more than I paid for it, well, maybe 45, given the discount I negotiated with the developer in exchange for a cut-price deal on the marketing of his next release . . .

Not one of life's natural sprawlers, however, carpet or no carpet, I was lying on the sofa, propped up sufficiently to be able to handle my wine glass and the CD remote, lightly pondering what to do about Ben View, contemplating what to wear to Potters that would have Jack Anderson begging for mercy and trying not to eavesdrop on Miranda's giggly phone conversation with Flora, in the kitchen. They were talking about the rules for The Powerpuff Club, a secret society they'd formed which, as far as I could make out, only had two members – themselves. Miranda was trying to think up a password – so far *girls rule* seemed to have the edge, after they had spent much of the earlier part of the call deciding what The Powerpuff Club members ought to *wear*. Maybe that's why they were permanently to be seen sporting matching pink baseball caps these days.

But back to Mrs Ferguson. *Ethically*, it ought to be obvious. I should make my intentions clear to her, face-to-face, and then urge her, in writing, to go ahead and put the house on the open market via another firm. Alternatively, a more diluted, yet still acceptable, course of action would be to still tell her that I fancied the house myself, but then to assure her of Blakemore's integrity in handling the sale, get her to sign something to the effect that she'd been told of my interest, advise my bosses at head office that I was interested in the house and had adhered to correct procedure in informing our client, and then instruct the Monitor Lizard, rather than me, to deal with the actual nuts and bolts of the sale.

But there was the big, red, irritating rub. Ben View Cottage was unique, beautiful, not in the slightest bit buggered about, and ripe for half the world to pin their renovation/isolation, Highland 'place to relax and unwind' dreams upon. And I knew damn well that half the world would do precisely that just as soon as they got wind that it was available. We'd be inundated with potential buyers from all walks of life, but the ones to worry about the most would be those from down south who wouldn't be able to believe their eyes at how cheap it was to buy their own little idyll – regardless of what asking price we set. So, we'd get dozens of over-excited Range Rover people who'd want to gut the place and fill it with seagrass, tartan throws and stowaway beds, and who'd plague us with questions about who they could get to clean and maintain the place when they weren't there, and did we know of anyone reliable who cooked?

Then we'd have to set a closing date, where a fixed time would be announced for sealed bids, and the highest one would inevitably be successful. Chuck into the equation the smattering of locals with more money than sense, add a sprinkling of panickers who knew they'd be competing with smatterings of people with more money than sense, and the sky would be the limit on how much the place would actually go for.

Explaining about closing dates in Scotland, to non-Scots, takes up a huge part of the Blakemore working day. The Monitor Lizard once went so far as to produce a draft leaflet to hand out, and whilst its tone was appallingly supercilious, like the reptile herself, I had to admit that she had a point. To paraphrase from Lizard-speak, it went something along these lines:

Listen up, you! When we set an asking price for a property, please on no account waste our time by even contemplating offering a lower amount! You may think you're being terribly shrewd, and so what if that's how it's done

65

in the south, but Blakemore can assure you that we've seen it all before! We don't prefix the price with the words 'Offers over' just for fun, you know! We have not just come down the Great Glen on a bicycle! This is how it works, please pay attention. Once Blakemore receives formal notice of more than one serious interest in a particular property, you will be advised of a fixed date and time upon which your best offer, in a sealed envelope, from your Scottish solicitor, must be in our hands. This is called the closing date. OK? When faced with this situation you must decide, after due care and the competent advice of your solicitor, surveyor and financial adviser, just how much OVER Blakemore's asking price you are prepared to bid. Is that clear? What part of 'Offers over' don't you get? Anyway, the highest bid will almost invariably get the house. So think long and well, and remember that a mark-up of 20 per cent on the asking price is nothing new to us, so don't feel you're doing us any huge favours. Goodday.

That's approximately how it went, anyway. Monica looked ready to spontaneously combust when I'd told her that whilst I appreciated her initiative, and whilst it would undoubtedly save us a ton of explanation, nobody ever sold houses by handing over a leaflet and then showing people to the door, did they? No, it was a bit like trying on clothes. The longer the assistant keeps bringing out stuff for you to try on, and the more trouble he or she goes to, the more likely you are to tap into everyone's basic feelings of obligation, and thus the more likely you are to part with your cash. Simple.

But back to Mrs Ferguson, and Ben View Cottage. Going through the correct channels with the sale of Ben View would risk my losing out on the house but at least, in theory, it would be *ethical*.

Only, you know, ethics can be queer, mutant fish.

What if you take other, *human* elements into account? I mean, couldn't you argue that the codes of conduct I was expected to follow were really, when all's said and done, designed to protect my own professional backside? What about Mrs Ferguson – what, ethically, would protect *her* backside? Now, I know it's not polite to refer to the backsides of the very old but there is a valid point to be made here – Mrs Ferguson could sign all the disclaimers in the world, Blakemore Properties' nose could be so clean in the handling of the sale that you could play a tune through it, but the end result would NOT be in the best interests of Mrs Ferguson! No, it wouldn't! Whereas, if I were to have a quiet word with her, and offer her an excellent, more-than-competitive price for the place, then what would I have achieved?

1. I'd have spared her the ordeal of having strangers poking round her home.
2. I'd have saved her an agency fee.
3. I'd save her any potential anxiety about timing, and being temporarily homeless if move-in and move-out dates didn't match up.
4. She could settle in front of the fire in her gorgeous riverside apartment, twenty-four-hour assistance just a bell-push away, happy in the knowledge that Ben View Cottage was safe in the grateful hands of her friend.
5. She could come and visit whenever she wanted – I'd make her some scones.

What's ethical about flinging a vulnerable old lady into the company of strangers, when I could protect her from all that?

So you see, ethics, schmethics. It was quite terrifying, really, to discover how easy it was to turn an ethical dilemma to your advantage. I realised that perhaps I should start reading the papers and watching the news more critically – clearly, ethics had situational angles and if you didn't look out for them, then, well – oh, I don't know, that way paranoia lies. But one thing was for sure – if you wanted something badly enough, you could find a way to justify it. I mean, Miranda had eventually swung the mobile phone argument in her favour by explaining how she'd feel safer having one when she wasn't with me, so all of a sudden the other argument *against* getting her one, that of spawning an uncommunicative couch potato, turned into a secondary issue – what price safety?

When I got to the office the following morning, I learned that Geraldine had taken the hint and was staying in bed to try and shift her cold, so Rod was manning the phones. Monica Izzard was out schmoozing the owner of a large sporting estate on the west coast, hoping to persuade him to succumb to Blakemore's second-to-none marketing charms, and shy Katy had gamely donned a name badge and was taking her turn at the front. I picked my way through the morning, haggling with a newspaper over advertising space, talking up a derisory offer for an Arts and Crafts-style semi in Nairn for the almost-not-worth-the-bother sum of one thousand pounds, and composing an elegant blurb to describe a dilapidated heap o' crap, the sale of which had been pressed on us by a long-standing client, in whose good books we hoped to remain, as he had odd bits of property all over the north which he was selling off one by one:

PYLONS' LEE
KINNAIRD VALLEY, INVERNESS-SHIRE

Attention D.I.Y. enthusiasts! Form an orderly queue, now, for one of the best investment opportunities to have arisen on the local market this year! At last, Pylons' Lee has come on the market, giving you your chance to acquire a traditional farmhouse in an idyllic setting, at a must-have price! We at Blakemore Properties are truly excited about the development potential of this compact, traditional home, located only an hour's drive from Inverness city centre in the picturesque Kinnaird Valley. Enjoy the gothic splendour of the Kinnaird dam and hydro-electric station just minutes from the front door, revel in the solitude, the treeless majesty of the moor, and the satisfaction which comes from having your own private water supply direct from the Black Burn behind the house, and full legal rights to construct your own, state-of-the-art septic tank and soakaway.

Once inside, we at Blakemore were struck by a single thought: this house is the perfect blank canvas upon which to paint a dream. With the enticing prospect of floor-to-ceiling renovation making the Blakemore creative juices flow, the discerning purchaser, after the immediate issues of wiring, plumbing, roofing, damp-proofing and flooring are attended to, can have free rein to create a unique layout within an unspoilt, traditional framework. Put the internal walls where you like! Or have none at all! Why not consider a spiral staircase, for that edgy, loft-style feel in the heart of the Highlands! One thing's for sure, you'll never be stuck for inspiration at Pylons' Lee! (See undernote for dimensions. Hard hat recommended for viewings. Viewers enter property at own risk, disclaimer notices to be signed when confirming appointments. Four-wheel-drive vehicles recommended for access track. Strictly no entry to hydro-electric storage compound adjoining the property.)

Satisfied, I escaped at twelve-thirty to meet Iris and Lisa for lunch.

The Coffee Sanctuary looked busy. Not Japanese tube train busy like the Next sale a few doors down (you would think they were giving away free Justin Timberlakes, the quantity of young females crammed into that place), but still busy enough to be a bit of a thought. I hovered at the door, whilst the rattling crockery, the slurping punters and the gluggily whooshing, state-of-the-art-deco machinery on the counter inside didn't give a monkeys whether I went in or not.

I didn't. Like the Little Match Girl, I gazed over the heads of the crowd into the very guts of the café, behind the counter, through the tiny gaps between the machines, catching flashing glimpses of ponytails, logo polo shirts, baseball caps, cocoa dredgers and mobile phones, and pondered the luxury leisure lifestyle experience only a few confident steps away – all I had to do was walk in and buy into it.

Still, I hovered outside, waiting for Iris and Lisa. I was a bit anxious we wouldn't find a seat when we eventually did go in; there were a few empty tables towards the back, but a queue of aspirational coffee-lifestyle shoppers was beginning to build up at the counter. However, I wasn't anxious *enough* to march in on my own and bag a table, risking a row from the staff, or worse, risking someone scary asking if the other seats were taken and having to say that they were when they obviously weren't . . . God, girls, *hurry up!*

It was Iris who had asked if we could meet here at lunchtime, which was a novel experience for all of us, as I couldn't recall the last time we'd been together before seven in the evening and without a wine glass in our hands. Like a breastfeeding mother having a let-down reflex, just

70

thinking of their names made me hear the sound of corks popping, and words like 'Chilean white', 'carafe' and 'tapas' swam tipsily round my head.

I was a Coffee Sanctuary virgin. This was a secret too dark and shameful to share even with Iris and Lisa – I'd kind of given them the impression I did designer coffee all the time, when in fact I did nothing of the kind. The only choice at my usual coffee shop haunt is – *or tea?* Here I would have to familiarise myself with a new language, or else risk exposure as an Anorak who didn't know her lattes from her macchiatos. Obviously, I could just guess – but I was anxious about that, too, in case I should inadvertently order the joke item on the board and get presented with a dressed crab. I squinted up at the blackboard behind the counter, but my contact lenses were a bit cloudy and I couldn't really make anything out.

After a few minutes, however, bored with watching grumpy shoppers and knots of parading teens (fat group, thin group, fat group, thin group) go by, I noticed that the squishy brown suede sofas in the window, the only comfy seats in the place, were just about to be vacated. Here was an opportunity too good to miss so I hurled caution to the wind and made my way inside.

The trendy young couple with their first child in a pram were in the process of leaving. I smiled in regulation, patient admiration and stood back as they began to shoehorn their cumbersome way to the exit.

Aha, but how did I know it was their first child? Well, the baby was wearing a bib with 'Thursday' on it, and it actually *was* Thursday (I'd bet you anything that underneath you'd find a vest saying *'made with 100 per cent love'* on it). The spotless navy and yellow pram had Land Rover wheels, a sleeping bag attachment, matching umbrella, Playstations One and Two on Widescreen strung across its line of vision on a piece of elastic, a proper changing bag

71

the size of the Millennium Dome and – oh – didn't I say? A grandparent hanging off the end of the whole arrangement to provide much-needed help for mum.

Further conclusive evidence of their first-timeness came in the *manner* of their exit. They nuzzled the pram wheels around the ankles of chairs in their path until their occupants looked up, to be greeted by grinning parents and grinning granny, the unspoken *'Budge for the beautiful baby and important, coping, us!'* in a dirty black think bubble above their heads, efficiently clearing their way like a US Army tank.

After a respectful pause (a quarter of a second) I threw myself into one of the sofas and flung my bag and jacket on the other. I gazed around the room, at the uncomfortable chairs, the litter-strewn tiled floor, the miserable-looking people who kept their coats on and who had great big flags on stands at their tables with pictures of what they'd ordered on them, and decided that the coffee was going to have to be quite exceptionally delicious if I was going to get any clue whatsoever as to why these places were so popular.

An arrestingly spotty male staff member, sorry, *crew* member, if the yellow lettering on the back of his polo shirt was to be believed, shuffled over to clear the table.

'There'th a plathe for dirty cupth over there,' he lisped, grudgingly starting to load his tray.

'What? Oh, sorry, they're not mine, I've just got here!' I replied, relieved not to be responsible for the mess and keen to engage with the lifestyle straight away. 'What, you mean, we're expected to clear up our own stuff here? Like in Mcdonalds?'

'Yeth.'

'That's good to know, er, Brandon!' His coffee-bean-shaped name badge had a gobbet of jam on it.

'There are thmaller tableth over there if you're by yourthelf,' he deadpanned, in that teenage, '*I don't give a shit if I sound rude*' voice that does my nut, as he rose with his tray, jerking his head to the wall at the far corner, where three sets of tiny tables, each with two scrapey wooden chairs, formed an alleyway to the toilets.

'Actually, sorry, but I'm waiting for some friends, thanks,' I replied. Sorry, thanks, sorry, thanks – for *what*, exactly?

'You're thuppothed to get your order from the counter before you thit down,' came Brandon's closing friendly banter, as he finished loading his tray up with the new parents' dirty cups and squirted disinfectant over the table and my lap with a spray gun. He then crouched down precariously, tray in hand, shooed the crumbs on to the floor with a green Jaycloth, and made his way back to the counter to talk about me. Or not. Like I cared what he did, nasty boy.

Moments later a shrill voice from the doorway made everyone in the entire place look up.

'*Wow! You got the sofas!*'

Lisa is very pretty, and is accustomed to attention.

She sailed over, tall and sorted in a long floral skirt, lime-green vest top and pink cashmere wrap, ignoring the interested looks she was getting, and plonked herself opposite me. 'Well done! I've never managed to get the sofas before – we can have a *Friends* moment – bags I be Rachel! How did you manage it?'

'I camped out all night. How are you?'

'Oh, fantastic, thanks, you?'

'Well, I was fine till I got here and had my butt kicked by a table-wiper about hogging the sofas.'

Lisa looked thoughtful. 'Better that than having your butt wiped by a table-kicker though, don't you think?'

'Yes, I suppose that would have been embarrassing, here in the window,' I agreed. 'He was only about twelve, too,

73

rude little shit.' I shot a dirty glance towards the counter, where Brandon was watching a piece of machinery glug and hiss, whilst excavating the adolescent wax from his left ear with his right index finger.

Louisa Alice Urquhart, or Lisa to those of us in the know, is a solicitor. She earns pots of money, wears great clothes and despises her job. She looked over at the hapless Brandon. 'He's probably only earning about a pound an hour, poor lamb. I bet he took a long, hard look at you and was overwhelmed by adolescent sexual tension. He's probably in constricted agony, over there, hoping no one'll ask him to move.' Lisa also has a very active imagination.

'Yeah, that'll be right.'

The arrival of Iris was much more low-key than that of Lisa, even though Iris's red and white checked mac looked stunning against her shiny black hair. Catching sight of us, she waved, furtively and at waist-level, before sidling past the other tables to join us.

'Hi, you two, sorry I'm late. Wow, the sofas!'

'I know', agreed Lisa, 'poor Anna here had to give the waiter a blow-job to get them.'

'Really? Was he nice?'

I shuddered at the thought and changed the subject. 'OK, what are we having? My shout.' I needed to get to the counter and swot up the menu and this was my opportunity.

'I'm a tall skinny latte,' replied Lisa, whipping out a mirror and applying more gloss to her fat mouth, which was the only plump part of her person. 'No food for me, thanks.'

'That's a little unkind,' I quipped, 'you're not in the least bit tall!' She glowered at me. 'Iris?'

'Macchiato, ta, with nutmeg,' she replied. 'And a cranberry muffin.'

'Naughty, naughty!' Lisa tutted. 'Given up on the Atkins

diet, have we? I noticed your breath wasn't too bad when you sat down.'

I left them to it. By now the queue had disappeared, leaving me with no time to attempt to translate the menu. The hep cat behind the counter, a tall, pale-skinned male with a tapering ponytail, was rattling crockery fit to bust but when he turned to face me he looked friendly enough.

'Yes, please?' he asked. I took a deep breath and reeled off the others' orders without mishap. 'That all?'

I scanned the overhead list in panic. The only two coffee types I recognised – cappuccino and espresso – didn't appeal and I wasn't going to cave in just yet and order a vile herbal teabag. 'Um, is there any chance of just having an ordinary coffee?' I ventured. 'I mean, these all look very nice but I don't like very strong ones, or very milky ones – I'd just like coffee with cold milk on the top – is that all right?' Suppressed feelings of insecurity were charging to the front of my head as I looked for signs of the hep cat (Keith) rolling his eyes, or giving his mates a *we've got a right one here* nudge but he merely flicked his ponytail and enquired, 'Standard? Jugular? Pianoforte?' or something like that.

'Mmm, yes please, thanks.' I was rewarded with the biggest mug of coffee I'd ever set eyes on. It should have had a joke slogan on it, like *'Do not use unless you have borrowed your bladder from a horse'*.

'I'm thinking about getting a tattoo,' Lisa mumbled a little later, through a mouthful of muffin. Iris and I looked at her in amazement.

'Really?' Iris squeaked. 'What of?'

'Dunno, really, maybe a Celtic cross, or a flower – something tender and meaningful. Any suggestions?'

'Where are you thinking of having it?' I asked, eyeing her lovely, creamy skin doubtfully.

'Round here, look.' She swivelled round and lifted her

vest top a little to reveal the perfect little downy hollow at the base of her back, already resplendent with two arrestingly tantalising dimples.

'I think you should just get a couple of eyebrows put in above those,' suggested Iris, poking each one gently with her finger.

'What do you think, Anna, what should I get?'

I frowned. 'Something useful, maybe, like your bank PIN number? No, Lisa, don't do it. You're too old for tattoos.'

'No, I'm not! You're never too old for body art! And thirty-four's not old, anyway!'

'It's pretty ancient, I'm afraid. Your thirties are way too late for tattoos. Or bizarre piercings.'

Iris nodded. 'And coloured mobile phones. And saying "cool".'

'And wearing cowboy boots with denim mini skirts,' I went on. 'And Boxercise. No, don't do it, Lisa. You'll regret it.'

'And you'll look like a slapper,' added Iris, for emphasis. 'Try Botox, if you want to start experimenting with your body.'

Lisa ignored that one and changed the subject. 'Anyway, Anna, what news of the lovely Mr Anderson?'

I coloured. And squirmed a little. 'We're going to Potters on Friday night.'

'*Friday?*' They chorused in alarm. 'That's . . .'

'He's off on a course for the rest of the week.'

'Ah. That's fine, then.'

I couldn't resist the next question to Iris. 'Did Pete say anything to you about Jack saying anything to him about me?' Then, 'Did that make any sense at all?'

Iris touched my arm. ''Fraid he didn't, but then, boys don't do that sort of thing, do they?'

'Mmm.' *Why the hell not?*

'If you like,' she went on, 'I could say something to Pete about saying something to Jack, asking him to say something about you so that Pete could say it to me and I could say it right back at you?'

'I fell asleep last night,' said Lisa, catching us off-guard.

'Sorry?' I said.

Lisa sat up, her hands clenched in her lap. 'You know, *I fell asleep!*'

Realisation. 'What . . . you mean . . . *during*?'

She nodded, gloomily. 'Right, slap bang in the middle.'

Iris was aghast. 'Lisa, you can't possibly have!'

'Well, I did.'

'Did Martin have to remind you this morning?' I asked, trying not to giggle.

'Nope. He woke me up to let me know.'

'And tell us, just how did that conversation go?'

'Well, he wasn't very polite, that's for sure,' she said, draining her mug.

'I'll bet,' agreed Iris. 'Although nodding off mid-bonk isn't exactly the height of good manners either, is it?'

'I suppose not.'

'Were you pissed?' I asked, paving a helpful line of defence.

'Nope.'

'Ah.'

'I find it easier if I'm pissed,' said Iris. 'I always find I can go through the motions quite energetically after a few jars.' Then, pointedly, at Lisa, 'And *then* I get to go straight to sleep.'

Lisa was nodding thoughtfully and I found myself staring at the two of them. Not great, is it, when two grown women, ostensibly settled in happy, stable relationships, talk about their love lives in such a dreary way? I should have been shocked, embroiled as I currently was in a thrilling lust-a-thon with a potential new man but thinking back to the latter stages of my time with Michael, to the sleepy, 'Oh well, all right, thens' and the resigned, 'Suppose it's been a while so I'd betters', I did kind of wonder, just who was having all the fun out there? Brandon and his contemporaries? Eeuw, what an icky thought.

'Mind you, it's OK most of the time,' added Iris, but Lisa didn't look so sure.

Chapter Five

First line uttered on my first date with Jack: 'Wow! You look nice!' OK, fine. BUT IT WAS ME WHO SAID IT, NOT HIM! Shit! When, oh when, *oh when* would I learn to stop trying so hard!

I had put a lot of thought into what to wear, though. After the fiasco that was the quiz night wedding outfit, I toned the clothing down to jeans (well, they *had* cost a hundred and sixty pounds in Harvey Nichols in Edinburgh), a tight white silk shirt from Thomas Pink, Pied à Terre spike heels, diamond ear studs and my solitaire pendant. The jeans had been a fantastic investment: they fitted incredibly well and made me wiggle when I wore them, but I had had a few anxious moments wondering whether perhaps Jack asked me out *because* of the way I was dressed at the quiz night, not *despite* it? Could it be perhaps he'd been waiting all his life to find a woman who dressed for the pub like it was a really, really big treat? Was he about to be outed as a granny-grabber?

'You're not half bad yourself,' Jack replied, leaning forward to kiss my cheek. Hmm, citrus – sandalwood? Bloody nice aftershave, anyway, and not too much of it. 'This is a really nice apartment,' he went on, looking over my shoulder into the hall.

'Thanks, we're really lucky to have it,' I replied, although 'Would you like to come right on in and throw me *on my king-size bed? You know, like in my Alastair Campbell fantasies?'* was what I was actually thinking.

'Well, shall we get going? Can't be annoying the *restaurateur*, now, can we?'

'Watch it, you.'

We walked downstairs. Andy's desk was deserted, but the lilies on the side table below the gilt mirror gave off a thick, heady scent which followed us into the cooling evening. But hang on, what was this? I stared at the tiny silver vehicle, towards which Jack seemed to be propelling me. It looked like a little battery. *A sports car?* At his age? Iris had told me he was thirty-nine. Hmm. OK, let's not be hasty, now. Plenty of men drive edgy little sports cars and are still nice, aren't they? This one was a real arse-grazer, though, metallic paint glistening, with little go-faster nostrils on the bonnet, and as Jack opened the passenger door for me and I dropped about four feet into the passenger's seat, the pale grey leather bucket seat chilled its way straight through my jeans and on to my skin. Perhaps it was a company car, though; maybe he hadn't had any say in choosing the make? So useful for, for nipping nippily from one construction site to another? Anyway, why shouldn't a single man with no ties drive a sports car if he wanted to?

'Hungry?' he asked, grasping the silver knob gear stick and easing the car off the starting line on to the track.

'Starving,' I lied 'How was the course?'

'Oh, not too bad. You been busy?'

'Definitely. The usual, you know?'

'Mmm. How's your daughter?'

'Miranda? She's fine, thanks. Off to the pictures tonight, then she's having a sleepover at her friend's.' Sensing a real danger that we were on course to exhaust each and every avenue of conversation available to us before he even hit third gear, not to mention the fact that I'd just let slip that I was going to be sleeping on my own tonight, I took some deep breaths and tried to relax. I glanced sideways at him, remembering the electricity between us at the quiz night, when that very profile was pressed up against me. He must be about six feet two, I reckoned – his head almost touched the soft-top roof of his silly little car, but as we zipped along the riverbank road and I felt the power of the engine, I took myself by surprise by beginning to rather enjoy the sensation of being a chick in a sports car, accessorising a big handsome bloke. Inverness didn't have a very generous serving of flash cars, and noticing people on the pavement turning their heads to look as we passed, whether they were thinking *'wanker!'* or not didn't seem to matter too much all of a sudden – because this was fun! Wheee! Gangway! Hot car with hot woman inside, coming through!

'Great car!' *Who said that?* Oops, me! *Liar!*

He smiled. 'Think so? Not sure if it's a bit of a middle-age crisis-mobile or not, but it's great to drive, that's for sure.' Thank God, he saw it too – so there *was* hope.

'I should be asking stuff like how many cylinders it's got, shouldn't I?'

'Well, you could, but I wouldn't be able to tell you. Ask me something easier, if you don't mind.'

'Hmm, OK. Is it a diesel?'

For some reason he found this incredibly funny, and I waited patiently until he stopped laughing for his reply. 'No, it's not a diesel. It's a petrol. I don't think this model does a diesel version, Anna.'

Funny how wibbly my insides went, hearing him say my name, even if it was only to take the piss. 'Jack' was a word I hadn't been able to bring myself to say aloud yet, although I could, I guess, have started slowly by asking if the car had a jack in the boot, or something. Whatever, by the time *Jack* parked outside Potters, I was beginning to unwind a bit, moulded into the confines of the bucket seat which my bottom had worked so hard to warm up, and looking forward to the evening.

Potters Restaurant hides down an underlit cobbled lane in the centre of town. Once inside the warm, clinky fug, a waitress took our coats and led us to a corner table, where a tea light shone hopefully up at us from the centre and a pink bud rose stood tall in a smoked glass vase. All of the other eight or nine tables were occupied, fortunately with nobody I knew, although Jack stopped for a moment to exchange a few words with a middle-aged couple seated by the window, giving me time to sit down and try to compose myself. My hair was loose, and I tucked a stray wisp behind my ear. Then I felt to make sure my blouse collar was sitting properly, turned the clasp of my pendant round to the back of my neck, discreetly rubbed the corners of my mouth to make sure my lipstick hadn't made a sideways bid for glory, and lastly, had a furtive stray-bogey patrol, touching my nostrils to check for unwanted bats in the cave (this precaution is highly recommended – take it from one who failed to do it once and spent an entire evening with a little something fluttering above her top lip each time she exhaled). All fine. Thus, by the time Jack came over and sat down opposite me, I was the most gorgeous thing on the planet and he was one seriously lucky bastard.

But, you know, what happened next was quite unexpected.

Did a jumbo jet crash into the building opposite, and put a little dampener on our lovely, lovely night? Or did Jack smile, revealing a full set of dentures which then slithered out of his mouth and plinked into his water glass? Maybe the waitress shrieked from the other end of the room, 'Jack Anderson, how can you show your lousy face in here with that tart when me and your five kids are holed up in the Refuge?' Or could it be that the walls of the restaurant suddenly collapsed outwards, like a clown-car? Well?

Nope, nothing so bland. What happened was, well, we just looked at each other. For absolutely *ages,* pushing the frontiers of first-date eye contact far beyond any regular horizon I'd ever encountered before, and as the moments edged by, I felt my head begin to swim. We were probably only intending one of those *'Well, then, isn't this nice!'* sort of pleasant exchanges but somehow when our eyes met, they simply stayed put. I looked into his brown eyes as he looked into my green ones, and I felt all of my boundaries falling away until the safest place on earth was right here, gazing at Jack, and tearing my eyes away would be just too dangerous even to contemplate. The expression on his face was mesmeric, as though his whole body wanted to ask a question, yet something inside him held back any words, and the thrilling sensation of just looking, yet neither touching nor talking, was hypnotic. Something deep inside my common sense department was aware that it was about time a touch of foolishness ought to be creeping in, but there just didn't seem to be any room, it was as though our minds were carrying on a communication so private that even Jack and I couldn't be sure what they were up to. And I could *feel* him breathing. It felt, I realised, as though we were already in bed.

'I can't believe we've only just met,' Jack said eventually, in a low voice, still staring deep inside me.

'Me neither,' I replied.

'Can I get you something to drink?' asked the thin, blonde waitress, appearing alongside and slicing into our trance. Ah, well – if Jack had been about to murmur anything about skipping dinner and making a break for his place he'd lost his chance – and I'd lost mine.

So we ordered. Wine, then food. To think, I used to

imagine what it would be like, out on a date with a mature man, sitting back coyly as he appraised me over a menu and murmured, 'Shall I order for you?' in a masterful voice, turning his strong head sideways and flashing greying sideburns at me whilst I simpered and fluttered and concentrated on augmenting my decorativeness by sexily parrying his devastating repartee . . . bloody hell. Once you're actually in situ, on location with a bloke in a date situation, what on earth is to be gained by letting him think you can't decide what to eat?

'Champagne for de couple in de corner!' came Alessandro, the manager's – the *restaurateur's* – heavily accented voice, as he showily approached us, brandishing a camp-looking silver ice bucket on legs, which contained a chilled bottle of Moët. 'Courtesy of Signor and Signora Maclaren,' he went on, and began to untwist the cage at the neck of the bottle.

'Oh!' I exclaimed, wondering whether there had been some horrible mistake, and that we were accidentally being given someone else's booze.

'They really shouldn't have,' smiled Jack, accepting a frothing glass from Alessandro and raising it in thanks towards the couple he'd been speaking to a few moments before. They acknowledged by way of a gentle inclination of their heads, a mouthed 'Good luck!' from Mr Maclaren and a comical thumbs-up from Mrs Maclaren. I smiled at them, feeling myself turn pink. This was a little embarrassing.

'I sorted out some work for them a few months back,' explained Jack. 'Managed to stop the hill behind their house from slithering into their kitchen.'

'Did you, now? My hero,' I replied, with a flutter. Alessandro melted away. 'So, we're a couple now, are we? That's fast work!'

'Without even going through an interview process, as well,' agreed Jack. 'Impressive!'

I leaned forward and touched his arm. 'Go on, then, interview me – let's see if I'm up to the job!'

'Hmm, well, first of all, we need to establish what position you're applying for . . .' he gazed appraisingly at me. 'How about, "Executive Arm Candy"?'

'Perfect.'

'So, Ms Morris, would you describe yourself as a team player?' He was leaning towards me, his fingertips touching in an appraising, prayerful pose.

'Good God, no – what a horrible thought!'

'Anna, being a team player is supposed to be something *desirable* in an interview situation . . .'

'Try that on Bill Gates. Next question, please, Mr Anderson – sir?' I could tell he liked that one.

'How are your interpersonal skills?'

'My what?'

'Your interpersonal skills – how are they?'

'I suppose interpersonal skills are another desirable interview trick to have up one's sleeve?' I queried – heavens, all Blakemore had wanted to know during my job interview was how many houses I thought I could shift over a twelve-month period. Anyway, Jack was nodding patiently. I tried to think of a reply that wasn't filthy, settling on, 'I'd put it to you that that's a rather interpersonal question, Mr Anderson – *sir* – and if you don't move on to a more professional line of interviewing I shall have no alternative but to call security.'

'Call if you like – I've given them all the night off,' he answered, looking brazenly down the front of my blouse with a wicked grin. 'OK, let me think, now. Aha, here's a good one that was used on me once, years ago – what would you wish to have carved on your tombstone?'

'Mmm, that *is* a good one,' I responded, playing for time. 'How about, *a hot piece of ass*?'

And so on – how he probed – how I parried! How he

85

tossed out the clevers, and how I churned out the funnies! Never had a conversation been so witty, so urbane, so downright smart – not in Potters, anyway, that's for sure. I'd found my intellectual equal – not that that was necessarily anything worthy of winning any awards, but it was a lovely feeling to spark off someone with such ease. Our first courses arrived, and when I told him he was shellfish for not letting me have a second langoustine, and when Jack said it took pluck to play the harp, we both threw back our heads, laughed loud and long, basking in the happy glow of the evening.

'What's your least favourite word?' I asked, re-igniting the interview theme.

'Fuselage, definitely.'

'Fuselage?'

'Yup. Fuselage. Scariest word in the English language. You only hear it after plane crashes, you know, *'Fragments of fuselage were spread across a hundred square miles'*, that sort of thing.'

'Not keen on flying, then?'

'Definitely not. So unnatural. And *bulkhead* – that's another bad 'un. Anyway, what about you, least favourite word?'

'Traditional.'

'Why's that, then?' he asked.

'It just gets so overused at work that I don't really know what "traditional" is any more. I've even heard it applied to an Art Deco bungalow with two different loft extensions.'

'It makes me think of curtseys, somehow,' he mused. 'Like you should curtsey in the middle of saying it.'

'Really? Go on, then,' I urged.

He looked round the room. 'Maybe later.'

I was still musing. ''Pamper' – hate that one. And *"jus"*.'

'Mmm. I'm not sure about "climax",' Jack went on. 'It bothers me a lot, somehow.'

'Performance anxiety?' I purred.

'No, never that. Behave yourself.'

The food was delicious. My fish in white wine was fabulously fresh and yummy, full of tarragon and lime, and instead of toying coyly with my plateful, as would befit a gal on a first date, I wolfed the lot, plus a couple of forkfuls of Jack's duck in cherry sauce. We managed to finish the entire bottle of Moët between us, and Jack had insisted on letting me choose a white wine to have with my fish, whilst he ordered Burgundy for himself. Once we'd started talking, we didn't stop. I told him all about Miranda, although I didn't say anything about Omar, nor did he ask, about work, the Monitor Lizard, Rod, Mrs Ferguson and her glorious cottage, my ingrowing toenail, my chronic aversion to swimming pools, not to mention the vital nugget about how my wisdom teeth had been extracted under general anaesthetic when I was nineteen even though they weren't causing any discomfort and didn't he think that could be viewed as a bit of an unnecessary intervention?

'And you?' I finally remembered to say, quite a lot later.

'Me what?' he replied with a smile.

'Your life, I want to know about it. Have you ever been married?'

'Nope.'

He didn't seem perturbed about the question, so I ploughed on. 'Do you think you ever will?'

'Are you offering?'

The glint in his eyes was teasing, and sexy. Right now, hormones ablaze, I wouldn't have minded if I was.

'Well, I hate to disappoint you,' I half-whispered, 'but marriage isn't really at the front of my mind right now.' The expression on his face when I lifted my eyes towards him was like an electric shock.

'So what is?' he whispered, taking my hand.

'Would you like to see the dessert menu?' interrupted the waitress, placing two cards in front of us and disappearing, without waiting for our reply.

'Well?' he persisted.

Now he really had me flummoxed. 'Well, what?' That didn't come out quite as teasingly as I'd intended – more like that teenage holidaymaker in an amusement arcade.

'Would you like some pudding?'

Pudding??

I moved my menu to one side. 'No, thank you, I never go all the way on a first date.'

'Ah. Perhaps some coffee, then?' Now his expression was unreadable. I didn't want the evening to end; yet the thought of inviting him in when we got back to my apartment was, frankly, terrifying. And to think, I'd told him at the start that I had the place to myself for the night!

'Coffee keeps me awake at this time of night.'

'Excellent! Two coffees, then?' he smiled. 'Just kidding.'

'Jack, I'm really nervous, all of a sudden,' came flying out of my mouth.

'Why, what's the matter?'

'I don't know; I think I've just forgotten how to behave on a date – my brain's overheating with "what ifs" and "supposings", and I can hardly think straight any more.'

For a few moments he said nothing, then he gave my hand a squeeze. 'I'm glad you said so – I'm nervous too.'

I looked at him in surprise. 'Really? You don't seem it.'

'I'm having a great time – you're a lovely woman, Anna, and I'm terrified I'm going to do or say something that'll blow it.' He shrugged and took a gulp from his water glass.

'Wow.' That was the best I could do.

'Do you think we can just stop thinking? Go with the flow?'

I shook my head violently. 'Nope. No way, no can do.

I'm a manageress, Jack, I *control* things! Can't possibly go with any flows. Sorry.'

Trying to be flippant, I realised with a jolt that what I had just said was absolutely spot on. However relaxed I felt in Jack's company, and however much champagne and wine I'd put away (quite a flipping lot), now that the evening was drawing to a close I was totally chewed up about what the heck to do next – so much so, in fact, that I was subconsciously reaching the conclusion that the best thing to do – at least, the *safest* thing to do – would be to say goodnight to him as fast as possible and get myself off to bed.

Jack still held my hand, even as Mr and Mrs Maclaren rose from their table and waved goodnight at us with knowing grins, like they were going to burst into excited giggles as soon as they were outside, and talk about us all the way home.

'So, no coffee, then?' he asked.

'Sorry, no, thank you.'

He motioned to the waitress for the bill, and asked her to ring for a taxi, as Alessandro came bustling over.

'Signor Anderson! Let me put your bee-ooteeful car in de garage round de back! Is no problem! You enjoy your meal?'

'It was wonderful, as usual, Alessandro, thanks very much.' Jack handed over his keys along with his credit card. *As usual? Car keys?* Jack was obviously a regular. Something about this made me slightly shifty, although rationally I knew that was unfair. Why shouldn't he have been here before? It was the best place to eat in town, after all, and it would've been a bit of a disappointment if he hadn't been familiar with it. But, who had he taken here before me? I knew I'd have to put Lisa on to a major fact-finding mission if this was going to go much further – and I really hoped it was, only, well, perhaps not tonight. I'd pushed my luck far enough, had a lovely dinner with a lovely man who seemed to like me too, and if there was one thing I was certain of, it was that I wasn't going to entice him upstairs for – coffee – just yet. Shame, though, what with Miranda away, and all.

Did I want him? Too bloody right I did. I hadn't had sex with a man for two years, truth be known. And even though I thought I didn't miss it, turning down the advances of a sexy available man who showed all the signs of wanting me, before he'd even asked the question, was dodgy behaviour on my part, to say the least. But deep down I had a real feeling of unease at the idea of bringing someone back to my home just because Miranda happened to be away for the night and I could do it without her being any the wiser.

We were last to leave Potters; Alessandro locked the door behind us, after kissing both Jack and me exuber-antly on both cheeks. Alessandro had called a taxi for us, and as we clambered into the back of an ancient Mercedes estate driven by a wiry old man who looked as though he existed on tobacco and brown ale, Jack slung his arm around my shoulders. I cuddled up and looked up into his eyes. He smiled, and at last, we kissed.

Andy was back behind his desk in the hallway of Fyrish House, watching, as we both got out and stood, awkwardly, facing each other.

'Shit.' Jack was fumbling around in his jacket pockets. 'Double shit.'

'Let me pay for the taxi,' I said hurriedly, leaping to the conclusion that he hadn't brought any cash with him.

'No, no, don't worry, I'll do it when I get back to my place,' Jack replied in a distracted tone.

Ah. Not coming in, then – or was that up to me?

'So what's up?' I asked.

'Nothing, forget it.'

'No, tell me!'

'I've left my flat key at Potters. I forgot to take it off the keyring.' He exhaled noisily, and rubbed his forehead.

I raised my eyebrows. 'That's a good one!'

'No, really, it was an accident, honest!'

'Yeah, right!' My voice was playful, but Jack clearly wasn't playing.

'I'll get the taxi to take me back that way.'

'But Potters is closed,' I pointed out. 'There won't be anyone there.'

'They might still be clearing up, if I hurry – God, what an idiot I am!'

'Well, you could stay here . . . if you like . . . ?' I walked two fingers up the sleeve of his jacket, and performed a gold-standard sexy gaze up at him, from under my eyelashes. I seemed to have subconsciously changed my tune about the staying over thing.

The taxi driver was showing signs of impatience – it must have been the busiest time of the week for him, and he could have been off, back into the town centre, for a more lucrative pick-up by now.

'No, Anna, thanks all the same. I'd love to come up, but, well, I'd better not.' He leaned down and kissed me again, lightly, on the mouth.

'Ah.' By now I was feeling a little bit competitive. 'But I wouldn't mind!'

In the great, flirtatious scheme of things, '*But I wouldn't mind!*' must rank as one of the biggest stinkers of all time, mustn't it?

He smiled.

'So, what's it to be, then?' the taxi driver called out, extremely irritably.

'Goodnight, Anna. Thank you for a lovely evening.'

He climbed into the front seat of the cab, and blew me a kiss. I heard him say, 'Travelodge, please,' to the driver, who slammed the old Merc into first gear and skidded down the drive, leaving me standing on the pavement, feeling quite disproportionately popped.

'That didn't . . .' began Andy.

'Please, don't say a word!' I replied, stomping past him and punching the lift call button, snapping my nail in the process. 'Bugger!'

'And a very good night to you, too,' wafted through the crack in the lift doors, from Andy, as I made my solitary way up to bed.

Chapter Six

Apart from the excitement that was my private life, this particular Tuesday was creeping towards the humdrum. The Monitor Lizard was in a particularly foul mood, as the offer she'd received on The Elms, a crumbling townhouse which had been on our books for eight months and which Rod had nicknamed 'Crackhouse View', owing to its location opposite a squat, had fallen through. She was breaking the news to the deceased owner's niece on the phone, and her face was a constricted powder-keg of suppressed fury as she attempted, quite gamely, truth be told, to deflect the blame away from Blakemore Properties.

'... yes, Mrs Oswald, but the latent defects uncovered in the survey report on The Elms couldn't possibly have been picked up ....but it's the job of the solicitor, not ourselves, to seal the contract on your late aunt's house ... no, the purchasers weren't bound to complete without ... Mrs Oswald, I really must interject ... Mrs Oswald! *Be quiet!*' There was a long pause, punctuated by Monica's overbreathing. 'Mrs Oswald, Blakemore most certainly has put a great deal of effort into ... sorry? You're what? Of course you still have to pay our costs!' Her eyes rolled to the ceiling and she made an upmarket *duh!* gesture. For a moment I thought she might actually go as far as raking her hand through her helmet of hair, but things didn't get quite that bad, and as she shook her head and listened to what was presumably a tirade of fury on the other end of the line, all of a sudden she became eerily calm. The hush was palpable. 'Pardon? Well, Mrs Oswald, I don't see what difference that would make . . .' she darted a glance in my direction, and my heart sank. 'Mrs Oswald, I shall if you insist but I assure you I am better placed . . . no, no, excuse *me*, but I think you'll find . . .' those large nostrils were cauldrons of indignation – no flames as yet, but it was early days. 'One moment, if you please.' I took a deep breath, knowing what was coming. 'It's for you, Anna. Mrs Oswald would like to speak to the *manager*.'

Oh, buggery fuck. Training, girl, training. What had I been taught on a thousand mind-scrambling courses? Feedback. Empathy. Not taking it personally. Support the staff. Blue sky, brainstorm, role-play, pie chart, breakout, workshop, boiled sweets, lime cordial. Rod, passing behind my chair, paused to give my shoulders a reassuring rub. 'Brace yourself, missus – tell her to naff off and sell her heap of crap herself,' he advised in a whisper. 'I'll get you a coffee.'

I still jumped, though, as Monica put the call through to my extension. When it comes to situations like this, the main objective is damage-limitation, trying to pacify the client so that she goes away thinking we're on her side and trying to help, and doesn't make it her mission to drag Blakemore's name through the mud all over town.

Mrs Oswald was the wife of one of our local district councillors and The Elms had been allowed to become badly neglected by her infirm maiden aunt for over twenty years, before one day last year when the old lady's window cleaner had arrived for his monthly contract visit, peeped through the sitting-room window as he worked, and spotted her, sitting upright in her chair, stone-dead and, as he put it, 'going off a bit'. The post-mortem had revealed that she had sat there, undiscovered, for at least three weeks.

So I suppose, rationally speaking, Mrs Oswald's over-riding emotion towards the house was probably one of guilt at having been shown up as a neglectful niece (or at least it bloody should have been), and now that the sale had fallen through and she still had the house on her hands to deal with, I knew that she needed someone upon whom to vent her anguish. So, looked at that way, being snarled at by a Monitor Lizard with her dander up perhaps wasn't the best of starts. Ah, well, batten down the hatches, here we go. I straightened up in my seat and lifted the phone.

'Mrs Oswald?' came out in my bedtime story voice. 'It's Anna Morris here, the manager. We were all so sorry to hear from your solicitor that the buyer has withdrawn – let's see what we can do to help, may we?' And as I settled in for a long one, and Monica whapped the file on my desk and stalked out for an early lunch, I had a feeling that the day was set to go from humdrum to worse.

Amongst the glamorous and illustrious functions of Blakemore Properties is our handling of an exclusive port-folio of prime residential letting opportunities. Luxury apartments for the discerning businessperson, holiday hideaways for the discerning holidaymaker, desirable family homes for the discerning desirable family (no pets, smokers, toddlers, mirror sunglasses, dodgy cars, white leather L-shaped sofas, vertical blinds, wallpaper with borders), gloriously luxurious stately homes for the lux-uriously discerning bigwig – our buzz-phrase is that we don't handle anything we wouldn't happily live in ourselves. The only notable exception to this is 'Frostpocket', a botched barn conversion which skulks in a gloomy hollow twenty miles away, where the only thing built to last is the damp problem, but we were conned into taking that one on by the owner telling us that there were shooting rights which went with the lease. There weren't.

I'm training Rod up to handle most of the rental places, and so far he's shaping up to do a brilliant job. He's ruthless about obtaining bank and employers' references and when it comes to requesting a deposit from prospective tenants, he's hard as nails (although he prefers to think of himself as 'firm but fair'), on the principle that the person who can't come up with a month's rent as a deposit without a squeak will cause problems later on, and so gets rejected on the spot. I call him my rent boy, sometimes, when he's been good, and he says, 'Thank you, madam'. Honestly, one of these days, the Christmas night out, perhaps, we'll probably stumble into a full-on spanking session . . .

Later on I was approaching the end of my recovery period from my conversation with Mrs Oswald, when the door opened and a burly, surly (one of them was even curly!) couple came in and walked over to Geraldine's desk.

'Good morning!' chirped Geraldine, whose cold was mercifully better. 'How may we help you today?' I glanced over my shoulder and noticed that Rod had shot off out of sight.

'We would appreciate talking to the manager immediately,' drawled the man, in a thick American accent. Oh, God, not again. Still time to go out and see if Tesco need a checkout girl – I could start right away. The wife, who stood about five feet nothing in her fat white sneakers, was the one with the curly hair, and she wore a quilted white anorak with a fur-trimmed hood, and sky blue jogging bottoms, which teetered right off the top edge of the pouchy scale.

'May I take a note of your names, please?' continued Geraldine.

'George and Carol without an e Leversedge,' replied the man.

'And may I ask what it's in connection with?'

'Our rental praaahperdy.'

'And that one would be . . . ?'

'You mean you don't know? Honestly!' put in the wife, planting her hands approximately near her hips. She turned to her husband. 'You see, honey? This is what we're up against!'

'It's Sunnyholm.'

Sunnyholm. Sunnyholm. I thought hard. Which one was . . . *Sunnyholm!* It had been Rod's first solo rental assignment – what the heck was the matter with Sunnyholm? I glanced over my shoulder again. Rod hadn't reappeared from through the back, so I got up and nipped after him. After checking the coffee room I discovered him on the landing where we keep the photocopier, hiding behind the door.

'Rod?'

'Yes, boss?'

'What's up with Sunnyholm?'

'Sunnyholm?' He stroked his chin, deep in contemplation. 'Nothing, I don't think.' Then, as he slunk out from behind the door and leaned against the photocopier, facing me, he added, '*Everything.*' His entire body signalled unmitigated gloom.

I gawped at him. 'Rod? What's up? *Tell me!*' I put my hands on his shoulders and tried to get him to look directly at me, but he shrugged me away.

'I'm sorry, Anna, but Sunnyholm's been going a bit pear-shaped for a while, now. I didn't want to tell you . . .'

'But why? What's up?'

He shook his head and took a deep breath. 'It's those two, the Leversedges. They've been . . . well . . . they've been giving me a bit of a hard time, actually. Complaints, that sort of thing. I thought I had it under control but . . .' He looked genuinely nervous and took some deep breaths, bracing himself to ask, 'Well, Anna, would it be all right if I didn't have to go out and speak to them?'

97

I was gobsmacked. This was so unlike the feisty Rod I knew and loved – only an hour before he'd had us all in stitches when he'd offered to provide sandwiches for an elderly lady who seemed hell-bent on spending the entire day viewing every single thing we had on our books – and then he gallantly went out and bought her some when she'd missed his gentle sarcasm completely and accepted, requesting tuna mayonnaise with no onion.

'Of course you don't, not if you don't want to. You leave them to me. Did they look at the house before they took it on?'

'He did, four times. She was still in the States.'

'Four times, eh? *Right.*'

I poked my head around the door and called through to Geraldine, loud enough for the Leversedges, who were still standing at reception, to hear:

'Would you be kind enough to show Mr and Mrs Leversedge through to our meeting lounge and let them know I'll be with them shortly?'

'Perhaps you should have offered them some pies to keep them going until you get there,' Rod said gloomily, as I closed the door and turned to face him again.

Sympathetic I may have been, but I definitely wasn't in the mood for flippancy, and if Rod was going to get me to clear this one up for him, didn't he have a bit of a cheek to be cracking jokes? 'OK, spit it out,' I demanded. 'Just why have we got Mr and Mrs Angry America in our office? And how afraid should we be?'

He sighed, suddenly looking even younger than his age, turning his head this way and that, like Miranda does when she's been cornered for a telling-off, and hunching his shoulders.

'OK, here goes,' he began. 'You know Sunnyholm was the first rental place you gave me to do on my own?'

''Course I do.'

He looked so earnest, in his grey suit and shiny tie.

'Well, you know how pleased you were when I got the Leversedges, and how their references checked out so well, and how the rent's been coming in bang on time from his employers, and how the owners of the house think the sun shines out of our corporate rear ends?'

'Ye-es?' A horrible thought struck me. 'Oh, God, don't tell me their cheques have bounced!'

'No!' he almost shouted. 'Nothing so simple!'

'WHAT, then?' I snapped back. Now he was making me nervous.

'Well, a few days after they moved in, they faxed through a list of defects.' He reached into his jacket for his wallet, and pulled out a very shabby piece of folded A4 paper. 'This one.'

'Really? You never told me!'

'Course I never told you! It's *my* property!'

'What sort of stuff's on it? I thought Sunnyholm was in good nick, wasn't it? Isn't that the one with the whirlpool bath and the jumbo larder fridge?'

Rod nodded and opened out his list. 'Yup. It's also got, let me see, now, a slight tear in the underside of an upstairs bedroom rug, a lampshade with a scorch mark on the inside, some scratching to the glasswork inside the refrigerator, a lack of an indoor clothing airer . . .'

'But there's a tumble dryer!' I put in. Rod didn't seem to hear me.

'. . . no airtight cookie storage facilities, an insufficiently powerful power shower in the second en-suite bedroom, too few guest towels, a coffee table in a colour of wood which does not match the other drawing-room furnishings, only six dining-room chairs in a house which potentially sleeps eight, an offensively tinny doorbell chime . . .'

'Stop!' I couldn't believe my ears.

'. . . no room for fish cutlery in the cutlery tray, insufficient napery . . .'

'Napery?'

'. . . an underpowered lawnmower and a partridge in a pear tree. Or rather, insufficient partridges in a sub-standard pear tree.' He handed the list to me and chewed his lip. I glanced down it, noticing that Rod had marked various ticks and asterisks in red ink all the way down.

'When did this arrive?'

'Oh, a few weeks ago, now.'

'Why didn't you show it to me?'

He shrugged. 'Thought I could sort it all out myself. I didn't want you to think I'd stuffed up on my first solo property.'

'What did the owners say when you showed them all this?'

Rod reddened even further. 'Well, um, I haven't actually told them, Anna.'

'You *what*?'

'I couldn't!'

'Yes, Rod, you could! This stuff's nonsense! The owners should have been warned we had a potential issue brewing . . .'

'But the Leversedges were my choice of tenants – it's not the owners' fault they're picky . . .'

'Picky? *Picky*? Don't you mean obsessive? Or just mad?'

'It's him, Anna, George Leversedge. He's been banging on about shoddy detailing for weeks now – it just got to me, that's all.'

'I still can't believe you didn't tell me. Or the owners,' I said, shaking my head.

'But, Anna,' he protested, 'I couldn't come crawling back to you about my first solo assignment, could I? And another thing, I assured the owners at the start that they could leave everything to me, so, well, I've sort of been getting things fixed myself.'

I stared at him in disbelief. 'What, you mean, you've been running around replacing all this stuff?'

He nodded.

'With your own money?'

He nodded again.

I sank back against the wall. 'But Rod! These people are *at it*! There's practically nothing on this list that merits fixing at all, let alone out of your own pocket!'

'But you should hear them!' he burst out. 'They've been going on and on about the smallest thing and make out that they've been duped into taking on a defective place . . .'

'Which they haven't! Good God, Rod, how much have you spent?'

He shrugged in defeat. 'Don't know exactly. About six hundred, by now. The new coffee table was a bit of a killer.' Plunging his hands into his trouser pockets, he appeared younger than ever. Another thought occurred to me. 'Did they *know* that you were paying for the stuff yourself?'

He nodded, glumly.

'OK, OK, let's think about this. They've sent you a wish-list, and, like Jimmy Savile, you've been granting them one by one.'

'Jimmy Savile?' queried Rod.

'Never mind – historical reference. Anyway, why are they here now?' I persisted. 'Looking for world peace and an end to all hunger?'

Rod shook his head. 'Well, I'm pretty sure it'll be the lawnmowing. I couldn't afford to upgrade the mower this month, so I've been cutting the grass for them myself, only I couldn't make it at the weekend . . .'

'Sweet, flipping heck!'

'. . . or it might be the lampshade. Mrs Leversedge

wanted coral, but apparently the one I bought them was peach . . .' He looked downwards and chewed his lip. 'Tell you what, if you keep them talking for an hour or so, I could nip up and firebomb the place, so's we can get them to move somewhere else?'

'They'll be looking for somewhere else, all right,' I muttered, stalking back out front.

But before I went to confront the Leversedges in the meeting lounge, a welcome surge of common sense led me over to my desk, where I sat down, ignored the inquisitive glances from Geraldine and the Monitor Lizard, looked out the lease documents, and quickly read through them, scribbling a few notes as reminders of what I saw as the main issues.

A few minutes later, I found George and Carol Leversedge perched on the edge of the larger of the two cream sofas in the meeting lounge, hunched over cups of coffee to which they had helped themselves from the machine in the corner. *Of course they took the coffee,* I snarled to myself, as I made a face which approximated a professional smile – what else might they have managed to get while they were here? Ah, yes, biscuits! I saw that our shortbread plate was nearly empty – they were chowing down on the lot, greedy, grasping, freeloading bullies! Oh! And dear Carol had helped herself to some brochures, a town map and a handful of paper hankies! Bless!

Bless, my arse.

'Mr and Mrs Leversedge, I'm Anna Morris, office manager. How may I be of assistance?'

It took a moment or two of rocking back and forth for George to rise to his feet, and when he did, he offered me a firm, corporate handshake, as though he'd finally found someone he could do business with. Carol opted to remain seated – there was one last biscuit to see off, after all. Or maybe she needed a pull from George, whatever.

'Ms Morris, Carol and I felt it would behoove us to talk with you in person so that we could discuss some of the difficulties we're not comfortable with concerning our rental property . . .'

'So I understand,' I responded, suddenly more ready for him than I had ever been for anyone. How DARE he intimidate my Rod! 'Am I correct in my understanding that you furnished Blakemore with a list of items with which you were unhappy?'

'You are.'

'And is this it?' I held up Rod's tatty sheet of paper. Mr Leversedge squinted at it.

'It is.' Carol Leversedge sat up a little, and folded her arms.

'And might you let me know the reason for your visit today?'

'Certainly.' George Leversedge reached into his pocket and produced a small black notebook, which he flicked through briefly before settling upon a page covered with a sprawly list. 'We had an agreement regarding the lawn-mowing arrangements, which last weekend was not adhered to. Furthermore, a replaced lampshade was not in the shade specified by my wife. This is unacceptable. The dinner napkins supplied were of an inferior white cotton fabric, when my wife specifically stipulated for ivory linen. We are concerned by the excessive noise produced by the dish-washing machine and require it to be replaced with a more silent model.' His wife nodded along to his words. 'We would be more comfortable if a security system were to be installed to safeguard both us and our belongings . . .'

'Mr Leversedge . . .' I began, to no avail.

'One moment, ma'am. We are concerned at the efficiency of the central heating system as our bills have far exceeded those to which we are accustomed in the States. Furthermore . . .'

'ENOUGH!' I shouted. Yes, *shouted*. Amazingly, George Leversedge, taking the hint, shut up, although he was breathing heavily. I faced them both, and steeled myself. There *was* something intimidatory about these two, and I couldn't quite put my finger on it, but I felt a wave of sympathy for Rod, having this to deal with on his first solo rental assignment. 'I think I get the picture. I have studied the list you gave my assistant Mr Dunsley, and found almost nothing upon it which merits action on the part of either Blakemore or our clients. Mr Dunsley has gone to great lengths, and great personal expense, to satisfy your demands, and I can assure you that if I had known of his actions in personally funding replacement items to your specification, I would not have allowed them. I find your requests trite, unnecessary and downright greedy, and I am furious that you have come here today demanding more, when an apology would have been more in order.'

Got 'im. He looked like he had been hit by a truck. 'An apology?' he repeated. 'That property is unfit . . .'

'On the contrary, Mr Leversedge,' I cut in, 'Sunnyholm is an excellent property in full working order, which I understand you viewed on four occasions prior to accepting. If there had been any impediments to your comfort or safety, these would have been picked up prior to your moving in. I find your demands unacceptable, and your intimidatory treatment of a valued member of my staff quite despicable. You knew that he was funding your demands personally, yet you allowed him to proceed. That, to me, is an unpleasant way to behave.' Was I afraid? Was I running out of steam? Thankfully, that would be a no bloody way.

'You have no right to talk to your clients like this!' Carol Leversedge exploded, which was not a pretty sight.

'Mrs Leversedge, I have never in my career had call to talk to my clients like this. Fortunately for me, you are not my clients. You have been allowed to occupy one of our client's houses because we have obtained references to the effect that you are eligible for consideration as tenants. In the light of what I have discovered just now, I'm afraid I must take the view that those references were erroneous, and that it would be in the best interests of our client if we were to terminate the lease agreement forthwith.'

'You what?' spluttered George Leversedge, advancing towards me, jowls a-tremble. 'I cannot believe I'm hearing this! You have no right . . .'

'On the contrary, Mr Leversedge, it is you and your wife who, unfortunately, have no rights. If you look at your lease agreement, you will see a clause which stipulates that tenants must not behave in a manner which causes nuisance, intimidation, or which places the general public, our clients or their agents – which is us – in a state of fear and alarm.'

'You're kidding, right?' Carol Leversedge had heaved herself to her feet, and was standing squarely beside her husband.

'Certainly not, Mrs Leversedge. Now, I don't quite know what's at the root of all this . . .'

'Your defective property! That's what's at the root of this!'

'You can't throw us out – we'll sue!' God, she was slappably smug, that one.

'Mrs Leversedge, I would look forward to that. Meanwhile, your notice to quit will be in tonight's post, which will allow you eight weeks to find an alternative place to live.'

'But it took five months for us to find Sunnyholm! We'll never find anywhere as good . . .' she stopped mid-sentence, as realisation of their predicament hit home. Her husband gazed at his feet.

'I can quite believe that, but I wish you luck with your search. Good day.' I turned to leave.

'Wait up!' George Leversedge came after me and touched my arm, quite gently, although I flinched all the same. 'Are you serious?'

Turning back to face him, I replied, 'Perfectly, Mr Leversedge. Your behaviour towards a young man on my staff whom I value enormously has been completely out of order. Sunnyholm is a top-of-the-range Inverness property, and you were lucky to secure it. I had several other potential takers for it, and I shall have no difficulty re-letting it.'

'I TOLD you we should never have moved here!' Carol Leversedge wailed at her husband. '*Why* did we have to move?'

'I'm sorry, sweetie,' he faltered. 'I did my best . . .'

I stared at them in astonishment.

'Not good enough!' she spat back, then, in a softer voice, 'Oh, God, I'm sorry too, sweetie.' Now she looked – almost – penitent.

George Leversedge put a hand on his wife's shoulder, then slowly turned to face me again. 'Ms Morris, you're probably right. I guess my behaviour has been a little over the top, I see that now. Carol honey, do you mind if I explain a few things to Ms Morris?'

She nodded, dabbing her eyes with a tissue. One of *our* tissues.

George Leversedge sighed. 'Carol didn't want to come over here. I persuaded her on the basis that we'd be living in a beautiful Scottish home, surrounded by beautiful countryside, and that soon we'd have lots of new friends, and we'd be flying home every three months to visit the family . . .'

'Every *two* months,' she corrected.

'OK, OK, every two months. Anyway, I promised her I'd find us a beautiful Scottish mansion house to live in – maybe even with a butler . . .'

'A *butler*?' I repeated, incredulously.

'I thought all big houses had them, here,' she mumbled.

'Ah.'

'I arrived a month before Carol, and my job was really good, only, well, the package I was offered shrank dramatically somewhere in transit, so the trips home were only to be twice a year, instead of every two months, and the mansion . . .'

'Became Sunnyholm,' said Carol.

'Yup, the mansion became Sunnyholm. It's only just within our allowance. And there's definitely no butler.' After a short pause we all allowed ourselves a smile.

'Sunnyholm could have been anywhere and it wasn't going to be good enough, I guess. I just want to go home!'

'But we can't, sweetie, not for another seventeen months, anyway,' her husband reminded her in a soft voice.

'I know, I know.'

We all stood in silence for a few moments. Carol Leversedge seemed so crushed, that even though I was angry with them for being so cruel to Rod, I was beginning to pity her lonely situation. And as for him, well, poor old sap, going round rental houses trying to find a mansion with a butler, knowing that his wife didn't want to come in the first place and would hit the roof when she saw that her new home lacked both trout loch and turret . . . it must be strange, being a stranger in a foreign land, even if the basics are meant to be the same.

'Ms Morris, on reflection, would you permit us to apologise to Mr Dunsley and recompense him for his expenditure?'

Wow, I had won. But their miserable faces took the edge off any impulses to punch the air which may have been creeping in. However, I thought for a bit before caving gently in. 'Mr Dunsley has spent nine hundred pounds out of his own pocket, Mr Leversedge.' Well, it'd be nice if poor old Rod could get a bit of beer money out of all this, wouldn't it?

'I can bring that over in cash in twenty minutes.'

'Very well, I think that would be appropriate.'

'And please may we stay?' asked Carol Leversedge in a very, very small voice.

God, it's ugly, that little mean streak that made me really, really enjoy the few deep, troubled breaths I took as I looked as though I was wrestling with my answer.

'I'll consult with Mr Dunsley, but I imagine that will be in order,' I replied. Besides, we'd never get that amount of rent from a private rental from anyone else.

I shook their hands and left the room to go and find Rod, ignoring the female voice which followed me out of the meeting lounge saying something about still wanting some proper linen napery. Rod was just where I'd left him, although he made a pathetic show of being busy, by attempting to photocopy a cardboard box.

'Well?' he asked, not nonchalantly at all.

'They want to see you, right now,' I said sternly. 'What's this I hear about you neglecting to clean their windows?'

Chapter Seven

Geraldine's choices of clothing were a wee bit of a sore point in the office sometimes. She knew damn well that, as our receptionist, she held the golden key to the portal that revealed the path to the bliss of being an exclusive Blakemore client, so why the heck she'd chosen to dress for work this morning in combats and trainers was beyond me. The Monitor Lizard took one look at her as she sat down at her desk this rainy Tuesday morning, sniffed in disgust and then turned her attention pointedly towards her computer. She began typing furiously – no, really, furiously – think of a Road Runner cartoon where he's hijacked a train, and he's looking out the side of the cab as it barrels full steam ahead, letting off the whistle, steam everywhere – *that's* what the Lizard looked like as she whacked seven shades of shit out of her keyboard.

Actually, I was pretty peeved with Geraldine myself, and realised that I'd have to have a word with her at some point. And when would be a better moment than right now? The office was empty – well, apart from the small, silent girl from Valerie's Flowers who was redoing the arrangement on the dining-room table in the window, all that was going on in the office this morning, the day after Leversedgegate, was the click of Monica's fingernails on her keyboard, and little ripping noises as Rod applied double-sided tape to the photographs of Beachcombe

Manor – a modern, over-designed, five-bedroom, four-bathroom monster built from bright red bricks shipped from somewhere preposterously inappropriate like India and situated on the seafront in Nairn, which was likely to sell for at least double the asking price owing to its proximity to the first tee of the golf course.

Furthermore, when Geraldine stood up, she revealed the word BENCH in huge embroidered letters on her backside – making me wonder whether I ought perhaps to put a notice on her chair saying ARSE, so that she knew where she was. I walked over to her and perched on the edge of her reception desk.

'Geraldine, can I have a word?'

She looked up from her timesheet and smiled at me. 'Sure!'

It had gone eerily quiet. I glanced over at Monica, and realised that she had begun mime-typing, as the clicking noise had mysteriously ceased.

'Um, this is a little awkward, but your clothes . . .'

'Yes?' Geraldine stroked a hand down her slim thigh.

'Well, they're not quite right for the office, wouldn't you say?' I could feel myself reddening – I knew I sounded like my granny. Perhaps I should have done this somewhere private? Ah, well, too late now.

'Oh! But they're new!'

'Yes, well, they're just not quite appropriate for reception, that's all . . .'

'The top's fine, isn't it?'

The top was a tight, black, long-sleeved V-neck T-shirt, which showed off her gorgeous, twenty-year-old figure to perfection, and her name badge, 'Geraldine Howie', with its Blakemore chimney logo, hovered pertly above her left nipple. I knew what the Monitor Lizard would think – but in fact, on reflection, I saw that the look, from the waist up at least, was rather good.

'Yes, Geraldine, the top's fine, but I'm afraid I'd like you to can the combat and trainer look and wear more office-type clothing. I'm sorry.' I ended up with one of those grimacey faces which was meant to convey reluctant authority and sisterly solidarity in the name of fashion, but probably just looked like a big old grimacey face.

Geraldine cocked an eyebrow and met my grimacey face. 'Would you like me to go home and change?'

'Don't be daft. We'll start tomorrow.' I stood up. 'I'll expect to see brown tights, lots of pleats . . .'

'And wobbly knees!' finished Rod, who'd been lugging in as well. 'Dame Edna glasses! Oh, sorry, Monica – no offence!'

'These are Christian Dior!' Monica sniffed, touching the rim of her pointy blue glasses with her right index talon. Aha, so she *had* been listening!

Geraldine took a call. Then she looked up and said, 'That's Jack Anderson on the line for you, Anna.'

I skipped like a teenager back to my desk.

'Jack!'

'Hi, Anna – how's things?'

'Fine, thanks, you?'

'Oh, you know. Just snogging in the bath, so I thought I'd ring.'

'Pardon?' *What had he said?*

'I said, I was just sogging in a hot bath – been on the go since five this morning, so I've taken a couple of hours off to freshen up.'

'Ah.' I checked my loins. Was there anything stirring at the abrupt visual picture of Jack chest-deep in hot bubbles in the middle of my working morning? Could be!

'Want to come over?' His voice was teasing, smiling.

'I might get wet,' I murmured.

Vague splashings and swishings from the other end of the line confirmed Jack's location. Hmm – a curious and

111

troubling intrusion. Mind you, wasn't it rather an odd thing to do after only one date, ringing me up to tell me he was in the bath, and inviting me to join him?

'Risk worth taking, I'd say,' he remarked.

I looked up and saw a man in his forties open the door for his elderly female companion, and my heart lurched guiltily as I saw Mrs Ferguson, wrapped up against the wind in a brown tweed coat and cream mohair hat, enter the office. However, I smiled and waved at her, gesturing to Geraldine to show them into the meeting lounge.

'Well?'

'Sorry, Jack, what were you saying?'

'I said,' he repeated slowly, 'it's a risk worth taking. Coming?'

'Don't be daft, I've got an office to run.' I felt slightly irritated – how could I possibly drop everything? He must have known that, surely, or did he think I was just playing here? Running my Barbie Deluxe Office with its Fully Working Parts? 'Can we make it later on?'

'Lunch, then?' he persisted.

'Done. Where?'

'Round here if you like – how about it? Say, twelve o'clock?'

A *nooner*! My stomach lurched at the prospect of a private lunch with a squeaky clean Jack Anderson. 'OK, see you then.'

I put the phone down, hauled my brain back into work mode and shot through to welcome Mrs Ferguson before I could reflect on the day to come. Geraldine, combats or not, was doing a grand job, handing out cups of coffee and chatting brightly about the weather.

'Mrs Ferguson!' I beamed. 'Welcome to my world! No, please don't get up.' I crossed the room and gave her an awkward peck on the cheek – something we'd never done before and, judging by her rather rigid reaction, an alien gesture to which she was unaccustomed. But she smiled warmly at me just the same, and clutched my hand with her small, papery one for a moment. It was icy cold.

'Hello, Anna. You'll have met my son James, have you not?'

I had not.

'This is Mr James Ferguson,' put in Geraldine, displaying immaculate training as she presented him to me flamboyantly, and he stood to shake my hand. The pressure of his clammy fingers turned my knuckles white, and I winced. 'May I get you anything else,' she went on, 'or shall I leave you to it?'

The combats and trainers had never seemed so irrelevant. 'No, thank you Geraldine, we'll manage fine from here.'

'Ms Morris . . .' James Ferguson began.

'Anna, please,' I cut in, as I sat on the sofa opposite.

'Whatever, my mother has been keeping me informed of developments regarding her relocation to Inverness, and I have travelled up here specifically to ensure her that best interests are protected.'

I hadn't expected to take to Mrs Ferguson's sons, and this first impression was a little short of promising. James Ferguson's appearance at first sight was reassuringly 'local' – quite tall, with large, strong facial features, interesting, grey eyes, his mother's straight nose and even, yellowish teeth, but the Highlander in him had been forced aside by what looked to be sharp, Savile Row tailoring, a well-tended greying moustache and blue enamel cufflinks, which glinted in sharp contrast to the pinstriped pink shirt which would never have made it to the shelves of any store in Inverness, let alone the gold slide which held his maroon knitted silk tie fast to his chest. He looked as though he had made a bit of an effort about the feet for

113

his return to the sticks, however, as his feet sported exquisite brown brogues, which could well have been cobbled by the original shoemaker's elves, so lustrous was the leather and so carefully worked the stitching. I'd been around long enough to recognise a bit of bespoke, so I had.

'James is very busy,' added Mrs Ferguson proudly, although her face seemed a little strained. I thought of how she used to tell me all about his 'business', always jetting away to big, sod-off conferences all over the world – I think the last one had been in La Manga – one of these places where the men golfed ('golved'?) in between sessions, and their wives got taken on luxury tours round jewellery shops.

'Well, I'm delighted to meet you at last, Mr Ferguson. I've heard a great deal about you from your mother, and I can assure you that her best interests are my absolute top priority.'

He sniffed.

'Your mother has always been a great friend of both me and my daughter, and we're very fond of her.' I sounded like a patronising nurse in a retirement home, patting one of the old dears on the hand whilst talking over her head. 'She's trouble, this one, she is!' Mrs Ferguson took it on the chin, though, smiling throughout.

'Of course, of course,' James Ferguson put in. 'Now, this, this, apartment . . .'

'Cedar Park,' I prompted. 'Yes?'

'How much is it?' He extracted an electronic organiser from his breast pocket and it clicked into life with a horrid bleeping noise and a flash of blue light, which bounced off his tiepin and on to the ceiling.

I hadn't expected this to be the first question, but at least I knew the answer. 'It's a fixed price of £136,000,' I replied, looking at his mother anxiously for her reaction. She gave none.

'How much?' he spluttered.

'A hundred and thirty-six thousand pounds. Quite pricey, I know . . .'

'Pricey? *Pricey?* That's daylight robbery! That's . . . that's extortionate!' He snapped the organiser shut and leaned towards me. 'You can't expect an old lady to pay that sort of money for a piddling little flat in Inverness – are you mad?'

'Now, James, let's listen to Anna, shall we?' Mrs Ferguson said calmly, patting her son on his knee. He eased her hand away like it was an irritating spider.

'What else have you got?' he demanded.

'Sorry?'

'What others have you got that aren't so expensive? She doesn't need a, a full-on *penthouse*, you know . . .' then he seemed to catch himself, and his voice lowered and softened a little '. . . I mean, what we're looking for is a small, comfortable, ground-floor place with no garden and a measure of security – somewhere easy to keep, you know what I'm getting at?'

You mean somewhere cheap, don't you, you vile man?

I gathered my thoughts. Poor Mrs Ferguson was now looking a little uncomfortable – she loathed confrontation, I could tell, and this was in danger of turning into one.

'Well, James is right, Anna, I don't need the lap of luxury!' she whispered, suddenly seeming very, very small.

'Mrs Ferguson – Mr Ferguson, may I explain a little about Cedar Park before you dismiss it out of hand?'

'Go on, then,' Mr Ferguson said, gruffly. His mother nodded.

'Well, first of all, I have to put it in context. Property prices in this area have soared over the last three years – there's a combination of reasons for that, but it's an unavoidable statement of fact. Some say that we're only just coming into line with the rest of the country – we've been a backwater for so long – but now, with new industries coming in all the time and huge pressure for housing, we've seen enormous leaps in values lately.'

'Doesn't help us much, though, does it?' James Ferguson sounded sulky, like a child, and I'm sure I caught a tiny glimpse of amusement in his mother's eyes as she gave him a sideways glance.

'Well, yes and no,' I replied. 'You have to bear in mind that these increases apply across the board, and if you take into account a house as lovely as Ben View Cottage, in such a unique location, I have no doubt that you will be able to realise a price for it which will make the Cedar Park apartment quite easily attainable.'

'I know we'll get a good price for Ben View . . .' Mr Ferguson began (*We*? You mean *'my mother'*, surely?) '. . . but what sort of surplus would we be looking at if we have to shell out a hundred and – how much did you say? – grand for a flat? Mmm?'

I stared at him. 'Thirty-six.' He didn't beat about the bush, did he?

'Go on, dear,' Mrs Ferguson prompted.

'OK, well, you asked what else you could get instead of Cedar Park. The answer to that, in terms of purpose-built secure retirement property, is currently nothing. Inverness is a small city, Mr Ferguson, as you know, and there are no other developments of this type currently under construction, to my certain knowledge.'

'But that's just Blakemore Properties, isn't it? There are loads of other estate agencies in town, and then there are the lawyers' windows – they're *full* of flats for sale!'

'No, really,' I insisted. 'Your mum's welfare is really important to me, as I said, and ever since I had that conversation with her at Ben View, I have made a point of monitoring the entire market to see if there were any alternatives available, in order to maximise her choices, and I am certain that, unfortunately, there are currently none.' Plus, I'd been feeling so darned shifty about my ulterior motives that I wanted to assuage my dodgy conscience by doing as much groundwork for her as I could. Oddly enough I kept this particular thought to myself.

'Are you absolutely sure about that?' he said, doubtfully.

'Completely, although you are of course at liberty to make whatever enquiries of the other agencies, and the property developers, in town, in order to satisfy yourself . . .'

'I don't have time for that!' he whined. 'I have a demanding executive position in London!'

'James is very high up, you know,' Mrs Ferguson affirmed, patting his knee again. It could be my imagination, but I swear she was beginning to look amused by her son's bumptiousness.

'Quite,' I replied. 'So, the way I see it you have three options. You can either give Cedar Park some consideration, or else you can bide your time and wait for other, less . . . *pricey* alternatives to come on the market.' I looked Mr Ferguson in the eye as I kind of hissed out the word 'pricey' – at least he had the decency to drop his eyes.

'And the third option?' Mr Ferguson asked.

'The third option is to do nothing, and stay put.'

'What do you think, dear?' Mrs Ferguson asked her son.

'I don't know,' he mumbled.

'Anna?' she looked at me kindly. 'What do *you* think we should do?'

I thought for a few moments before speaking. 'Well, as your agent, I'd be telling you again that Cedar Park is an absolutely stunning and well thought-out development in a beautiful part of town, where the inside attention to detail is of the highest standard I've ever seen in this part of the world. I'd be telling you that you would have twenty-four-hour warden assistance, security gates and cameras, a cleverly landscaped garden, a bus service at the gates which runs into the town centre every fifteen minutes, an open fire if you want one – the warden even carries the coal in for you – proper wooden windows and doors, a prescription delivery service, all the chiropody, hair-dressing and grocery services you could wish for, home help as required, and a view of the river to die for.' She raised her eyebrows at my unfortunate turn of phrase and smiled. 'Sorry!' I grinned, and smiled back.

'And as my friend?'

'As your friend, I'd want you to be absolutely certain that you feel that this is the right move for you – never mind what others say – no offence, Mr Ferguson – but if you want to stay on in Ben View Cottage and just see how it goes, then I'm sure that your family and friends, including me – even Social Services, they're very good, you know – will rally round to see what can be done to make arrangements and improvements so that you can continue to be happy there for a long time to come.' Boy, was I glad to get that off my chest. I stared pointedly at Mr Ferguson, to see if there was any reaction at being implicated in the 'looking after mother' team, but I saw none.

'What if she was *your* mother?' Mr Ferguson asked, a little more contritely this time. 'She can't go on living up at Ben View indefinitely, you know, it's getting ridiculous!'

'Well, it would be nice if she were my mother, even though there's nothing wrong with my current one, and if that were the case, and if it was clearly decided that a move had to be made, then I would have no hesitation whatsoever in snapping up Cedar Park.'

'Hmm.'

'Besides,' I added, in a conciliatory voice, 'Cedar Park's an excellent investment.' *Well, once an estate agent . . .*

'That's as may be,' he said, his brow furrowed and shiny, 'but not at that price. What can you do for us?'

'Sorry?'

'Come on now, Anna – *fixed price*? What nonsense! I know a thing or two about property – I've dabbled, you know, and I know an opening gambit when I see one, so, I repeat, what can you do for us? *For my mother?*'

'What, you mean in terms of reducing the price?' I queried softly.

'That's exactly what I mean,' James Ferguson affirmed, sitting forward and easing up into his negotiating stride.

'James!' his mother scolded. 'Don't be making Anna uncomfortable, now!'

'It's all right, ma, Anna's an estate agent – she can handle it!'

Meaning???

'Mr Ferguson, unfortunately with Cedar Park the price was set in advance by the developer – the sales contract was given to us on a fixed-price basis, meaning we have not been afforded any leeway with the price negotiation.' I thought it best to give it to him straight, rather than flannel about. I needed James Ferguson on my side, whatever his mother decided to do.

'Well, that's not very good, is it?' he replied, huffily. 'Obviously you will need to explain to the developers in this instance that a discount is in order.'

This was verging on the unfair. 'And they will proceed to ask me whether there are any other interested parties to whom the apartment may be released instead,' I replied in an even voice.

'To which your answer would be?'

I looked him in the eye. 'The truth, of course – that there are several.' I turned back towards his mother. 'Mrs Ferguson, I have held this place for you as I said I would, but in terms of the price, there's nothing I can do.'

'Of course, of course, dear – don't you be worrying yourself! You've plenty worries without me, I know that!'

'Oh, but there is,' James Ferguson cut in, a slow smile creeping over his face.

'Pardon?'

'Something you can do – you know there is, don't you, Anna?'

His voice now had an oily, boardroom quality doubtless forged in a thousand air-conditioned, pot-planted and modern-art-strewn offices high above the mean streets of the City of London.

'What do you mean?' He had me this time; I was baffled. The only thing which crossed my mind was the vague notion that he was going to ask me to sleep with him, but surely he wouldn't attempt that particular tack with his *mother* in the room?

'Your *commission*, Anna, of course – I take it Blakemore will be charging a hefty commission per sale with this development? One thing my property dabblings has taught me is that the agent always creams off, what is it with this one, Anna, three per cent? Four?'

'James!' his mother turned on him, outraged. 'That's no way to speak to Anna!'

'Calm down, mum, it's Anna's job to negotiate, isn't it, Anna?' He wore a look of triumph like a child at a birthday party who'd managed to scoff ALL the meringues, AND keep them down, before the other children got to the table.

'Oh, absolutely.' *And if your mother wasn't my dear friend I'd currently be negotiating with Northern Constabulary to release me on bail after I'd smashed the stainless steel coffee machine over your mean little head, you, you arse.* How, I wondered, could Mrs Ferguson have spawned such a dud?

'However,' I went on, 'unfortunately, or fortunately, whichever way you'd like to look at it, I have already deducted Blakemore's commission from the figure I quoted you. You will see from our advertising material and our website that these apartments are on the market for sale at a fixed price of £140,000. And if you like I can show you my copy of our contract with the developers which states that we are paid a flat rate of four thousand pounds per sale.'

'Oh, Anna . . .' Mrs Ferguson began '. . . you don't need . . .'

'You mean you're doing this for . . . for *nothing*?' her son spluttered.

'As I said, Mr Ferguson, your mother is a friend.'

My, but the moral high ground's a bit of a chilly place when the icy whiff of ulterior motive whistles up your skirt, isn't it? I mean, what I'd said was true, but my motives for not charging a commission to Mrs Ferguson had been far more to do with guilt than altruism. Certainly, the sale of Ben View would almost certainly realise more than enough to pay for Cedar Park, but I saw from the start that my not charging a commission would benefit both of us – her finances and my conscience. We'd already done extremely well out of the other Cedar Park sales – and for very little effort on our part, as well. The apartments were so lovely, and in such demand, that they'd virtually been walking out of the office by themselves. All we'd had to do was swan proudly around their warm interiors, stroking the turned wood door handles and pointing out how easily the chrome monobloc taps switched from 'jet' to 'diffuse' . . .

Mr Ferguson was wrestling with himself, which was a mad, bad, ugly sight to behold. Presently he turned to his mother. 'Well, ma, what do you say?'

'I say we should go ahead,' she replied.

'Fine.' He straightened up and looked at me. 'We'll take it. I mean, my mother would like to take it. You're absolutely sure it's a good investment?'

'Completely,' I replied, wearily. *Cash cow. Dripping roast. Dead cert. Prime piece of real estate.* God, I wished he wasn't sitting in front of me any more. Then I pulled my face into its most dazzling, estate-agent-smile shape and thought about what to say next, but Mrs Ferguson got there first.

'Em, excuse me a wee minute, the both of you?'

'Yes?' we chorused, this time wearing matching indulgent looks as we ceded the floor to her tiny frame.

'I don't suppose you'd be letting me see it first, would you? I don't want to be a nuisance, but this fireplace you're telling me about . . .'

'Of course!' I overdid. 'I was just about to say just that!' I wasn't. It had slipped my mind. 'Can you come now? I've got . . .' I looked at my watch. It was twenty to twelve – I wouldn't have time to show them round and then get to Jack's in time to inspect behind his ears to make sure he'd washed them properly. 'Ah. No I haven't. I've got a twelve o'clock . . . appointment which I'm not going to be able to change. Bother! How annoying! Erm, tell you what, I'll ask Mr Dunsley . . .'

'Isn't that that nice Rod you keep telling me about?' Mrs Ferguson cut in. 'The one who leaves a wine gum on your desk when you're having a bad day?'

'That's him! At least, he still hasn't owned up to the wine gum thing, but I'm sure it's him . . . anyway – can I ask him to take you there? My twelve o'clock . . . ah . . . meeting . . .'

Judging by the twitch of her eyebrows Mrs Ferguson had twigged where I was off to, the saucy old minx. Her son, on the other hand, adopted the knowing nod of the fellow professional with the full diary, and mumbled something vaguely coherent about how they ought to have made an appointment but there you go, busy, busy, busy.

But there was a problem. It had been dawning on me for the past few minutes that this could very well be the only opportunity I'd have to speak to Mrs Ferguson about my buying Ben View privately, whilst she had a member of her family – albeit rather a poor quality one – beside her. It was a scary prospect, but, surely, saying something now would be my only hope of coming across as a straight-up person who really was on her side? I realised perfectly well that she and her son could go and look round Cedar Park, decide that it wasn't right for her, and slam the whole thing into reverse but surely this was the best – the most neutral – time to have a go?

I took a deep breath, then let it out again. I couldn't do it – it felt so wrong! And yet – I thought of Miranda, free to run on the hills and play at the waterfall – I thought of being the owner of the cutest cottage in the cutest valley in the Highlands – I thought that whatever I offered Mrs Ferguson, I would get back with knobs on in the event of throwing a wobbler and having to re-sell – I thought of the birch trees, the chanterelle-hunting expeditions, the blaeberry and white chocolate muffins I could make on a reconditioned range after purple-fingered berry-gathering trips – I thought of drinking wine in the lee of Ben Seilagan, raising my glass to its majesty and promising to always live in its shadow . . .

'Mrs Ferguson, Mr Ferguson, there's something else.'

Mrs Ferguson was smiling kindly at me. 'You'd like to buy Ben View yourself.'

I gawped at her like a hooked fish. 'Sorry? How . . . how did you know?'

'You what?' her son echoed, slowly catching on. '*You* want it?'

I nodded, and twisted my mouth. 'I wanted you to know that right now, before you go to Cedar Park, so that even if you decide not to go ahead, I will have been completely honest with you.'

'But – it's unethical!' James Ferguson could sense his fat profit slithering to the floor, and he didn't like it one bit.

'Wheesht, James, it's no such thing,' his mother scolded.
'But . . .'

'Actually, it's not *unethical*,' I faltered. 'There are rules governing this sort of thing, but I thought it would have been unfair of me not to make my intentions clear at the earliest possible stage. I wondered, Mrs Ferguson, whether I could save you the torment of showing people round your house – all that uncertainty, all those strangers – by offering you, say, whatever the surveyor of your choice values the house at plus . . . ten . . . no, *twenty* per cent?'

God, I hated my miserable, scheming old hide sometimes. I searched the cobwebby recesses of my psyche to think of something friendly to say that would pull my squalid little punt back from the brink.

'And your legal costs – I could pay them as well?' was the best I could do. Not the best friendship-restorer, but a useful sweetener under normal circumstances, nonetheless. Mrs Ferguson's face was calm and inscrutable – she had guessed I'd want her house, I just hoped to God she didn't think any the worse of me for it. Her son, however, was doing furious mental calculations, the effort of which were practically making his tiepin slide down his front.

'Ms Morris . . .' he began.

'No, James, let me speak to Anna.' His mother was becoming more fragile and saintly by the second – I wanted to pop my own eyeballs out with a teaspoon in a quasi-religious act of contrition, but settled instead for a small, humble look.

'Anna,' she started. 'I have always known that you love my house, and even before I spoke to you about the chance of me moving to the sheltered accommodation, it was on my mind that you might have an interest, so don't you be worrying about what it is that I'm thinking.'

'Thank you,' I said, from the bottom of my cringing, miserable heart.

'Ben View Cottage is my home, and I don't want it going to just anyone, who won't look after it, or who'll demolish it and turn . . .' she faltered at the idea of her home being knocked to the ground '. . . and build a bungalow, or, or a new holiday house . . .' she broke off again, her eyes filling with tears.

'I know, I know, it's the scourge of the north, isn't it?' I said quietly, nodding my head and thinking guiltily about the few quid I hoped to make from the odd summer let when I knew Miranda and I wouldn't be there. 'Whole communities, laid to waste, for a few holiday houses which lie empty for most of the year . . .'

'Anyway, I've been having a wee lookie at the market myself, actually.'

'Have you?' her son gasped. 'Where?'

'Oh, you know, in the papers, on the web, when I'm in town with the post bus, that sort of thing – it can be quite absorbing, can't it, Anna?' I nodded again, wide-eyed this time. 'What a price hike has been in it, these last few years!'

'Quite,' I managed.

'On the *web*? Ma, you, you *surf the web*? But you don't have a computer!'

'Yes, but the library does, James, now don't be inter-rupting.' James Ferguson flicked me a 'Would you credit these old dears!' conspiratorial look, which made me feel even more shabby, so I ignored it.

'I've been noticing a considerable discrepancy between the town and the rural markets, wouldn't you say so, Anna?'

Again, I nodded.

'I mean, the average city property has sold for approxi-mately 15 to 25 per cent above the asking price, particu-larly in the late spring to early autumn. Depending on individuality, amount of land, extra features, that sort of thing, some houses have been known to be selling for up to 35 per cent above the asking price – now would you credit that, Anna? James?'

'Well . . .' I don't know which one of us said that.

'But then if you have a wee look at the country market, well, would it not be fair to say, Anna, that, in business-speak, that *all bets are off*?'

'Sorry?' Did she mean she wasn't going to sell?

'Rural homes are at an all-time premium – I've heard of a couple wanting to convert their local electricity sub-station into a two-bedroom bungalow – for £100,000! I'm telling you, Anna, the world's gone mad!'

'You said it, Mrs Ferguson.' Hang on, I didn't realise that that sub-station story was public knowledge! That was one of Blakemore's finest – and most confidential – hours! We'd all gone out for lunch after nailing that one!

'Anyway, the current year's projections show that the market is holding up strongly against the threat of price stabilisation – even price reduction – which is endangering the south-east of England and for that reason, and also because my late husband . . .' she put her hand back on her son's knee '. . . your dad – liked the excitement of a wee gamble, I'm going to chance Ben View on the open market, to gauge the extent of the interest, before I'll be thinking about looking at private offers.'

'Ah,' I said.

'Been off on a course?' her son asked, finding his shirt collar to be intensely uncomfortable.

She ignored James's sarcasm. 'Plus, I'll be enjoying the company – it'll be nice to see some new faces up the glen, not to mention some of the others who've knocked on my door recently to ask if I'm thinking of selling up!'

'Have they?' I said in surprise, although common sense should have reminded me that Ben View was exactly the sort of place which would attract all the opportunistic chancers of the day to risk . . . people just like me, in fact.

'Yes, Anna, and although I'm very fond of you, and I very much hope you'll be successful if I do *definitely* decide to sell, I've never been in the property market before, and this is my only chance – it's so exciting, isn't it? No wonder you love your job!' Her pale eyes shone as she smiled at me.

I smiled back, relieved, in a strange sort of way. 'Fine. Great, in fact!'

'Well, that's settled, then, is it? Shall we go?' James Ferguson stood and helped his mother to her feet.

I shot out of the room and briefed Rod, who was helping Geraldine stuff our fortnightly newsletter, *The Update*, into stout white mailing list envelopes.

'OK, so it's red carpet time, I get it!' he said brightly, after nodding his way through all my instructions. 'Leave it to me!'

'Yes, but don't overdo it,' I cautioned. 'Mrs Ferguson looks frail, but she's sharp as a tack.'

'And you love her,' he said, gently.

'Correct.'

He strode over and introduced himself. 'Rod Dunsley, delighted to meet you both! Now then, Mr Ferguson, if you'd just allow me to assist your wife with her bag . . .' he gave me just the tiniest wink.

'She's not my wife! She's . . .' James Ferguson spluttered, before cottoning on and laughing – a gesture that improved his demeanour no end – shame it was just a shade late in the day for me to start changing my opinion of him.

'I can see I'm going to have to be keeping an eye on you!' said Mrs Ferguson merrily, taking Rod's proffered arm.

'I shall enjoy that!' he answered. 'Shall we sally forth?'

'Just one more thing, if you wouldn't mind. Anna?' Mrs Ferguson called me over, as her son went outside to start the car.

'Yes?' I replied.

'You do know about the land that goes with Ben View, don't you?'

'The garden? Oh, absolutely – I wouldn't dream of disturbing all those rhododendrons – I know your husband loved them. And the shed's easily repaired . . .'

'Ah, yes,' she cut in, nodding. 'But there's five acres of hillside, to the left of the Seilagan Burn at the side of the house that goes with it – you can't do much with it, but it's nice to have, you know.'

'Really? How lovely!' I trilled, my mind turning somersaults. Wow, five extra acres alongside! That turned Ben View into one hell of a tasty prospect for redevelopment . . . I'd simply assumed her boundary stopped at the rickety fence, overlaid with honeysuckle and falling down in places, which surrounded the cottage. Having a bit of extra land would make it far more desirable for developers and people with big ideas . . . Rod was thinking the same as me, I could tell from his raised eyebrows as Mrs Ferguson allowed him to guide her out to the waiting car.

Chapter Eight

Jack's little car, perkily parked at the door, pointed the way towards his flat, which was tucked away in Spencer Road, a side street set about two hundred yards back from the river. I'd handled the sale of one or two of these flats in the past, and, whilst it wasn't my favourite location in town, I suppose it could have been worse. Plus, hadn't he said he was only renting? The development, by a country-wide building firm called Ardenfield Construction, had been slow to sell when it was completed two years ago, but then, all of a sudden, when Inverness began to mushroom like a Klondike gold-mining town, all twenty-four flats sold out within a three-week period, mainly going to smart buy-to-let investors. And sure enough, its central situation had shown it to be a magnet for young professionals, newly moved up for work, who wanted somewhere modern and convenient for the town centre, and who were prepared to pay an over-the-odds rent for the privilege. Those investors would have pretty much doubled their money already in purely capital terms since then, to say nothing of the monthly income, which would be more than covering even the heftiest of commercial mortgages. The council tax was fairly steep in this neck of the woods but at least the mains gas supply meant that the running costs would be low . . . oh, for pity's sake! Don't you think, as I wound my way towards the door, that my mind ought to have been more on the man waiting for me inside the place, rather than on the place itself? But still, as I appraised the white-harled exterior of the unambitious four-plex, taking in the screamingly ugly vertical office blinds which adorned every window, the satellite dishes like clumps of mushrooms – or ears – below the eaves, the forlorn little pink and green swing on the patch of lawn allocated to the flat next door to Jack's – I found that I was mentally girding myself to brush aside Jack's apologies for his low-grade temporary surroundings, to reassure him that he'd chosen wisely in terms of location at least, and maybe even to offer to put him on our mailing list for something a bit more, well, a bit more *him* . . . who knew?

Impulsively, I'd stopped at Marky's corner shop and bought the most expensive bottle of wine that Marky had to offer. It was a South African Merlot, caked with dust, from the top shelf, and priced by hand at £12.99. I knew it'd be nice as I picked up this very bottle most weekends at Tesco for a fiver. I was wearing my sexy raincoat too, the retro, double-breasted one which I'd belted and buttoned securely, right to the neck – would I get the chance to tease him that, underneath, I was completely naked? The thought made me flush, all over, as I rang the doorbell, and jumped at the tinny but unmistakable sound of a *Star Wars* ring-tone.

'Anna! We meet again!' Jack, who had put some clothes on, looked delighted to see me, and stepped forwards to kiss me on the cheek – there was that faint scent of aftershave again! Yummy! 'Thanks for coming – come on in!'

I followed him into the tiny vestibule, which opened grudgingly into a dark, narrow hall, carpeted in what felt like emery board, in an unclassified shade of dark blue. A round paper globe lampshade was the sole item of furnishing, and it appeared from its condition to have lost at least one argument with Jack's head.

'This is nice!' I chirped far, *far* too brightly to have been the truth in any remote sense of the word.

Jack, who was leading me through to the sitting room, turned and looked at me kindly. 'No, Anna, it's not *nice*, it's a flat, and rather a poky one at that. Meet my lounge!'

His 'lounge' was a magnolia cube, furnished with a foam modular three-piece suite in coral chintz, a smoked glass coffee table in black ash veneer, and a gas fire in a teak-effect surround. These items, quite patently, were the ones which had earned the flat the description 'furnished', and a swift appraisal of the far corner (although 'far' meant only about eight feet to the other corner of the room) showed up an enormous hi-fi, a gigantic collection of CDs, displayed on about eight vertical chrome towers, and one huge, fuck-off plasma TV, which was currently showing the lunchtime news on an exceptionally widescreen, making the blonde female newsreader look gratifyingly like an Oompa Loompa.

'Oh!' I exclaimed, as I took a proper look at the poster above the TV.

'What is it?' queried Jack, relieving me of the bottle of wine and taking it through to the kitchen (or 'galley kitchenette', if we're going for strict accuracy, here, so titchy was it), 'feeling out of your depth amidst all this grandeur?'

'No, of course not – it's your poster!'

'What about it?'

'Well, it's Ewan McGregor!'

'Ten out of ten for observation!'

'Yes, but I've got exactly the same one on the wall in my en-suite at home!'

'Have you, now? Wow, my perfect woman!'

I winced. What the heck was Jack Anderson doing with Ewan McGregor on his wall? Could he possibly do the same things that I did when relaxing at home on my own, in the bath, gazing up at that very image? Surely not!

'Actually,' he went on, 'it's not strictly *Ewan McGregor*, is it? It's Ben Obi Wan Kenobi, Jedi Knight! And thank you for rubbing in the "en-suite" thing – I've just got a bog-standard bog in this place. Like a glass?' He pulled the cork expertly out of my dusty bottle.

'But, you have a *bath*, don't you? That's what lured me round here in the first place, if you remember – the sound of you, soaping yourself off . . .' with a wanton surge of God-knows-what I walked towards him, removed the bottle from one hand and the corkscrew from the other, laid them down on the square foot of available kitchen worktop, slid my arms around his neck, and kissed him.

His response was immediate and engulfing. His hands felt their way over my back, pulling me closer towards him, as he kissed me right back. His tongue found its way into my mouth, where it explored and teased, and I found myself, literally, becoming weak at the knees – I hadn't realised it was an actual physical phenomenon until then, but I managed to murmur something about having to sit down and so, after drawing back a little to kiss my hair, my nose, my forehead and my neck, he caught my hands and led me towards the bedroom.

Now, how on earth could Ardenfield Construction have described this unappealing little cell as a *double* bedroom? And did they think that by installing mirrored wardrobe doors along one wall, they'd pull off an illusion of space? Well, it didn't work – all we could do, once we'd squeezed our way indoors, was, well, jump on the rumpled bed, where Jack rolled on top of me and began loosening the belt buckle of my coat which, yes, I was still wearing. I fumbled to undo the buttons until Jack, quite firmly, eased my hands down to my sides and murmured, 'Here, allow me.' So I complied and lay back, writhing only a little, and allowing Jack, very slowly, to kneel astride me and take my clothes off.

Underwear, now there's a thing. Personally, I'm very much in favour, but only if it's the very nicest, silkiest, slippiest that I can find. I'd learned from a very wise person, years ago – actually it was a cunning sales assistant in a gorgeous little lingerie boutique in Glasgow so maybe she had just a tiny wee vested interest (although vests didn't figure in this particular shop at all), that a woman's underwear formed a foundation for not only her physical appearance, but also for her entire state of mind; that a woman's underwear gives out clear instructions to the woman herself; thus if you are a wearer of big pants they will surely contain enough room to hide not only your self-conscious arse, but also your self-esteem. Similarly, if you favour sports bras and snug white briefs, then the chances are you are doing an extremely efficient job of whatever it is you are doing, and jolly well done – where would the rest of us be without you? So, cottoning on (again, though, you won't find a great deal of cotton in my drawers) to the wisdom of the undies shop guru, from that seminal day onwards, I became an avid acquirer of a very beautiful and personal collection, and only ever bought gorgeous, handmade, silk and satin smalls. They cost a fortune, but you really, honestly can't put a price on the way they make you feel.

No worries, then, as Jack eased the zip of my skirt down and slipped it off, revealing one of my favourites – palest pink silk knickers adorned with hand-stitched tea rosebuds.

'Wow, but you're gorgeous!' he said, smiling appreciatively. Despite it having been ages since I'd done this, and even though Jack was making all the right moves, a little part of me remained curiously detached, as I helped him with my blouse buttons, which were tiny, and numerous. It was absolutely beyond me why builders of apartments like these seemed to insist on creating plaster swirls and spikes in their ceilings, as though this were some sort of asset to the interior of a room – I mean, these things are fine on Christmas cakes but did builders realise how much it costs to get someone in to scrape the bloody stuff off?

'You'll need to sit up, so I can take this off,' Jack whispered, easing his hands behind my back and helping me sit up. I clung to him as though I was being rescued from a pond, then raised my arms so that he could remove my silk camisole. That aftershave was definitely a turn-on, I decided, sneaking the chance to bury my face in his neck and inhale the hot, male scent.

'Oh, shit! Sorry!' Somehow Jack got the angle all wrong as he pulled the silk upwards. My lovely camisole ripped up the whole length of the front seam, where the hand stitching had formed a delicate rose trellis pattern, and my breasts sprang out, taking even me by surprise – although rather a nice one, I realised, once I'd got over the shock.

But it was all too much for Jack. He sort of moaned, whipped off his clothes, revealing, as expected, a lovely, firm body in a . . . well, in a high state of readiness, pulled the duvet back, engulfed me in it then jumped in as well. Then, just after he'd done so, he lay completely still.

'Em, Anna?' His voice was tense, and strained.

'Yes?'

'I . . . I'm not sure I'm going to be much use.'

I smiled wickedly, rolled on to my side and ran my hand down the length of his body. 'Doesn't feel that way to me,' I answered, easing myself on top of him and looking deep into his eyes. Gee, whiz, it's like riding a bike, isn't it? Once learned, never forgotten – *oh, Jack Anderson, see to my cobwebs!*

Well, as the naughty Valentine goes, 'Brace yourself, darling, for the best twenty seconds of your life!'

'Sorry.'

'Don't be.'

'Well, I am.'

'Well, you needn't be.'

'I ripped your top!'

'I noticed.'

'That was rubbish.'

'Thanks.'

'No! Not you – me!'

'Don't be daft – it takes two.'

'Yes, but I feel terrible.'

'Don't.'

'How are you?'

'Me? Just fine.'

'Good.'

'Feeling better?'

'A bit.'

'Good.'

'Are you warm enough?'

'Positively hot, in fact.'

'Ah. Would you like me to . . .'

'No, but thank you for offering.'

'Rightio. Can you stay a bit longer?'

'Definitely!'

'Great – I've made lunch!'

'What? Oh! How . . . lovely.'

I hadn't actually taken any notice of Jack's underwear when he'd whipped it off, only a very few tragic minutes before, but as I watched him dress, I mused that perhaps pale blue Y-fronts were the most practical everyday solution for today's busy construction engineer? Weren't bad pants on a man better than '*I'm gonna get laid tonite!*' thongs and things? They were a bit hideous, though. I mean, I'd rather see him in something like that than a, a black *pouch*, or long johns – no, actually, long johns would have been quite fun – whatever, I guess the lingerie rules are probably fairly gender-specific. Jack had his sports car to buoy him up for the day, and I had the secret sensation of raw silk next to my skin – provided it hadn't been ripped in half by hasty men during awkward nooners, that is.

I dressed again, slowly, in the remaining clothing I had brought with me which was still intact, and walked shyly into the 'lounge', where Jack had set up a foldaway table with two glasses of red wine, a pint glass filled with bread-sticks, and a bowl of Cheesy Wotsits.

He came over to me and kissed me lightly on the lips. 'Moving swiftly on, would you care to take a seat?'

'Thanks.' I checked my watch, as a displacement activity, or a reality check, or something – anything that wasn't connected to unsuccessful shagging. Miranda would be out in her school playground, only a couple of miles from where I sat, running around with Flora and her other little friends, sharing secrets, inventing games and feeling safe. Meanwhile her mother, who to be fair hadn't had sex for ages and was probably due a bit of excitement, was sitting self-consciously at what was to all intents and purposes a picnic table, wondering what to say to the man she'd just been to bed with, on their second date, as he walked towards her and handed her a plate containing . . .

'Modom, *voilà!*'

A sandwich.

A bloody sandwich!

He must have caught my expression, as the next thing he said was, 'I'm afraid I'm not much of a cook, but I do appreciate taste sensations – and this one, though I say it myself, is a bit of a speciality of mine!'

I looked at him encouragingly. 'It looks just fine – thank you. What is it?'

'Well, I'm not sure if I know you well enough yet to divulge the secret recipe – can you be trusted?'

'Absolutely not.' We grinned at each other.

'Taste it and see if you can guess.'

So I did. The white bread was soft and squidgy enough, no worries there, but the filling? Shards of sharp stuff that felt like crisps lacerated the roof of my mouth, and then a salty metallic tang gave me a stabbing pain in the centre of my forehead.

I forced it down, and looked at his expectant face. 'Go on, then, you've got me. What is it?'

'Marmite, and crushed Sour Cream and Chive Pringle! My own invention! Fantastic, isn't it?'

'Mmm!' Oh, well, at least there was wine to drink.

'So, do you have to get back to work this afternoon, or shall we do something together instead?' asked Jack through a huge mouthful of sandwich.

'I'm afraid I'll need to get going in a minute,' I replied. 'Got tons to do in the office, then I'm taking Miranda to Brownies after she finishes school.'

'Ah, that's a shame.' He reached over and caught my hand. 'I was hoping we could, well, try again?' He suddenly sounded shy. 'I'm really embarrassed about, well, screwing up, if you'll pardon the expression.'

'Don't be, really – we both rushed things a bit, didn't we?'

He nodded. 'I feel about fifteen years old.'

I raised my eyebrows in disapproval. 'Were you shagging at fifteen?'

''Fraid so.'

'My, quite the early starter, weren't you?'

'It's not the early start that's the problem, it's the early finish that's not so impressive . . .'

'Oh, for heaven's sake! It was fine! You were fine!' I drained my glass and stood up. 'Now, I have to get going. Thanks for . . . lunch.' The skinny strap of my ruined camisole hung out of the top of my bag. Jack stood up and tucked it gently back in.

137

'You haven't finished your sandwich.'

'I know. Sorry.'

'Can I see you again? Please?' he asked, as he helped me back into my coat. I buttoned it securely around myself, turned, and looked up at him. He really was quite beautiful.

And then we kissed. This time it was a real kiss, stripped of lust, and excitement and nerves, just a no-nonsense, full-on, movie-magic kiss. It reminded me of our connection at Potters, and at the quiz night, when we hadn't been silly and lunging and impetuous, when we'd just been true to ourselves and enjoyed the force of our attraction and for some reason, when we drew apart, I laughed.

'Of course you can! God, we're a pair of daft buggers, aren't we? You'd think, at our age . . .'

'. . . we'd have done things a bit more carefully,' Jack finished, with a smile. 'You're great, Anna.'

'Goodbye, Jack. Call me!'

'You can count on it!' he called after me, closing the door – with a rather cheap, chipboard click.

Where was my gentleman with the greying sideburns? Where was the handbag with the tortoiseshell clasp?

I kept my head down and my coat tightly belted around my top half, which felt exposed and vulnerable without my pretty camisole, as I pounded the pavement back to the office, trying not to feel like a two-bit hooker and convinced that everyone I passed knew exactly what I'd been up to. Why hadn't he offered to drive me back? Just what, precisely, had been nice about that particular inter-lude? Had there been any actual need to jump his bones today, just because he'd made a flirty phone call from his bath (acrylic, in 'pampas')?

Thinking about it, and being totally, totally honest, I hadn't wanted sex. I'd just wanted to be wanted by someone who wanted sex. And, thinking back, I wasn't sure if he'd wanted it either. God, I was such a turkey.

138

That feeling was nothing compared to the looks I received from the others in the office, when I got back to my desk. Katy glanced up from her accounts desk, sniggered, then looked down again and began shuffling invoices. Geraldine said 'Hi Anna, nice lunch?' before she and Katy sidled through to the meeting lounge 'to clear some cups'. Once they had closed the door (I could hear muffled spluttery giggles almost immediately), the Monitor Lizard had me all to herself.

'You're very flushed,' she observed, from over the top of her Dame Edna specs.

'Well, you know, it's a bit nippy out there!' I replied in a fake normal voice. 'Rod not back yet?'

'He rang to say he was going for lunch after he'd finished showing your *friends* Cedar Park.'

'Ah. Did he say how the viewing went?'

'No. He didn't. Nice . . . *lunch?*'

'Yes, thank you.' I sat down and turned my flaming face away from her. Just WHAT was it that made me look so guilty?

OK, back to work. I needed something to do that would stop me thinking about what had just happened. It was too awful! How cheap can a girl get? I gazed at the half-typed sales particulars I'd abandoned earlier.

ROSE VILLA

Blakemore is very proud to present Rose Villa, a prestigious city-centre home of high quality in an enviably convenient location. If you're looking for lively city living, then look no further than this delightful townhouse! Rare are the opportunities to acquire residential property which sits directly on the High Street, where Inverness's full range of prime retail outlets are, literally, on your doorstep! Ideal for those who spurn the car-owning philosophy, Rose

Villa's quality triple glazing acts as a first-rate buffer from the buzz of the outside world, creating a sanctuary of convenient centrality . . .

I tried to resume where I had left off – pondering whether 'centrality' was a real word and wondering whether to deign to ask the Monitor Lizard, but she had nobbled the well-heeled customer who had come into the office to enquire about one of our properties. *Centrality.*

Just then the phone rang, and as Geraldine was still 'clearing cups' with Katy in the meeting lounge, I picked it up.

'Good afternoon, thank you for calling Blakemore, I'm Anna – how may I help?'

There was a pause. 'Anna? Is that you?'

A slow shiver crept up on me at the sound of the deep, clear voice, and I felt my body begin to tremble. No! It couldn't be! And *why why why* hadn't I called Geraldine through to do her sodding job and take the call first?

'*Omar?*' I whispered. 'Is that you?'

'You remembered! Yes, Anna, it's me. I do hope you don't mind my calling, out of the blue like this . . .'

Out of the blue. Literally, Out Of The Blue. The blue of my mood, the blue of my lunch date, the blue mists of my past – *Omar was on the phone!*

'Well, I, I don't know what to say – how are you?'

'I am well, thank you. And you, how are you – both?'

Now I was terrified. Omar must want Miranda – he was on his way up with henchmen, court orders and a great big stick and he wasn't leaving without – *his* – daughter! *Stop, world!*

'Um . . . fine?' The receiver rattled against my earring, such was the force of my trembling hand. Even the Monitor Lizard peered round her well-heeled client to look at me in disapproval. Not that that was anything new, mind.

'Anna, you sound afraid! Please, don't be; I have been so worried that you would feel this way if I rang! I just thought, well, that I . . . well, this is very difficult . . .'

'It certainly is,' I managed – although his voice was just as gentle as I remembered.

'Anna, please, I promised you that I would not get in touch, but, well, I'm in London.'

'*London?*' I kind of barked. 'Where? I mean, since when? For how long?'

'A month, already. I have begun ambassadorial work for Jordanian industry.'

'Really?' Well, what else can you say?

'Yes. It's a twelve-month posting, at present. And you, how is the world of property in the Scottish Highlands?'

Silently I cursed again at having been the one who had picked up the phone. He'd think I was a receptionist! Over the years, in some of my most private, reflective moments, I'd run through countless imaginary scenarios of meeting up with Omar again, generally involving me looking my absolutely most glamorous and sorted, hoodwinking him with coy flirtations and gentle dismissals, then sweeping away, leaving him to torture himself with a lifetime of might-have-beens. There, in the safety of my mind, I could compartmentalise the Omar I knew, like a holiday scrapbook, to be dwelt upon when it suited me, and then put away.

'Oh, it's very busy, you know. I'm . . . manageress.' How disgustingly feebly I spoke! Hardly surprising from a woman who'd just had her underwear ripped off, but still, it would have been nice to have had a few days' prior warning of this one so that I could have spent some time in rehearsal.

'That is wonderful – many congratulations.' I could hear genuine warmth when he spoke.

'My receptionist's on her break, so I'm manning the

phones, otherwise I wouldn't have picked it up . . .' I tailed off, wondering if I could have found anything more crass to say if I'd tried, before deciding – probably not.

'I understand.'

'Omar?'

'Yes?'

I took a deep breath. 'What do you want?'

'Anna, do not be alarmed! Please believe that I have no wish to intrude where I am not wanted! I promised you that, did I not?'

'Yes – yes you did, but you were going back to Jordan then!'

'I know, but just because I have returned does not invalidate my word.'

God help me, but I believed him.

'I'm sorry, Omar, it's just such a shock to hear your voice,' I said, more softly this time. 'It's been a busy day, you know.' No, he would never, *ever* know the day I was having.

'Perhaps I should have written you a letter, but I don't think I would have found the right words,' he replied.

I paused, allowing his words to seep into my panicked skull, before asking, 'Why, what did you want to say?'

'Well, you must feel free to say no, but . . . may I meet you? And Miranda?'

I couldn't speak. The question hit me like a Flintstones' club. And yet, and yet . . . somewhere, beneath all that fear, was the realisation that a little part of me had ached to hear that very question for almost nine years.

Chapter Nine

It was time to tell Miranda everything.

Omar and I had talked on the phone for almost an hour that afternoon – I'd switched the call through to the privacy of the meeting lounge, evicting Katy and Geraldine, whereupon I'd slammed the door behind me, composed myself as best as possible under the circumstances (deep breaths, voice control, let him speak) and tried to catch up with the past nine years. And although there had been moments during our conversation which almost recaptured some of the warmth and connection which we had so revelled in when I'd been in London, by the end of the call, as soon as I replaced the receiver, I had experienced a curious delayed shock reaction, trembling all over and wondering dizzily if I was about to pass out. My God – he'd got me *swooning*! Does anybody *swoon* any more? How does one *swoon*? Only Jane Austen's lovely Fannies *swooned*, didn't they? Anyway, whatever, by the end of the call not only was I frazzled and swoony, but I had also arranged that I would travel to London – on my own at first – to meet up with him, suss him out face to face, see what the past nine years had done to him, check him over for kidnapping tendencies, that sort of thing, and when I'd said as much on the phone, he'd scored an immediate few points by agreeing with alacrity. He did offer to travel north to visit us, but that prospect had terrified me – just imagine, opening my front door to Omar! Omar in my cinnamon sitting room! No, I'd realised – it was far too early for that . . . but then, what had I been thinking, *far too early*? Had I already made the decision that he was going to become part of our lives at some stage in the future?

So here I was, sitting nervously in my car outside the Jubilee Hall at five to eight in the evening, waiting for Brownies to finish, composing the words which would best describe how Miranda had come into being and realising, not for the first time, that niceties such as 'So you see, you were so *wanted*!' and 'Your father has always loved you very much!' were simply not available. Miranda had to be told that she had been an accident and that now, from nowhere, the man who had helped cause that accident wanted to meet her. What a privilege that was for him! And why the heck had I agreed?

As I worried myself into a frenzy in my car I half-watched a knot of other mothers, who leaned on the post and rail fence which surrounded the depressing, seventies' architecture of the Hall, chewing the fat.

It was all so ordinary. Nice women, most of them, busy, like me, bringing up their kids as best they could. There was Siobhan, who cooked different meals for each of her three children every night, depending on what they requested. And Harriet, who didn't have a telly. Sheena minded children, and had turned over an entire room of her house to murals, paints and toys and Beth did the books for her husband's plumbing business. Lesley had arthritis and walked with a stick, Juno got a new Range Rover every year (her current one was so big and square it looked like she drove around not only in the Range Rover, but in its garage as well) and Helen did therapeutic massage on a fold-down couch in her front room. Briony – now she was a strange one; once, a few months ago, she'd come up to me, out of the blue, in Tesco.

'*Miranda has such a lovely olive complexion, doesn't she?*' she'd asked.

'*Her father is Jordanian,*' I'd replied, wondering why Briony hadn't just moaned about the weather, like normal folk.

'*Ah! A little Arabian princess!*' Briony had beamed, before barrelling off towards the deli counter, her curiosity satisfied. It was the first time I'd ever been quizzed about Miranda's skin, and it set me wondering whether there were loads more people lurking out there, speculating lasciviously about my murky past.

Anyway, Brownies was the one time of the week when Miranda was really atrociously dressed and as soon as her brown jogging-trousered, custard polo-shirted, supermarket-freezer-department quilted waistcoat-wearing, trailer-trash baseball-capped little self had jumped into the front seat of my car, I turned towards her, and smiled. She gave me a strange sort of look in return.

'What's up, mum?'

Miranda knew the basics. She knew that she had a daddy, but that he lived on the other side of the world and we couldn't all live together because lots of mummies and daddies don't live together, and that's a shame, but hey, we're all right, aren't we? She also knew that her daddy had cared about her enough to give us money so that she would always be looked after properly. That was it – no more. I had never, ever lied to her by saying that her daddy loved her – how could he?

A year or so back, when she'd asked if we could go and visit her daddy, I'd quickly replied that it was too far to travel and amazingly, she hadn't pushed the point. And then when she wondered aloud why her daddy didn't come and visit her I'd just said that he wasn't able to because of work, and quickly changed the subject. Whether she had a junior defence mechanism which prevented further probing, or whether her trust in me was such that she knew implicitly that I'd fix the situation if I could, who knew? I didn't have the guts to try to find out. But time was running out. Miranda was nearly nine. Soon she'd ask me again, and wouldn't be fobbed off with vague nonsense about distances and difficulties – she watched enough children's TV to know how to argue for Britain and soon, adolescence would come a-knocking and what would that add to the mix? Perhaps Omar's call was a timely working of fate which ultimately, whatever the outcome, would at least protect her from deceit?

'I had a phone call from your daddy this afternoon.'

'Really?' Miranda's eyes lit up with a mixture of surprise and curiosity. 'My real daddy?'

'Yes.'

'What for?'

'Oh, just to say hello, and see how we both are.'

'Did he sound funny, phoning from the other side of the world?'

'Well, do you know, Miranda, he's not on the other side of the world just now – he's down in London!' I tried to keep my voice light and conversational, scanning Miranda's face the while to try to judge her reaction.

She looked at me quizzically. 'But that's *this* country!'

'Yup, it is indeed, poppet!'

'Can we go and visit?'

'Well . . .'

'Please? We can go on the London Eye, and see the Queen's palace, and go shopping!'

OK, so the immediate need for stress counselling, trauma management, time off school to come to terms with it all, paediatric psychology and a punchbag had receded somewhat. Did Miranda's unruffled reaction mean that I had done an unbelievably good job as a parent, or an un-believably bad one?

'Well, maybe, some day.'

'But won't he have gone by then?'

'Oh, no, love – he's come to London to *live* – for a while, anyway – a whole year!'

'Oh, good! Flora went to a place called the Rainforest Café when she went to London on holiday – can we go there?'

'Course we can!' I said, relief penetrating every inch of me as I realised that, so far, at least, she was fine. 'But I'm going to go down and see him by myself this weekend . . .'

'No way!' Her whole body slumped downwards in disappointment. 'Can't I come too?'

'Miranda,' I said, gently, pinching her chin and turning her head round to look at me. 'I haven't seen your father for nine years. We haven't spoken at all until today. I have to go down on my own to make sure that . . . well, to make sure that it'll be OK for him to meet you.'

'That's not fair! Can't I decide that?' she asked, chewing her lip. 'What if you don't like him and I do? Or what if you like him and I don't?'

She had a point. I frowned, and massaged the steering wheel. The other Brownies and their mothers had trickled away, and we were alone in the car park. A light breeze agitated the birch trees which rimmed the gravel parking space and, out on the road, my scrambled thoughts were further punctured by the thumping '*doof doof doof*' of the stereo in the lime green Vauxhall Nova which flashed past my line of vision, driven by a taut-faced boy who looked, at the very most, twelve.

'Mum?' Miranda said at length.

'Yes, my love?'

'Do you think he'd like me better if I was a boy?'

'No, darling, I don't. I think he's going to love you just as you are.'

147

And that was precisely what bothered me the most. I started the engine, and turned for home.

Oh, the gloom. Gloom upon gloom, adding to my morning malaise as I sat in the office the following morning.

Mains of Blusterystones
Morayshire.

Dear Ms Morris,

My husband and I have been considering putting one of our properties, East Blusterystones, on the market for sale. For several years we have been renting this property for holiday lets, and it has been well used by sporting parties for stalking and fishing. However, because the upkeep and administration have become somewhat onerous, we are contemplating a sale. Our motive is not primarily to realise money – my husband's investments and family have more than provided for us satisfactorily, and I enjoy considerable success with the sale of my paintings. Of course I do not sell all of my paintings – many are donated to charitable causes and have contributed substantial sums to their recipients' coffers.

We require full details of the services you offer, plus a detailed breakdown of your charges. I might add that we have a great friend who is in the property business, albeit on a somewhat larger scale than here in the Highlands, who has been supplying us with help and advice on asking price, plus the best places in which to advertise. I shall expect that your company's logo takes up not more than 5 per cent of any advertisement. I shall also require a written breakdown of your sales strategy. My husband and I require a service of the utmost discretion and propriety, and will wish to be fully involved and informed

148

*at each stage. We have also had a number of approaches
from private prospective purchasers, and would caution
that we may not ultimately require the services of an estate
agent at all. However, in the interests of fairness to all
parties we have consented to explore various selling
options. As this is a charming property which will I have
no doubt 'sell itself' we would anticipate this factor to be
brought to mind when you fix your charge.*

*Perhaps you could contact me at the above address to
request an appointment so that we can discuss the matter
further, in particular, your costs.*

Yours sincerely,

Lady Francesca Underhill

Holiday cottages of the aristocracy were almost invariably
horrible, dingy shockers, eagerly rented by hordes of men
in tweed, for whom tawdry details such as threadbare
carpets, scratchy baths and damp old beds brought them
blissfully back to the twelve childhood years they'd invariably spent at boarding school. I massaged the sides of the
letter, feeling the coarse vellum against the pads of my
fingers, and trying to ignore the paper cut which the sturdy
envelope had made on the side of my thumb, as I'd
unwisely slit it open with my bare hands. I foresaw months
of tedium and high-class bullying, topped off, if we were
lucky, with a tepid sale of an undoubtedly shabby lump
of a house, and a monumentally large squabble over our
fees. Don't ask why I knew – you just have to have been
an estate agent for a few years to sniff 'em out. And if I
had a quid for everyone who had a friend 'in property'
. . . Lady Francesca's family crest looked a bit like a sleeping
toad – perhaps designed in her likeness? Whatever, this
was without doubt one for the Lizard. These cold-bloods

really ought to be encouraged to stick together.

'Monica?' I said, brightly.

She looked up sharply from reading the paper, cross at being caught on the hop. 'Yes? Just checking this week's layout.'

'Quite right, too. Got a dodgy one here, wondered if you could give me any advice?' Buttering up was, quite simply, the only way to go.

'Well, I'm very busy just now, but suppose I can spare a minute.' She folded up the newspaper – I noticed it was one that we never used for advertising, but anyway – and peered at me over the top of her Dame Edna specs.

'It's a holiday home in Morayshire . . .'

She rolled her eyes in disgust, as I knew she might. 'Oh, God, a holiday home? I thought we weren't taking on any tin-pot tiddly holiday homes? Haven't we . . .'

'Yes, I know,' I interrupted, 'but the owner . . . let's see now . . .' I made an exaggerated show of running my finger down the paper to find the name. 'Ah, yes, some Lady Underhill or other . . .'

'Not Lady *Francesca* Underhill?' the Lizard exploded. 'The *painter*?'

'That's the one!' *Bingo!*

'Marvellous woman! So creative – so *elegant*! What did you say she was selling?'

'Well, it's just a holiday home, I'm not sure if Blakemore'd be interested, quite honestly – we're pretty busy at the moment . . .'

'Of *course* we're interested, Anna!' She gave me a look which was a scary mix of astonishment and pity, that I could be such an unwavering pleb for saying such a thing, and eyed up the letter which I was making a show of surveying doubtfully. 'Clients like Lady Francesca Underhill don't grow on trees, you know!'

In ponds, perhaps? 'Well, I . . .'

'Have you spoken to her yet?' she asked, as I stifled a giggle at the note of panic in her voice.

'Not yet, that's what I wanted to ask your advice about, Monica. I mean, this place is forty miles away, and there's no guarantee we'd get the sale to handle, judging by the tone of this letter – don't you think we ought to pass?'

'*Pass?*' she spluttered. 'Absolutely not! Believe me, Anna, just let me handle this one and the sale's in the bag – I just *adore* Lady Underhill's work! Such a patron of local charities, as well! Extraordinary woman!' Monica was actually *patting her hair*!

I paused to consider. One, two, three. Then I slowly shook my head. Four, five six. Chewed my lip in a torment of indecision. Seven, eight, nine. Drew in a slow, reluctant breath. Ten, eleven, twelve . . .

It was too much for her. 'Let me go and meet her, Anna – you *have* to!'

Furrow the brow. Thirteen, fourteen, fifteen. 'But it's only a *pitch*, Monica, sounds like she'll be approaching several sellers – probably some of the other nationals, judging by this letter . . .'

'I'll go in the evening! On my own time!'

Double bingo! 'Monica, I couldn't possibly ask you to do that!'

There was a snort from behind me. Rod had been lugging in and had clearly rumbled me. If I turned round now and caught his eye, all would be lost.

'It's no trouble! No trouble at all! May I have the letter?'

'Oh, Monica, are you sure?'

'You definitely haven't spoken to her yet?'

'Definitely not.' Fear not, Lizard, my trying Scottish vowels have yet to irritate her titled ear . . .

'Then I'll do it. Honestly, Anna, *Lady Francesca Underhill*!' She whizzed out from behind her desk and snatched the letter from me, gasping with relief as though she was a junkie who'd just got her hands on a class A illegal substance. I watched her closely as she scanned the contents. She frowned a little, and for a moment her eyes flicked warily in my direction, before she settled herself, ran a scarlet fingernail sensuously over the embossed letterhead, and picked up the phone. I tried to get back to work, but couldn't help noticing her straighten her back and wipe the bled lipstick from the corners of her mouth, before she spoke: 'Ah yes, good day. Might it be at all possible to speak with Lady Francesca Underhill?' I could see how much lizardly pleasure Monica was deriving from her opportunity to address a bit of gentry.

An email flashed up on my computer screen, from Rod: *You are a truly unscrupulous woman. I like that.*

I grinned and typed back: *Get back to work, boy.*

An hour or so after I'd unloaded Blusterystones on to the Monitor Lizard, I overheard Geraldine put a call from Mrs Ferguson through – to *Rod*! Rod glanced in my direction and shrugged, before picking up the call. But my attempts to eavesdrop on his half of the conversation were thwarted by the irritating matter of having a couple of people sitting eagerly in front of me who seemed hell-bent on putting in a ludicrously high offer for Arden, one of our more mundane bungalows.

There hadn't been anyone sniffing round Arden for weeks, and I'd been busy only the day before consoling the jittery seller, whilst also coaxing more money out of him for a spruced-up advertising campaign – not that the couple in front of me knew any of this, of course. Oh, but it was *'perfect'* for them, as the wife insisted on telling me, while her husband nodded vigorously. *Honestly.* I almost felt like throwing them a bone, telling them that they really ought to be leaving the negotiations to their solicitor, and that a bit of shrewd bargaining would quite possibly have us knocking a fair few grand off the asking price for this one – there wasn't a single other soul who'd shown the sign of wanting it so obviously a closing date was out of the question – it'd be a case of grabbing the first halfway decent offer with both hands. Arden had been on our books for three months and I was sick of the vanilla, uninspired sight of it – but well, a Blakemore client is a thing of beauty and a joy for ever and mine would be over the moon at getting the full price for this place so I kept my mouth shut and my ball-breaking sales negotiator's face on.

But this, this sweet young couple, eager, and tender as a pair of soft-boiled eggs, sitting shiny-eyed in front of me as they scanned my face for a longed-for 'yes' to their verbal offer, almost had me cracked. It wasn't the hard-nosed, pushy ones which got to me, on the contrary, I usually really enjoyed the rough-and-tumble of a bit of back-and-forth bargaining – it was these, these *schmuckos*, who just needed someone to tell them that they were hurling *way* too much money our way . . . oh, whatever. But sometimes I caught myself wondering whether there might be a type of person who actually *enjoyed* paying over the odds for a house; maybe it made them feel that they were injecting extra quality into a place, or something. Don't get me wrong, that's fine and dandy most of the time, but when you have a nice, straight-up couple who are simply letting their desperation cloud their judgement – well, I just felt a bit of a toad for not helping them out.

Rod was talking animatedly to Mrs Ferguson. I could see him smile, and nod, using his expressive hands to emphasise his words.

I turned back to face the couple, who were by now so eager that they looked as though they might burst, 'Well,' I began, 'I'll take my client's instructions on your verbal offer and explain that you have still to speak with your solicitor, although it may be some time before I can get back to you.' I thought of my client, Graham Kingsland, glanced at his mobile number which was right in front of my nose and knew that if I dialled the number I'd get through to him right away – however he'd be more than likely to let out a disbelieving whoop of joy if I told him that I had cash buyers practically sitting in my lap. Graham would almost certainly be in the pub at this time of day.

'This house has been on the market for some time, but there has been a flurry of interest lately, and, whilst we were not envisaging setting a closing date for offers right at this moment, it may well be that my advice to him would have to be to hold off accepting any offers at this stage.' Stretching the truth a bit, there. The flurry of interest comprised the couple sitting in front of me, and, well, nobody else. But, strictly speaking, I hadn't *lied* to them, and I had a duty to Graham Kingsland to gauge the strength of their interest as fully as possible, didn't I?

They looked at each other and a little nod passed between them. I froze. *No! Don't do it! For heavens sake! Pull back! Pull back!*

'Ms Morris,' the husband began, 'if it would help our cause any, we could stretch to another five thousand, if that might convince the seller to let us have the house?' His wife clutched his hand. Flipping heck.

Oh, I'm sure that won't be necessary – your current offer will almost certainly be more than adequate!

That's what I ought to have said.

'Really? Well, if you're absolutely sure, I think that would be an excellent idea! Leave it with me, I shall lay your revised figure before my client and revert to you as soon as possible – hopefully by close of business today. It's most unusual in the current climate to accept a lone offer without first testing the market at a closing date, and of course nothing is final until you have taken independent legal advice, but I shall of course keep you informed.' I stood up and ushered them out, waving away their profuse thanks, before hurrying over to Rod's desk, where he was just winding up his call with Mrs Ferguson.

'Yes. No bother, see you then – mind how you go now . . . sorry? Well, I do have something of a soft spot for raspberry, now you come to mention it . . . no, I wouldn't dream of it! Well . . . ONE jar, then, I'll look forward to it, but only if you let me bring you some Murray Mints – it was Murray Mints you said you liked, wasn't it? Wonderful! Sorry? Yes, I'll tell her. Thank you very much indeed! Bye!' He replaced the receiver and gave me a thumbs-up. 'What a great old girl! Sends you a hello. I can see why you're so fond of her, Anna.'

'So, she's all right?' I held my breath.

'She's fine! Green light situation for Cedar Park, and we're going to see her to measure up Ben View at four o'clock. I checked your diary earlier so's I'd know when you were free.'

Something curious happened to my insides – Mrs Ferguson was going ahead! I realised, as I stuck a post-it note on my computer screen saying '*Ring Graham Kingsland in the morning*', that my desire to own the cottage was more than just an idle whim – I practically had the Aga technicians in measuring up already. British Racing Green was a great colour for Agas – but then, perhaps a nice, classic cream, for a country bolt-hole? Two-oven or four? Whatever, I loved that cottage. I loved Mrs Ferguson, too, but if she'd truly decided that it was time for an easier life in town, and it finally appeared that she had, then I had to have it! I could afford it! A four-oven AGA would be over the top for Ben View, two would be plenty – I could spend the saving on some really top of the range limestone for the bathroom, or maybe a little conservatory . . .

'And are you *absolutely* sure she's all right?' I repeated, needing to hear it again.

He nodded confidently. 'Perfectly – I think she's quite

excited about it, now she's seen Cedar Park.' He sat back in his chair and folded his arms in satisfaction. 'Lovely job!'

A thought occurred to me. 'Hang on, though, Rod – oh, bugger and sod it! I can't really go and measure up, can I, being one of the interested parties? I'll need to hand this one over to Monica to head up, I suppose.' God, but that was a depressing thought. I glanced at Monica, who was still chatting with Lady Francesca Underhill and had turned into a sycophantic puddle of malleable awe; her eyes were huge and she appeared to be agreeing with everything Her Ladyship had to say on the other end of the line.

'No, you don't!' said Rod.

'Why?'

'That's what Mrs Ferguson and I were discussing just now – she wants you to be involved, and doesn't mind in the slightest that you might be one of the bidders.'

'But . . .'

'She really knows her onions, doesn't she? She asked me to draw up a letter that she could sign, confirming that she knows of your interest but still wants you to handle the sale. Told me she knew I'd keep you in order.'

'Did she, indeed?'

'Yup – anyway, I'm off out to buy a bag of Murray Mints. Back in five.'

He touched my shoulder on his way past, and stopped to open the door for a heavily built salesman who was struggling through with what looked like a tempting array of water-cooler systems.

'Wants me to be involved?' I spluttered. 'Hang on just a minute, Rod, who's in charge here? Isn't it up to me to decide whether you're coming with me, not the other way round?'

Rod smiled. 'Sorry, boss, but Mrs Ferguson did specifically ask for me. We had a really good laugh when we were over at Cedar Park – she was talking about buying a telescope to spy on the neighbours!'

'But she's *my* friend!' I whined, sounding about six years old.

Rod softened. 'I think she's trying to look after you, Anna – she knows you want the house, so she's maybe wanting to set you at arm's length from the process by speaking to me first. And personally, I think she's right – are you all right there, mate?' The water-cooler rep had left Rod holding the door open and was rummaging in the boot of his car, parked on the double yellow lines at the door, for ever-larger display models. 'She trusts you, Anna, simple as that – how many more, guv?' he called to the suited-up backside which was struggling to get what must have been their elite cooler out of his boot – it had 'Excelsior' written on the side, after all.

'Or maybe she's got the hots for you,' I muttered, still feigning my sulk.

'Well, you know how I feel about older women,' Rod replied brightly, before giving up on the salesman and setting off at a run for the sweetie shop.

'Monica?' I called over to the Lizard, who had finally wound up her call to Lady Francesca with what looked like a kind of desk-curtsey and was now doing her best to look busy. 'Would you be kind enough to attend to our gentleman caller?' I sidled off through the back to pour myself a cup of tea before she had a chance to reply, although I caught her audible '*tsk*' squarely in the back of my head.

Chapter Ten

Jack hadn't called. It was three days since our nooner, and Jack hadn't called. I had barely slept a wink since; my brain was too busy trying to process my actions into an acceptable segment of memory with which I could comfortably live for the rest of my days. And Jack hadn't called. Nor sent flowers – although come to think of it that would have been embarrassing – I wasn't sure if I wanted a thank you, or an apology, or anything which drew attention to the fact that an incident of a sexual nature had taken place for which he felt that a token of his, his . . . nope, couldn't find the word yet, it was much, *much* too soon . . . was in order. Anyway, *Jack hadn't called* – did I say?

Luckily, just as I was about to fizz into a little green puddle on the floor of the office, like the Wicked Witch of the West, Iris popped in unexpectedly to see me, so I had someone upon whom to vent my rage. She was dressed in her nipped-in black Armani suit and her hair was pulled into a glossy knot at the back of her head. I couldn't decide if she looked devastatingly professional, or a bit like a cinema manageress. The Monitor Lizard was out showing a property, and Geraldine was on a late lunch. Rod and Katy were preoccupied, so we weren't overheard.

'You have to ask him out for lunch,' Iris giggled, after I'd filled her in with every single one of the details, and she'd listened, nodded, tutted, and finally, exploded with laughter. 'Take him to a restaurant, somewhere busy, so that you can be sure you'll keep your clothes on. God, Anna, I can't believe he *ripped* your clothes off!'

I frowned. 'But if he *was* interested in seeing me again, he'd have got in touch before now, surely?'

'Not necessarily, from what you say. My bet is he's terrified of you . . .'

'But . . .'

'Having inadequacy issues, probably.'

'You reckon? He wasn't inadequate, as such . . . well . . .' Up until now the only feelings of inadequacy to which I'd given any credence had been my own.

'Definitely. I mean, what you've just told me sounds like a short story straight out of *Loaded* magazine – you're telling me you walked into his flat, ostensibly for lunch, but then you dragged him off to bed, where he ripped your clothes off, is that *approximately* what took place?'

'No! Well, yes . . . yes, it was,' I stammered. 'Although if we're being completely honest here I might have to ask you to delete the "ostensibly for lunch" bit.'

'He's probably fantasised about that sort of thing since he was sixteen . . .'

'Way before that,' I interrupted. 'He lost his virginity at fifteen.'

Iris gasped. 'No! The slut! Anyway, nobody truly wants their fantasies to actually come true in real life – how terrifying would that be? I mean, for instance, I may *dream* about being shagged senseless by three farm-boys, after they stumble across me pleasuring myself in their haystack on a searingly hot day, but I'd never actually, *really* put on a loose white gypsy top, with no bra, in real life, and set out across a field . . .'

'All right, I get the picture! Thank you, Iris. Iris?' I had momentarily lost her; she had glazed over and was staring into space with a distinctly *hungry* expression on her face.

'Sorry? Oh yes, anyway, back to Jack. In the sack. On his back.'

'Har, har.'

She shrugged. 'Sorry. Well, he is disgustingly good-looking, and you get on well with him, don't you?'

I pondered. 'Well, yes, I think so, at least I *thought* so – if I can blot out the worrying stuff like the bad flat, and the shocking sandwich.'

'Is he the sort of guy you think Miranda would take to?'

'Miranda? Goodness, I have no idea! Heavens, Iris, that is a very perceptive question!' It was also the single one which I had not permitted my brain to contemplate. 'Would Miranda like Jack . . . well, to be fair, we have only been together three times – at the quiz night, where we were both drinking, at the restaurant, where we were both drinking, and, well, that third time as well – I've no idea what he'd be like with her . . . hmmm, should that be worrying? Shouldn't that have been my first thought?'

She shook her head. 'Not necessarily, but it sounds to me like you ought to give him a call to see if he's up for meeting you in some nice, daytime setting – not that daytime's any protection from you, you *harlot* – and start all over again.'

I grinned. 'OK, you're right! I'll call him.' I checked my watch. 'Oh, sorry, Iris, it's great to see you, but I've got to go out and measure up a place in a few minutes . . .'

'Hang on!' she interrupted, slapping her hand down on my desk. 'I'm not just here to sort out your love life – I'm here as a client!'

'Really?' I stopped shuffling papers, like a winding-up newscaster, and stared at her. 'Don't tell me you're moving! You've got a gorgeous house!' She did as well; it was a huge, detached grey granite dream of a place set in an acre of garden on the south side of town – we'd get four-fifty for it, no problem.

'Well, no, not exactly, it's just that, well, Pete's inherited a bit of money from his uncle's estate, and we're looking for ways of investing it, so I told him we needed to come and speak to you.'

'Really? That's very nice of you! Would you care to just write me a cheque now, and I'll invest it in some of the nicest shoes you've ever laid eyes on?'

She wasn't smiling. 'Seriously, Anna, it's a ton of cash – three hundred grand!'

'What? *How* much?' I spluttered.

She nodded, solemnly, as though the information was some sort of enormous burden. 'Three hundred thousand pounds. Pete knew his Uncle Ivor was worth a bob or two, but, well, the actual amount came as a real shock when we were told, the other day.'

'I bet it did.' I thought back to the day nine years ago when I'd opened Omar's letter with a million pounds in it. That had been a bit of a shock, too. 'So, won't you need to get yourselves a financial adviser?'

She nodded. 'Perhaps. But we do definitely want to spend some of it on property, that's really why I'm here – not that listening to the nitty gritty of your afternoon of porn hasn't been worth the trip in itself, I hasten to add – but we've always hankered after the notion of having some rental property to get stuck into. I'm sure I must have mentioned it to you at some point, haven't I?'

I nodded, vaguely. Everyone I'd ever met in my entire personal and professional life said something along those lines to me at some point or other, so there was no reason for Iris to be any exception, even though I couldn't recall a thing about what she may have said to me. 'Definitely, I remember it well. So, what sort of thing did you have in mind? There's an apartment in Hunter Street on for 78,000 at the moment –you'd rent it out no bother, as it's so near the hospital and the college – or were you planning two or three flats? Personally I wouldn't go for the larger family property; you'll have real problems getting good, long-term people for that type of place. Oh, and go for a new or new-ish build – you don't want to be saddling yourself with maintenance bills. Or a garden, either – go for something on the first or second floor, definitely. Then you won't have a garden to look after, and female tenants tend to like the security of being up at least one flight of stairs. Shall I get a portfolio of potential matches together for you?'

'Well . . .' Iris was looking a little swamped. Clearly this was more of a prospect than she'd bargained for.

'Don't worry about leases, contracts, that sort of thing – I can sort out a full factoring service for you! Rod Dunsley – you know, the cutie-pie? He'll do references, leases, inspections, advertising, that sort of thing. I mean, there'll be a commission charge, obviously, but believe me, it'll be worth every penny for the peace of mind it'll bring you! Now, how many flats did you have in mind? Because, between you and me, if we were to consider the Hunter Street development, I'm sure you could do a deal on three or four of them – you'd be on the piggy's back! Sorted!'

'Anna?'

'Yup?'

She was squirming a little. 'Well, that wasn't really the sort of thing Pete and I had in mind, to be honest.'

'But I thought you wanted advice!' I whined, watching my Hunter Street kick-back payment slither off down the street.

'Yes, but, well, it wasn't so much the flat rental market we wanted to get into – we were thinking more along the lines of a holiday cottage, you know, somewhere nice and secluded, tucked away somewhere, with lovely views, that Pete and I could use as our weekend bolt-hole during the quiet times of year. We don't mind doing a bit of upgrading; in fact, I'm quite excited about a spot

162

of interior design! What do you think? Are we off our heads?'

Ah. My head did a slow-motion clockwise semi-circle and my jaw wandered slackly from left to right. 'You mean, some sort of cute little cottage, not too far from here, in an idyllic situation?' I said, in a sort of dead, robotic drone.

'That's right!'

'Nice and secluded, but within weekend reach of Inverness?' I droned. 'Precisely! Are we in cloud cuckoo-land? Do you know of anywhere?' Iris's eyes were shining – isn't that a song?

'Well, unfortunately, yes, Iris. Yes I do.'

Shy Katy in Accounts was a closet computer minesweeper addict. Rod had touches of it as well – once or twice I'd heard them bragging to each other about stuff like how they'd taken four seconds off their expert level score, or how they'd worked out what to click when you had a 1-1-2-1 combination, or else they'd be whining miserably about some terrible incident or another when they'd only had two cells to reveal and were on course to shatter their records but had been forced to take a guess and been blown up within sniffing distance of glory – it was all a bit of a mystery to me. I'd be aware of them clicking away, usually during their lunch breaks, oathing and cursing discreetly when they got themselves blown up, high-fiving and *yessss!*–ing when they managed to clear the board.

This, however, was *not* their lunch break and, since Iris had left, full of enthusiasm at the prospect of getting her hands on Mrs Ferguson's cottage, I was not in the sort of frame of mind just to ignore the quickie minesweeper session which had kept them occupied whilst Iris and I had talked. I was ready to snap some necks, truth be told.

'Bastard!' Rod hissed, evidently having just been blown to kingdom come.

A few feet away, Katy seemed to be having more success. 'A hundred and forty-six seconds! Wooo!' She punched the air, eyes still fixed glassily on the screen.

'Get out of here!' Rod jumped out of his chair and sort of danced over to check her screen. 'You've just beaten my best score! You witch!'

'Congratulations accepted!' Katy simpered. 'Sheer skill!'

'How many guesses did you have to make?'

'Just the one – top right-hand corner – I left it to the end. Wowser! Must post that up on the website . . . oh! Hi Anna!'

I had sidled over to her desk, and was glaring down at her with my arms folded. God, I just felt so crap, and it looked as though I was about to take them with me. 'I'm so sorry to barge in, children,' I began, 'but I was just wondering whether you were planning to schedule in any actual *work* this afternoon?'

Katy looked instantly abashed. Rod, however, just grinned at me. 'You've got your stern face on, Anna!' he joshed, swivelling round a full circle in his seat, without using his hands. 'Suits you!'

A little depth charge of fury caught me utterly unawares and I rounded on them both. 'Actually, guys, I am getting thoroughly cheesed off with you two taking the piss! Could you please go and do something useful and lay off the computer games until you get home and your mothers let you play with your own ones? Honestly, I'm going to have to remove that sodding minesweeper programme from your machines if you don't stop buggering about on it!'

They both looked like they'd been whacked with a stick. I had never, ever, raised my voice to them in the office before, but this chummy little twosome had just insinuated themselves so far up my nose it was going to take antibiotics to get them out.

'Rod, I haven't seen you anywhere *near* the mailing list for days now!' I thundered on, like a steamroller. 'Which means, while you've been arsing around with Katy, this office has been putting its reputation at risk by not keeping people up to date with what's going on!'

'I'm sorry, Anna . . .' Rod did sound a bit horrified, which, at that moment, I decided was a very good and desirable state for him to be in.

'Well, I'm sorry too!' Now this was the sort of phrase I used with Miranda. *Mummy's sad too!* I stepped back and glowered at them both. 'I *trust* you guys! And you're taking advantage – well, I'm afraid it's going to have to stop. Katy?'

'Yes?' came out in a tiny little whisper from a young woman with the deepest scarlet face I had ever seen outside Corkers Wine Bar after Lisa has put away too much Merlot.

'Please get on with what you were doing. Which account are you *meant* to be working on?'

'Em, I'm charging up . . . em . . . the . . . oh, what's their name . . . that funny name . . .'

'Come on, Katy, we're all meant to be intimately acquainted with each of our clients! *Especially* at feeing time! These are the small details that give us our edge!'

She was rustling her file – I was taken aback to see that her hands were trembling. Oh, God, just because I was in a stinking mood, did I really have to make everyone else suffer?

'Em, it's Leonard and Tracy, but I can't remember their surname,' she whispered.

'Butt!' I interrupted. 'Leonard and Tracy Butt – well, I suppose I should be pleased that you knew their first names. Right, come on, you two, Rod, get on with updating that mailing list . . .'

'Yes, boss. Sorry.' Rod shot off, his sarcasm dissipating like smoke into the tense office air.

Breathing deeply, I began to soften up. 'That's OK. Let's forget about it, shall we? Katy, will you *please* get back to charging up those Butts?'

After the immediate, pregnant pause, it must have taken a good fifteen minutes for the three of us to finally stop laughing.

So, buoyed up by the goodwill in the office, I went back to my desk and dialled Jack's mobile.

'Jack Anderson,' came the brisk, I'm-at-work voice.

'Anna Morris,' I shot back.

'Hey! I was just thinking about you!' *Promising!*

'Well, naturally. How've you been?'

'Good, thanks – are you around this week?'

'That's why I was ringing – how about lunch sometime?' I kept my voice as light as possible, although I noticed I was doodling strange, gothic symbols of doom on my notepad.

He laughed, making me squirm with embarrassment. 'Lunch? Or, you know, *lunch*?'

'Behave yourself, I meant lunch, as you well know. Lunch *out*, somewhere.'

'Ah. Actually, I'm working on a site thirty miles away this week, so I'm not around at lunchtimes. But how about going out for a drink, say, tomorrow night?'

'Tomorrow? Why not? Great! I'll see what I can do about a babysitter, and if I find someone, I'll meet you at the Yew Tree at, say, eight-thirty?'

'Great – see you then – oh, and Anna?'

'Yes?'

'I'm looking forward to it.'

I put the phone down and was just about to ring Lisa to ask her to babysit, when Rod appeared at my shoulder and said, 'I'll do it!'

'What?'

'Babysit Miranda – I'd love to!'

166

For some reason the very idea filled me with a surge of horror. 'Rod, no way!'

'Why not? Miranda's a wee star, we get on great when you bring her into the office, and I'm not doing anything else tomorrow.'

'I couldn't possibly ask you to put yourself out like that!'

'Go on, Anna, it's no bother.'

'Well . . . what about your girlfriend? Won't you be seeing Heather?'

'Nope, nor any night, actually, that's been well and truly over for a month, now.' His face winced a little as he spoke. 'Actually, I could do with the distraction, and bedtime stories may well be just the thing.' Now he was playing with the end of his tie, looking young, and vulnerable.

'Oh! I'm sorry to hear that . . .'

'Don't be, it's fine. We hadn't really been getting along for quite a while.'

'Ah. Well, I'm sorry to disappoint you, but Miranda reads her own bedtime stories – you're more likely to be nuking the hell out of each other on the Playstation.'

'Sounds like my perfect night in! So I'll be round at about eight o'clock?'

That's really the test of a person, isn't it – can you leave them alone to care for your child? Well, in Rod's case, absolutely, totally and utterly. Without the merest shadow of a doubt. It just seemed really awkward, somehow – the thought of Rod and Jack meeting up, not that they necessarily would – no, they definitely wouldn't – Jack wasn't even going to get to the foot of my stairs tomorrow night, especially with Rod inside – imagine! 'Thank you, Rod. That'd be great. OK, shall we head off to Ben View?'

'It's the two of you that's in it!' Mrs Ferguson greeted us at the door with a smile, and clasped each of our hands.

'Yup, reinforcements today, special customer!' Rod said, pressing the bag of Murray Mints into her hand.

'Away with you! There's no need for this! But thank you – see and remind me about the jam later on.'

'No bother, that's why I'm here, after all!' They smiled at each other.

'So how are you?' I asked as we walked inside, feeling once again like that six-year-old school kid muscling in on the attention.

'Oh, not too bad, you know. There's been a lot of visitors lately, actually. But you'll be wanting to get going, won't you? Where would you like to start? I've tidied up as much as I could, but I don't know if you'll be wanting to move the furniture . . .'

'Mrs Ferguson, it looks lovely, really,' I said, looking round the sitting room with its floral everything. 'I hope you haven't worn yourself out.' Looking at her more closely, she seemed distinctly strained, and her hands were trembling. She always had a slight tremor, but today it seemed more pronounced. Now I felt a little bit like a bailiff come to throw her out for non-payment of debt.

'Not at all, not at all.'

'Your son isn't here, then?' I asked tentatively.

'No, but he'll be phoning me later. And yourself, I expect, to see how we're getting on.'

My heart sank. 'Ah, lovely. Right then, Rod, will we make a start?'

'I'll put the kettle on,' said Mrs Ferguson, slipping away with a sort of respectful demeanour which made me feel even more horrible.

'OK,' Rod began, 'I'll hold the beep-beep machine, and you do the words.'

A kind of autopilot kicked in as we moved from one little flowery room to the next. It was bright and sunny outside but the house had a chill about it, suggesting damp, and traces of old-lady neglect. The sitting room had three doors, one of which led directly into Mrs Ferguson's bedroom, a musty time-warp, where specks of dust hovered in the slices of sunlight which slanted through the window and came to rest on the lemon-yellow candlewick bedspread. The dressing table was an Art Deco master-piece, probably original, with plastic doilies squashed beneath glass tops, and on top of that lay a brown lacquer hand mirror and matching hairbrush, silvery strands of hair trapped between the bristles.

I bent to touch the cool edges of a thickly carved crystal scent bottle, which had a tiny hose leading to a little crochet-wrapped balloon squirter, finished off with a red tassel, and, on the other side of the dressing table, a matching crystal bowl held dusty cotton wool balls. Right in the middle, in a yellowing silver frame, was a black and white wedding photograph of Mr and Mrs Ferguson on their wedding day. Mrs Ferguson was dressed in a thirties-style ankle-length gown, showing pale satin shoes with a single ankle strap, and her headdress was a straight veil which was fastened by a circlet of what looked to be lily of the valley, my favourite flower. In one hand she held a trailing bouquet of white lilies, and her other arm was linked through that of her groom, soberly dressed, clean-shaven, yet quite clearly proud as punch. It was all so poignant, so deeply personal, and so reminiscent of a bygone age that all at once I found myself dangerously on the verge of tears.

'Anna?' Rod's voice broke in softly. 'Come on, we've got a job to do.'

I nodded and hauled myself together. 'OK – right! Where were we? Two power points, wall-mounted night storage heater, sash and case window with southerly aspect, two fitted cupboards, one housing hot water tank and fusebox . . . oh, godfathers! I hate this!' I slumped against the wall. 'It still doesn't feel right – I feel like . . . like a burglar, or something!'

Rod walked towards me, fishing in his pocket. 'Here, have the red one.' He pulled out a tube of wine gums and offered me the top one. 'Red wine gum for a blue lady?'

I smiled weakly. 'I talked her into this, Rod. This is her home – she should be allowed to . . .' I broke off, put the wine gum in my mouth, and shrugged.

'Die here?' he suggested with a shrug.

I nodded. That was exactly what I'd meant.

'Well, maybe,' he went on, 'but Anna, she's decided to move on – we all do it, and why should her decision to have a change of scene be suddenly tragic just because of her age? Isn't it a bit patronising of you to think that way?'

'Well . . .'

'And just because *you* want to buy her house doesn't automatically make it the number one environment of choice for everyone in the whole world, does it?' He spoke gently, but there was a certainty in his voice which began to reassure me a little. 'Personally, I think this is an impossible place to live – I mean, I love the hills, as you know, and I'd kill for these views, but, well, there's peace and quiet and there's *peace and quiet*, isn't there? This place is miles from anywhere! Even I'd get a bit spooked here at night – just imagine being ancient, Anna, with bad legs, and gout and stuff, and hard of hearing, and being woken up by noises and bangings in the night?' He gestured out the window, towards the miles of moorland, and shook his head slowly. 'There'd be no one to hear you scream . . .'

'You're a great big chicken, Rod Dunsley,' I said, smiling at him, and sniffing.

He nodded in hearty agreement. 'Yup, but nice with it. Now, can we get a move on? It's brass monkeyville in here.'

Mrs Ferguson was arranging cups and saucers on a tray

as we returned to the sitting room and walked towards the door on the other side of the room, which led to the second bedroom and the cloakroom at the back of the house.

She touched Rod's arm as he passed. 'I'm not actually hard of hearing, son,' she said, 'But you're right about the other ailments – old age doesn't come along by itself!'

I gawped at them both. Rod put his hand to his mouth. 'Oh, Mrs Ferguson, I'm terribly . . .'

She laughed at him and interrupted. 'Wheesht you and don't be bothering!' She looked towards me. '*Both* of you. And you're quite right, Mr Dunsley, it's not very nice to be hearing that an old person can't enjoy a change of scene. I've got nothing but gratitude for you, Anna, you've found me a lovely new home. Now go on and be getting finished before your tea stews.'

The second bedroom was even more freezing than the first. Unheated, with the small, decaying window peering straight out on to the looming embankment behind the house, you could tell that Mrs Ferguson had tried to inject some cheer with her ambitiously floral decoration. The twin beds were covered in counterpanes of thickly embroidered crimson net, and the wallpaper reached an all-time zenith of floweriness by being entirely covered in fat globe chrysanthemum blooms of every possible, and *im*possible, shade. I sniggered as I thought of Mrs Ferguson's son, tucked up and shivering, surrounded by flowers and pink gauze as he drifted off to the first-class executive section of the Land of Nod.

'It's like diving into a drum of jelly beans,' Rod commented, as we tapped the back wall to try to ascertain whether there might be a fireplace beneath the plasterboard. Hmm. I'd have to install some decent heating before I could put Miranda in here – maybe under the floors if the foundations were up to it, but so many older houses

171

didn't have any foundations at all, they were just built up from ground level and then left to settle, which most of them did, quite happily, for centuries. And *lights*, for heaven's sake – some halogen spots on a dimmer mechanism, definitely! While the electrician was at it he could wire up a sound system through the whole house, and a computer cable . . .

'Got the measurements down, Rod?' He nodded. 'Good. What do you think, price-wise?'

He scratched his head. 'Well, normally I'd say around a hundred and thirty for the house, given its location, but you say there's – how much land with it?'

'Five acres, apparently. Just heather, I think – wouldn't be any use for a garden – far too steep and acidic, unfortunately.'

'Couldn't we sell it separately as a house site?'

'Nah, I don't think so – it's a conservation area up here, the planning department would take a machine gun to anyone trying to put up any more buildings, so I don't think it'd fetch all that much per acre.'

'Might be worth a phone call to the council, though?' Rod suggested. 'I could give it a go if you like.'

'Well, OK then, but don't get your hopes up. I agree with you about the cottage, though, if we put it on at one-thirty we'd get offers of loads more than that at a closing date. It's going to appeal to all sorts of people – the local people who want a holiday house to rent out, the folks down south who want a holiday home for themselves . . .'

'The curious hermit-types,' Rod put in.

'Yup, curious hermit types, not to mention Miranda and me, the speculative investors . . .'

'Dodgy closed cults?'

'Dodgy closed cults, folks who want to knock it down and build something bigger – all sorts, really.'

172

Rod nodded. 'It'd be a top spot for stag weekends – or séances! Just imagine, lighting candles, getting the old tarot cards out . . .'

'Hmm, Mrs Ferguson would love to think her house was being used as a den for the occult – let's go through; I'm gasping for a cuppa.'

'Is there any more information you'll be needing?' Mrs Ferguson asked, waving away my offer of help and shakily pouring tea into the thin china cups. 'What about the deeds for the house?'

'Aren't they with your solicitor?' Rod asked, helping himself to a scone and jam.

'No, no, I've got them here – my husband put them in the wardrobe in the spare room.'

'Well,' I said, 'it'd be a good idea to hand them in to your solicitor – they'll be safer there, and he or she will need them when it comes to drawing up the documents of sale, and then they'll be handed over to my . . . um, I mean, the new buyer's solicitor.'

'Delicious scones, Mrs Ferguson,' Rod spluttered quickly, as crumbs scattered all over his lap and on to the carpet. 'Oops, sorry!'

She patted his knee. 'Don't you be worrying about those. I've got a wee baggie of them for you to take home with you to have with the jam!'

'We'll need to take a few photographs of the outside before we leave,' I put in, 'and then we'll get back to the office to have a chat about what sort of asking price to put on it. Is that all right with you?'

She waved her hand dismissively. 'Yes, yes, whatever you think best.'

'Did *you* have any thoughts about the price?' Rod asked her all of a sudden. I stared at him in surprise – somehow, it seemed inappropriate. Although to be fair, this was a question which I'd trained him to always ask prospective sellers – it was a good idea to gauge where they were coming from in terms of their expectations, so that they didn't flounce off elsewhere in fury if we came out with a figure which was way below what they had in mind. But somehow, with Mrs Ferguson, I found the question impertinent. 'Or your son, perhaps, has he mentioned any figures?' Rod ploughed on.

Aah, good point, I acknowledged, silently. *Rod, my young Padawan, I have taught you well . . .* undoubtedly the Very Important James Ferguson, who 'dabbled', would have a few ideas on the price front.

'No, not really,' she replied, after a moment's pause. 'I'd be quite happy to accept your guidance on price and such-like. You did say that it would bring in enough to pay for the new flat?'

I nodded. 'Definitely, I have no doubts about that. Rod and I think it'll do very well indeed – only . . .' I stopped, wondering if it was a bad idea to mention the possibility of a separate house site, particularly as getting permission for it was such an unlikely prospect.

'What is it?' she pressed.

'Well, I'm just a tiny bit bothered about whether it might be an idea to put it on the market in two separate lots, the cottage as lot one, and the five acres as lot two as a building plot – it's not very likely that planning consent would be granted, but if it was, then you could do well financially . . .' I tailed off. Her body language said it all; she clasped her hands together, looked downwards, and was shaking her head slowly. 'Whatever,' I pressed on. 'Can we go back to the office and have a think about it, and I'll ring you later with some more ideas?'

'Or would you be happier if it was all kept together?' Rod put in, gently.

She looked at him in gratitude. 'Well, it would be nice

174

if it could be kept together, that's what I was saying to the gentleman who called to visit me this morning.'

'Oh?' said Rod in surprise. 'What, was this "gentleman" a friend of yours, or something?'

'No, no, nothing like that – he just popped up and knocked on my door – very flashy sports car he was in!'

I felt my insides go a bit funny.

'Anyway,' she went on, 'he was a charming man! He told me he had been looking for a place like this for . . . oh, what did he say, now?'

'Go on,' I breathed.

'Well, I can't quite remember now, but it was something about a client of his who needed a shooting lodge! Yes, that's right – a shooting lodge! I told him that Ben View was no shooting lodge! Imagine that!' Her hands had gone from trembly to fluttery – clearly this 'gentleman' had made quite an impression on her.

'What else did he say?' Rod asked evenly.

'Well, he said he worked for a building firm, and that they had a customer who was prepared to pay a very high price for the right place, and that he'd been keeping his eyes open for somewhere for a long time . . . here, Anna, are you all right? Let me get you another cup of tea.' She moved creakily over to the tray and refilled my cup, which I held out to her with some difficulty – now whose hands were trembling! 'Are you cold? I'll put some more coal on the fire.'

'No!' I exclaimed, reaching my free hand out to prevent her from lifting the heavy coal scuttle. 'No, I'm fine, really – just a little surprised, that's all. Tell me, did you know this person?'

She looked at me a little strangely. 'Know him? Of course not! I thought he must have been speaking to your office or something like that, otherwise, how could he have known that I was selling?'

'How, indeed?' repeated Rod, turning to look at me. 'Mrs Ferguson, Blakemore would never just tell people to show up unannounced and make enquiries about your house, isn't that right, Anna? *Anna?*'

You know, if you've been on the verge of tears already in one day, as I had been when I'd gazed at the little relics of Mrs Ferguson's past, then that wibbly feeling really doesn't retreat too far away for quite some time. I had to take some deep breaths before replying. 'No, absolutely not. Mrs Ferguson, did you get his name?'

She nodded. 'Oh, yes – a Mr Anderson. Very nice young man, he was. He said he worked with a big building firm in Inverness – what is it now . . . Fairfax, or something?'

'Lomax,' I murmured back.

Rod looked as though he was seething. 'Mrs Ferguson, did he make you an offer for the place?'

I held my breath.

'Oh, yes, a very good one, as well! A hundred and forty thousand pounds! Fancy that!'

'And what did you say?' Rod persisted, although softly, this time.

'Well, I asked whether his offer included the extra land as well, and when I told him about the five acres, he seemed very pleased!'

'I'll bet he was,' I hissed. 'What did he say when you told him about that?'

Mrs Ferguson shook her head. 'Well, he just excused himself at first, and went back to his car to make a telephone call, but as you know, Anna, you can't get the reception for these mobile phones up here, so I let him use my telephone.'

'That was very kind of you,' smiled Rod, whose knuckles were now somewhat white.

'So, I waited for him in here, and when he came back, he raised his offer to – wait for this, Anna – £155,000!'

Rod whistled. I couldn't speak. To think, Jack had been

in this very house, wheeling and dealing, on the information I'd given him over dinner! On our first date! It was too . . . too *freaky* for words.

Eventually, I raised my head and looked at Mrs Ferguson. 'That's a very good offer, in my opinion,' I said, forcing my voice to stay calm. 'Do you think you might go ahead with it? You don't need to feel any obligation towards me . . .'

'Anna!' Rod burst out, furiously. 'You can't say that!'

Mrs Ferguson smiled at me, then, obviously noticing how deranged I must have looked, got up, crossed to where I was sitting, put her arms round me and gave me a hug. 'Gracious, Anna, do you think I came down with the last shower? Of course I didn't take it! I told him to speak with the lovely Anna Morris at Blakemore, who was taking good care of my interests. Now, who's for another scone?'

Chapter Eleven

BEN VIEW COTTAGE

Here in the beautiful Highlands there are few locations that remain genuinely untouched by the march of progress. But Ben View Cottage is just such a place, nestling in substantial grounds at the head of Glen Seilagan, and it is with great pride that Blakemore now offers it for sale. This is truly a once in a lifetime opportunity to acquire a charming cottage with a productive garden and five acres of wilderness land, in the heart of a conservation area, with outstanding views, and yet within reasonable travelling distance to Inverness, with its myriad amenities and transport links.

The current owner, who is reluctantly selling owing to health reasons, has preserved the character of the house, whilst maintaining the characterful garden and, although the house would benefit from a degree of upgrading, it contains many original features which make Ben View Cottage a truly unique choice.

Offers over £140,000 are invited for the house and land. Viewing strictly by appointment with the selling agents. See overleaf for details.

It was quite a job, sorting out my apartment for Rod coming round to babysit. I'd reckoned on a five-minute spruce-up, but as soon as I got in the door, chores bred chores and it took the best part of an hour and a half to get the place spotless. What the heck had I been thinking, agreeing to let one of my staff have the run of my home? I might as well go to work naked; might this perhaps be a staff-bonding step too far? Take my bedroom, for example. Now Rod was hardly likely to go in there, was he? Oh, come on, *was he heck.* As soon as Miranda fell asleep, my bet was that that'd be the first place he'd check out, so, after picking the pants and tights off the floor, scrubbing the en-suite, hiding my razors and dental floss, arranging my Penhaligons bath oil bottles beside the bath, replacing the towels and hoovering, I changed my sheets. Then I sprayed them lightly with lavender water. What if he were to, to pull my duvet back, press his face longingly against my mattress, and inhale?

But it was poor old Miranda who really got the hard time. 'Go and tidy your room!' I barked as I sailed past her, my voice muffled by the armful of sheets in front of my face.

'Why?'

'Because it's a mess, and I don't want the babysitter to think we live in a pigsty.' I called this out from the depths of my massive, embroidered duvet cover as I nearly pulled my shoulder joints out of their sockets attempting to wrestle the top ears of the duvet into their rightful corners.

'Is the babysitter going to sleep over?' Miranda asked, innocently. 'You don't go to all this fuss for Iris, or Lisa, or granny . . .'

I glowered at her. 'What? No! Of course he isn't! He's just a friend who's helping me out for the evening. Now just do it, please! I want to see all those books back in your bookcase, the dirty clothes in the laundry basket, shoes on the rack by the door, games in the toy chest . . . oh, and Miranda?'

'What *now*?'

'You will be polite to Rod, won't you? And go to bed when you're told, but no later than nine o'clock, OK?'

'OK, OK!' She flounced off, in that slender, flouncy way that only young girls can carry off to perfection – the rest of us lose the art of the flounce, along with the rest of our innocence, somewhere in adolescence.

Flustered, I went through and lit some scented candles in the sitting room but then, realising that only calculating minxes with hidden agendas light candles for boy baby-sitters, I swiftly blew them out again. I did hide the really trashy magazines, though, and dust the TV set.

Then, more or less done, I stood back and sighed.

All Rod had said to me as I drove furiously back down the glen to the office after we had bidden farewell to Mrs Ferguson had been, 'So, am I still on for babysitting tomorrow?' to which I'd replied 'Too bloody right!' before realising that perhaps those weren't the prettiest manners nanny had ever taught us and adding, 'If that's all right with you?' Rod had just nodded, and spent the rest of the journey gazing out of the window at the dark, blameless hills, which were zooming past far too quickly for a single track road. And today, in the office, he didn't mention Jack Anderson once.

He rang my buzzer at three minutes to eight, and as I let him in, Biddy danced and whirled at his feet, whimpering with joy at having a new person to sniff, and I was startled by how different he looked from his usual get-up of grey suit and tie. I'd seen him dressed in civvies often enough before – at the staff barbecue, on weekend house-viewing sessions and just bumping into him in town, but it was definitely a different Rod who walked into my apartment, smiled like the teenage visitor he practically was, give or take six years or so, bent to make a fuss of Biddy and said, 'This is a really lovely flat! So, where's Miranda?'

I led him through to the sitting room where Miranda sat, as prophesied, engrossed in the Playstation. She looked up for long enough to say hello to Rod, then flicked her attention straight back to the screen. Biddy went back to the chewbone in her basket, job done.

'Miranda!' I snapped. 'Put that thing off and say hello properly!'

'It's fine, really,' said Rod. 'I know what it's like when you get on to the higher levels on these things – exit at your peril! Hi, Miranda – want to show me what stage you've got to?' He crossed the room and sat on the sofa beside her. 'Wow – *Harry Potter and the Chamber of Secrets*! What room are you in?'

'Flourish and Blotts,' she replied. 'Want a go? You need to *flipendo* all those barrels.'

'Thought so,' Rod replied, taking the console she offered him, and giving me a furtive thumbs-up.

'Erm, excuse me?' I ventured.

'Yes?' they chorused, not taking their eyes from the cyber-Harry on screen.

'I've set a tray with tea and coffee and stuff in the kitchen, Rod . . .'

'I'll show him where it is,' Miranda called over her shoulder. 'Have fun, mum!'

'Yes, have . . . *fun*, Anna,' Rod repeated, not looking at me either, as I reversed out of the room, feeling like a gawky interloper, and closed the door.

The Yew Tree's gimmick is that it doesn't have a gimmick. There's none of the Oirish, you won't get tapas, it doesn't have forty-eight different flavours of Lithuanian vodka, there's never any live music and nor is there an ear-bleeding disco. The word 'available' isn't chalked up anywhere on the food blackboard and there is no fluorescent lighting creeping up from the backs of mirrors. Nor is there a sign to tell me to wait to be welcomed. For those reasons it's my favourite pub in Inverness. It's not a wine bar, either, although Iris, Lisa and I had cleaned it out of more bottles of Chilean white than I cared, or was able, to remember.

I saw Jack immediately, sitting in one of the four red leather booths which were punched out against the back wall, looking extremely relaxed, one arm stretched along the back of the seats, just like he had done in the Maltings on the quiz night, only then he'd had me encircled underneath it. My tummy gave an involuntary jolt as I recalled the long, warm thigh, and then it gave a different, awkward kind of jolt as our doomed attempt at intimacy in his flat swept across my brain like a comedy in-head movie. Whatever, I had to stay focused – this man had some major-league explaining to do.

'Anna!' he beamed.

'*Jack!*' I answered, ladling more sarcastic sweetness into that one syllable than I'd previously thought possible. *OK, matey, it's crunch time.*

He stood up and walked over to meet me, clasped my elbows with his hands, leaned down and kissed my cheek. *Fuck,* but he smelt good. Lemony, sandalwoody, and just a suggestion of something that could have been bergamot or could have been some cunning aftershave ingredient like badger semen, one of those pheromone things which they chuck in to the mix to appeal to the lower levels of the female consciousness but WHATEVER, there was just a hint of it and it overlaid his basic, scrubbed-up man smell like crackly icing on a particularly scrumptious cake.

'What can I get you?' he asked.

Two hours of oral sex, a massage and a soapy bath, thanks, in any order you like . . . 'Oh, just a gin and tonic, thank you. Shall I go and sit down?'

I walked over to the booth he'd just left, and sat down to wait. The bar was half empty – or half full, if you will. The punters were mostly about my age, some a little younger, a random mix of after-work foursomes who had forgotten to go home, odds and ends of singletons, bar-proppers, people-watchers, no-hopers, interlopers, window-gazers, navel-gazers and a query group of under-agers.

'So, how have you been?' Jack asked, placing my drink on the table and sliding in to sit beside me.

I turned to look at him. 'Come on now, Jack. I'm not happy, surprisingly enough.'

He swigged his pint and then looked round at me in surprise. 'Sorry?'

'I said, *come on*, Jack, talk to me! I spent a very enlightening afternoon with my great friend Mrs Ferguson yesterday – but then, you probably know that, don't you?'

I'm sure some of the colour drained from his cheeks. Replacing his pint on the table, he sighed. 'Ben View Cottage?'

'Ten out of ten, Sherlock.'

He was raking his hair, sitting up a bit, twisting his mouth, all sorts of things a body-language expert would have a field day with but as it was, any clues he might have been giving out went criminally to waste as I waited for his reply. 'I was going to tell you about that,' he began, 'but I wanted you to get settled first.'

'*Settled*? Or drunk, perhaps?' I enquired. Well, at least it didn't look as though he was going to try to deny it.

'*Settled*, Anna – I've been looking forward to seeing you.'

I raised my eyebrows. 'Really? Why didn't you call me, then, or have you been too busy wheeling and dealing behind my back to pick up the phone?' That sounded a bit needy, so I didn't give him the chance to reply. 'Jack, would you like to tell me just what the *hell* you were playing at?'

'Anna, I know this looks bad – I didn't know when – or if – you were going up to the cottage, or I would have spoken to you first, but let me explain . . .'

'Mrs Ferguson is a very old lady, Jack, you can't just go knocking on doors like that!'

'But . . .'

'And our conversation was *private!* What I told you at Potters was in confidence!'

His demeanour shifted a bit on hearing that. 'Well, actually, I'm not so sure about that one.'

'What?' I spluttered. I was beginning to quite enjoy the gondola-ride to the upper hand, and wasn't prepared for Jack having much to say for himself by way of defence.

He paused before going on. 'OK, I did go to see Mrs Ferguson yesterday morning – she's lovely lady, isn't she? She gave me a jar of raspberry jam on the way out!'

'But you had no right, Jack!'

'Anna, come on! I work for Lomax Group! I've been scouting around for a property in an isolated rural location for one of our biggest clients ever since I came up here!'

'Yes, but . . .'

'Listen, part of my brief is to secure a rural, kick-ass site for one seriously wealthy lucky bastard to build a state-of-the-art holiday lodge and ponce around being Lord Muck to impress his colleagues – Lomax does a ton of work for him already, not to mention the contract we'd get to build the lodge itself . . .'

'Well, lucky ol' you,' I droned, squishing the chunk of lime in my drink against the side of the glass, and licking my fingers.

184

'As soon as you mentioned Mrs Ferguson's cottage, I suspected that it may be a possibility, so I spoke to my MD and got the go-ahead to make an approach as early as possible.'

'How about waiting until it went on the market? What's wrong with competing fairly, like the rest of us have to do?' Oooh, pots and kettles . . .

'What's wrong with not?' he shot back. 'What's wrong with offering top dollar for the place – way more than the place is worth, and saving Mrs Ferguson the upheaval of showing people round?'

I bit my lip. This was precisely the sort of reasoning I'd been using for my own ends just recently – he could have been quoting directly from the central regions of my head. 'But it's not right!' I said eventually. 'You know that – I feel kind of like you've betrayed me, Jack. You can say what you like, but approaching Mrs Ferguson to try to cut a deal, without telling me, was a bit sneaky. Not to mention . . .' I tailed off, biting back the train of thought which, if spoken aloud, would show me up as a great big fat money-grabbing hypocrite.

'You'll lose your commission if you don't get the sale?' Jack said, softly.

I half smiled at his perceptiveness, and nodded.

'Lomax would see your firm all right, Anna – you know that – gee whiz, this conversation isn't exactly going the way I wanted it to!'

'I'm surprised you wanted to have this conversation at all – did you think that you'd be able to agree a sale with Mrs Ferguson without me knowing what you were up to?'

'No! Anna, let me explain!'

'Go on, then – let's hear it.'

He took a couple of deep breaths, as though wondering how to begin. 'Well, in the first place, you didn't tell me that the place was *definitely* going to go on the market, so

185

theoretically I was only checking out something that you might not ever have become involved with.'

'Not good enough,' I growled.

He held his hands up. 'Fair enough, I accept that. So, secondly, all I can say in my defence is that I didn't tell you about my going to see Mrs Ferguson, and I didn't tell Mrs Ferguson that I knew you, so that I could protect you.'

I snorted, which was not pretty. *What had he just said?* 'Oh, why, thank you, kind sir! Pass me my fan! You went behind my back to Mrs Ferguson, *to protect me*?'

He nodded. 'Absolutely! I went up there, specifically to offer Mrs Ferguson a large price for the exclusive right to the house, so that I could do a deal without telling you, and you would not be compromised in any way because you'd known nothing about it – think about it, Anna!'

'I *am* thinking about it!' I frowned. 'And I'm none the wiser!'

He put his hand gently on my knee. 'Come on, now, you've been in the game long enough to know that off-market property deals go on all the time, haven't you?'

'Well, Jack, as I work *within* the market I'd be hardly likely to know all that much about off-market deals, would I?'

'But it's hardly illegal, is it? And you know I would have found out about Ben View before it went in the newspapers anyway, whether I'd been speaking to you or not, wouldn't I?'

It took a moment or two for this to sink in. I looked at him quizzically. 'Why? How do you mean?'

He laughed. 'Come on, Anna! I've spoken to your firm a couple of times in the past, with this client in mind . . .'

'Not to me you haven't . . . oh!' I jolted as I recalled the Lizard's comment that she may have spoken to a Jack Anderson in the past.

'No, not to you, obviously – if I'd got *you* on the phone

I would have made a point of asking the owner of the sexiest voice in Inverness out for a drink on the spot, wouldn't I?' The hand which was resting on my knee began slowly to move up and down my thigh, just a few inches up, then a few inches down. A few up . . . then a few down, up . . . down . . .

'Monica Izzard? My senior sales negotiator?'

'That's the name! I haven't met her in the flesh, but my guess would be she's, what, fifty-ish, loads of make-up, bit of an attitude? Mucho scary, in fact?'

'We do try,' I said, primly.

'Anyway, she was a bit off-hand to start with, but she did promise to let me know as soon as she heard of anything. She'd have been on the phone about this one any day now, I'm sure about it, judging by her ruthlessly efficient telephone manner.'

'No, she wouldn't, Jack!' I broke in. 'Monica may be a scary old witch but she'd never risk tipping you off about places before they were actually on the market . . .' My voice tailed away. Wouldn't she? A shiver worked its way upwards from the base of my spine, and I turned to face Jack. 'Tell me,' I said, slowly, 'and please be honest, did you do some kind of private deal with Monica? Because if you did . . .'

'Of course I bloody didn't!' he burst out, whipping his hand away from my thigh. 'I told you, Anna, I haven't done anything dishonest! OK, I jumped the gun and went up to visit Mrs Ferguson after you mentioned her cottage. OK, I admit I was a bit taken aback . . . a lot taken aback, truth be known, by how frail and kind of vulnerable she was when I got there, and I began to feel a bit bad for not announcing my intentions by phone or whatever, but, Anna, really! I had to do something before it hit the market because once I'd properly clocked Ben View's location on the map, I realised straight away that it was perfect for my client, and if it was perfect for him then it'd be perfect for about a squillion other people as well, and that here was an opportunity to do a quick deal to everyone's advantage!'

'But . . .'

'Let me finish, please,' he implored, roughing up the corner of his beer mat between his fingers. 'I didn't feel brilliant about it, of course, but, Anna, this is just the way it works sometimes in the construction industry. I desperately need a bit of an edge with this client – so much rests on Lomax continuing to get business from him. He's made millions renovating warehouses in Liverpool and now he wants to get a foothold in the Highlands. But no, my idea of a competitive edge does NOT extend to asking for inside deals from scary women on the other end of a telephone line – just the earliest *possible* tip-off – so you see, I'd probably have been the first to find out about Ben View in any case! I really, really wanted to protect your reputation, Anna!' He squeezed my knee again before leaning in closer. 'Well, your *professional* one, anyway!' he winked, and I whacked him. He was looking directly into my eyes. 'You told me about a fantastic-sounding property over dinner, and all I did was to follow it up. I thought that by doing things this way, you'd be cut out of the loop completely, so if there did turn out to be any crap hitting any fans, none of it could blow your way!'

'Thank you for that nice image.' Now I didn't know what to think. 'And just when were you planning on telling me all this?'

'Oh, tonight!' He looked away for a second, then back at me. 'I was going to ring you, but you got there first. I had every intention of 'fessing up to you this evening, before you found out what I'd been up to from someone else – although it didn't quite turn out that way, obviously.'

'Obviously.'

Most of the suits were finally draining their glasses and beginning to shamble their way, briefcases in hand, back to their cars and no doubt, their brassed-off spouses. It looked like the Yew Tree was going to be able to close early for the night, as there were only about six of us left now, and I for one had no intention of making a night of it. The barman was leaning against the counter, reading a newspaper.

'Well,' I said, presently, 'I'm just not sure about all this. Although I am damn sure about one thing – if I'd had a whiff yesterday afternoon that Mrs Ferguson was uneasy about your, your *visit*, I'd be kicking your butt from here to the other side of the room by now, but yes, I do also see now that your approach, technically, may not have done her any actual harm.'

Relief spread all over his face. 'Thank you.'

'But how exactly do you mean, when you said that Lomax Group would "see my firm all right" in terms of lost commission?'

He smiled. 'Oh, come on, that's easy! We've got blueprints on the go for a couple of cracking developments in town, and we're going to need a lot of help shifting them – what do you think?'

I looked downwards. Jack squeezed my thigh, ever so gently. 'For a dirty lowdown shark you're redeeming yourself just a tiny bit,' I murmured, before suddenly, and inexplicably, thinking about Rod – his stony silence as we'd driven back from Ben View, and his air of slight disapproval as I'd headed out of the door to meet Jack – he'd felt betrayed too, although not by Jack – by *me*. I placed my hand over his and gently moved it. My gin and tonic had all but disappeared, and Jack motioned to the jaded barman to bring over another.

'So, what do you think, Anna? Date or dump? If I owe you an apology, and I probably do, then I apologise. Truly.'

189

Hmm. Part of me wanted to break out into a beaming smile, gush 'That's OK!' and throw myself on him, but something – Rod's doubtful face perhaps, held me back. Plus, there was one more thing I still wasn't convinced about.

'Anna?' He peered round at me.

'Be honest, Jack,' I said, meeting his eyes. 'Were you *really* going to phone me today?'

'Yes!' he replied instantly, before inhaling sharply, his face twisting into an expression of severe doubt. 'Well . . .'

'You weren't, were you?' I held my breath. Jack was now ripping the shit out of his beer mat. Gently, I eased it from his grip and placed what was left of it in the ashtray in the centre of the table.

'Well, to be truthful, yes, I *hoped* I was going to ring you today. Apart from anything else, I'm going to be away at the weekend, and I wanted to see you before then. But I was terrified.'

'Good!' I snapped back.

'For one thing, I felt you probably wouldn't be fussed about hearing from me too soon after, well, after that time at my flat, and for another, I wasn't really relishing the prospect of having to have this very conversation. I was really worried you'd take it the wrong way.'

'Well, I have to say you had pretty good reason to feel that way,' I said softly.

'Yup, fair enough. So I think the honest answer is that yes, I wanted, I *had* to speak to you today, but no, I probably wouldn't have had the guts to actually make the call. I would have done my ostrich impersonation and made things much worse. But Anna?'

'Yes?'

'I like you a lot and I can't stop thinking about you. I've thought of nothing else, since . . . since that lunchtime, er . . .'

190

'Encounter?' I suggested.

'Encounter,' Jack agreed. 'Unfinished business, and all that.'

'Eeuw, I wouldn't put it like that – I've been turning scarlet every time I thought about it!'

'Really? That's a shame – there was so much that went on which was really very promising, don't you think?'

'I don't think like that – I'm a girl, Jack.'

'I had noticed.'

I sat back, folded my arms, and looked at him. His face was pink and he looked as though he didn't know what to do with his mouth. And he couldn't look at me. 'Well,' I said, 'it was horrible – a never to be repeated experience. Made me heave, to be honest!'

He put down his pint with a thud. 'Anna, that's a bit . . .'

'Utterly shocking! You should have been ashamed of yourself!'

'Well . . . I . . .'

'And if I ever find myself confronted by a comedy sandwich like that again, we are most definitely history, OK?'

I got home earlier than I'd expected, and as I turned the key in my front door and tiptoed towards the sitting room, my heart was doing a conga at the prospect of explaining myself to Rod. Then instinctively, or perhaps to put off the moment, I veered left and opened the door to Miranda's room. The fairy lights around her bed were still on, and beneath them she lay, gently illuminated in shades of lilac and pink, sleeping like an angel, with Biddy curled up languidly on top of the covers at her feet. Her hand was resting on her favourite book, *Tom's Midnight Garden*, which she was reading for the umpteenth time, and I smiled as I slid it from her, marked the place she'd reached, and placed it on her bedside table. It had been my favourite at her age, too. Then the gentle kiss which I placed on her forehead was as much to do with giving myself courage as bidding her goodnight and as I left her room and strode towards the sitting room, I paused at the hall mirror to check my reflection. I felt that Jack's lingering farewell kiss must be somehow visible on my mouth, like a traitor's mark, that Rod would notice it and I'd be condemned as an underhand, scheming shagabout . . . but of course all I could see was my own anxious reflection through tired, shifty eyes.

Rod was reading the newspaper.

'Oh!' I exclaimed when I saw him. 'I thought you'd be watching telly, or still on the Playstation!'

He put the newspaper down and stretched. 'Nah, not fussed. Besides, I wanted to be sure I'd be able to hear if there was anything up with Miranda. She's a great kid, Anna – we've had a lot of fun!'

'This really was kind of you, Rod, I'm very grateful.'

'It was no bother, really, my pleasure. How was your evening?' A hint of chill entered his voice at this, which I tried, but failed, to ignore.

'Well, it was all right, I guess . . .'

'Anna, I know it's not any of my business . . .'

'Yes, yes it is, Rod, I know I owe you an explanation.'

'Did you chuck him?'

I smiled at him. After the Yew Tree, it was like a refreshing breeze to come back to Rod's directness.

'Nope – nearly, but no, I didn't.'

'Ah.' Rod sank back in the sofa.

'And are we still handling the sale of Ben View, or has he relieved us of the burden?'

'Of course we are!' I retorted, sharply. 'That was never in doubt!'

'Wasn't it?'

'No!'

192

'Thanks to Mrs Ferguson', Rod pointed out. 'She could easily have done a cracking deal with . . . *Jack* this morning, couldn't she?'

I sighed and sat down, resisting a strange urge to cuddle up on the sofa next to him, and settling instead for the squashy gold chenille armchair opposite. Kicking off my shoes, I curled my legs underneath me. 'Maybe,' I said eventually. 'But she's kind of special, isn't she? Somehow I think she would have instructed him to do business with Blakemore even if he'd offered her twice that amount.'

'They don't make 'em like that any more,' sighed Rod. 'Do you think she knew that he was your . . . that he knew you?' Rod didn't meet my eyes.

I shook my head. 'No, don't think so. I did mention him to her last time I visited, but I don't think I told her his surname, or what he did . . . no, definitely not. She would have said something, anyway, I think – she's not one for hidden agendas. Look, Rod, Jack explained his motives for going up there yesterday morning, and although he didn't do anything illegal, he's not very proud of himself, and he apologised.'

'Think so, too.'

'Anyway, I'm sorry, too, if all this had made you think less of me . . .'

'Don't be daft.'

We sat in silence for a few moments, until Rod began folding up the newspaper. I played with a bobble of wool on the sleeve of my cardigan and wondered what to say to encourage him to stay a bit longer, so that we could talk some more and I could try to melt the ice crystals that were forming between us.

'Would you like a cup of tea? Or a nightcap?'

For a moment I thought he was going to say yes, but after a short hesitation, he shook his head. 'Nah, thanks,

I'd better be going. Got an important property to launch on to the market in the morning!'

'Tell you what, though,' I said, furrowing my brow and standing up to show him out.

'What?'

'Soon as you get in tomorrow, could you change the price on the particulars to "offers over 155?"'

'How much?' he gasped.

'Offers over £155,000 – we've got one buyer in the bag already who's prepared to go higher than that, so why don't we go for it?'

Rod looked doubtful. 'It's tempting, but isn't it a bit of a risk? I mean, won't a starting price that high scare off the bulk of the interest we're banking on attracting – and what then if Lomax Group go cold on the idea? Mrs Ferguson . . .'

'. . . trusts me. Mrs Ferguson trusts me, and I'm going to get her a price beyond her wildest dreams.' Then I added, 'Even if it turns out to be me who's writing the cheque.'

'*You?*' Rod exclaimed. 'How much are the guys at head office paying you?' Then, he swiftly added, 'Sorry, that was rude.'

'I'll manage.' I smiled, trying not to let myself think about the wisdom of committing such a large sum of money, which was supposed to be for Miranda's future, to a project which was in danger of morphing from a flight of romantic fancy into an all-out competition.

'If you say so, but Anna, don't you think you may be a bit close to this one to make a proper judgement? I thought we were pushing it a bit at 130, to be honest, and I'd hate to see you, or Mrs Ferguson, get hurt.'

I touched his arm. I wanted to give him a hug and tell him he was wonderful, but I didn't – he'd have thought I was losing my marbles. 'You're a good mate, Rod.'

194

He looked down at my hand, which was still resting on his arm. 'Think about it, Anna,' he murmured. 'It's not worth . . .'

'Rod, we're going to milk its one-offness for all it's worth. Places like Ben View are like gold dust, and it'll be our job to make that fact absolutely clear to everyone who goes to look at it.'

'But . . .'

'Don't worry, we're going to pitch for some sky-high offers for Ben View when it comes to a closing date, and I'm sure, even at the higher price, we'll find enough interested parties to whup the Lomax Group's ass!'

Chapter Twelve

'Comfy' is a really dire word in the world of clothing. *I wear it all the time because it's comfy* is not a statement, in my opinion, to be proud of. It conjures up an image of letting your tummy hang out fatly in some monster garment with an elasticated waist, as you loll smugly in the knowledge that you're just as comfy as can be. How about fleece – now *that's* comfy! Any particular shade, madam? No? Not fussy? We've got some real shockers for you to choose from – the peach is especially comfy . . .

It's how it makes you *feel* – personally I'm much more at ease (at ease, mind, not comfy – big difference, *huge*, in fact) in my gorgeous little bras and knickers, wearing nicely put-together clothes on top that fit properly, than slobbing around in comfy ol' trackie bottoms, comfy sweatshirt and comfy trainers. Better to be concerned about walking straight in high heels and a tight skirt, than worried about bumping into someone – anyone – in clothes more suited for an eighteen-month-old child, surely?

Such were the thoughts that entertained me as I parked my car and boarded the first-class compartment of the Caledonian Sleeper train to go and meet Omar in London. My little brown leather suitcase bulged with my overnight things and a single, knock-out new outfit: a cropped jacket in chocolate suede, coffee silk vest top, tight black bootleg trousers and fabulous killer heels. But this evening I deigned a nod towards the comfy end of the spectrum by wearing black, heavy, silk jersey wide-legged trousers, a grass-green cashmere turtle neck jumper and my most 'accommodating', that's so as not to use the other word, kitten-heel mules.

It's a much-maligned service, the sleeper. I guess, if I'm honest, the term 'sleeper' is a bit of a misnomer as the jolts, shudders and titchy beds seem to spend the night hell-bent on keeping you awake as you barrel south, sideways, through the night, but as a means of getting from Inverness to London it's unbeatable. Think about it, if you were to travel down by aeroplane, you have to check in, what, two hours early? Then fly to Gatwick or Luton, both of which claim to be London airports but in fact live a good hour or so outside, and don't even get me started on things like baggage collection, delays and the sheer lunacy of being about 36,000 feet up in the sky, sitting in a thin tube of silver metal which is maintained by a company that's only charged you a fiver for your ticket. It's as bonkers as a bag of bunnies.

Whereas, if you go on the sleeper, what happens? You spend the evening with your daughter, pack your stuff in a leisurely fashion after tea, deliver said daughter to her grandparents for the weekend, get yourself to the station, hop on board ten minutes before departure – and go to bed! Then, the next morning, a lovely person brings you breakfast in bed and a newspaper, you snap up your roller blind to look out of the window – and you're in London! It's magic! How does that work, then?

My portly sleeper host showed me to my room, asked me what I wanted for breakfast, then left me alone to nest, as the train creaked into life and began pulling the Highlands out from under me.

All at once I was in Barbie heaven – miniature everything!

Even the bed! The courtesy sponge bag disgorged a little flannel, weeny soap, a hygienic hand-wiping sachet, disposable razor and a foldaway toothbrush and Lilliputian tube of Colgate encased in a phallic fat black plastic tube which had definite potential for use later on. So very thoughtful!

Plonking myself happily down on the bed, I took out my mobile and rang Miranda to wish her goodnight.

'Hiya, sweetheart – are you all ready for bed?' I asked, as her clear voice answered.

'Well,' she said, slowly, 'I am, I mean I've got my pyjamas on and I've cleaned my teeth but granny and grampa are having a movie night tonight, so I'm having to stay up with them. Is that OK?'

I pictured the scene, and hugged myself happily. 'Course it's OK! What are they watching?'

'*Bedknobs and Broomsticks* – grampa says it's his favourite, and granny's made popcorn! And I've got lemonade in one of grampa's wine glasses!'

'Well, that sounds lovely, but you must make sure you give your teeth a really good scrub before you eventually get to bed. Is Biddy behaving?'

'Yes – we've taken her for a walk and now she's asleep in the utility room.' My parents weren't wild about dogs – Biddy was lucky not to be in the garage, but it would be a novel change for her from her little warm den at the foot of Miranda's bed.

'That's good. I hope she doesn't make any noise later after granny and grampa have . . .'

'Mum?' she interrupted, her voice suddenly anxious.

'Yes, honey?'

'You won't tell him . . . daddy, I mean . . . that I sometimes forget to do my homework, will you?'

'Of course not!' I exclaimed. 'As if I'd tell him a thing like that!'

'Or that I took my Powerpuff Club things in to school when you told me not to?'

Realisation was creeping over me that Miranda was fully aware that my trip was a sort of audition for family membership, but while I'd been viewing it as a chance for me to check Omar out, poor Miranda was sitting, in knots, at my parents' house, believing that my intention was to tell Omar all about her, so that *he* could decide whether *she* was worth bothering about! The thought made me tremble all over. What a thing for an eight-year-old to endure over a whole weekend! Perhaps I should have brought her with me after all – for her sake – to hell with Omar, I could have protected her if things didn't go well ...

'Darling, don't you worry! All I'm going down for ... hello?' The train was heaving itself up towards the belly of the Cairngorm mountains and my phone reception was beginning to peter out.

'Mummy?' came her faint voice.

'Miranda!' I shouted. 'I'm going to tell him how wonderful you are! Hello?'

'... OK ... 'night ... love you ...'

The phone beeped at me, then gave up the ghost, and died. I sat staring at it in anguish. I *think* she heard me ... oh, God. This was one hell of a potential mess. It hadn't truly occurred to me properly until that moment that, if Omar did turn out to be different to how I recalled him – if he'd become sly, or dodgy, or had plans to share custody of Miranda – heaven forbid, then I'd have no alternative but to refuse to allow him to visit, and return home and have to break the news to Miranda that yes, I'd seen her daddy, but no, she wasn't going to get to meet him for herself. Then I'd just have to sit back and perhaps wait for a letter summoning me to a custody hearing to come flying through the letter box. And Miranda would think it was all her fault. Wonderful.

199

I looked at my watch. It was barely nine-thirty. There wasn't much point in undressing and getting into bed this early, so I swished on some lipgloss, fished my book out of my suitcase and wobbled through the narrow passageway to the lounge car for a nightcap.

The dimly lit lounge car was almost empty, apart from a knot of four hearty hill-walkers with happy, exercised faces and skinny legs in tight stretchy trousers with stir-rups and piping down the sides, getting stuck into cans of lager – and one solitary and very familiar-looking man who was earnestly tapping information into a dinky silver tablet computer. Ah.

'Hello, Jack,' I said, approaching his table and sitting down in the chair opposite.

'Anna!' he cried, looking astonished but not entirely displeased to see me. 'Stalking me now, eh? Fantastic!'

'You should be so lucky!' I replied, and nodded towards his empty glass. 'Another drink? It's about time I bought you one.'

The attendant, a round young woman, roly-polied up in her Scotrail thick woollen jumper, brought over two brandies and set them in front of us. Jack closed up his computer and leaned towards me.

'You didn't tell me you were coming south this weekend!' he said. 'What's on?'

I took a large gulp of brandy and immediately began to unwind a little. 'Ah, now, I could tell you,' I replied, mysteriously, 'but *should* I, that's the question? I mean, who knows *what* you might do with the information . . .'

He smiled good-humouredly and raised his glass. 'Fair enough, I deserved that.'

'I'm going to meet Miranda's father,' I said quietly.

'Oh.' He looked at me for a long few moments, then looked away. A roar of outdoorsy laughter from the hill-walkers punctuated the pause.

'I haven't seen him since . . . since before she was born,' I went on, realising that, given the nature of our relationship, he was owed at least a little more information than the small details I'd hitherto volunteered. 'He's been abroad, and now he's back, well, back for a year, at least, and he got in touch to ask if he could meet Miranda. So I'm going down to check him out first, on my own.'

He nodded. 'Sounds like a good idea. Have you spoken much on the phone?'

'Only the once, last week.'

'You didn't tell me when we were at the Yew Tree . . . OK, sorry, it must be strange for you . . .'

'It is. Very.'

Outside, the sunset to the west cast the hills in gloomy shades of burnt orange. Occasional lights flickered from isolated cottages and beside the train, the A9 with its busy car headlights accompanied us on our way.

'How do you feel?' There was genuine concern in his voice which, weary, nervous and worried about Miranda, I appreciated.

'Apprehensive. And curious, as well. It's been a long time . . .'

'Is he married?' Jack cut in.

I smiled at him. 'No, he's not. But don't worry, whatever happens, I have no immediate thoughts of him playing a major role in our lives in future – he just wants to meet his daughter, and, well, I suppose he's entitled to that. After I've grilled him to within an inch of his life about his intentions, of course. Who knows whether he'll want more than one visit? I think he's just finally become curious, that's all.' I wondered just how much of that sentence I actually meant.

'And what does he say . . .'

'Jack, can we change the subject, please? It's tomorrow's

201

issue, and I'm getting tired. What are you heading south for?'

'Just a trade show – boring, boring, boring. All about supposedly revolutionary new building materials, you know, better for the environment, harder wearing, much more expensive, that kind of thing.'

'Hmm. Really?' Wrinkling my brow, I thought hard for a few moments before saying, 'You know, Jack, I can't think of a single interested question to follow that up with, is that OK? Remember when I asked you if your car was a diesel? I'm having one of those moments.'

He laughed, and I joined in. So, as we couldn't talk about Omar, or Jack's trade show, and definitely not about Ben View Cottage, we started trading spurious witty comments about what the hill-walkers might have been up to instead. And when we'd exhausted them, we moved to less catty waters, like London, and holidays, and later, as my third brandy threatened to make me slide to the floor and start snoring, stupid cars. Here, we both had quite definite views.

'Smart cars, Jack, what do you think?'

He shuddered. 'I always want to press my thumb on their roofs and just *flip* the silly little fuckers on to their backs, don't you?'

'Ha! Spoken by a man who drives the titchiest vehicle in Inverness! Jack! *Jack!* What's going on with the sports car?'

'You don't like it?' He caught my hand and feigned a melodramatic sob. 'And to think, the salesman told me I'd have women flinging their knickers at me as soon as I got it out of the showroom! I'll sue!'

The glint in his eye was definitely a little bit arousing. 'Well, I did enjoy being in it, but – oh, I don't know. I want to tell you how ridiculously impractical it is but I know that in doing so I'll show myself up as officially an old bat with a daughter to think of, so I won't.'

He glanced under the table and shook his head. My kitten-heel Gina mules were just visible under my trousers. 'And you say my car's impractical? Where are the safety belts on *those*?'

'That's different.'

'Oh, really?'

'Shoes are power.'

'And my car?'

'Is ridiculously impractical. I told you.'

'No, you said you weren't going to say that, so I erased it from my memory. You do give me a hard time, Anna – first you insult my sandwich, and now my car – two of the things I hold most dear in life! Now, then,' he leaned forward and gently stroked my cheek. 'Would you like to go to bed, or shall we start trading Lada jokes instead? I know some great ones!'

'To bed? You mean . . .'

'Yup! I mean *together* – let's go for membership of the Mile Long Club, shall we?'

'How ridiculously impractical would that be?' I laughed.

'Good practice though, for trying it in my car some time, wouldn't you say?' The hill-walkers went eerily silent as Jack stood up, leaned across the table and kissed me, slowly, yet insistently. When he drew back he reached for my hand and I knew with a rush of excitement that the toothbrush holder was safe for the time being. 'To think, the only company I'd been expecting tonight was hot chocolate and a book,' I breathed, as together we swayed our way to my room, which lay closer to the lounge car than Jack's.

Once inside, I locked the door and all hell broke loose, as we began grappling with each other in the tiny, over-heated compartment. Standing, at first, Jack pressed me hard against the wash-hand basin, kissing my mouth, my

203

neck and my hairline, his breath fast and rasping, whilst I deftly undid the buttons of his shirt. Then together, we dropped down on to the bed and as my hands roamed all over his incredibly toned torso, he drew back a little, pulled my jumper over my head and gently eased me on to my back. All the while the train rolled south, juddering and clattering into the night, while piece by piece my clothes were expertly removed.

'Careful, now!' I giggled as he unhooked my bra strap.

'Don't worry, I've been practising since last time,' he gasped.

'Sorry?'

'I can now remove a pillowcase without the pillow knowing a thing . . . wow, Anna, this is most definitely the only way to travel!'

And then we were both naked. Jack eased himself on top of me on the tiny little bed, where it swiftly became apparent that any sideways movement by either of us would end in disaster.

I started to giggle. 'This is impossible!' I squealed, clutching him to me and feeling the contours of his shoulders beneath my fingernails. 'Hang on, Jack!'

'I didn't think there'd be quite . . . so little . . . room . . . ah!' he moaned as he entered me.

I closed my eyes and concentrated on the sensation, and as I did so we both suddenly heard, loud and clear, the sound of the person in the next compartment brushing their teeth.

'Shit! Better keep the noise down,' Jack hissed.

'I'm not saying a thing,' I whispered, pulling his head towards mine and kissing him again.

We moved, slowly, as best we could on the tiny bed. It was like making love on an ironing board but somehow, the difficulties only added to the excitement and as Jack moved against me, just as I had surrendered myself completely to the pure, if somewhat stifled, sensations, all of a sudden the train gave an enormous jolt which sent us both crashing off the bed and on to the floor.

'Ouch!' I landed squarely on top of him, and raised my head to look into this startled eyes. 'Are you all right?'

He smiled languidly back. 'Why, good evening, Ms Morris – what brings you down here?'

'Shhh!' I giggled. 'Where were we?'

'Just about . . . here, I think. Tell you what, let's just lie still and let the train do the work, shall we?'

I nodded and closed my eyes. 'Mmm, although I have to say that doing otherwise isn't really an option . . .'

So we lay together, squashed in a heap on the floor of the compartment, which, luckily for Jack, was carpeted, and gradually felt the motion of the train take over. The space was so tiny that Jack had to keep his knees bent, and I lay astride him like a cowgirl aboard a western saddle. I closed my eyes and clung to him and finally, had to practically sink my teeth into his shoulder to stop myself from shrieking with long-suppressed joy.

'Thank God it didn't stop at a station, back then,' gasped Jack.

Later, as we half-sat and half-lay back up on the little bed, I asked, 'Do you think we're destined always to have strange sex?'

'Sounds quite tempting, I have to say,' he replied, lazily. 'Think the guy next door heard us?' Jack was languidly pulling on his clothes.

'I hope not. I'm going to have to cower in here for hours tomorrow morning until I'm sure he's safely off the train.' Then I gave a huge yawn. 'Hey, Jack, speaking of tomorrow morning, I hate to have to do this but I'm going to have to throw you out soon. I've got a big day tomorrow, and you've got your, your bricks, and things, so . . .'

'Fair enough,' he replied, kissing the top of my head

before standing up and stretching. 'Sleep well, gorgeous – don't fall off the bed, now!'

London. There's no smell quite like it. The muggy, sprawling bustle of Euston Station is a perfect urban whack in the face for a girl newly arrived from the Highlands. It sort of forces you to get with it; to walk briskly, head down, purposefully, and make like you're one of the crowd.

Jack had popped his head round the door to say a quick goodbye, as he had to run for another train to take him to his trade show somewhere far, far out in the 'burbs. I'd scrubbed up fairly well – it's amazing what you can do with only a basin of hot water, a Scotrail flannel and a mirror if you have to – and as I clipped across the station concourse and down the steps to the taxi rank, I was aware that a man was walking very close behind me.

'Good morning, Ms Morris – I believe you had a pleasant night?'

It was George Leversedge.

I flushed so deeply that I practically passed out and had to pause for a few moments to recover and to let him amble chortlingly on his way. I breathed a huge sigh of relief when I reached the taxi rank queue and found that he wasn't there. I used the ten minutes or so of queuing to gather a measure of composure together and try to prepare for the meeting to come. Come on! I scolded myself. Omar can only make you nervous if you let him! He's got everything to gain, and you've got nothing to lose, so head up, girl, and go check him out!

We had arranged to meet for coffee at the Stafford Hotel in St James's, which apparently was close to Omar's apartment. I'd contemplated booking myself in there for the night before deciding against on the grounds that there would be no way on this earth I'd be able to get the phrase

206

'I've booked a room here for the night' out of my gob without sounding like I was trying to pick him up.

I'd never have found the hotel myself in a million years. Rolling past St James's Palace, I tried to peer through the windows like the excited Highlander I was, imagining it stuffed to the gunwales with minor royalty and obsequious people with improbable titles like 'Equerry', or 'Lady of the Bedchamber'; perhaps a duchess or two having a leisurely Saturday morning, slouching around in monogrammed silk housecoats and crested slippers, dogs at heel – or perhaps wearing huge, floppy straw hats and getting stuck into a spot of light pruning in some private security-conscious plot, and hurling traitorous weeds into a heritage trug.

On we went, up, along, round and down, ever-decreasing lanes, which ultimately, a bit like Glen Seilagan, narrowed to a point where, at last, the taxi driver stopped and a doorman, liveried in a frock coat of royal blue, positively *leaped* from the hotel steps to open my door. I had to skirt awkwardly round him in order to pay the driver – how do these Audrey Hepburn types manage to stay so elegant, with all of the serving-clutter that goes with their class?

The entrance hall was tiny – more a lobby, really, and I flustered over to the reception desk, where I stopped, straightened up and attempted to compose myself.

'I'm due to meet a . . . a friend here for morning coffee,' I said to the receptionist.

She smiled back in a not unfriendly way. 'Certainly, madam, have you booked?'

Had I? 'Well, I'm not sure, really. The name would be Ghez – Mr Omar Ghez?'

I held my breath while the receptionist checked her book. It was so *weird* being in the same building as him! My senses were becoming flayed with anticipation, which the near silence of the discreet lobby did little to allay. 'Ah, yes, I have the reservation here. Mr Ghez hasn't arrived yet – may I show you through?'

We walked into the lounge, which, in contrast to the narrow reception lobby was bright and beautiful, lined with low white-clothed tables set for morning coffee. Little groups of lovely women, most of a certain age and all bearing a greater or lesser resemblance to Goldie Hawn, sat and tinkled their cups and chatted in that languid, confident way that shrieks, *My hairdo cost three hundred quid! So up yours!* There were few, if any, men, or maybe they were so elegantly and discreetly attired that they had simply disappeared into the background.

The waitress turned towards me. 'Mr Ghez has requested a quiet table, madam, and as the lounge is almost full this morning, I wonder if you would care to follow me through here?'

So on we sailed, down the narrow corridor towards the rear of the building. Damn. The last thing I wanted was a quiet room – in imagining our meeting my mind's eye had us perched in some large, opulent, marble lobby full of chic sofas, busy, clicking heels, foreign voices on mobile phones and suede *objets d'art* in challenging cube shapes, but not . . . this!

'This is our American Bar, madam, I hope you find it comfortable. Would you care to choose where you would like to sit?'

I stared around the room. The American Bar was a vision of purest green. From the diamond-patterned carpet, to the deeply buttoned, cracked leather sofas which lined the walls, to the semi-circular bar, which even had a green leather pad upholstered around the outside edge of the counter, perhaps there to cushion executive heads as they plunged towards the deck after one rare single malt too many.

The walls, too, were dark green, though barely visible behind hundreds of framed photographs, sketches, engraved plaques and shields, and paintings. Sporting scenes, mainly, interspersed with some upper-crust cartoons, drawings of aircraft, rugby team photos, the occasional regiment, standing to attention . . .

. . . but the ceiling! The waitress had disappeared. I looked up, blinked, and looked again.

It was hung, from end to end with boys' stuff – baseball caps, polo helmets, model aeroplanes, old school ties, sporting pennants – just how the *hell* do you dust all that? And how posh do you have to be not to care?

Plumping for a the table in the bay window at the top corner, I sat on the semi-circular sofa which hugged the wall and saw that above my head in this little nook the baseball caps were so tightly hung, peaks pointing downwards, that they resembled multicoloured fish scales, swimming futilely against a tide of model Spitfires and public-school tat.

Well, Omar, I thought to myself, you've confounded me again. Already, and I haven't even set eyes on you yet! Why here? Why this, this, gentlemen's club? I peered more closely at one of the signed photographs on the far wall. Yup, that would be Margaret Thatcher, all right.

The bar opened on to a small terrace, which was furnished with wrought-iron tables and chairs – painted bottle green – what else – and the one or two voices which trickled in from the occupied tables had American accents. This must be a perfect spot for wealthy American visitors, I mused, giving them a hint of Old Boy England with a slice of Way Back Home. Rarely, had I felt so out of place.

Glancing at my watch I saw that I was still fifteen minutes early. I had thought that the traffic would be impossible in central London at that time of the morning but, misjudging the Saturday lull and forgetting about the effects of the congestion charge, I had zipped through the mean streets with the ease of a George Bush cavalcade.

But then I froze. The only perceptible change was the faint sound of some floorboards creaking in the corridor outside the bar, but I knew. *He was here.*

'This way, sir, please,' came wafting through.

And then, I saw him.

'Anna.'

I stood up. 'Hello, stranger,' I replied.

I had forgotten how tall he was. And how graceful, as he moved towards me, and held out his hand.

When in London . . . I'd expected double kisses but, as though hypnotised, I slowly extended my right hand. He caught it gently by the fingertips, raised it to his lips, and kissed it, sending an electric shock right through me. I fought competing urges, to throw myself on to him in an enormous hug, or to pick up my bag, squeak and run for my life.

'You look very beautiful,' he said, as he sat down on the green armchair opposite. 'More beautiful than I remembered.'

I blushed like a girl.

The maroon-coated waitress handed Omar a menu.

'Have you ordered?' he asked.

I shook my head.

'Coffee?'

'That would be lovely.' I could have done some real damage to a gin and tonic but I guess, at ten in the morning, that that may not have been a very good idea.

I looked at him. He was dressed in an immaculate navy blazer, with a pale blue shirt and slightly darker blue tie. His thick black hair was cut far shorter than I remembered, but it suited him – his strong, smooth olive features, liquid brown eyes, beautiful, even teeth – somewhere in the turmoil that was my head I found a smug moment to

210

congratulate myself that, on the whole, most of the men in my life were distinctly easy on the eye.

While I was busy staring at him, he looked around our curious, green surroundings, then frowned. 'This is not what I had planned, Anna, I asked for a quiet table, but I did not intend to meet you in a *bar*!'

'Well, I did wonder!'

'I shall request a table in the lounge. It's brighter there.' He made as if to get up but I laid a hand on his arm.

'Don't, Omar, this is fine, really.'

'But . . .'

'Honestly, it doesn't matter!'

The waitress reappeared and covered our table with a thick, white damask cloth. Then she produced a yellowing silver bowl piled high with white and brown sugar lumps, and topped with little tongs, closely followed by a matching milk jug and chunky cylindrical cups and saucers, heavily patterned with garlands of flowers and finally, a chunky pot of coffee, which she poured for us, splattering a few tiny drops on the pristine cloth. It was only after she had gone and we were rejoined by the thick silence that I began to wish that I had agreed with him, and that we had indeed moved to the bright, happily clinking lounge at the front.

'Too late now, anyway!' I smiled. 'It's a bit different from the hotel – the last time – but none the worse for that. So, how are you? What have you been up to for all these years?' The words came tumbling out but I managed to stop myself from bumbling headlong into saying, 'Oh, and thanks again for the million quid, it's been terribly useful . . . ' Shhh, girl! Calm down! I lifted my cup – good, no shakes – and tasted the coffee. It was a little over brewed for my taste, and not quite hot enough – but maybe, I thought, self-doubt creeping back like limescale on a London kettle, that's the *correct* way to serve coffee?

Omar's cup remained untouched. 'I'm very well, thank you. It's been a long time, hasn't it?'

'It sure has,' I replied.

'And how is my . . .' He stopped himself, and I caught my breath. 'How is Miranda?'

Thinking of Miranda seemed to make everything all right. I became unassailable. 'She's great, Omar, she's very beautiful, and so bright! She's doing really well at school, and she's got loads of friends, although she's very close to one particular girl called Flora – they do almost everything together. And she's got a little dog – a miniature dachshund called Biddy, who's adorable, sort of caramel coloured, really friendly, Miranda's great at looking after her. She goes to Brownies, although you should see the stuff they make them wear these days, it's appalling, and she goes to tap-dancing lessons, and piano – oh, and she's trying to get me to allow her to have her hair cut short, but I'm not sure – there's plenty of time for that sort of thing when she's older, in my opinion, and she's just pestered me into letting her have a mobile phone – apparently everyone else had one and she felt hard done by because I'd always said no but she said there is a good argument that they're useful as a safety measure, what do you think?'

Despite my words coming out with no spaces in between them Omar seemed to listen intently, nodding and smiling before laughing aloud – he did have a lovely, warm laugh. It brought even more memories surging back, of the fun we'd had during our week together.

'Why, Anna, are you asking me to become involved in a parenting decision *already*?'

I laughed, and didn't reply. *Was I?*

'She sounds wonderful. I wish . . .' He paused, and all of a sudden I pitied him. There was something about his body language, the faint catch in his voice, that brought home to me a little of what he might be feeling. 'I wish I knew her,' he finished, simply.

Reaching over, I squeezed his hand. 'She's very like you, I think,' I said.

'Really?' He beamed.

'Yes, she's, well, very contained, and dignified, for an eight – nearly nine – year-old. I often think she appears far older than her classmates. And she's very accepting of things – I suppose she's had to be.' He looked away. 'I didn't mean that as a criticism!' I added hastily.

'Didn't you?' he said, turning back to look at me.

'No, definitely not!'

'Do you think, if things had been different, that we might have been able to be together?' he asked, in such a low voice that even in the silence of the green bar I had to lean a little closer to pick up his words.

This was most definitely truth time. I searched for the words. 'Well, probably the thing to remember is that things *weren't* different, Omar. We both made our choices, didn't we? And we hardly had time to get to know each other properly, so . . .' Stopping mid-flow, I looked straight into his eyes, and then continued, 'No, I don't think we would have been together.'

He nodded, gazing at his coffee cup.

'And you – what do you think?'

'I think that one of the reasons we had such a wonderful time together nine years ago was that we were – are – such different people. You were like a breath of air to me, Anna, so much fun, and so exciting!'

I grinned, my nerves beginning to lift into the air and drift upwards to dance around the coating of ridiculous hats on the ceiling. 'Thanks!' Oh, well, if I was struggling to be languid and sophisticated like the Goldie Hawns out front then I could do a lot worse than 'fun and exciting', sitting here with by far the best-looking bloke in the place, couldn't I?

He smiled back, and then became suddenly serious. 'Anna, what we did, the time we had – I do not make a habit of it, you know – it is not usual for me to . . . to . . .'

'Pick women up in hotel lounges?' I suggested. 'I guessed that, Omar, don't worry. Me neither – that time with you was most definitely a first, an experience I can't see myself ever repeating . . . oh, but it was great! I didn't mean I regretted . . . oh, you know . . .'

He reached across the table and laid his hand on my shoulder. 'Perhaps we can stop worrying now about how things looked back then? Or we'll never get anywhere. I had a wonderful time with you, a time which I would have held in my heart for the rest of my days even without . . . Miranda.'

'Thank you. Me too. Omar?'

'Yes?'

'It's good to see you again.'

He smiled. 'And you.'

I reached into my bag and pulled out the small, dark grey suede book which I had spent some time preparing. Then I handed it to him, without a word.

He looked at me quizzically, then turned to the first page. 'Oh!'

I had put my favourite photograph of Miranda right at the front, rather than build the little album up chronologically, starting with one of those frightening, crumpled, newborn shots. Instead I had chosen one I'd taken last summer up at the waterfall in Glen Seilagan; Miranda had been walking ahead of me, trying to keep up with Biddy. We'd been in ridiculously high spirits as it was a crisp and tangy early summer morning, the sun was just beginning to release its warmth and I had an enormous rucksack on my back which was packed with a disposable barbecue, sausages, fizzy pop and marshmallows. Despite the heavy rucksack I'd managed to sneak my camera out from a zipped side pocket, and increase my pace a little until I was just behind Miranda, but she hadn't realised how close I'd come to her. Then, I held the camera up, called out, *Boo!* And pressed the shutter just as she wheeled round in delighted surprise. The photograph captured just about everything I wanted to say to Omar about her – her beauty and spirit, the shining eyes, beaming smile, all caught in semi-profile – although I little realised when I took the picture that it would find its way here, to the fusty back bar of a strange hotel in St James's, being stared at in wonder by Omar.

'This . . . is her?' he said, as I nodded, suddenly feeling a little emotional. 'But of course it is! How . . . so . . . sweet! She looks so happy!'

I studied his own face as he gazed at Miranda, framed in a similar semi-profile to his daughter's, and the resemblance became even more striking. So *that* was where these glorious eyelashes came from! Then, slowly, he began turning the pages, gently easing the tissue paper back from each new image, smiling, shaking his head and occasionally biting his lip. I couldn't for the life of me think what to say – having lined up a little speech about each one, somehow it now seemed inappropriate to interrupt Omar's first encounter with his daughter.

He reached the final picture – Miranda almost a year ago, blowing out the candles on her eighth birthday cake. I had thought about not putting this one in; it seemed as though showing him pictures of events he'd missed out on and would never have was kind of rubbing his nose in it, but on balance I had left it in as it showed my parents on either side of her and I wanted Omar to see the other people who were in her life – dad was holding the cake, and mum had her hands on Miranda's shoulders as I took the picture in the gloom of my curtained-out kitchen. Plus, the glow from the candles illuminated her face so beautifully that the picture made the final cut through sheer artistic merit. She truly was a lovely child. We sat opposite each other, her parents, both filled with pride and emotion, joined for ever, yet inhabiting entirely different worlds.

'I've often thought about sending you a photograph of her, Omar.'

He had begun, softly, to cry, pulling a large white handkerchief from his pocket and dabbing his eyes. Again, I leaned forward and laid my hand on his arm, unsure of what to say. I certainly hadn't expected him to be the one in tears – to think, I had been afraid to meet this man!

'But, well, I was afraid to, for all sorts of reasons – you told me not to get in touch, and I couldn't bear it if I sent a picture and you couldn't care less . . .'

Again, he nodded. 'It would have been nice,' he whispered. 'I see that, now.'

'And I was afraid, as you know,' I went on. 'I still am, Omar. Miranda is my whole world . . .'

'I told you,' he cut in, gently, 'you must not be afraid. I owe you a great debt of gratitude, that you have raised this . . . this beautiful child and that you have agreed to see me this morning, to even *contemplate* allowing me to be introduced to her. It is a great deal more than I deserve.'

'But Omar, *I took your money.*' It was no use, this little nugget of a fact just had to be aired. OK, for almost nine years I had allowed my conscience to be more or less at rest on the subject, but I couldn't have Omar sit there and talk to me of gratitude when . . . or could I? Hang on – was I actually saying that my entitlement to the million quid gave him entitlement to Miranda? In giving me the money, was I acknowledging that he'd purchased an option on her life, on *both* of our lives, to be taken up on his whim?

216

At least my bald statement made him finally dry his eyes and put his handkerchief back in his pocket.

'Anna, all I did was try to help in the most feeble, easy way I had open to me.'

'Yes, but under the circumstances . . .' tailing off, I realised that I didn't have a clue how that sentence would have ended, so why I had embarked upon it, apart from to fill the silence, was anyone's guess.

'I have plenty of money,' he said, simply. 'And I have spent the last nine years berating myself for buying my way out of my responsibilities.'

'But Omar, I didn't want you! And you didn't want me! Don't you remember? We had a good time, and then we called it a day – now we've both spent some time this morning explaining to each other how out of character our behaviour was when we got together, so we both know that we're nice people really, but, Omar, neither of us intended for me to get pregnant!'

'That is true,' he admitted. 'But as soon as I knew I ought to have come to get you. I ought to have married you, Anna.'

I gawped at him. He looked a little like a penitent schoolboy, hauled up before a strict teacher, reeling off the words he thought she wanted to hear.

'Omar! Come off it! I would have turned you down! You know that!'

'Would you?'

'Well . . .'

'Truly?' He was smiling, just a tiny bit.

'I think so. OK? I *think* so.'

We were disturbed by a small clutch of elegant American ladies, who drifted into the bar, floorboards a-creaking, and moved straight on through to the terrace, whipping monster sunglasses down from the tops of their shiny heads to their suspiciously wrinkle-free eyes.

Outside the bright sunshine made the terrace a tempting prospect, but we were too embroiled, sitting just where we were, under our preposterous canopy of caps. A waiter bustled through to take their order – four decaf lattes, and although I can't swear to it, I'm certain that when an authoritative female voice called him back to request a glass of iced water, he replied, '*At once, Ms Hawn . . .*'

Omar closed the photograph album, and pushed it reluctantly across the tablecloth towards me.

'Please, keep it,' I said. 'It's for you.'

Here was no child-snatching psychopath. Here was no towering businessman with the clout of his millions brandished, ready to browbeat me into submission. Here, put simply, was Miranda's daddy.

'I don't think I can bear the idea of sharing her, that's all,' I said, thus finally speaking aloud the last of my fears. 'She's . . . she's my right arm, my whole life . . .'

'I understand,' he said. 'I have asked too much.' He leaned back in his chair, defeated, and clutched the photograph album I had given him close to his chest.

'But . . .' I began.

'Yes?'

'She wants to meet you.'

'Does she?'

'Yes.'

'That is wonderful! May I?'

'Yes. Yes, you can. You must come to her on her birthday.'

Fortnum and Mason. Did you ever see so many pots of jam under one roof? I danced around them in a blur, before skating over to one of the chocolate counters and ordering a large box of handmade truffles to give to my parents to say thank you for looking after Miranda. Then I bought Miranda a lollipop the size of a saucer. After that, my sense of purpose deserted me and, like a child abandoned in a sweetie shop, which I kind of was, I stood in the middle of the store, utterly and totally flummoxed as to what to do next. I had a day and a half of London shopping, all to myself, and a perfectly nice room booked for the night in a perfectly nice hotel in Piccadilly. I had shoes to shop for, dimity little morsels of costume jewellery to attend to, Jo Malone to visit for lime, basil and mandarin bath oil, espresso to drink at Bibendum, Joseph to clean out of summer basics and an exhibition of the history of Art Nouveau to take in at the V&A. Then I was supposed to hop back on to the sleeper tomorrow night and go and find Jack, who was booked on to the same return train.

But all I wanted to do was go home and cuddle my daughter. I knew that the sleeper didn't run on Saturday nights, and as the Fortnum and Mason shoppers whirled around my knees and I stood, forlornly clutching Miranda's lollipop, probably looking like some tragic extra on the run from the child catcher in *Chitty Chitty Bang Bang*, wanting to drop to my knees and howl for somebody to make everything all right, I reached a decision.

I walked out of the shop, hailed a taxi on Piccadilly which took me back to left luggage at Euston, where I picked up my suitcase, then all the way across the city to Gatwick, where I waited for three hours before boarding the evening flight to Inverness. And as the big city disappeared below me and we flew north into the gathering evening, I knew, as I gazed out of the window at the orange clouds below, that Miranda would from now on have two parents in her life.

Chapter Thirteen

Biscuits in the office – are you for or against? Do you subscribe to the politics of the packet? Because if you work in an office and don't then I suggest that you are either a blue-sky thinker on a higher plane from the rest of us, in which case get your CV hot-footing in to Blakemore immediately, or else you are the office outsider – you don't quite fit in, do you? Got something going on, haven't you? Is it your marriage? Are you on the take, perhaps – one hand in the petty cash – something along those lines? Anyway, whatever it is, sweetheart, we're on to you . . .

Geraldine does the grub run on a Monday morning, restocking the tearoom with biscuits, milk, instant coffee (the real coffee machine in the meeting lounge is really for the punters and to be completely honest, its coffee isn't all that great) and teabags. As befits my managerial station, and because I love them, she gets me a packet of ridiculously costly Duchy Original Lemon Biscuits, handmade by fairies from royal flour, crested butter, refined sugar hand-stripped by pandas, and Commonwealth lemons – because I'm worth it. Geraldine herself has never quite grown out of her childish passion for pink wafers, and even although she puts away about nine at a time per tea break, she still manages to have that perky little figure – really makes me feel my age, she does. How *do* her bosoms defy gravity like that? Cunningly cantilevered little cantaloupes, that's what they are. I know for a fact that it's those boobs that got us Insch of Stour, one of our most scrumptious ever properties, to sell – its dashing young owner, Jeremy fforsythe, couldn't take his eyes off them the other week when he visited the office to make a vague enquiry about selling, and by the time he'd left we had the place in the bag and Geraldine had an invitation to lunch.

Shy Katy in Accounts has us all puzzled, though, as she always goes for bourbon creams. She really is a dark horse, that one. I mean, if ever a biscuit was brought out as a joke, surely it's the bourbon cream? Just what is it that's nice about them? That bitter charcoal, hardcore cocoa taste that coats your teeth and has to be forced down your throat with scalding mouthfuls of coffee has no place on the tea-break table of the civilised world, if you ask the rest of us in the office. Yet if you quiz her about just what she thinks she's doing as she dunks yet another in her Gold Blend it only encourages her and she races over and offers you one, like she's on a divine mission to convert you to her gang – The Church of the Modern Day Bourbon Creams – so you just have to let it go, and shake your head and lament, quietly, the loss of another young soul from the delights of the hobnob, the boaster, the jammy dodger – even the bourbon cream's respectable cousin – the *custard* cream.

Is there such a thing as biscuit racism? Is it imperative to add that colour has got nothing whatsoever to do with it? Some of my other favourites are absolutely *covered* in chocolate! Step forward, Penguin! Yes, you, Wagon Wheel! Gypsy creams – Mrs Ferguson's choice – that's a persecuted group as well in some (family) circles but not here! Oh, no! We *embrace* the gypsy cream! In fact, we positively embrace it but then positive discrimination in the biscuit world is a bit New Labour for Blakemore so let's just stop at 'embrace', leave the 'positive' part out of it, and *move on*, brothers and sisters!

Being a slim, fit young bloke, Rod's idea of a mid-morning snack is to nip out to the baker's on Union Street and come back with a pie and a sticky, white-iced doughnut filled with fake cream, scoff them, in that ravenous, collie-at-lunch male way, and then he'll start planning which takeaway he's going to invade for lunch. Occasionally he'll go on a health kick and ask Geraldine to get him some energy bars, something deeply figgy, pruney and oaty, so that he can 'optimise his performance' or whatever it is that they promise so evangelically to do. It's always a good opportunity to take the piss a little, whenever I see him indulging in the vile little chewy horrors because as his boss I am hidebound by certain protocols which prevent excessive ribbing and vindictiveness – '*Skipped breakfast? Don't worry! Here's something Naomi the orang-utan regurgitated earlier!*' I quip, or, '*Low potassium getting you down? Enjoy a taste-free Crud bar and feel your levels go through the roof!*'

Ah, but the Lizard ingests *her* biscuits by stealth. Geraldine stopped asking her what kind of biscuit she wanted ages ago as she tired of being rewarded with a pained look and a shake of the head. 'If you have a proper breakfast there is absolutely no need to pig out on biscuits in the middle of the morning,' she claims. And yet, and yet . . . why is it that Monica repairs alone to the tearoom after the rest of us have finished, brandishing a herbal teabag and the *Daily Telegraph*, stays closeted in there for a good twenty minutes, and returns with a constellation of crumbs down her front? Why do my Duchy Originals only last half the week? Oh, we've tried to catch her out – the number of times Rod has tiptoed up to the door, then flung it open, hollering, 'Telephone, Monica!' just to try and catch her in the act of putting away a Duchy Original or two, but you know? He's never succeeded once in finding her in flagrante with even so much as a pink wafer. 'She must just lash out her tongue like an iguana and pull them into her gob in a fraction of a second – *whap*!' he opined one day, executing a demonstration with a rubber band and a bottle of Tippex.

It was a brisk Wednesday afternoon, and Ben View Cottage had just hit the market at the beginning of the week. The phone had started ringing at two minutes past nine on the Monday morning, and by the end of that day Geraldine had put eighty-seven sets of sales particulars in the post, and emailed out a further twenty-four. Requests for viewings were coming in thick and fast, and a quick call to Mrs Ferguson revealed what I had suspected, that the Ben Seilagan road had been chock-a-block all week with a steady stream of cars which had driven up, paused furtively at her front gate, then turned, and gone back down again.

'Some of them have even rung the doorbell!' she exclaimed when I rang her up to fix a time for us to carry out the first round of viewings.

'Oh, Mrs Ferguson, that's terrible! People are so rude, aren't they? They know perfectly well they should organise viewings through the office.'

'Well, they're very grateful for the cup of tea and scone, anyway.'

'What, you've been *letting them in*?' I exclaimed, horrified at the picture which was forming in my head – Mrs Ferguson, bustling unsteadily to and fro with trays of tea for brazen strangers . . .

'Well, why wouldn't I?' she chuckled. 'They've come a long way, and I wouldn't be wanting to turn away potential customers, now, would I?'

'That's true, but these people are just chancing their arms, Mrs Ferguson! I see it a lot – people who think they're being crafty by trying to outwit the system and do a deal direct with the seller . . .' Oh, crapola – here we go again – trumpeting the merits of the very system I had myself hoped to subvert just a couple of weeks ago. 'It's not on, you know! Have any others made you any offers, apart from . . . that first person?' That would be Jack Anderson, by the way, who was coming round for dinner tonight, to meet Miranda.

'Well, one or two of them have, in fact. I had a couple yesterday who said they had the money in cash and could let me have a cheque today, if I wanted!'

'Honestly!' I whined. 'The cheek of some people!'

'Don't you be worrying, now, Anna,' Mrs Ferguson soothed. 'Was I not telling you before that I was looking forward to trying out the market – some of these people think that just because I'm an old lady I came down with the last shower!'

'Yes, that's fair enough, but from what you're saying I have to say I'm a bit concerned for your safety, Mrs Ferguson – really, you can't just allow strangers in like that – I don't want to alarm you, but, well, you're miles from anywhere – who'd come to help?' That wasn't a very good attempt at not alarming an old lady now, was it?

'Och, away, you!' she scolded. 'James is here with me, and he sends them all off to register a formal interest with you at your office, and to wait for the closing date like everyone else. After they've had their cup of tea, of course. Well, it's a long run back in to town.'

'James?' I echoed, feeling a little gloomy thud somewhere around the pit of my stomach.

'Oh, yes, James is up to supervise the sale – I thought he'd have been in touch with you by now? He's wanting to discuss one or two things with you.'

'Ah. How lovely,' I lied. 'Well, I'll look forward to seeing him again – I've provisionally lined up a whole day of back-to-back viewings tomorrow, as you know . . .'

'Yes, that'll be right – James will be dealing with all that.'

'Oh? But I thought you wanted to be in charge . . .'

'He's sending me off in a taxi to Inverness for the day, so that I don't have to be worrying myself with all these people poking around the place. He thought it would upset me. He's very thoughtful sometimes, you know! And he thinks I should buy a new couch for the new flat, although I don't know why – the old one's done me fine this last thirty years!'

I sensed the faint tone of bewilderment in her voice, but tried to ignore it. 'So, are you saying that when I come up tomorrow, to spend the *entire day* at your house showing no fewer than eighteen sets of potential buyers around your house, that *James* will be there to . . . help me out, and you won't?' I asked, faintly.

'That's right, dear. Will that be all right?'

'Oh, perfectly,' I lied again. 'Although I'll miss seeing you.'

'Don't you be worrying – I'll be leaving enough scones to keep you going all day! And there's some more jam for Miranda as well – see and remind James to give it to you before you go, now.'

Like that would happen. 'Mrs Ferguson, there was no need . . .' I faltered, but she had bidden me farewell and put the phone down.

'How is she?' asked Rod, so I explained. He screwed his face up at the prospect of my spending a whole day with James Ferguson, but then said, 'Do you think Mrs Ferguson would like me to take her to lunch, as she's in town anyway?'

'Rod!' I beamed. 'That's so sweet!'

'Hey, I'm just a sweet kind of guy, you know,' he

simpered back, licking his finger and stroking imaginary sideburns.

'Katy'll give you some money from petty cash...' I began, but tailed off when I caught his withering look.

'I think I can just about manage to buy lunch for one of my mates, Anna,' he said, not unkindly, but I definitely felt a little like a mummy who'd just had an offer of extra pocket money for good behaviour turned down.

And still the enquiries flooded in. Geraldine was becoming a little sarky, truth be known, as more and more people on the other end of the line asked her the same old questions.

'How may I help? What...not... *Ben View* Cottage? Just remind me...oh, yes, now, let me see, I *think* I've got the details here somewhere – let me just check the file, now...ah, yes! I see *it is* still on the market!' The rest of her spiel came out in the sort of flat monotone which only just rose above earning her a ticking-off. 'Would you like me to send the details and do you think there is the possibility of your requiring to view the property because if so I must advise you that the viewing schedule is being strictly controlled owing to the sensitivity of the area and the considerable amount of interest in this particular Blakemore property and I could offer you one time-slot only and if you couldn't make that and were unable to advise us of your cancellation you may incur a cancellation fee of forty-five pounds to cover our expenses and I can offer you tomorrow at twenty past three and may I have a note of your name, address, contact number and also your solicitor details, please?'

Still, at least it got her off the phone and on to the next call nice and quickly.

Back home that night, Miranda was at last becoming excited about the prospect of meeting her daddy in just

226

over a week's time. Meanwhile, at the other end of the kitchen, *my* excitement had more to do with the imminent arrival of Jack, who was due at any moment. I'd cooked moussaka, which was a speciality of mine, assembled all the ingredients for a Greek salad, and bought fresh figs and gooey cheese for pudding. That eternal dilemma about just how much effort to go to when you're cooking for a man! Not too much fiddly stuff, the aim was for effortless flair. I decided that in this instance it was probably appropriate to spend a little time actually cooking the main course, but just to throw something expensive on the cheeseboard for later, and *definitely* not to concoct a starter. I had some Kettle Chips in the cupboard for emergencies, but the very idea of crisp-type snacks still brought me out in a cold sweat after the Pringle sandwich débâcle in Jack's flat, so for now they could stay firmly put.

'Mum?'

'Yes, poppet?'

'Remind me, is this Jack who's coming tonight your . . . boyfriend?'

I put down the tub of olives, which had just splattered oil on to my shirt, and turned to her. 'Well, I don't know, Miranda. We're only just getting to know each other, really. I wouldn't exactly call him my boyfriend. I just want you to meet him, like I told you. Is that OK?'

She looked puzzled. 'Well, it's fine by me, so long as he's nice, but what will my daddy think when he comes up on my birthday, if you bring your boyfriend?'

'Oh, that's an interesting question!' I trilled madly, playing for time. How could I explain things to Miranda when I couldn't yet explain them to myself? And if that was the case, what business did I have inviting Jack round in the first place? Was I in the process of doing untold damage to Miranda's psyche? Had that been done already? Any more scary questions, while we're at it?

'Well, I just want to be sure everyone's going to be friends,' Miranda went on.

'I'm sure everyone's going to be really good friends,' I said, walking over and kissing the top of her head. 'Like I told you, Jack is a new friend of mine, and we're just going to have dinner together tonight. Tell you what, I don't think we'll have him at your birthday, do you? Just you, Biddy, me, granny, grampa, Flora, and . . . daddy.' Seemed obvious, once I'd said it.

Miranda beamed up at me. 'Are you sure he won't mind?'

'Quite sure.'

'Mum?'

'Yes?'

'Please can I just have you and daddy on my birthday? That would be the best, *best* present?'

My first instinct was to laugh off the request but she looked so earnest that for once I tried to fit myself into her shoes and when I did I saw that the dream of having both of her parents spend the day with her had been hitherto only that – a dream – so I nodded, and said OK.

The doorbell rang. *Places, ladies. Eek!* I hurried across the hall to open the door and Miranda, emboldened by our chat, followed. Jack was standing, looking distinctly nervous but faintly delicious, all shaved and scrubbed-up and tall and things, smiling at both of us from behind a large bouquet of lilies.

'Hello!' I said.

Miranda stepped out from behind me. 'Hello! I'm Miranda, and I want to say that I hope it's all right if you don't come over on my birthday even though you're mum's friend.'

What had she just said? I held my breath.

'Ah, yes!' Jack exclaimed, hunkering down to get a bit closer to her. 'You're nearly a birthday girl, aren't you?'

Miranda nodded proudly.

'Then these must be for you, then, mustn't they?' He fished in his pocket, pulled out a box of After Eights, and handed them to her. 'I hope you have a lovely day, and maybe you'll tell me all about it afterwards? Can I give the flowers to your mum?'

'Certainly,' she replied solemnly. 'They're very nice, aren't they?'

'Ten out of ten,' I whispered, gratefully, as Jack got up and handed me the flowers.

'Did you get After Eights because age nine comes after age eight?' Miranda looked impressed at the thought.

'You know, I'd love to say yes to that, but I'm not nearly clever enough!' Jack laughed.

Just then Biddy came bustling over and began sniffing around his trouser leg. I looked at him in mock expectancy. 'Well, you may think you've made a good start, but there are actually *three* women in this house, Jack . . .' I quipped, as I made to take his jacket.

'Mmm, so I see.' He looked downwards for a moment, then, delving into his other pocket just before I whipped the jacket away, grinned sheepishly before producing a small, slipper-shaped chew toy, which he crouched down to offer to the already won-over Biddy. For an instant I was lost for words. I hung his jacket on the coat hook behind the door.

'God, that dog's shallow,' I said, as, gift in jaws, she trotted waggily back to her bed. 'I thought we could eat straight away, is that all right?' I asked as I led him towards the kitchen. 'Dinner's ready, and Miranda and I are starving, aren't we?' Miranda nodded vigorously.

'That's fine, Anna, I'm starving too, and something smells good!' Miranda slipped out of sight into the kitchen as Jack bent and kissed the back of my neck. 'Aha, thought so – it's you,' he whispered.

I had warned Jack that Miranda was excited about the prospect of meeting her father, but it would have taken a man with the patience of Job not to have been at least a little bit irritated by the number of times she kept casting the fact up, as we ate our moussaka and salad.

For instance: 'My daddy's coming all the way from London specially for my birthday!'

And: 'Mum says my daddy's really looking forward to it.'

Plus: 'Mum, what sort of present do you think my daddy will bring me?'

Or: 'It's going to be a great birthday, isn't it, mum? With daddy there?'

How about: 'What's daddy's favourite colour?'

And the tricky: 'Mum, where will daddy sleep when he comes up?'

And yet Jack, sitting at my round glass kitchen table on the chrome and leather chairs which cost a fortune from Heals, with one of my forks in his hand, and his elbow on the table as he ate my meal, his hair haloed in the over-bright glow of the halogen spotlights overhead, the trees, my trees, rustling gently through the window which was right behind him, his open-necked shirt revealing that tautly contained hollow beneath his Adam's apple, a hint of chest hair, a suggestion of five o'clock shadow – he was just so damned *decorative* – my kitchen hadn't seen anything this bloody tasty since the night a few weeks ago when Miranda and I had made ourselves ill by dunking Cadbury's Flakes into a tin of condensed milk.

Sure, I felt uncomfortable, deflecting Miranda's barrage of questions and trying to catch Jack's eye to give him apologetic looks, but at a more basic level it was absolutely lovely to have him here, in my warm home, sitting around my table, eating my food, smiling at my daughter. And if he was fed up with Miranda he certainly didn't show it.

In fact he seemed to speak to her in a remarkably grown-up way, asking questions about her school, and her friends, even picking up on the pervasive daddy/birthday theme by inviting her to tell him what sort of presents she was hoping for.

'Well, I'm kind of hoping for some new tap shoes, and maybe some lip gloss – Flora's got bubblegum flavour but mum says I'm not allowed gum so maybe strawberry, or something like that?'

Jack laughed. 'I thought children nowadays all wanted things like Playstations and computers and DVD players in their rooms? You seem to have a remarkably restrained wish-list, Miranda – well done!'

'Thanks!' she replied, pleased by the compliment. 'But I've got all these other things already anyway so why would I want two of them?'

I hid my head in my hands, but Jack only grinned. 'Well, why, indeed? Quite right!'

Lots of people, particularly childless ones, overdo it when they meet kids, popping their eyes, tickling (is there anything worse than a man who tickles?), getting down with the young 'uns, but Jack was so accepting that his Brownie point tally just climbed higher and higher as the meal went on. I was still slightly blown away by the dog toy thing, actually. For a man, particularly a man like Jack Anderson, whom I still held in the 'unstructured but promising raw material' category, to think enough, to *bother* enough, to bring a present *for the dog*! Wasn't that really tapping into some depth of understanding about my family, its smallness, its fragility – or was it just a severely lucky strike on his part? Or was it a bit weird?

Miranda was more than happy to disappear off to her bedroom immediately after dinner after I told her she could watch TV in bed for an hour and that she wouldn't have to help with the dishes.

'It's funny,' I said to Jack, as we cleared up together. 'I'd been looking forward to showing Miranda off to you, but she was a bit of a pain tonight, wasn't she? All that stuff about . . . Omar's visit.'

He smiled as he rinsed out the wine glasses. 'She's lovely, Anna, don't be too hard on her. She's got a huge occasion coming up, so it's no wonder she wants to talk about it, and . . . about *him*, as well.'

'Yes, well, I'm sorry about that.'

'Don't be!' Jack protested. 'It's fine!' Then, drying his hands, he turned and leaned against the sink, looking at me as I closed the glass-cupboard door. 'But, you know something, Anna?'

Somehow I didn't like the sound of this. 'Go on,' I mumbled, facing him.

He scratched his forehead. 'Well, timing-wise, don't you think maybe, well, maybe I should back off a bit, until all this is sorted out?'

Bugger!

He walked across the kitchen until he was standing squarely in front of me. I flicked the tea towel over his shoulder and he pulled me gently into a slightly hesitant hug.

'I mean,' he went on, speaking into my hair, 'you've got enough on your plate without me cluttering up the place at the moment, haven't you? Miranda's got a relationship to build with her father, and you're going to have to be around for her twenty-four seven – and around *him*, as well, aren't you?'

Drawing back, I looked into his lovely brown eyes. He had become unfathomable. Inscrutable. Impenetrable. Bloody sexy, as well. I rose to the challenge. 'No, Jack, don't be silly! Omar's only coming up for one night and if you think for one instant that he'll be sharing my room, well . . .' I sighed, a bit crossly. 'Of course there's going to be . . . room . . . or whatever you'd like to call it, for you! We're together – aren't we?'

'Did you tell Miranda's father that we were?'

'That's not fair – he didn't ask!' I snapped back, stung into defensiveness.

'Might have helped a bit if you had, I must say,' he said softly.

'There wasn't time . . .' I said, lamely, as I filled the coffee jug. 'Jack, there's no need to be worried, or jealous . . .'

'Isn't there?' he murmured. 'Anyway, it isn't that. Now that I've met Miranda and got to know the living, breathing child who's got a momentous event coming up in her life, I don't want any of you to be cluttered up with unnecessary complications.'

Panic was beginning to rise in my chest. 'But, Jack, I wouldn't exactly describe you as a complication,' I said, going back over to where he stood and laying my hand on his forearm. 'Well, not in a bad way, anyhow. Omar . . . well, Omar and I may not have spoken about you in London, Jack, but we did speak about *us*, as in he and I, and we both knew that there was nothing between us . . .'

'Apart from your daughter.' Now his voice definitely had an edge to it.

I furrowed my brow in annoyance. 'Well, obviously – that was a bit of a low blow, Jack.'

'Exactly! Or *was* it, Anna?' Jack's whole body became suddenly agitated. 'This is precisely the problem! I get the feeling that it's the type of situation we're going to come up with all the time if I don't clear off for a bit! I'm going to be torn up with jealousy – OK, Anna, I admit I'm jealous – who wouldn't be? And I'm going to have to be always watching my gob to make sure I don't say anything out of turn or make any comments which you're going to pick up on, or I'm going to kick myself afterwards for – I don't want to do that sort of thing! Maybe it's a failing of mine,

233

but I need things to be straightforward! I mean, I don't mean dumb, brainless straightforward, but, well, *open* straightforward! I can't bear the idea of watching my every move around you and Miranda when you've got other things to concentrate on – and maybe that's selfish of me – maybe this is why I've never been married or anything, but, well, there you have it.'

'Jack . . .'

But he didn't seem to be quite done. 'It's like when we were at the Yew Tree, after I goofed up so spectacularly by going up to Ben View Cottage, and then I couldn't face ringing you to own up! I knew I'd crossed a line and I was almost, yes, *almost*, ready to let our whole relationship go rather than face up to you! I was pretty sure that I'd ruined whatever good opinion you may have had of me – oh, I don't know. What does that make me? A coward? A perfectionist? Immature?'

'Jack,' I repeated.

'And maybe that's why I drive a sports car and live in a rented flat, as well – who knows? Who knows *what* I choose not to deal with in my life? Growing old, being tied to a mortgage, speaking out of turn when we talk about Miranda meeting her father . . .'

'Jack, you don't need to explain yourself to me!' I interrupted, finally claiming his attention by putting my hand on his hot cheek and gently pulling his face down closer to mine. There hadn't been anything intimidating about his tirade; on the contrary, seeing him open up like that, to reveal himself in such an impassioned way, instead made me feel wretched for having stirred all that stuff up in the first place. 'I'm sorry I said it was a low blow when it wasn't, but, Jack, I'm actually quite enjoying finding all this stuff out about you for myself, thanks very much, which is why I don't want you to "back off a bit" while Miranda and I get ourselves through to the other side of this!'

Oh, God, *didn't I*? Truth be known, wouldn't it actually be a great deal more straightforward if I could deal with Omar's visit, his meeting with Miranda, without the added pressure of having to explain to him about my brand-new boyfriend?

I think Jack must have seen the flicker of doubt in my eyes as I spoke my reassurances. He sighed, smiled and kissed me lightly on my mouth.

'No coffee for me, thanks, Anna. If you don't mind, I think I'd like to buzz off and have an early night.'

And my arguing was all used up. I followed him out to the hall and watched lamely as he picked up his jacket. Biddy, sensing a walk, gatecrashed the scene, sat down pleadingly in front of him and began whining.

'That's what I feel like doing,' I mumbled. 'Don't go, Jack.'

He kissed my cheek. 'I'll phone you. Good luck with everything.'

And he left. I listened until I heard his little car scrunch away, then turned back towards the kitchen to pour the coffee down the drain.

Chapter Fourteen

'Can you let me know how you propose to fund the purchase? Because I would caution you that we are not in the market to entertain time-wasters! Coffee?'

James Ferguson's approach was nothing if not to the point. We were on our third set of viewers, and so far, whenever the doorbell had rung he'd elbowed his way to the front of the house so that he'd reach the door before me, before giving the prospective purchasers an invasive-looking once-over with his small, glittery eyes.

It was clear that Mrs Ferguson had worked very hard to spruce up Ben View Cottage for the visitors. Fresh flowers warred with the wallpaper in the sitting room, and by the fireplace, the brass coalscuttle gleamed almost white with its hard-won shiny lustre. There was a strong smell of polish yet most of the furniture didn't look as though it had appreciated the attention all that much – the sideboard, so dark it was almost black, which meant that the glossy patina added by a coat of beeswax somehow made it look brooding and sinister. If anything, the extra cleaning, the extra plumping and polishing, prinking and primping, only served to show up the shabbiness of the interior in even sharper relief than usual and as I surveyed the edges of the brown linoleum kitchen flooring which were lifting up with age, I experienced an unwelcome moment of panic that perhaps I had been over-selling Ben

View Cottage – *even to myself*. Gazing into the sitting room at the faded sofa and armchairs, I had to admit that James Ferguson was quite right to suggest to his mother that she should spend the day hunting out a new couch in Inverness. You could strike matches on that scratchy, looped fabric with its threadbare arm-caps and uncomfortable, undulating seat pads!

Realisation caught me, unwillingly, that Ben View Cottage was a whole lot diminished without its hospitable little occupant. That a large part of the attraction of the place was the happy, toe-wriggling knowledge that a visit to Ben View meant scones, chat and a general looking-after by a dear old lady in her time-warped, fairy-tale den. Was this not just the Place of the Granny-On-Tap? And would my rural retreat, idyll plans be blighted by melancholy and regret if I were to buy the place and find that the previous occupant, prior to handing over the keys, had cynically removed the 'Mrs Ferguson' fixture?

James Ferguson had treated me to a pep-talk when I had arrived, at quarter to nine.

'Now then, Ms Morris, we *have* got a very busy day today, haven't we? Eighteen appointments! Should get some more than decent offers out of that lot, eh?' He rubbed his hands in cartoon glee and I forced a cheery nod.

'Yes, I hope so.'

'OK, OK, so here's the game plan. I'll show them round, treat them to a bit of a tour, explain where it'll be possible to extend, point out the features, that sort of thing. Then *you*, Anna' (he jerked both hands towards me as though I was a bin bag that needed taking out) 'can give them the information they need about offering, closing dates, that sort of thing, and perhaps, if they look half-decent, offer them a cup of tea? We'll need some sort of code as to who's half-decent and who's not – of course it should be obvious for most of them but, let's see, what do you say I clear my throat when I walk past you in the kitchen, if they're a bit of a no-no?'

We were standing in the kitchen now, and I was gazing down the drive to see whether the first viewers were on their way. They weren't. Can't say I cared much what he said as I was beginning to lose my way a bit, shrouded once again in melancholic thoughts of Mrs Ferguson leaving this place for good. I had never, ever been so affected by a sale before.

'Could you stick your Jeep round the back, please?' I asked, after a pause, appraising the huge lump of shiny new metal which was taking up half the drive. 'We need the driveway clear so that people have plenty of room to manoeuvre.'

James Ferguson, patently proud of his super-sized four-wheel-drive, had opened his mouth to protest but then he thought better of it, tapped the side of his nose in an *Aha, I see what you're doing there!* way, and ducked off. When he returned, I suppose it was only natural for a man like him to try to claw back the upper hand.

'Ms Morris,' he began, 'you do know, don't you, that my brother and I are not entirely happy about you handling the sale, given that you have expressed an interest in buying the house yourself?'

'Well,' I began, but he interrupted.

'My mother is vulnerable. *Very* vulnerable. She has a great capacity for trusting people, and she seems to be particularly fond of *you*.'

He practically spat out the final word. 'I'm fond of her, too,' I ventured.

He shook his head doubtfully. 'Yes, well, that's as maybe. But this, this, *arrangement*, you handling the sale – it's not right, is it?'

My heart had begun to pound. Not really out of anger,

but because he was, in some ways, dead right. Come on, it didn't look all that good, did it? 'Well, I have to say I do share your discomfort in some ways, Mr Ferguson, but all I can do is remind you that Blakemore's handling of the sale is entirely above board and ask you to trust me, as your mother does, to do the best possible job for her.'

'But that's just it!' he burst out, jamming his hands on his hips, and then lowering his voice to a spooky hiss. 'She trusts you *too much*! I have a feeling that my mother is going to accept your offer for the house, regardless of whether we get higher offers at the closing date, as some sort of, of *gesture* to you.' I opened my mouth to say something by way of protest, to no avail. 'Ms Morris,' he went on, silencing me before I had begun, 'I'm not necessarily blaming you for this situation, but my brother and I both feel that, once mother has had her fun playing around with the market, she'll go along with whatever price you offer. Our mother is – or rather *was* – a very intelligent woman, but she's old now, she has different values, different requirements, and I feel that one of her priorities is to hang on to your friendship, to keep in with you so that she has an ally when she moves to Inverness. Do you get what I'm saying? It's hardly fair to her family, now, is it?'

He was standing quite close to me now; I could smell his warm, agitated breath as it bounced off the lapels of my jacket. His forehead was moist and shiny, and as I tried not to let my eyes fall on the pink blotches that were forming on his neck above his Jermyn Street Collar, my brain shrieked *Think! Find a lifebelt for your drifting reputation, Morris!*

'Not really,' was the best I could do. 'I'd never allow your mother to do me any special favours!'

'Wouldn't you?'

'Never.' Oh, flipping heck, there goes my brain again, drifting back to my earlier attempt to buy the place privately. Was that or wasn't it an attempt to ask Mrs Ferguson for a favour?

'Not even if mother were to insist? To say she's doing it as a kind of thank you for finding that, that horrendously expensive place at Cedar Park?'

I was puzzled, now, as well as cross. 'Has she actually said anything to you?'

'Good grief no! Mother would never worry me – it's not in her nature! That's why I have a duty to look out for her interests, even if it means speaking very frankly, Ms Morris – Anna.'

'Well, Mr Ferguson – *James,* as we're speaking frankly, all I can do is to tell you that I am unaccustomed to having my integrity called into question and you appear to be making something of a habit of it.' *Ooh, what an excellent start! Wonder where that came from?* 'I repeat, I am going to bid fairly and squarely for Ben View Cottage when the closing date is set and if I am unsuccessful, then I shall reluctantly wish the lucky purchaser well, and move on. OK?' Thank God, my assertiveness gene had woken up in the nick of time.

He had taken a step or two backwards as I was speaking. I glanced out of the window and saw our next set of viewers pulling in at the gate. Judging by their car – a big, shiny Lexus, they had plenty of money, but by the looks of both the car and the clothing of its occupants, they'd never be interested in a renovation job like this one. The wife's creepy French manicure, displayed as she clutched the car door to heave herself out, confirmed my suspicions, the slightly sour look on her face providing a reassuring double underlining. Hmm, no cuppa for this lot. I moved away from James Ferguson to go and greet them at the door, disregarding his earlier instructions about loitering in the kitchen.

He caught my arm as I passed. I turned sharply round

to look at him and when I did, I saw that the shiny forehead had sprouted tiny beads of sweat, and he was breathing heavily.

'Anna?'

'Yes?' I replied, trying to calm myself, although we both jumped when the doorbell rang.

'Promise me something.'

I narrowed my eyes. 'And what might that be?'

'Promise me that if my mother accepts your offer and it's lower than the highest bid we receive on the closing date, you'll pay me the difference, in cash?'

'What?' I exploded, as the doorbell rang out again.

'You heard.' His eyebrows beetled horribly as he spoke – he might have been an actor, or a pimp, or, well, anyone, other than the son of Mrs Ferguson! Maybe there had been a horrible mix-up in the hospital when he was born and somewhere out in the world there exists a truly vile couple who scratch their heads and wonder every day just how their son turned out to be such a thoroughly nice bloke?

'But why on earth – your mother can accept whatever offer she likes, and anyway, I've already told you, I wouldn't . . .'

'*Just say yes!* Otherwise I'll make a formal complaint to the Association of Estate Agents or whatever they're called – I've done my homework, I've . . .'

'Yes, yes!' I cried. 'You've *dabbled*! You said!' Oh, God, that did it, I lost the plot. Shaking free of his arm, the doorbell rang for a third time, this time accompanied by loud knocking and audible tutting noises of impatient disapproval. But I didn't care. I had a reputation to defend, and anyway, the couple on the other side of the door weren't going to buy the house – I'd bet my life on it. 'Why on earth do you think you can threaten me with a complaint when I haven't done anything wrong!'

He smiled at that one. 'Well, maybe you have, and

maybe you haven't, who knows? We'd just have to wait and see what the Association decides, wouldn't we? And in the meantime . . .'

'What?' *You odious little heap of puppyshit.*

'I would be very interested to read what the papers would make of the story, wouldn't you? I'm sure Blakemore wouldn't like *that* sort of publicity, now, would it? Now, if you would move aside, we have customers, I think.'

He brushed past me and opened the door, offering oily apologies for his tardiness and leading the unimpressed-looking couple into the sitting room. I was left leaning against the kitchen sink, breathing heavily and totally, utterly furious.

As predicted, they didn't stay long. Even as they poked their heads round the kitchen door to glance round the kitchen (I didn't bother to introduce myself), they were muttering about 'needing room for an en-suite', and 'new windows' and 'gut it and start again', so after they left James Ferguson and I found ourselves alone in each other's company anticipating the next viewers, who were, according to my schedule, Iris and Pete. James Ferguson, presumably sure of his victory, had stalked into the sitting room and was standing lording it in front of the fireplace, so I took a deep breath and followed.

'*James,*' I cooed. 'I've been thinking. Can I just run your proposal past you again?' Perching myself on the edge of the sofa, I clasped my hands deferentially on my lap and looked shyly up at him. 'I mean, we are both *businesspeople*, after all?'

James Ferguson lifted his chin, lowered his eyelids and then, turning towards me, smiled very, very slowly. 'Absolutely – let's do business!'

'OK.' I cleared my throat. 'Let's say, for example, I put in an offer at the closing date of, oohh, it's a toughie – say,

£159,000 – I think it might go for something around that level, don't you?'

'Well, we would sincerely hope so – that at the very least,' he replied, licking his already wet lips.

'And supposing, *hypothetically*, of course, that your mother is indeed planning to let me have the place, regardless of there being higher offers on the table.' I stood up and started pacing the room, deep in concentration, like the girls in the old *Charlie's Angels* TV programme, in the final sofa scene where they have to run through the whole plot again for the benefit of slower viewers.

'Ye-es?'

'Well,' I twisted my face into an expression of puzzlement and attempted to look as though I was thinking really, really hard. 'What would stop you getting a friend – or should I say, an *accomplice*, from putting in some sort of ridiculously high offer which, if I agreed to your, your *blackmail*, I'd then have to match?'

'Blackmail?' he spluttered. 'I hardly think so! You're hardly one to speak about ethics, Ms Morris!'

'Oh, really? Tell me, Mr Ferguson, have you really convinced yourself that I'm up to something to such a degree that you think those papers you're planning to tip off won't be equally interested in your, your *indecent proposal*?' Eeuw, but that wasn't a very good phrase to use. Too late, now I had to deal with the greasy mental image of James Ferguson having sex.

Well, at the very best what I'd hoped to get out of that was him experiencing an *I've-met-my-equal* moment of truth, where he'd tap the side of his nose, maybe smile wryly – shake my hand, perhaps? What I actually got was far more troubling. I hadn't noticed but his face had grown considerably pinker over the past few minutes, and to my horror I saw that James Ferguson's lower lip was trembling. Not *another* crying man!

'It's just so unfair!' he burst out, before storming out of the sitting room to the spare bedroom – *his* bedroom, once, and his brother's, presumably, and slammed the door. I gawped at the space he had just left. Even Miranda at her most popped had rarely achieved such a diva-strop of an exit. Good grief, he was . . . jealous? Of my relationship with his mother! And so, I deduced, if he had decided that it was a bit late in the day to win back any more of his mother's affection, then at least he was going to try and come out the other end with a wodge of cash with which to console himself. It was almost enough to make me begin to pity him, were it not for the fact that he was a slimy toad.

I went through to the kitchen and put the kettle on, noticing with relief that Iris and Pete's car had just pulled up outside.

It only took a minute to appraise them of the situation – not that they were listening much, they were far too busy being utterly and completely blown away by Ben View and its surroundings.

'Where can you buy inglenooks?' Iris squealed as she glanced at the brown tiles of the fireplace. 'This wall – it's just *crying out* for an inglenook! Isn't it, Pete?'

Pete spent most of his time during their visit on or around the doorstep, just gazing around him and nodding blokeish approval. James Ferguson had reappeared and gone outside to sit in his Jeep, with barely an acknowledgement to Pete as he brushed past him at the door.

I sidled up to Pete. Iris was beginning to do my nut, verbally redecorating Ben View from top to bottom, and I needed a gasp of fresh air.

'So, Pete, what do you think?'

'It's very nice,' he replied.

'Nice enough to put an offer in for?' I persisted.

'Pete – I've found some original parquet!' came bellowing out from indoors.

244

'Better be, by the sound of things,' he shrugged.

'Um, Pete, you do know that Jack's been scouting around this place as well for some big Lomax client, don't you?'

He nodded. 'Heard something along those lines, yup.'

'Well, mightn't your interest cause some problems at work? This is already the House of the Multiple Complications, believe me.'

He smiled, watching the hills. 'How much could we get per week on holiday lets?'

'Make it nice inside – four fifty. Easy. Bank on a 50 per cent annual take-up and you won't be disappointed.'

'Quite the little property encyclopedia, aren't we?' Iris quipped, sidling up between us and flinging her arms around our shoulders. 'We'll take it. How much do you want?'

'You'll just behave yourselves and wait for the closing date like the rest of us. I'm having a go at it myself, I should warn you.'

'You?' Iris exclaimed. 'Is that, you know, legal?'

'Perfectly,' I replied, wearily. 'Coffee?'

After Iris and Pete left to gear themselves up for the closing date, the remainder of the viewings droned on interminably, and James Ferguson, who had eventually got out of his Jeep and returned indoors, sat and brooded in the corner of the sitting room like a big patch of damp. By the end of the day I wasn't seething quite so much and I was actually beginning to see a shadow of the little boy who had grown up here but who, as soon as he was old enough, raced away to the bright lights and better things. '*He's very high up, you know.*' His mother's words danced around my head, but the sight of the boy, almost crouched in his childhood sitting room and only a short sulk away from stamping his feet, told of an inner turmoil which no quantity of sharp

245

suiting could clothe. Perhaps the prospect of the childhood roots which he had been so keen to cast off being pulled up from under him was beginning to hit home. Whatever it was, he withdrew from taking part in the viewings and left me to it.

Here are some of the questions which were put to me during my longest day:

'Does it have a Broadband connection?'

'Do you know of anyone round here who cooks?'

'Come on, love, cash is king – how much, to close this deal right now?'

'So do we call this a cottage, then or is it more properly, a *croft house*, or a *but 'n' ben*, or even a *clachan*?'

'Do you know of anyone around here who cleans?'

'Could we put a gate up at the end of the road to preserve our privacy, do you think?'

'Do you know of anyone, a *couple*, perhaps, who could help out with the garden, do a bit of cooking for guests, spot of cleaning and laundry?'

'Are there any limits on how many stags I can shoot?'

'Why is there no shower?'

'I don't suppose there's a gas main up this way?'

'Do you know of anyone super who cooks?'

'Do you have anything larger?'

'Are there any limits on the number of static caravans I could put on site?'

'Could you find the name of someone who could do a bit of cooking?'

'Would you care for a wine gum?'

I had never been so pleased to see Rod in my life, and, without thinking, threw my arms around his neck and hugged him whilst James Ferguson tutted, and bustled off to help his mother up the path.

'Sorry,' I mumbled, as I drew away. 'Been a pig of a day.'

Rod said nothing, but he did tuck a stray wisp of my hair behind my ear, before letting me go. The gesture sent a little shock through me – somehow it felt more personal than if he'd kissed me – I was clearly going out of my mind.

'Do you know,' Mrs Ferguson said when she came level with me, 'for only £170 extra I could have insured my new couch against accidental damage?'

'You didn't, did you?' I asked in horror.

'Are you mad? Does anyone?' She shook her head. 'No doubt there are some old dears out there who'd be taken in by that sort of thing, but not this one! Now, James, be a good lad and put on the kettle, and while you're there you can get out a jar of jam for Anna's wee lassie, and then you can both tell me all about the day you've been having!'

I got back to Inverness around six and drove straight to the Howarths' house to pick Miranda up. Patricia let me in and waved away my apologies for being a little late.

'Don't worry, they're engrossed – look!'

Miranda and Flora were jiggling around the sitting room to a DVD of Busted belting out 'Glad I Crashed the Wedding'. For a few moments neither girl spotted us as we stood in the doorway admiring their self-conscious moves.

I frowned at the bouncing boys on the screen, leaned close to Patricia, who was watching them as well and whispered, 'What exactly did these children think they were going to *do* after they crashed the wedding? Let off stink bombs?'

Patricia giggled. 'Shh! You sound like a big old git.'

'I *am* a big old git.' Miranda and Flora spotted us and dropped instantly to the floor in embarrassment. 'Don't worry, girls, we used to do exactly the same when we were young and supple!' I trilled, attempting to cool their pink faces with reassurances.

'*Talkies*, we called them!' Patricia hobbled melodramatically into the centre of the room as Flora and Miranda embarked on their complex Powerpuff farewell – high fives, hands on hips, quick wiggle, index finger angled to chin, comedy hands, air-kiss, and a double thumbs-up, with a wink, to finish.

'Bye, Miranda – see you at the party!' Flora returned to the DVD as Miranda retrieved her schoolbag and heaved herself over to my side.

'Bet you can't wait to meet my daddy!' she chirped back, before surreptitiously taking my hand as we walked to the car.

Chapter Fifteen

Iris was looking languid in chocolate corduroy jeans and a duck-egg blue cashmere polo neck. Lisa, however, had the appearance of a woman who hadn't slept for a week. Devoid of make-up, her face was blotchy and her hair, usually effortlessly pretty, hung grimly to the sides of her head as though it had lost the will to live. I led her into the sitting room to join Iris, where she sat down heavily, and belched.

'What's up with you?' Iris asked her, accepting the glass of ice-cold Pinot Grigio which I poured for her into one of my favourite slender glasses. 'You look knackered.'

'Do I?' she replied in a dull voice. 'Thanks.'

'No, really, you look like crap – what's the matter?' Iris and Lisa's relationship had always been on the punchy side but Lisa winced at the insult, all the same.

'Nothing's up. I'll be just wonderful in another two days. Leave me alone.' She was sprawled across the sofa like an untidy throw.

Iris and I looked at one another, and Iris rolled her eyes.

'Detox?' we chorused.

She nodded.

'Ah.' I poured a second glass and offered it to her, but after wrestling with herself for a few moments, she shook her head.

'Not *another* detox, Lisa – which one is it this time? The South Beach Celebrity Apocalypse?'

'Sorry, Anna, but do you think I could just have some water?' She hauled herself upright.

'I think this'd do you a bit more good,' I wheedled, wafting the glass under her nose.

'Go on, Lisa mate, one won't hurt,' insisted Iris.

'No!' she protested, waving the glass away. 'This is, oh, what's it called again . . . *The tyranny of friendship!* There's a whole chapter in the book on coping strategies for this sort of thing but I skipped it because I didn't think you two would give me a hard time . . .'

'Sorry?'

'Look, guys, I have to stick with it, just for two more days. Don't try to put me off – please! If I don't thin down my colon mucus I'm going to be in deep gastro-intestinal shit in a few years' time, so I've made a really good start, and if you were real friends you'd be supportive.' She drew her knees up to her chin, and hugged them grimly.

There was a short silence. Then Iris whispered, 'I don't think there's any sort of response to that, is there, Anna?'

I shook my head.

'Don't suppose you've got any organic apple juice, please?' Lisa asked dully, as I was about to sit down.

I trudged through to the kitchen and rummaged in my cupboards, returning with one of Miranda's little cartons of the stuff and handing it to her. I suppose it would have been friendly to have decanted it into a glass but something sadistic inside me really quite enjoyed watching her rip the Cellophane off the straw with her teeth and ram it into the carton.

'Delicious,' she affirmed defiantly. 'Cheers, girls. All grist to the mill for dislodging those evil mucus plaques!'

'Marvellous,' said Iris, in a sort of trance.

'You should try it, you know,' Lisa went on. 'Just five days of apple juice, water and herbal sachets . . .'

'No thanks.'

'Really, it's not difficult . . .'

'No thanks, Lisa.'

'Or if you find it too hard you can add in some raw broths . . .'

'LISA!' I shouted. 'Are you on commission?'

'Is it a closed cult?' put in Iris. 'Have you gone over to the dark side?'

She smiled, and then went in for the kill. 'Well, you know, all I'll say is that some expelled mucus plaques have been known to be up to *three feet* long, so there! How'd you like that bunging up your bum?' Game, set and match.

'I think I preferred it when you were doing those Carol Vorderman ones,' I said with a shudder. 'The budgie food, the smoothies, the juicer . . . they all seem so tame now, somehow.'

'Oh well, all the more wine for us, I guess, Anna,' shrugged Iris, reaching over and topping up her glass.

Miranda drifted in, swaddled in her snuggly retro tartan dressing gown, scooped up a handful of crisps, and drifted out again, giving Iris and Lisa a cheeky smile. She paused when she spotted Lisa sucking on one of her juice cartons, but said nothing, for which I was grateful.

Iris was staring wistfully at the door after Miranda had gone. 'That child gets gorgeouser by the day,' she murmured. 'Is she dating?'

'At eight years old? I hope not,' I giggled. 'I'm going to ply her with ponies to put off the evil moment as long as possible. The whole idea's too horrible to contemplate.'

'Quite right, and so overrated,' affirmed Lisa, her carton imploding rudely as she drained the last few drops from the corner. 'Wish I'd stuck with ponies.'

'Might explain the apple affinity,' nodded Iris. 'Anyway, Anna, my pet, how's things with you?'

'Omar's coming up to visit,' I said, flatly, deciding

against any warm-up remarks and getting straight to the point. 'Next week, for Miranda's birthday.'

There was a hefty silence, as they gawped at me.

'But . . .' Lisa choked, 'didn't you say that . . . he'd never . . . I mean, that he didn't want . . .' She was making swirling gestures with her hand, her head waggling.

'I know. But he is, and he does.'

Iris just stared.

'Give me that wine. Now.' Lisa hauled herself to her feet and grabbed the glass which I'd left on the table in front of her. 'It's all fruit, anyway, isn't it?' She drank half of it in one gulp, and then looked for a moment as though she might pass out as the alcohol crashed its way into her freshly laundered system. 'Aah, fantastic,' she moaned. 'Now, where were we – oh, yes. Oh, no, I mean, of course, erm, so, how did this come about?'

'Out of the blue, really. He just rang me up at work . . .'

'The cheek!' Lisa spluttered, slugging more wine.

'No, no, it was fine, really,' I said quickly. 'He was nice.'

'Nice?' Lisa repeated.

'Yes – nice. Y'know I was in London last weekend?'

'Ye-es,' said Lisa, whose brain had raced into overdrive, before she gasped loudly. 'You didn't!'

'I did.'

'No!'

'Yes.'

'And?'

'Well . . .'

'Well what?' Lisa had slithered off the sofa and was sitting on her bottom on the carpet, shuffling over to the wine bottle on the coffee table.

'Um . . .' I suddenly didn't know where to start. I'd asked them round especially to 'fess up what was going on, but when it came to the crunch, I couldn't think how to begin explaining myself.

'Anna,' said Iris, gently. 'Why don't you start at the beginning? Lisa and I will *shut the fuck up* until you're done, won't we, Lise?' She fixed Lisa with a scary glower.

''kay then,' agreed Lisa, scowling back. She stood up, wobbled alarmingly, and grabbed the wine bottle roughly by the neck. 'We'll need to have another of these at the ready, though, won't we? Take it there's more in the fridge?'

I nodded as she swayed towards the door, looking flushed, and famished. 'Grab the cheese box as well, would you?' I called after her. 'Oatcakes in the tin, plates in the cupboard above the microwave.'

She made a thumbs up sign over her shoulder. 'Bloody good shout, missus, won't be a tick.'

Iris was shaking her head slowly. 'Why didn't you say something sooner? I mean, this is a bit major, isn't it?'

'Yup,' I nodded, staring at the fire.

'Anna, has he . . . threatened you or anything?'

'No, no, nothing like that, don't worry, he was . . . fine.'

'Does Miranda know?'

'Oh, yes, she knows – she's being amazingly level-headed about it all; at least on the surface.'

'Really?' Iris sounded surprised.

'I know, it's strange,' I admitted. 'I've been trying to fathom her out ever since I told her, and the only explanation I can come up with is that it's expecting rather a lot for a child to feel strong emotions about meeting someone who's a stranger – I mean, what I'm trying to say is, well, it's *huge*, isn't it? A massive moment for her, but just because you or I think she should be wetting herself with nerves and excitement and whatever else doesn't mean she needs to play along and do just that, does it?'

'Guess not,' Iris said, doubtfully.

'Why can't calm anticipation be just as valid a reaction for a kid? It's certainly better for her nervous system, isn't it?'

'Um . . .'

'I mean,' I ploughed on, 'the more I think about it, the more I believe that Miranda's *programmed* to have just me as her family – well, along with my folks and her Uncle Alasdair in New Zealand and you two honorary aunties, of course – it isn't as though she's had anything tangible *missing* from her life, is it? I mean as in something she's had, and then not had – does that make sense?'

Iris frowned. 'Only kind of.'

This made me cross. 'Oh, come on, Iris, of course it does! Miranda's fine about it all because Miranda's fine! I've made sure she's fine!'

'So you mean,' Iris began slowly, 'she's never said that she wished she had her father in her life?'

Lisa emerged from the kitchen carrying a tray, hastily loaded up with wine, biscuits, cheese, the remainder of the quiche I'd had in the fridge, a tub of nutty Boasters and a bunch of bananas, as I pondered Iris's question.

'Well . . . come to think of it, she did occasionally ask the odd question . . .'

'Like what?' Iris pressed, as Lisa banged and clattered the food and drink around, her body planting itself between Iris and my line of vision. I was grateful for the break in transmission, actually, because there was something so intense in Iris's face as she looked at me, and something very close to panic rising inside me, that I realised she had gone and mussed up an issue which I had hitherto been careful to keep spotlessly neat.

'Well . . . I suppose . . . she sometimes says she wishes she had a daddy at home, like Flora and the rest of her friends, so that she can go swimming more, or at school concerts, when the parents fill the rows and the teachers welcome all the mums and dads . . . then she makes little comments afterwards, that sort of thing.'

'And how do you deal with that?' asked Lisa, rapidly

254

bringing herself up to speed on the conversation, which, judging by their intense looks, was one which both of them had been longing to have.

'Well . . .' How did I deal with it? I turned away and gazed at the fire. Neither Iris nor Lisa moved an inch as they waited for me to reply. *Miranda was fine!* How did I deal with it? *Did* I deal with it?

'We're not judging you, Anna,' Iris put in. 'We think you're wonderful.'

'A wonderful old evil detox-assassin,' affirmed Lisa, reaching for the neck of the wine bottle.

'I've just realised how I deal with it,' I said at last. 'I *flood* her. I bring my dad in, and my mum; I send her to Flora's or haul Flora round here. I ruffle her hair and tell her to never mind. I give her puppies and mobile phones, and tell her we're the A-Team, that we look after each other, all that sort of thing. I whirl her off to the cinema, and if things get really tough, I quickly remind her that lots of children have only one parent, and some poor wee souls don't have any at all, so a nice hefty dose of guilt usually puts paid to any more serious probing on her part.' I looked at each of them in turn and grimaced. 'Nice, huh?'

'Understandable,' said Iris, after a moment. 'She's only little, after all.'

'Guess so.' But I wasn't convinced. Little, yes, but still . . .

'OK, Anna, from the top,' said Lisa. 'Omar phoned you at work, out of the blue. Then what?'

Iris was pulling the cork out of the second bottle, and stood up to refill my glass, followed by her own. 'Take your time, we've got all night.'

'OK, well, I felt a bit of a plonker at first because I picked up the phone instead of Geraldine so I spent the first wee while convincing him I wasn't the receptionist. But his voice made me shiver, all the same – he sounded so nice – just like when we were together. He was nervous, definitely, but just as polite as ever, apologising for calling un-announced, reassuring me that he hadn't turned into a gun-toting child-snatcher, and just . . . just asking if he could see me – and meet Miranda, that's all.'

'What do you think changed?' Iris asked.

'He promised he wouldn't, after all,' added Lisa.

'I know! But I get the impression that this had been creeping up on him for a while. He doesn't have any other children, and well, I guess nearly nine years is a long time to know you have a child in the world and never see her, isn't it? Anyway, he's been seconded to work in London for a while, so he rang me up, simple as that.'

'Anna?' said Iris, quietly.

'Yup?'

'What do you think he'd do if you had refused to allow him to visit?'

The question surprised me, partly because I realised that it was one I had simply never properly considered. 'Well, now that I've been down to see him, I am fairly sure he would have been disappointed, but I don't know if he'd have made a scene, or anything. However, I am equally sure that he would have tried again at some point . . .'

'So you felt pressured?' Lisa probed, narrowing her eyes.

'No! No, I didn't, actually, it wasn't like that. In fact, I felt completely . . . *safe*. Otherwise he wouldn't be coming up here, that's for sure.'

'So you went to check him out in London – good call,' said Iris. 'First impression?'

'Mind-blowing, to be honest,' I said with fervour. 'He's very good-looking . . .'

'That much is obvious, judging by Miranda,' Lisa offered.

'Yup, well, it was funny, we had this really good talk,

256

after we'd got over some of the awkwardness. I showed him photos of Miranda, and they nearly finished him off; he got quite emotional at that point.'

'What, you'd never sent him any before?' Iris asked in surprise.

I shook my head. 'Nope; he didn't want any involvement, remember, and I accepted that.'

'But he helps out financially,' Lisa said. 'You mentioned that in passing once before, as I recall.'

Ah. Yes. Well, perhaps now was the time to tell them the truth. My heart began to hammer against my ribcage, and I chewed my lip.

'Anna?' Iris prompted.

'Yes. Well, he helped out financially, at the beginning, just the once.'

'What?' Lisa spluttered. 'Only once? The cheeky bastard! And now he just expects . . .'

'He sent me a million pounds.'

In the ensuing astonished pause, I was vaguely aware of Avril Lavigne shouting angrily out of the CD player in Miranda's bedroom, a couple of lorries thrumming past in the road below, and the crackling of the fire. Iris nodded slowly, as though the story was beginning to fall into place.

Lisa's eyes were bulging. 'What a great guy!' she quipped. 'Wasn't I just saying that?'

'I've wanted to tell you a few times, in the past, but just never really found the moment.'

'You didn't need to, though,' said Iris. 'We all keep stuff to ourselves.'

'I know. And obviously it was meant for Miranda, not me, and I did manage to invest it carefully so that the money I've spent came out of income, rather than capital . . .'

'Those Clydeside apartments you told us about?' Lisa put in.

I nodded. 'You must have wondered where the finance came from?'

'Not really, I think I just assumed you got some sort of business loan as you're in the trade, or something. Wow, Anna, that is a mind-blowing amount of money!'

'Yes, but it's an embarrassment, too, in a way, kind of like a pay-off, or something, to buy my co-operation . . .'

'Bollocks to that!' Lisa spluttered. 'Obviously Omar's minted, and if there was any paying-off being done, it was to buy a clear conscience for him, no?'

'Kind of tacky, though, don't you think?' I pressed, determined to exorcise my demons by being shown up as grasping and shallow if it was the last thing I did.

'Tacky schmacky. He did the second most honourable thing, if you ask me. Did he propose, by the way? When you told him you were pregnant?'

'Course not!' I shot back. 'And I would have turned him down if he had, he knew that. I think.'

'Is he married now?' asked Iris.

I shook my head.

'Girlfriend?' she pressed.

I paused for a second, and pondered. 'Don't think so – he never mentioned anyone, and I wouldn't have dreamt of asking when we only met up for such a short time – *way* too personal.'

'You think so?' Lisa looked puzzled.

'I *thought* so,' I affirmed. 'At the time. I definitely didn't want to give him the impression that I was, well, angling for information – he had enough to cope with that day. And so did I, come to think of it.'

'Fair enough,' Iris said, as Lisa shrugged. 'Ah well, I guess I won't have a cat's chance in hell of getting Ben View, if Miss Moneybags here is going for it.' She smiled weakly at me over the top of her glass.

'Yes, you will, Iris, I'm not going to offer anything too

bonkers – it's Miranda's money I'm playing with, remember.'

'Fair enough – whatever, let's not think about that. So how are you feeling?'

'*Frazzled*,' I replied with fervour.

'Anna?' This was from Lisa. She was looking grave.

I looked back into her eyes. 'Yes?'

'Lend us a tenner, will you?'

There was a moment's pause, a heartbeat, and then, to say that I exploded with laughter wouldn't even come close to doing justice to the snorting, cackling, rib-aching paroxysms which suddenly engulfed my entire body. Iris and Lisa joined in and we howled, and we roared, and we wept, and we rolled around, and we knocked over the cheese board, and we thumped cushions, and every so often when one of us sat up and tried to say anything it just came out like an anguished, unnatural squeal until finally, several minutes of uncontrolled agony later, Lisa put the tin lid on the whole orgy of mirth by jumping up and having to run to the toilet.

I didn't dare go near the mirror as I mopped my face with tissues, knowing I'd be all shiny and red, with smudgier black eyes than Avril Lavigne herself. And I didn't care a hoot. Iris was looking none too composed either; her nose had just blown a little bubble, for one thing, and her cheeks were on fire, like mine. Lisa didn't go red, ever, she was a porcelain doll compared with Iris and me, but her embarrassing dash to the lavatory (farting all the way, if the full, mortifying truth is to be told) more than made up for any advantage in the dignity stakes which may have been afforded by her peachy complexion. Clearly her detox was working.

'To think,' Iris gasped, 'I'd been fretting over telling you about the money Pete's inherited! We always thought you'd be struggling to get by on your own, didn't we, Lise?'

'More fool us,' Lisa agreed, returning from the loo and flopping gratefully back on to the sofa. 'We often used to bitch about how you always had such great clothes, on a single income.'

'Not *bitch,* exactly,' Iris corrected. '*Discuss in a caring way* is more like it.'

'You didn't!' I giggled.

'Oh yes,' Lisa affirmed, matter-of-factly. 'Iris thought you probably managed by dressing Miranda out of charity shops and feeding her porridge and baked beans . . .'

'And you decided she was in a credit card debt spiral, didn't you?' Iris countered.

'Yes, or in hock to one of these loan sharks with shades and burly minders.'

'Pete was kind of hoping you were a high-class hooker on the side, Anna. He will be disappointed.'

'Will he? Oh, tell him I'm sure we can come to some sort of arrangement.'

I was beginning to feel giddy. Too much wine, and the delicious lifting and sharing of my secret, so that in a matter of minutes it had morphed from an awkward burden into a confession, and then a fact, then a joke and finally, history. I wished I'd told them ages ago but at the same time it was nice that it had come out this way, informally, in private.

'Are you going to introduce Omar to Jack?' Iris asked.

'Good grief, no!' I replied, instantly. 'It's not as if, well, Jack and I are barely even a couple yet . . .'

'I like the sound of that *yet* you said just there,' Lisa murmured. 'Take it it's going well, then?'

I blushed. 'Well . . . it *was*. He's laying off a bit until after Omar's visit – giving us some space.'

'Ten points for that,' said Lisa, approvingly.

'And he's . . . he's *good* for me,' I went on.

'Good for you, eh?' Iris repeated thoughtfully. 'What,

like drinking lots of water and not squeezing your spots? That's not very . . .'

'Horny?' Lisa tried.

'Frisson-ish, is what I was about to say.'

'At least horny's a real word,' Lisa grumbled. 'Anyway, what do you mean, he's *good* for you? I think I'd prefer it if you'd said he was *bad* for you, for some reason. At least that would be . . . what was your non-word again, Iris?'

'Frisson-ish.'

'Yes, that! Frisson-ish!'

I smiled as my insides churned over gleeful words like 'horny' and 'Jack' and 'couple'.

'What's he like in bed, then?'

'Lisa!' Iris burst out. 'Leave the poor girl alone – or at least, if you're going to be blunt, could you please frame your questions a bit more carefully?' She turned towards me. 'Now, madam, who's better in bed – Omar or Jack?'

'Aha, I see your point,' Lisa admitted. 'It's all in the wording. Anna?'

They looked at me expectantly. Had I been sixteen, in a soap opera, and without a glass in my hand I would have chucked cushions at them, but instead I settled for an outraged squeal and some furious head-shaking. 'I'll never tell!' I wailed. 'Never! Or not until I've had a chance to make a proper judgement, anyway.'

This was just perfect for them, and it wasn't until I'd said it that I realised the ambiguity of what I'd just said.

'So, you *haven't* slept with him, then?' quizzed Iris.

'Or have you booked both of them together for a night when Omar gets here?' put in Lisa. 'A sort of bonk-off?'

'Noooo! I just mean I haven't had an opportunity to check Jack out . . . properly, yet.'

'Sorry, Anna, but can we just go back a stage? Have you shagged him or not?'

'Yes.'

'And?'

'And what?'

'Was he any *good*, you awkward turnip! You know exactly what!' Lisa slapped her hand to her forehead in frustration.

'For someone who claims to have fallen asleep during sex you're peculiarly interested in my love-life, madam,' I replied, primly, playing for time.

'Of course I am!' she retorted. 'That's because it's interesting! And mine isn't!'

'Well, I don't know if I'd call it interesting, but at least it's kicked off again, so that's a start.' I felt disloyal to Jack as soon as I'd opened my mouth.

'What, not so great then, with Jack?' Iris ventured. 'Shame that, I mean, him being so good-looking, you'd think, well, you two, early days, been a while . . .'

'Iris, leave it!' I shouted. 'That's enough!'

'Sorry,' she said quickly, biting her lip and glancing at Lisa, who was also a bit shamefaced.

We sat in silence for a bit, lost in thought as I pondered the situation. With Omar coming up to visit – would he leap on me? Or I on him? For old time's sake? It was a curious, out-of-control thought. I mean, it had been wonderful in London, *really* wonderful. But so long ago . . . and yet, we had a child! Something about that thought almost made me think that it'd be acceptable – friendly – setting a seal on the rightness of our creation of Miranda . . . oh, for heaven's sake. Intellectualising naked lust (for that's what it would be) is impossible. *Has* to be impossible, otherwise it'd stop being naked lust and become something much more boring.

'I don't know,' I said, eventually. 'In some ways I wish Jack hadn't come along now – or I wish Omar hadn't popped up now – my head's turned to mince with it all.'

262

'Nice dilemma,' Lisa murmured.

'No, it isn't! It's like, I've only got one chance to do the right thing, and I haven't a clue what the right thing is at the moment!'

'You'll just have to play it by ear,' said Iris. 'See what happens.'

I nodded, doubtfully. 'I know, but I'm useless at that. I like to know what my options are at all times, and this situation just seems so . . . random.'

'Well, try to remember your basics,' Iris went on. 'You say Omar's a great guy . . .'

'Yup.'

'And he's Miranda's dad.'

'Yup.' Like I could forget that one.

'But he's been off the scene for nine years, and has reappeared at his own convenience.'

'Yup, I suppose.'

'Better late than never, though,' Lisa commented, helping herself to her fourth cracker and slicing a large wodge of Brie to go on top of it.

'True,' I said, doubtfully.

'And you're getting on well with Jack – he's . . . *good* for you?' Iris didn't sound sure.

'Well, yes, actually. I think I understand where he's coming from – he's a lot like me, business-wise . . .'

'Bollocks to that!' Lisa spluttered, sending crumbs all over the carpet. 'Do you fancy him?'

'Yes. Definitely. I think. No, *absolutely*. Rod's not so sure . . .'

'Rod?' said Lisa, looking confused.

'From the office. He's . . . well, he's a good mate.' Goodness knows why Rod's opinion had just come crashing into play right at this moment.

'OK, so that's clear,' said Iris, smiling. 'Listen, Anna, you're going to have to play this really carefully, you know.'

'Oh, I know. It's about what's right for Miranda, more than me, after all.'

Iris frowned. 'Yes, perhaps, but don't you think what's right for you will be best for her, though? I mean, for one thing, you're not going to have to decide anything when Omar's here, unless the right course of action becomes bleedingly obvious, one way or another.'

'And if you find yourself under pressure, run a mile,' added Lisa.

'Thanks, you two,' I said, staring back towards the fire and wondering, not for the first time, whether Blakemore needed a feisty single mum to open up a happening new branch at the North Pole, or on the moon.

Chapter Sixteen

Following my hell-day at Ben View there was a further smattering of eager viewers and eventually, with ten formally registered notes of definite interest (mine, Lomax Group, Iris and Pete, the static caravan guy, a couple from Sussex, a couple from Kent, a couple from Gloucestershire and three locals), it was time to set the closing date.

I sat at my desk on a very rainy Thursday morning, checking the diary. Next Friday, the 19th, would probably be best, the day after Miranda's birthday. Fridays were traditional days for closing dates and with holiday homes in particular you have to move fairly fast before people begin to go cold on the venture. Hmm, two problems there – that clashed with the Young's Insurance Services party, at which we were all expected to show face, and it was the day Omar returned to London. Still, presumably Omar would be leaving first thing in the morning – Miranda was at school, after all, and if I made the closing date twelve noon on that day, then it would give us the whole afternoon to go through the offers with Mrs Ferguson, and presumably also her appalling son, contact the successful bidder (a task that wouldn't take long if, as I still hoped, that successful bidder turned out to be me), then get to Young's later on in the afternoon to get stuck into some free alcohol.

Of course, given that technically I shouldn't be too

closely involved with Ben View I now had to make the Lizard think that that date was all her idea.

Monica had visited Mains of Blusterystones the night before and had been notably quiet about the experience ever since she came in this morning. I had been furtively watching her as she scanned, with a frown, the photographs which the FastFoto, the express picture company, had just biked round to the office, and now I was just waiting, like a little crocodile (just by looking at her I had become imbued with the terminology of the rainforest), for the right moment to open my jaws and just, just *snap!* at her.

'Monica? Excuse me?' I wheedled, getting going on a bit of verbal foreplay.

She rolled cool eyes through 360 degrees before focusing them beadily in my direction, although she did not reply. If I was a tasty jungle-flying insect I'd have been a goner.

'How'd it go at East Blusterystones?' I had to choke back a Ross-from-*Friends* splutter of laughter as I asked the question. 'Did you have fun with Lady Francesca?'

Monica narrowed her eyes (a reminder that they did, after all, have lids) and looked at me suspiciously.

'Was Lady Francesca nice in the flesh?' Seeing that Monica was picking up on my tone of voice I softened it a bit by adding, 'I've been on the web, checked out some of her stuff – wow, Monica, she's a real player!' Whether she was or not would remain a mystery because I had done no such thing but isn't that one of the main points of the Internet? To facilitate the fabrication of fibs?

Monica nodded, uncertainly. 'Yes, she is undoubtedly successful, Anna.'

I looked more closely. 'But? Don't tell me there's a but! Come on, Monica, show me the pictures.' As she stood up to bring the photographs over, I added probably the most unwise and risky comment that had ever flown out of my mouth. 'Do you know something, Monica? Whenever I type your name in my computer it always warns me about my spelling and suggests "*maniac*" as an alternative! There's no justice, is there? Do you think perhaps it's a Bill Gates conspiracy virus, set up to shield Clinton?'

Geraldine, ever the eavesdropper, gasped.

Monica, however, chose not to punt back my little attempt at repartee. Or banter. Or rudeness.

'Anna – did you know anything about this property before I said I'd take it on?' she asked, a little frighteningly.

I glanced through the pictures, as she returned to her chair. It was worse than I feared. East Blusterystones looked to have been thrown up (in both senses) around the 1950s. It was a square, white-harled, single-storey old meanie of a cottage with metal window frames and a roof that wasn't pitched quite steeply enough to allow anything other than the most leisurely of rainwater run-off. A few sheds lay at jaunty angles round the back, and hanging down the walls of the house, green slime from years of leaking gutters tipped like stalactites from the eaves.

'No, nothing, Monica, honest. Not great, is it?' The internal photographs were a scream – it was as though the house had been deliberately distressed for a dress rehearsal of the poorhouse scene in *Oliver Twist*. 'Interesting stencilling in the top corners, though.'

'Stencilling?' Monica queried, peering more closely at the glum sitting room. 'Up there? Ah, no, that would be damp.'

I looked more closely. 'Oh, so it is.'

'I think, quite honestly, that we should give this one a miss,' Monica said, slowly. 'It's . . .'

'A disgraceful heap of utter crap?'

'Quite.'

'Bad luck, Monica.'

'Never mind. I shall hand-write a letter to Lady Francesca to let her know, as she is so sure it will sell itself, that she should just let it get on with it. Do you think that would be disrespectful?'

'Definitely. Go for it. Er, Monica, I don't suppose I could help you take your mind off it by asking you to give some thought to the Ben View closing date? I mean, it'll need to be fairly soon, but, obviously, the date is entirely up to you. Fridays are best, and this Friday's a bit soon, oh, let me see, and the Friday after next might be a bit far in the future . . .'

Monica glanced at her diary as my ramblings sank in before saying mildly, 'So, Anna, are you trying to say that I should decide, all on my own, to set the date for Friday the 19th?'

We smiled at each other. The first, real, warm smile we had ever shared.

'Yes, please.'

'Well, the 19th it is, then. I'll get the letters typed and in the post tonight.'

'Thank you. And I'm sorry about your wasted trip to Blusterystones.'

She grimaced. 'Well, you just never really know what people are truly like, do you?'

I nodded. 'How right you are.'

'*Nice one, boss,*' flashed up on my screen as Rod grabbed his coat to make a dash for the bakery in Union Street.

'Buns, anyone?' he called out.

'Not for me, thanks,' Katy whispered.

Geraldine, sounding lively on the phone, talking to Jeremy fforsythe about the huge amount of interest we'd had in Insch of Stour, did a vaguely pornographic mime which told Rod that she wanted a ring doughnut, *dripping* in soft icing.

'Anna? Bun?'

I pondered for a second, and then remembered Omar's imminent arrival, the whip-like Goldie Hawns at the Stafford Hotel, and the importance of sultry, slender superiority when he next laid eyes on me. 'No, thanks, Rod. I've had a huge breakfast.'

Rod had his hand on the door handle when Monica suddenly spoke up. 'Oh, Rod?'

He turned towards her. 'Yes, Monica?'

'Do you think you could get me a nice bit of Bakewell slice?'

'A . . . a what?' Rod echoed, looking puzzled, as did we all.

'Monica! You're joining in the bun run!' I burst out. 'That's wonderful – a breakthrough, in fact!'

'What's wrong with that?' Monica retorted, though looking a tiny bit pleased at the attention nonetheless. 'I'm feeling a little . . . *dangerous*, today – dash it, Rod, make it *two* nice bits of Bakewell slice . . . no, no, cancel that . . . make it one bit of Bakewell slice and a pineapple tart, there's a good lad. I'll settle up with you when you get back.'

'Rightio!'

Rod bounded off with such enthusiasm that I was reminded of the time, not long after I started at Blakemore Inverness and before I'd got to know him so well, when I'd oh-so-wittily asked him whether his name was short for Rodralab as there had to be a bit of Labrador mixed up in him somewhere and it was his instant reply which had earned him my lifelong respect: '*Spot on! But it's usually only other dogs that pick up on it*' – I knew then that I'd found someone on my wavelength. How dull the office would be without him!

Instinctively, my hand felt for the little wisp of hair, the one which he had tucked behind my ear at Ben View.

*What would happen if, when he came back from his bun run,
I was to pull him into the photocopier room, ram him up against
the wall, press myself hard against him, undo his trousers, slide
my fingernails down his bare torso and lick every goddarn inch
of him until he cried out for mercy? Would he snarl that I'd
taken my time getting round to this and he was going to make
me pay for making him wait? Well? Or . . .*

'Do you know why I asked for a nice bit of Bakewell slice,
Anna?' Monica asked, driving our brand-new friendship into
a veritable designer outlet village of uncharted territory.

I had to attempt a mental emergency stop on the Rod
thing. 'No! Do tell!'

'They're Dusty's absolute favourites, the scamp!' She
had gone all gooey and cake-like, herself, what with the
pink jacket, and cherry cheeks, and all.

I knew it was going to be wrong; I knew it before I
opened my mouth, but I was feeling a little hot under the
collar so out it hopped anyway, the mental *whoah, bimbo!*
protection mechanism trailing a mere nanosecond behind.
'Oh, do you have a dog, then, Monica?'

She closed her eyes and shook her head. 'Dusty is my
. . . my *gentleman friend*, Anna – Ernest Urquhart Miller –
but he has been called Dusty since his army days.'

'*Gosh*, Monica' (something about her saying '*gentleman
friend*' made me want to respond in kind, with a *gosh*, or
a *golly*, or a *cripes*), 'to think, after all this time, I never
even knew his name! What a chump I am!'

Somehow the throwback mood seemed to hit all her
right buttons and she brightened visibly. 'Not to worry –
how was a gel to know?'

'*Pax!*' I squealed back, without knowing what it meant.

The phone rang and Geraldine, who may or may not
be even cleverer than she lets on, mimed an old-fashioned
switchboard operator plugging in a dozen or so wires
before cocking her head to one side and taking the call.

'So the pineapple tart must be *your* favourite, then, Monica?' I ploughed on.

'Well . . . it is and it isn't, really. It's what I always get when . . . oh, never mind. Must get on with those closing-date letters!'

'When what? Do tell!' I prodded. Well, we were mates now, weren't we?

She sighed. 'They're the ones I buy when Dusty's dentures rub his gums raw and he has to leave them out for a while – he can eat the centres out of pineapple tarts with a spoon. Now, where's that Ben View list – ah, here it is – back to work!'

And the barrier shot back up like a Bond film gold-mine door. I had probed too far and she had revealed too much, so we got back to work. Unsure what to think of Monica in her new guise as a human being, I turned towards my monthly sales analysis sheet but couldn't begin to make any progress because to my profound gloom I saw that George and Carol Leversedge had entered the office and were standing squarely in front of my desk, blocking the light from outside.

'Good morning,' I said, forcing a smile. 'How may we help?'

'We'd like to speak with Mr Dunsley, if we may.' George Leversedge's voice was calm, but there was an edge to it. I craned my neck around the outside edge of Carol Leversedge and spotted Rod about to burst through the door, arms full of paper bags with twisted ears at the tops and the beginnings of cream seepage down the sides, before he clocked his clients, executed some nifty footwork of which Michael Jackson would have approved, and shot off up the street.

'He's with clients at present,' I replied, smoothly. 'I'll make sure he calls you on his return. Good . . .'

'Never mind, you'll do,' charmed Carol. 'We would like

271

to request some garden furnishings. Sunnyholm has failed to be served with such.'

'Pardon?'

'Our rental property is not fully seasonally functional as it lacks garden furnishings for the summer, a factor which we consider a seasonal necessity.'

Carol Leversedge reached into her faded denim shoulder bag and pulled out a Scott's of Stow furniture catalogue. 'We have circled a number of possibilities,' she honked, opening the catalogue and laying it in front of me to display the wealth of outdoor entertaining solutions which lay within.

'Now before you say anything,' put in George Leversedge before I said anything, 'because I know you will raise this as an issue, no, there is no provision within the terms of the inventory for garden leisure furnishings but we are of the opinion that this is an unacceptable oversight on the part of your company. Garden furnishings are an essential part of life and when you are purporting to offer for rent a property which you purport to be of high quality then it becomes essential that the fundamentals for outdoor as well as indoor seating and tabling are provided for.'

As they stood, side by side, quivering with correctness, I caught a glimpse of Rod doing another furtive fly-past outside.

'Mr Leversedge, are you implying that this is some sort of *human rights* issue?'

'That would be the case, yes, ma'am, I am.'

'Yes, he is,' echoed his wife, stoutly.

They were prepared to go to the death on this one, I could feel it from the force of their breathing, and from the determined way she clutched his shirt sleeve with both hands while he spoke, urging him on, as though she were a rider, and he a horse. I was going to need every ounce of training, every morsel of tact, every scrap of patience, to get through this one without bloodshed. I would have to draw on all my years of expertise, my in-depth rental knowledge, my experience of playing Solomon when conducting reasonableness tests on issues varying from how many pet gerbils to allow in a one-bedroom flat, to how many collapsing chimney pots constituted an unsound structure . . . and if Rod Dunsley scurries past that window one more time I'm going to haul him inside by his ear and slam his cream bun in his face. Then I'd have to lick the cream off and just what would the Leversedges think of that, then?

'Well?'

'Well, what?' I replied, petulantly.

'I've decided the "Calypso" range would be most appropriate for our needs . . .'

'Sorry,' I began, 'but you do realise that there's no way on this earth you're going to bully any more stuff out of us, so why are you trying?'

They liked that one. It mined deep, deep into the septic scab of their hard-done-byness. And as they flinched, I felt their pleasure.

'Ah, we knew you'd be hostile,' breathed George Leversedge.

'This is what we're constantly up against,' added his wife.

'Remember the tale of the man sitting on the mountaintop overlooking the village?' This was from Monica, who had risen from her chair and walked over to shake hands with the Leversedges. We all looked at her in surprise.

'Excuse me?' they chorused.

'Oh good, you haven't. Well, long ago, a man was perched on a hillside, looking down on his home town, when a traveller came up to him and asked him what the town they were looking at would be like to settle in. The man asked the traveller what the town he had left behind was like. "Oh, it's a terrible place," the traveller replied. "Full of thieves and unkindness, greed and anger." So the man said to the traveller, "Well, that's just what you will find in this town." Now . . .' Monica was pacing round the office, conducting her own words with her hands – Geraldine and Katy had stopped work and were lugging in as well and the Leversedges and I, stunned by the interruption, were docile as baby koalas. Rod surged past the window again. '. . . would you like me to tell you the second half of the story or have you worked it out already for yourselves?' We gawped at her thickly. 'You know, new traveller, same man, same question, *nice* town this time, nice people, well, that's exactly what you'll find here – the end? Now, if you'll excuse me, I'm off out to rein Rod in before my nice bit of Bakewell slice disintegrates.'

As she sailed out of the office and Geraldine and Katy exchanged baffled, *wait till we get a chance to talk about this one* glances, I was left with a somewhat shell-shocked pair of Leversedges and a brain of scrambled egg.

It was Carol Leversedge who spoke first.

'So, anyway, are we gettin' the furniture?'

'No.'

'Oh, I think we are,'

'Well, you're not.'

'We'll buy it ourselves and deduct the cost from our rent.'

'I'll have you thrown out if you do.'

'No, you won't.'

'Yes, I will.'

'You can't do that.'

'I can and I will.'

'You're a bully.'

'You're the bullies!'

'Bully.'

'Bullies!'

'Honey, call the cops.'

'Race you!'

Oh, they left, eventually. It was an interesting exercise, that one, because although my training went totally out the window, or at least it must have done to have allowed the scene to develop into a full-blown slanging match, the fact was that I hadn't been in the least bit intimidated by them. So much had happened, recently. I'd been accused of dirty dealings by James Ferguson, picked up and semi-dumped by a sexy man with one or two disappointing lifestyle choices, contacted by the father of my child who wanted into our lives, and allowed into the private world of the Monitor Lizard. All it would take now would be for Rod to make a pass at me . . .

'Anna?'

'Yup, Rod?'

'You busy this lunchtime?'

Surely to God . . .

'Depends,' I ventured. 'Why?'

'Just wanted to get going on the new window display – that dining-room table's getting on my wick now.'

'Oh, OK, fine.' *What had I been expecting?*

'Shall we discuss the new display over a spot of lunch?'

He seemed a little shifty. It was time to take control.

'OK, fine – what did you have in mind?'

'Well, I thought maybe a garage theme, but with house pictures instead of topless women on the wall – well, maybe just a couple of topless women as well, but . . .'

I'd meant for lunch, actually, but no matter. 'No, Rod.'

'OK, bikinis, then? No nips?'

'Tell you what,' I said, as my twelve o'clock clients arrived at Geraldine's reception desk, 'why don't you nip

275

out to Marks & Spencer and get us some sandwiches, and we can have a chat about it then?'

'Fine.'

They had a familiar look about them, my twelve o'clocks. What was the name again? I glanced at my diary. Henry and Daphne Maclaren, Waterbank, Beauly. Geraldine showed them into the meeting lounge and I followed and introduced myself. They were a pleasant-looking couple in their fifties, he was very tall, with a shiny bald head and grey sideburns, and she was about my height, dressed in an olive-green pleated skirt and beige rain jacket, with a large single pearl in each earlobe, a tight perm and gold glasses.

'Did you enjoy the champagne?' was the first thing Daphne Maclaren asked, as I invited them to sit and poured us each a cup of coffee.

'Oh! Of course! *Potters!*' I exclaimed. 'Yes – thank you so much for that, it was terribly nice of you!'

'We think the world of Jack,' her husband added. 'How is he these days?'

The mention of his name sent a shiver of something between pleasure and panic through me. 'Oh, he's . . . he's fine! Just great!' Well, as far as I knew, anyhow. He was doing just grand when I let him slip away. That had been a week ago, and he hadn't called, not that I'd really expected him to. I'd agonised about ringing him, or sending an email, at least, but saying what? That I hoped he'd stick around until I was ready for him?

'Did a marvellous job for us at Waterbank, as I'm sure he told you,' Mr Maclaren continued. 'We owe him such a lot – the house was in some danger, but his work on the bank behind the house has been first class – it's remedied the problem completely, in fact – no more worries!' He retrieved a small sheaf of papers from his jacket pocket.

'Here's a copy of Jack's report – would you care to have a look at it before we go on?'

'We'd really like you to – please?' Mrs Maclaren added.

So I read quickly through the report. Fifteen pages of Lomax-headed paper, with Jack's name and engineering qualifications printed at the bottom. It was certainly impressive, fluently written, explaining the full extent of the landslip problem and the measures taken to secure the bank and prevent a recurrence, all backed up with diagrams and statistics which meant absolutely nothing to me, and glowing reports from various surveyors and council officials who had inspected the completed job.

'Shame we've got to sell up, in many ways. We love the house, but it's too big for us now, so we're moving down to be closer to our daughter in Perth. Do you think you would be able to handle the sale?' He looked at me eagerly.

'You come highly recommended!' his wife added, with a naughty smile. Then she fished in her bag, and took out a photograph. 'This is the house.'

It was bloody huge. More of a country pile than a house, really, three storeys of shining granite, a round turret on one corner and a stone archway above an enormous, vaulted front door. I saw immediately that it was in good nick – there was no moss on the roof, the slates looked in perfect condition, and the large sash windows were painted pristinely white. It was delicious.

'There's a stable block as well, round the back,' said Mr Maclaren, 'and a gate lodge at the end of the drive – have you brought a picture of the lodge, Daphne?'

She had. I could practically see the candy canes and liquorice allsorts that went into its construction, so edible was the design, and another photograph of the grounds, with their lily loch, wild-flower meadow, all-weather tennis court and new, covered swimming pool, told me that this one was something of a peach.

'It's beautiful,' I said, with feeling. 'You must be terribly upset to be moving.'

Mrs Maclaren nodded. 'Thank you,' she said, quietly. 'We are.' Then she turned to her husband. 'I told you she was the one for us!'

'No you didn't,' her husband chided, 'Jack Anderson did that!'

It was the excuse I needed. After they had gone, I picked up the phone and dialled Jack's mobile.

'Thank you, Jack,' I said, when he answered. 'For Waterbank.'

'Shucks, it was nothing – you'd have got it anyway,' he replied. 'How are you?'

'Fine, and you?'

'Not too bad.'

'Are you really?'

'Course I am.'

Rod came back in with the sandwiches. There was silence at the end of the line.

'How's Miranda?' Jack asked, eventually.

'She's . . . fine.' *Sticking to the ceiling with excitement and anxiety about meeting her father* . . . couldn't say that, either.

'She must be getting excited about her birthday?'

'Yes, she is. Anyway, just wanted to say thank you, again. Looks like you did a great job on the place, by the way, your report's mightily impressive.'

'Just doin' my job, ma'am. Take care, OK?'

'OK, bye, and thanks.'

'Right!' said Rod, brightly, and through a mouthful of chicken and bacon sandwich. 'What do you think of my garage idea? I've got some mates who run an MOT centre – they could give me all sorts of signs, and tools, and stuff, and Anna?'

'What?' I said, playing for time, not wanting to puncture his boyish enthusiasm too abruptly.

'I've measured the window – there's enough room to get a Mini Cooper in there! Course we'd need to take the glass out of the window to install it, but, wow, Anna, it'd hit the headlines!'

I poked at the slippery, slimy, evil pasta salad which Rod had got for me 'as a wee change', deciding that 'pasta' and 'salad' were two entirely different things. What was it about my men and bad food?

'Rod, we are *not* taking the window out to put a car in. Sorry. It'd be expensive and silly and . . .'

'*Silly,*' Rod repeated, turning instantly beetroot.

'OK, not silly, sorry, in some ways it's a brilliant idea, but more as an art installation than as a means of attracting customers . . .'

'You were fine about the bathroom display a few months back!'

'Yes, well, I take your point, but . . . but everyone could relate to that – even the very wealthy have to go to the toilet . . . oh, Rod, I don't know. Sorry. I don't know about anything these days – I'm turning into a great big waste of space.'

'Forget it,' he said, 'And no you're not – you're a top use of space, in my humble opinion.' Now he was beetrooter than ever. 'You're right, forget the garage idea. I just thought that as we have now done almost every possible different kind of room to be found in a house, that the garage was the next logical step, that's all.'

Something pinged inside my addled brain. 'You're right – we have done just about every room in a house, haven't we?'

'Think so,' agreed Rod, 'apart from gyms, or torture chambers, or those daft rooms people have with a rowing machine, sofa bed, electronic keyboard and computer workstation crammed all together in them . . .'

'But we haven't done *outside*, yet, have we?' Oh, but it was nice to be vile and nasty. 'Rod, when you're done with that sandwich, go and log on to the Scott's of Stow website and order some outdoor furniture by express delivery – the "Calypso" range, I think you'll find, is one of the most expensive – get some loungers, and a barbecue – what about one of those ridiculous patio heater things? We can stick the property details in the ground like seed packets on lollipop sticks . . . even lay some Astroturf! It'll be fab!'

And when we're done with that display, I'll be able to buy it at a knockdown rate and install it at Ben View.

Chapter Seventeen

It wasn't until I got him back to my apartment from the airport, on Miranda's birthday, that I realised just how out of place Omar seemed in Inverness.

The London flights which scream into Inverness Airport several times a day are always full of exotic curios. Tall, confident Goldie Hawns and their corduroy spouses, gaggles of young people with attitude who pluck skis and rucksacks and fishing rods from the single carousel before double kissing their drivers and disappearing who-knows-where to country houses for riotous times 'in Scotland', whence they are never seen or heard of again until it's time for them to wing their way back to civilisation and their real lives in London and the shires.

Not to mention the gruff oil workers in bomber jackets, who glug pints of beer at seven in the morning and fill the departure lounge with smoke, or the men and women in suits who travel up and down for presentations and meetings and conferences, briefcased and focused, or the foreign holidaymakers – what will *they* make of us all? Will the fact that it'll probably rain for the entire two weeks put a dampener on their summer break, or will we get away with it because of our bonnie hills and alleged, though unproven, douce charm? Our dear gentle, backward ways? Because believe me, if they think their whole stay's going to be a hoots mon scone-fest in the Ferguson tradition they're sadly Mcstaken – lucky if they find an unlocked public toilet half the time . . .

A familiar jealousy had washed over me as I watched the flight disgorge all this exotica. I was simmering a mixture of 'I could have done that too, you know!' alongside a pang of longing for the bright lights of the city. *Honestly*. I had plenty of money – I could move to London in a trice, ensconce Miranda in a private school where she'd have to wear a straw boater and play lacrosse . . . I could buy a flat, find a part-time job in a super-luxe estate agency which had a heady social life built into the office routine, and concentrate really hard on personal grooming, personal shopping and sundry other personal issues which don't figure so much up here, like parking, cosmetic surgery and designer chic. But would it make us happy? Would Miranda be safe? She'd hate to leave her school – she'd be gutted about not having her little Powerpuff chums around her. Would proximity to Omar make up for the lack of Jack? Or Rod? Good grief, it was all just a bit of a risk, wasn't it? Not to mention the fact that Omar wasn't necessarily going to be in London permanently, and then where would we be? Probably hot-footing it back up north, where the Lizard would have taken over my job and I'd have to apply to be her assistant and she'd cackle with the delight of turning me down.

Miranda sat silently by my side, pale, pensive and intent on scanning the faces as they descended the steps of the plane. I had taken the day off work and borrowed her out of school for the day. It was her ninth birthday, and I didn't care what the school thought. She was going to meet her father for the first time, a shocking, neglectful, throbbing thought. She only possessed one photograph of Omar, the one which he had sent up via email, at my request, the week before and which she had gazed at constantly, as though willing it to like her. After much consideration she had proclaimed that he looked '*nice*', an opinion she spoke quietly, for fear of contradiction. Her anxiety broke my heart, and although I told her a thousand times that she wasn't to worry about anything, the fact is she did little else but worry, and quite right too, all things considered. Dark circles under her eyes told of a sleepless night. She'd unwrapped her mobile phone and some other cards and presents as she sat in pyjamas at the kitchen table, saying something nice about each one, even the furry wombat sent from New Zealand by my brother, although her mind was elsewhere. As she left her new phone to charge up, she didn't seem bothered that it'd be at least twelve hours before she'd be able to try it out.

We watched as the plane landed heavily in a shimmer of fuel, and for a few seconds I thought of Jack and decided for the umpteenth time that he was quite right, the sheer arbitrariness of flight was quite baffling – I mean, if that lump of metal had come down any harder, what's to have stopped the back wheels buckling outwards and the plane completing its flight on its belly, in flames? *Then* where would we be?

It was essential that Miranda should come with me to the airport because I wanted it to be transparently clear to her that she was to be included 100 per cent in every aspect of Omar's short visit, but the busy arrivals hall and the commotion of the greetings and flounderings for trolleys which were going on all around made me think that perhaps this decision had been a mistake – although leaving her at home would have meant a childminder – or worse – my parents – being present when she met him . . .

'Is that him?' she said, in a small, high-pitched voice, as at last, Omar emerged from the plane and began descending the steps. I should have known he'd be last – he'd be hanging courteously back to let the elderly, the female, and the just plain pushy off first . . . how typical of the man I remembered, and a definite good sign . . .

'Yes, my darling, that's him.'

Nobody made any move to stop her as she jumped up from her seat and ran past the security desk and outside on to the Tarmac towards him – I guess nine-year-old terrorists are unlikely prospects in Inverness and anyway, her face must have shown that she wasn't going to be stopping for anyone. I stood up and followed, only as far as the floor-length window, where I watched as she approached her father for the first time.

Omar, at the bottom of the steps, stopped still in his tracks. His arms fell to his sides and the raincoat, which was slung over his arm, fell to the ground. He was staring in astonishment at his child. At last she reached him and stopped too, right in front of him, and looked up into his face. I thought my heart was going to explode out of my chest and splatter against the glass as I watched them stare at each other. The likeness was unmistakable – *inexcusable*.

I think Miranda spoke first. Omar's mouth fell open although he appeared to remain silent, but then he crouched down so that he was looking directly into her face. Miranda, without so much as a glance back in my direction, held out her right hand, and after only a brief second, Omar took it in his left, and kissed it. Then he spoke to her, just a few words. I desperately hoped they were 'Happy birthday' because she smiled, and nodded, and spoke back. Omar was looking down at her hand, held in his own. Two airport ground staff had to squeeze past them to climb the steps and check the plane, ready for the turnaround, and I crazily thought for a second that perhaps Omar might just turn and follow them back aboard, taking Miranda with him – hijack the plane, fly it away, but not only was this improbable, but Miranda was pointing back towards me in the terminal building from where I chanced

a little wave. They both waved back, Omar a little uncertainly, Miranda as furiously as a child on a rollercoaster
– which I suppose she was.

I expected Omar to get up and for the two of them to
come towards me, but they stayed where they were –
Miranda was by this time talking nineteen to the dozen
and on one or two occasions Omar laughed at whatever
it was she was telling him. A security guard was keeping
an eye on them and kept darting little glances towards me,
but so far he was leaving us all to it. Thank heavens. A
huge, bearded man in a thick, holed jumper jostled me as
he made for a stray luggage trolley which was parked at
the window just beside me.

'Sorry,' I mumbled. He ignored me and wheeled his
prize towards the carousel. Then there was a whoop as
an over-excited woman threw herself upon a pair of
lanky teenage boys wearing baggy skateboarding (or
snowboarding? Skiing? Heavy metal? How was I
supposed to know?) gear, before linking her arms
through one of each of theirs and waltzing them out of
the terminal building.

Miranda was talking about Biddy. I saw her hold the
palm of her left hand (Omar was still holding her right)
about eight inches off the ground, before waving her head
from side to side, demonstrating the dog's enthusiasm, or
something.

An announcement crackled out for passengers
Donoghue, Baillie and Fraser to report to the security desk
immediately. A short man standing close by tutted and
broke away from the group he was with, to cries of 'It's
rubber glove time!' and 'Keep your bum to the wall, Eddie
now!' ringing in all of our ears. It was a welcome distraction. When would Omar and Miranda report to me, then?

I stayed where I was, wondering about the strangeness
of being an interloper on their reunion. It was almost as

though I felt I didn't have any *right* to go and join them, that this was a family matter and it was being handled perfectly adequately by Omar . . . no, that thought would have to go. I marched towards the security desk, just at the same time as Omar stood upright, picked up his coat and, still holding Miranda's hand, began to walk towards me.

Miranda beamed as she reached me, looking from Omar and back to me with the utmost pride. 'Mum, erm, d . . . daddy's got a suitcase to pick up – he says it's got a present for me in it but I told him not to worry about getting me a present because how would he have known what to get?'

'That's fine then, Miranda, we'll wait here for the suitcase. Hello, Omar.' How the heck the tremble stayed out of my voice I shall never know. A klaxon sounded and the first of the luggage began to rumble through the screen and on to the carousel.

'Anna – thank you for meeting me.' His eyes were bright and I felt an involuntary surge of pity for him even though those shoes, that jacket, that grooming – they all told of a man who had enough money to buy as much pity as he'd ever need so any surplus from me would be a bit of a waste . . .

'It's no bother,' came out strangely from my dry mouth.

He leaned and kissed my cheek.

We all fell silent in the car, on the way back to my apartment. Miranda, sitting in the back, had shrunk into the seat and I could feel her eyes rove from me to Omar and back again. Words balled themselves up in my mouth but nothing came out, the nonsense about the weather, inane comments on the few, sparse landmarks which we passed on our journey back into town, all the things I could have used to buffer the silence, all stayed put inside my head as I stared straight ahead and just drove.

I did notice Omar nod in silent approval as he saw my apartment block. Andy the concierge instinctively sensed a VIP visitor as he bounded down the steps to help with Omar's case.

'Hiya missy!' he called out to Miranda. 'How's the birthday going? Still on for our date – clubbing, isn't it?' He jostled his way between us and was pulling the case – which was a bit on the large side for an overnight stay – from the boot with a flamboyant flourish when a thick scraping sound told us all instantly that a large slice of camel-coloured Asprey's leather suitcase had just scratched its way across the lower catch of the boot. I gasped, as Andy, who had gone white, turned the case over to have a look at the damage.

'Shit.' Andy let the case fall to the ground, scratch side upwards and we gawped at it helplessly.

'I'll replace it!' I barked. 'Don't worry, Andy!'

'It is not necessary, truly,' Omar said, calmly. 'Please, allow me.'

'Sorry, sir,' Andy said as he held the door for us to go inside.

Omar waved the apologies away and, relieved, we took the lift and entered the apartment.

'This is very lovely,' he murmured, as he looked around.

'Thank you.' I have to say I *had* gone a bit bonkers with the polish and dusters the night before and it *was* looking pretty darned good.

He crouched down and unzipped the scratched Asprey's bag, pulling out a large, lumpy present, clumsily wrapped in silver paper and tied with red ribbon.

'Happy ninth birthday,' he said, handing the parcel to Miranda, who beamed as she accepted the gift. Then he reached back into the suitcase, and pulled out a second parcel, identically wrapped.

'Happy eighth birthday,' he said, almost in a whisper,

hiding his eyes as he delved further into the case for a third parcel.

'Happy seventh birthday, my sweet.'

Miranda fell silent, as each parcel was pulled out of the case and handed to her. More and more, smaller and smaller.

'Happy first birthday,' the final gift, was just a tiny silver box.

I burst into tears, and rushed into my bedroom, closing the door behind me, where I threw myself on to my bed and sobbed my heart out.

'Anna, we have to talk.' When I emerged half an hour later, having pulled myself together and repaired the damage to my face, Omar took me gently by the arm and guided me towards the sofa, where he sat me down and took his own seat opposite. We had to kick our way through a heap of crumpled silver wrapping paper; Miranda had disappeared to her room and closed the door. I went in to try to speak to her, but she told me she needed some private time with her new things and her thoughts, so I left her to it.

'Do we?' I whimpered. 'Omar, I'm not sure what . . .'

'Please,' he interrupted. 'Please may I speak?' His eyes burned into mine and I began to tingle all over.

'Oh, OK then.'

I watched him compose himself. 'Anna, I need to tell you everything. There is a reason why I have come back to London.'

'Oh?' was all I could say.

'Back at home I . . . well, I was engaged to be married.'

Somehow this came as no surprise. I stared at him.

'My, fiancée, she is a doctor, she works in a hospital just outside Amman, only, things hadn't been going well between us for a long time, so we separated; and I just didn't know what to do.'

'So you came looking for us?'

He nodded. 'That was what prompted me to make changes in my life. I want stability, a marriage . . .'

'Children?'

'Of course. I had to get in touch with you – I am older now, wiser, certainly – I realise the importance of, of the next generation, the future, and all of a sudden I couldn't believe that I had a child whom I had never seen, had never wanted to see, because of what I saw as a mistake, a failing on my part. Anna, forgive me if that sounds heartless, but it is only recently that, well, that I have discovered that I care about my child, and now that I have met her, well, she is so much more than I ever imagined, I see how she looks like me as well as like you, and, well, do you want to know the truth?'

'Tell me the truth, Omar,' I said, looking into his eyes.

'I accepted the position which would take me to the United Kingdom for selfish reasons; I wanted to put some distance between my fiancée and me in the hope that it would make her realise of her own accord that she wanted to be with me, but also in order that I could get in touch with you to see whether . . . whether perhaps it is you that I should be with after all.'

'We all make decisions for selfish reasons, Omar.'

He nodded. 'Yes, yes I know that.'

The calmness which I felt was eerie. It was nice, to be faced with honesty. Whatever form it takes, I realised, the truth is always reassuring.

'I wondered about us, Anna. I wondered whether we would fall into each other's arms, that the past could be wiped away and we could begin again, but real life isn't like that, is it?'

I smiled. 'I wondered that as well, for a bit. It would certainly have been nice and neat, wouldn't it? Well, apart from your fiancée, of course.'

He smiled, thinking of her, I was sure of it. 'Of course. But, well, Anna, I am so confused! I almost wish . . .' he tailed off.

'What?' I prompted.

He sighed. 'I almost wish, or at least, *wished*, that you would make the decision for me.'

'Omar,' I began, *'please* – we've been through this already, back in London, haven't we? This is all just . . . too quick. I mean, I'm happy that you are here, but . . .'

'Don't say any more,' he broke in. 'I know. I know it is too quick. Finding you and Miranda has been a gift for me, and all I can wish for now – all I think I want to hope for, is that perhaps we can spend some time together – in the holidays, perhaps?'

Relief. Buckets of the stuff, flooding all the way down to my toes. 'Yes, Omar, let's do that.'

Miranda had put some loud music on, and soon we heard the sound of thumping footfalls coming from her room.

Omar glanced over his shoulder and smiled. 'That might be the dance mat; I was told in the toy store that young girls love them.'

'Well, Miranda's been asking for one for a while – her friend Flora has one which they play on all the time – good choice, Omar!'

'Thank you.' His face took on a smug look, which made me laugh.

'Would you like a cup of coffee? Then we ought to get going, I've booked a ten-pin bowling rink, I'm afraid, it was Miranda's first choice for her birthday treat.'

'Was it really?' Omar replied. 'It is something I used to enjoy too, when I was a child.'

'A family trait, then?' I teased. I stood up and went through to put the kettle on, nearly tripping over the ill-starred Asprey suitcase in the hall. 'Bugger!' I cursed. 'I'll show you through to the spare room, where you can get yourself settled.' The hairs on the back of my neck prickled as I said the words. I wonder – had he been expecting to share my bed? Had I been expecting him to?

Omar shook his head. 'Thank you, but no, I have made a hotel reservation. It is very generous of you to invite me to stay here, but I felt that it would be inappropriate, so I took the liberty of making alternative arrangements.'

Ah.

I took Miranda in a drink and told her we would be leaving in ten minutes. When I returned to the kitchen, Omar was standing there, holding what looked for all the world to be a property schedule.

'Anna, I hope you do not object, but there is another birthday gift which I would like Miranda to have.' He held the schedule out towards me and I took it from him, and sat down.

It was a highly glossy brochure (which would easily have cost thousands to produce – the photography was superb) of a new apartment block, apparently on the verge of completion in the middle of London. Overlooking the Thames at Battersea Bridge, it was a masterpiece of glass and steel, containing thirty-two luxury flats, with underground parking, concierge, gym and swimming pool. I flicked through the specifications, salivating, if a little confused.

'One of the companies I represent is building this,' Omar said, and I could detect the pride in his voice. 'They made me a gift of one of the apartments in the block, and if it is all right with you, I would like it to be Miranda's.'

'What?' I spluttered.

'Please, it would be for my benefit as much as for hers – obviously it would be held in your name, in trust for her until she comes of age, but imagine, Anna, perhaps, if you wish, you could spend time there occasionally; we could all see each other more often . . . Anna?'

'Wow,' was not the most elegant word in my vocabulary but it would have to do. Whenever I was in London I lusted after those sorts of Thames-side apartments like a greedy monster, and now, Omar was handing Miranda an absolute corker on a plate. Then I had a horrified word with myself for allowing my first thoughts to be of the *'whoopee!'* variety – this was a very big step which had to be thought through with enormous amounts of care and professional detachment. Or . . .

'That's a marvellous idea, and so generous. Thank you, Omar. Now, shall we make a move?'

Chapter Eighteen

Eleven o'clock the following morning, the day of the Ben View closing date. The remainder of Miranda's birthday had been a tremendous success; she had taken the extra-ordinary day in her happy stride. Bowling, burger bar, feeding the ducks, and finally a movie, we were quite the happy family, for one special day. Omar, who had changed into clothing which was as casual as he could muster (thank you, Ralph Lauren), seemed to enjoy every moment and late in the evening, as we dropped him off at his hotel and he and Miranda had shared a hug, Miranda was buoyed up by the fact that she was to see him again the following day, at my parents' house after school, before he returned to the airport for his flight back south. He was quite content to spend the bulk of the day on his own, he wanted to spend time getting to know his daughter's home town, in preparation for possible future visits. It had all gone just a little too well, I worried, as I sat down at my desk and popped the waiting wine gum in my mouth.

Quite often there's a buzz in the office when a major property has a closing date, but this one, although small in status and monetary terms, was particularly special for me. With closing dates usually set for twelve noon, what typically happens is that some offers are already sitting waiting for us along with the morning mail, and others are hand-delivered from local solicitors' offices, as the morning progresses. All have one thing in common – they are all clearly marked on the envelope: **Offer for Ben View Cottage** (or whatever property it is) – **not to be opened until twelve noon.** It's a courtesy thing, which also helps to ensure fairness – if all the envelopes are opened at once, after the deadline has passed, then there's no chance of anybody sliding on to the scene with a higher offer. That's the theory, anyway. There's a Blakemore office cautionary tale of the young inexperienced manager who'd accidentally opened an envelope containing an offer before the twelve noon deadline, only to have the would-be buyer's solicitor come panting in fifteen minutes before noon to demand his unopened offer back as his client had changed his mind and decided not to go ahead . . . that's a cardinal estate agency sin, by the way, because it makes you out to be untrustworthy and leaves you open to accusations of foul play, which in this case definitely had not been involved . . . OK, OK, I was very young, right? And it was a genuine mistake! Boy, did I have to do some major grovelling and sucking up about that one. My nose was brown for weeks.

But occasionally offers will come through by fax as well, and although we are obviously able to read what's written on them as soon as they come through, protocol dictates that we treat them as though they're written in invisible ink which only reveals itself properly after the twelve noon deadline and they get shut in my desk drawer until then.

Anyway, Ben View Cottage was going to bust all our previous records wide open, in terms of the number of offers we expected to receive. So confident was I of having a bumper crop of fat, promising envelopes to get my teeth into after twelve that I had even invited Mrs Ferguson in specially to witness the occasion, the downside of which being that odious James would have to be there too.

Rod and I were musing over who the lucky purchaser was going to be.

'My guess is it's that couple from Gloucestershire who've been on the phone every five minutes,' said Rod. 'The ones in the white Mercedes.'

'Nah,' I replied dismissively. 'The Lomax bigwig's bound to get it, whoever it is Jack's been acting for. I just get the impression that money's no object there.'

'Aren't they going to bulldoze the cottage and build some sort of fake colonial dinosaur?'

'I think you mean "gracious country retreat", don't you, Rod?'

He frowned. 'Isn't that what I said? I thought that was what I said – but what about *your* offer, Anna? Still going to go for it?'

'Oh, yes, absolutely – it takes more than a thousand other bidders, a potential conflict of interest court case and a blackmailing son to put me off – I think . . .' Gee, whiz. Did I really want the place? Yes, of course I did. Crossly, I wiped the doubt from my mind. I did want it – *I did!* Didn't I? OK, so I hadn't given it all that much thought these past few days but there had been one or two other things on my mind! The reappearing father of my child, for example, not to mention the boyfriend whom I might have allowed to slip through my fingers, Rod and his insistent, beguiling wine gums – it had been quite an episode, and it wasn't over yet.

'It's just . . . well, you don't seem all that excited about the closing date, that's all. Or is it just your nerves, getting to you?'

He was right, I wasn't. Yesterday afternoon I'd rung up and instructed my solicitor to compile an offer of £173,000, and ever since putting the phone down, I'd been trying to summon up some excitement, and brush off the doubts which just wouldn't go away. Although, come to think of it, wouldn't it be a bit hard of me to be excited when poor old Mrs Ferguson's world was being unwillingly turned upside down by an enforced sale due to her increasing infirmity? That was it! I wasn't excited because I was such a nice, compassionate person! *Phew!*

'Cool, calm, collectedness, that's what this is, Rod,' I replied. 'Just being my usual ice-queen self, that's all. Did you not know about my nerves of steel?'

He raised his eyebrows slowly, and I felt a little shiver run through my body.

'Oh, *them* – yes, I know about your nerves of steel, Anna.'

Urrrrrrr!

A thought occurred to me. I hadn't actually noticed any offer envelopes yet. 'Geraldine, where's this morning's post? Have you separated out all the ones marked as offers for Ben View?'

Geraldine looked puzzled. 'Sorry? Oh, the post! Yes, I sorted it first thing. Here's the Ben View offer.' She got up and brought me over a single envelope.

'Offer? *Offer?*' I bellowed. 'We should have about *six* on my desk by now! It's only an hour till the closing date! Are you sure?' I gazed in disgust at the envelope, noticing from the crest on the back that it was from my own solicitor's office. Huh, after all that anticipation, the only offer on the table so far was my own? Flipping heck, Mrs Ferguson and the lovely James were due in forty-five minutes for a grand opening ceremony – how was I going to explain to them that mine was the only bid? They'd think I'd been going round issuing Mafia-style death threats to the competition, James would call the police and I'd be all over the papers . . .

'Don't worry,' said Rod, feebly, looking worried. 'There's plenty of time – oh, thank God, there goes the fax machine.'

I rushed to stand over the machine to will the next offer out. Only it wasn't an offer. It was a short letter written on the Lomax Construction Group headed notepaper and signed by Jack, and it went like this:

Dear Ms Morris
This is to formally intimate, for the avoidance of doubt and for your records, that Lomax Construction Group will not be pursuing the interest which it has hitherto expressed in the subjects known as Ben View Cottage and land.
Yours sincerely
Jack Anderson
For Lomax Construction Group.

And he'd scrawled along the bottom of the letter: *Sorry, Anna, but I'm afraid we're doing a private deal to buy Waterbank from the Maclarens. Long story. See you sometime, J.*

I gazed in disbelief at the letter. Bastards! My plum candidates, pulled out – and the chief reason I'd pumped the asking price up to a level which would not have been shy to wear a sign round its neck saying *exorbitant!* Flipping heck, what now? The Lomax bigwig had buggered off to Waterbank, and there was absolutely nothing I could do about it.

And what of Waterbank? I raced over to the file and scanned its meagre contents. Mr and Mrs Maclaren hadn't signed and returned the contract letter which would have bound them and Waterbank to Blakemore for all eternity, so legally they were free to do whatever they liked with the place. Dammit! Normally I don't let new clients out of the office without signing the contract letter on the spot, but the Maclarens had been so nice – I'd thought the sale was in the bag . . . wanted to be all chummy . . . wanted to go that little bit extra, given that they were friends with Jack, and I was Jack's special lady . . . *bastards!*

I decided to run away. I'd sprint out of the office and join a travelling circus. I could wear an embroidered cloak and sell programmes at the entrance to the tent, and Miranda could fly the trapeze. It seemed to be the obvious thing to do.

'Here's one!' Geraldine called out, as she signed for a nice, fat envelope which was handed in by a burly bike courier who didn't even have the good manners to take his helmet off. He seemed mightily impressed with Geraldine, though, who today was wearing a crisp white blouse with the two top buttons undone, showing off her taut, creamy skin to perfection. He raised his visor, perched the left cheek of his leather butt on the edge of her desk, and said, 'So, been here long, then?'

I wasn't in the mood for office shenanigans, though, and he had definitely brought a bit of a petrolly whiff in with him. 'Rod, throw a stick and get rid of him, would you?' I called out, none too quietly. The biker took the hint and pushed off, and Geraldine went back to her keyboard, a little smile playing at the corner of her mouth.

No sooner had his motor bike parped away than a huge, earnest girl whom I recognised from the solicitors' round the corner swung into the office and placed another pleasingly plump envelope on Geraldine's desk.

'That's an offer,' she announced with massive importance before turning towards the door.

'So I see from the writing on the envelope,' replied Geraldine in a dangerously sweet tone of voice. 'Look!' she pointed at the envelope. 'Offer!' The girl looked suspiciously over her shoulder and Geraldine gave her a wave. 'Thank you so much for visiting Blakemore this morning, and good day!'

Then, hurray, the fax machine clicked into life once more, spewing out an eager offer of £162,000, from a local couple who passionately wanted to bring up organic hens and sell happy eggs with golden yolks and helpful fatty acids to the world. Huh, I thought as I looked it over – shame it wasn't going to happen at Ben View. A hundred and sixty-two grand? Who had they taken their advice from, Ebenezer Scrooge?

By the time Mrs Ferguson and odious James came into the office at precisely eleven forty-five, we had received a further two written offers, and one more by fax, of £168,000. I glanced at the enticing little stack of unopened envelopes on my desk. Hmm. The higher of the faxed offers was running mine just a little bit close – and who knew what sort of figures were contained in the unopened envelopes in front of me? There was still time to ring my solicitor and ask him to fax through an amendment to my offer, by putting another five grand on my total – where would be the harm in that, then?

'Well, Anna, what is it you're thinking? Are you getting the scent of victory in your nostrils?' Her pale eyes were full of mischief, a sight which filled me with relief – I didn't know what I'd do if she was emotional, or full of doubts, or anything scary like that.

I smiled. 'Come through and have a seat, Mrs Ferguson. I'm far more concerned about how *you* are today!' *And bring that horrible heap of crap of a son of yours as well, why don't you?* 'Mr Ferguson! How nice to see you again! Do come with me!'

James Ferguson grunted as he helped his mother through to the meeting lounge. It was ten to twelve.

I proudly laid out the two faxed offers and five unopened envelopes in front of Mrs Ferguson.

'Well, it's all looking pretty good right now!' I began. 'Seven offers, which is great, two of them by fax, and the higher one of those two is for £168,000!'

'Well, would you credit it?' Mrs Ferguson seemed amazed. 'Isn't that a marvel? James, isn't Anna a marvel?'

We both looked expectantly at James Ferguson, who just made a sort of nasal twanging sound but said nothing.

I patted him on the arm, brimming, suddenly, with self-righteous bravado. 'Do you know, Mr Ferguson, I've just got a feeling that we've got even better things to come in one or two of these babies!' I stroked the topmost envelope with my other hand, and beamed at Mrs Ferguson.

Just then Geraldine tapped lightly on the door, came in and laid yet another sealed envelope on the pile.

'Can I get anyone a cup of tea or coffee?' she enquired.

We all declined. I was far too excited by this stage to think about hot beverages and I was willing the clock to move forward so that I could rip open the envelopes and find out whether or not I'd got the house.

'Oh, excuse me, Mr Ferguson?' Geraldine went on, as she reversed towards the door.

James Ferguson appeared not to have heard; he suddenly became very interested in a speck of dust on the arm of the sofa.

'Mr Ferguson?' she repeated.

A sharp dig in the ribs from his mother reminded him of his manners. 'What?' he said, brusquely.

'Thank you for the offer, but I'm afraid I won't be free for dinner this evening – I already have a date for tonight.' She narrowed her eyes at him before flicking a meaningful glance at me and half winking.

'James!' Mrs Ferguson glowered at her son in disgust, and shook her head. Something about the way she looked at him told me that she wasn't entirely surprised by Geraldine's words. 'I thought you'd given up all this nonsense!' She leaned towards me and muttered, 'He told me he was going to be meeting up with a school friend this evening, the rag!' before treating her son to an absolutely filthy glare.

I looked up and mouthed at Geraldine, *'Insch of Stour?'*,

and grinned as she nodded sheepishly. Wow, nice one, Geraldine – Jeremy fforsythe was loaded, and cute as a button to boot!

'Oh, for heaven's sake, mother, it's not at all what you think! For God's sake, Anna, open these ruddy envelopes, it's practically twelve o'clock, isn't it?'

I checked my watch. 'Actually it's three minutes to – I can't possibly open any envelopes prior to the allotted time as that would be unethical, and as you have taken pains to point out to me on numerous occasions . . .'

'All right, all right, I get the picture, you can stop there.'

'I'm thinking it's about time you were holding your wheesht and letting Anna do her job, James,' his mother said sternly.

'Yes, ma.'

Then we sat in silence, living and breathing the final few seconds before I would begin to open the envelopes, but not finding any useful words with which to fill the space. Mrs Ferguson was wearing a navy lambswool jumper and trousers that were so far up the Beaufort scale of manmade, old-lady, no-need-to-iron comfort that even giving them the unforgivably residential-home title of 'slacks' was a bit racy. A large oval pendant, comprising a semi-precious chunk of orange and green polished stone in a curly wurly gold mount hung around her neck, and the collar of her cream blouse was tucked in on one side. She looked tense, annoyance at her philanderer-wannabe son notwithstanding, and although I wanted to ask her how she was feeling I knew she'd reassure me that she was fine whether she was or not so I kept my mouth shut and my eyes on my watch. At one minute to twelve there was a tap on the door and Geraldine hurried in and handed me a further envelope, this one heavy dark grey vellum, with OFFER, BEN VIEW COTTAGE thickly typed in bold capitals. I added it to the pile.

'Shall we start opening them, then?' I asked, as the second hand finally surfed past the twelve on my watch. 'I think it's time.'

'Go on, then,' said Mrs Ferguson. Her son said nothing, but he was beginning to sweat.

'Well,' I began. 'Obviously we've got these two faxed ones first – one for 162 and one for 168,000. Let's see now . . .' I quickly scanned each of the faxed offers in turn. 'Right, then, the lower one doesn't want to pay for the place for another seven months, and the higher one is conditional on planning consent being obtained for two more houses on the adjoining five acres. That's not very good, is it? Let's see what's in the others, shall we?'

I began with the grey one which had just arrived. Quite often last-minute offers were ridiculously high so maybe it ought to have been left until last, but I had decided, for some reason, to leave the envelope from my own solicitors until last.

'Well?' James Ferguson had foregone his sulk in favour of hurrying me up. His mother produced a spectacle case from her handbag and put on a pair of gold-rimmed reading glasses.

'A hundred and sixty-nine thousand, from a Mr and Mrs Lightbody . . .'

'Delightful couple!' James Ferguson burst out. 'Absolutely desperate to secure the place! Marvellous! Next?'

Again, his mother said nothing, merely inclined her head a little. I picked up the next envelope and ripped its head off. It contained a horrible little conditional offer of £140,000, from a couple by the name of Hunter whom none of us recognised. I shrugged and picked up the next one.

'It's a bit like opening Christmas presents!' I said, absently, to fill the silence which had descended.

'Only there's only one gift,' Mrs Ferguson murmured.

'Mmm, yes, I suppose . . . OK, let's see what we have next!'

It was Iris and Pete's offer and at £172,500, it was only a terrifying fraction below mine. My heart jolted when I saw how close it had run me, although James Ferguson was practically doing somersaults of glee when he saw how much lovely money looked to be coming his family's way.

'Just look at that!' he said, fatly. 'I had a feeling we'd pitched the asking price a little on the low side! We could have realised a far higher figure if . . .'

'Be quiet, James!' his mother scolded.

'Sorry, ma, but . . .'

'I mean it! Anna's done a lovely job. Now, Anna, dear, shall we have a wee look at the last ones? There's still three to go.'

And one of them was mine. Still I left it until last. To my amazement the first of the final three was also a bid of £172,500, from the man who wanted to put static caravans on the site; and the second last one was a disappointing attempt at getting a steal in the event of there being no other offers – a paltry 129,000, one of those lottery-ticket type punts which never, ever pay off. James Ferguson acted like the bid was a personal slight.

'Pah, that's a bloody insult!' he spat. 'Who do these people think they are?'

I saw his mother wince.

'Would you be kind enough to watch your language, please?' I asked, turning towards him and smiling. Bloody pain in the arse. Still, who cared? Ben View was mine! Only just – which was a huge relief: much as I loved Mrs Ferguson I'd hate to have secured the place by some sort of massive margin of about £10,000 – just think what I could have spent that sort of margin on . . .

'Well, Anna,' Mrs Ferguson said, as with trembling

303

hands I picked up my solicitor's letter, 'I take it this is your own offer? Or have you decided against buying Ben View after all?' She was smiling kindly at me.

I smiled back. 'Yes, this is mine. I know by the crest on the back of the envelope. It just happened to be at the bottom of the pile . . .'

'Just open it!' James Ferguson muttered, in a tone of extreme boredom. 'You'll know what it says, but we don't – I don't appreciate being played with!'

'Playing with you was the last thing on my mind, Mr Ferguson,' I assured him with fervour as I opened the envelope, pulled out the offer, unfolded it and, without checking it first, spread it out on the table, facing them. I kept my eyes on Mrs Ferguson's face as she peered closely at the wording.

James Ferguson was frowning. I guessed he'd be wrestling with himself, not wanting to give me the satisfaction of seeing him look delighted at the size of my offer, yet delighted with the size of my offer nonetheless. But I was more concerned about his mother's reaction, so I kept my eyes on her face, hoping and praying for the first expression to cross her face to be one of pleasure, or relief, that her home was about to belong to me.

She read on, impassively. At one stage, she even took her glasses off, polished them on the hem of her navy jumper, shook her head, and replaced them on her nose. I sat, heart racing, a child expecting praise.

Eventually James Ferguson spoke. 'Is this some kind of joke?'

'Sorry?'

'This offer – thought you said it was from you?' He thrust the letter towards me.

'It is!' I protested, picking it up and glancing at it – ah, something wasn't quite right somewhere.

'So when did you suddenly change your name to

Kenneth Hopkins, and think you could tempt us with a bid of one fifty-five?'

It was true. The offer in my hands was indeed written on the headed notepaper of the law firm I used, but the offer was on behalf of this unknown Kenneth Hopkins person, and the reference at the top of the letter showed that the solicitor who had compiled it had the initials I.G., which corresponded to Irene Grey, whose name was third from the bottom of the partners' list at the foot of the page, rather than the H.E. of Harry Emmerson, my own solicitor.

So where the *fuck* was my offer? 'I don't understand it!' I spluttered, and shot to my feet and out to the front. 'Geraldine! Monica – are there any other offers for Ben View lying around? Mine's not here!'

I searched my desk frantically whilst they cast around theirs and shrugged. Rod hammered the fax machine in case it had my offer in its memory and had decided to keep it to itself.

'Haven't seen any others,' Geraldine shrugged.

'You know if there had been any offers delivered to me I would have passed them over immediately,' sniffed the Lizard.

'Nope, nothing here, Anna,' Rod called over, after giving the machine several final sharp thumps.

'For heavens sake!' I groaned to nobody in particular. 'What's that idiot Emmerson been playing at? He knew perfectly well when the closing date was – Geraldine, you haven't taken any calls from him, by any chance, have you?'

She shook her head. 'Nope, definitely not. Been really quiet for the last hour or so, actually – no calls at all!'

'Right! I'll throttle him!' I snatched up my phone, just as the office door flew open and in blustered Harry Emmerson himself, cheerfully waving an envelope at me.

At the same moment, James Ferguson emerged from the meeting lounge, presumably to see where I'd got to.

'Phew!' Harry Emmerson said, jovially. 'Sorry about that! I take it you got my message?'

'Your . . . what?' I repeated, astonished that he had the gall to be smiling. He could be struck off for failing to submit an offer in time! Harry Emmerson was a genial man in his late fifties, with grey wavy hair, a fledgling paunch and a taste for brightly coloured silk ties. Today's was bright blue emblazoned with a golden solar system, and it lay across his left shoulder, blown back in his evident haste to get to me. Normally I thought the world of him; he had given me some excellent financial and tax advice in the past, and he'd handled my apartment purchase brilliantly, securing me a 5 per cent refund on the purchase price owing to 'excessive' building noise in the adjoining, incomplete apartment, but today I could have happily skinned him alive as he strode over to me and planted breathless kisses on either side of my face.

I stepped backwards from him and sighed. 'You left a message?' I repeated.

His eyebrows shot up towards his hairline, and would have made it had his hair commenced at approximately the starting point of his youth. 'W . . . what, don't tell me you *didn't get it*? I called about half an hour ago to say I was stuck in traffic on the A9 – caravan overturned, hell of a mess – been off down in Carrbridge seeing an old lady for emergency will instructions – on her last legs, poor old love, and then I lost reception for a while but I assumed you'd have received the message saying I was running late anyway . . .' He bent his knees slightly, the better to study my crestfallen face. James Ferguson was listening intently, for once not saying anything. 'I must say, though,' Harry Emmerson continued, 'I *was* a bit surprised to get your answering machine mid-morning!'

'Oh . . .' Geraldine was suddenly looking a bit uncertain, and she glanced under her desk at the tangle of wires which led to the sockets in the walls.

'What?' I snarled. 'What do you mean, you got the answering machine?'

'Oh, shit!' Geraldine shot backwards from her desk, and her hands flew to her mouth.

I felt a dull, aching thump somewhere in my insides. 'What's happened?' I asked, forcing my voice to remain calm.

Geraldine was breathing heavily. 'I've unplugged my phone headset by accident – I'm really sorry, Anna!'

'You've what? How on earth did you do that?' I squeaked.

'Well, the new water cooler's been getting on my nerves, making a horrible buzzing noise and heating rather than cooling the water, so I lost my temper with it and unplugged it . . . at least I thought I unplugged it . . .'

Rod, who'd been listening in, rushed round to the corner behind Geraldine's desk and rummaged about with the wires.

'Yup, water cooler's still working, phone's knackered,' he confirmed. 'You pulled the wrong plug, Geraldine. Bummer.'

I didn't know what to think, apart from a fleeting realisation from left-field that the Lizard seemed to be rather enjoying the spectacle, from behind her spectacles.

'The system would've gone on to its answering machine setting by default,' Rod went on, standing up and pressing some buttons on Geraldine's switchboard. 'Yup, you appear to have nineteen new messages! No wonder it was a bit quiet this morning!'

Geraldine was aghast. So was I, actually. I looked from her to Rod to Harry Emmerson to James Ferguson, hoping somebody would say something helpful.

'Does it matter?' This was from James Ferguson.

'Sorry?' I said.

'You heard, I said, does it matter? Is your offer higher than the others?'

I nodded.

'Well, that's all right, then!'

'No, it isn't,' I corrected him, quietly. 'I've missed the closing date.'

'Oh, come on, Anna!' Harry Emmerson came over to me and rubbed my arm reassuringly. 'So what? I'm sure, under the circumstances, we can relax the closing date time, can't we? I knew that as it was your offer, and as it was being delivered to your office, that you'd be able to extend the closing time given the exceptional circumstances! In fact, I'm bound to have evidence somewhere on my mobile phone that I'd tried to ring your office – come on, Anna! Lighten up! It's fine – just open it!'

'Quite right, too,' agreed James Ferguson. 'Load of old nonsense, all of it!'

'Especially when it's *your* offer, Anna! It's your office, you can turn back time if you want to!'

Geraldine, Rod and Katy had all given up any pretence of doing anything else and were watching the scene, engrossed, for all their different reasons. The phone rang and, without a flicker of hesitation, Geraldine whipped the answering machine back on.

James Ferguson glanced over his shoulder back into the meeting lounge. 'Look, Anna, if your offer's the highest then it's in my . . . I mean, it's in my mother's best interests to accept it, so come on, let's get it back in there and tell her it fell behind the desk, or something!'

'It's no worse than some of the things we've got up to in the past!' joshed Harry Emmerson, nudging me conspiratorially. 'And anyway, closing dates are mere protocols, made to oil the wheels of the selling process, nothing more!

It's not as if there's anything legally binding about having to be in possession of the envelope before noon, now, is there?'

'That's true,' I whispered.

'Excellent!' James Ferguson visibly relaxed.

'But it is *morally* binding, isn't it?'

Both men tutted, which gave me the confidence to go through with what my heart was screaming out at me to say.

'Look, Mr Ferguson, I've missed the closing date, it's as simple as that. I can't allow my offer to be considered along with the others.'

'But it wasn't your fault you missed it!' Harry Emmerson was evidently feeling a little shifty by now that he might be in danger of being implicated in some sort of negligence squabble over this one, so he was siding quite heavily with Ferguson. 'You're splitting hairs!'

'Quite right,' James Ferguson agreed. 'I don't give a damn about a few minutes' delay, so let's get on with it, shall we?'

I glowered at him. '*Get on with it?* Mr Ferguson, for what it's worth, it occurs to me that you have wasted no time in calling my morals into question on numerous occasions, quite unjustifiably, I would add, regarding the sale of your mother's cottage, and so it seems a bit rich to me that when there is the possibility of an advantage to be gained, all of a sudden you're encouraging me to behave unethically!'

'Ms Morris, I'm not really in the mood for another of your ticking-offs. Now, shall we go back through and open your offer, or maybe you could just tell us how much it's for?'

'Er, time I was off. Sorry, Anna, frightful mess! Be in touch!' Harry skulked off in a rather less energetic fashion than that of his arrival, and disappeared down the street.

'You have to think of my mother in all of this,' James

309

Ferguson went on, this time in a far more conciliatory tone of voice. 'She deserves . . .'

'She deserves all of us to be straight with her, as she has always been with us,' I said, before walking across to Geraldine's desk and silently feeding my unopened offer through the shredder.

James Ferguson made no move to stop me; he only murmured something that included the words 'bloody' and 'shambles', strode back into the meeting lounge, and slammed the door behind him.

'You did the right thing, Anna.' Monica spoke quietly.

'Thanks, Monica, that means a lot.'

'Well done, Anna,' said Rod and Katy together.

'I'm really sorry for screwing up,' said Geraldine.

'Don't be. It was a mistake, that's all. Why don't you give the water cooler guy a ring and tell him to come and take his useless heap of shit away? You'll need to switch your phone back on first, of course.'

Then I took a few deep breaths, and followed James Ferguson back into the meeting lounge.

'I'm sorry about your offer, Anna, but I think you acted very honourably. *Unlike some.*' Mrs Ferguson was standing up, and was glowering at her son.

'What, don't tell me you heard what was going on out there?' I gasped.

She chuckled. 'Every word. I remember telling you up at the house that there's nothing wrong with my ears – it's just the rest of me that's needing the sheltered housing! Now, are you all right?'

'Me? I'm fine – why shouldn't I be?'

'I just thought you might be feeling a bit upset that you won't be getting the house, that's all – or is that your brave face I'm seeing?'

Nope, it wasn't. I'd been so caught up in the drama of the moment that I hadn't allowed myself a second to let

310

the fact that I'd lost out on Ben View sink in. I sat down on the sofa opposite the Fergusons, and plunged my chin into my hands. I was gutted. No, hang on a second, I wasn't. Disaster? Umm, guess again. Maybe I was just in shock? Maybe tonight, after the Young's Insurance party, I'd break down into uncontrollable, keening sobs of loss and absence?

James Ferguson got up and stood with his back to us, staring out of the window. I thought he'd probably be about done with talking by now, but I was wrong.

'How much higher was your offer?' he demanded, in a low voice.

'James!' his mother scolded. 'It doesn't matter!'

'It does to me.' He turned round. 'How much, Anna?'

'Well . . .' I looked over at Mrs Ferguson for some sort of steer as to what to say. She just shook her head and closed her eyes. James Ferguson turned round and faced me, his face betraying a small measure of anguish for the situation, but a larger mask of curiosity for the sort of figures we were talking about. I ought to just tell him, to put him out of his misery. To miss out on £500 was peanuts – he'd feel a whole lot better if he knew I hadn't offered tens of thousands of pounds higher.

'Tell me, Anna,' he urged, 'just so that I can . . .'

'. . . sue me for the difference?' I jumped to my feet. 'Sue my office? You're not even my client – your mother is!'

'And I've had enough of all these squabbles! Sit down, the pair of you. Don't we still have to decide who *is* going to get the house?'

We sat down, breathing heavily. I collected up the offers and sifted through them, eventually laying the caravan man's offer alongside Iris and Pete's, and placing the others to one side.

'OK,' I began, 'the two highest offers seem to be very similar in all respects; both are requesting the same date

311

of entry, and neither contains any conditions which are in any way awkward or unusual.'

'That's good,' Mrs Ferguson nodded approvingly. 'So, shall we toss a coin?'

'Why don't we go back to them and ask each of them to increase their bids?' James Ferguson was either shameless or thick, or quite possibly both, but whatever it was, he was quite easy to ignore.

'The first offer is actually from two friends of mine – they want to do some sympathetic restoration work and eventually open the house as a top quality holiday rental property – from what Iris has told me, the place sounds as though it's going to be absolutely gorgeous! Not that it isn't gorgeous already, mind!'

'Is that right, now?' Mrs Fergsuon was smiling to herself. 'A holiday home, eh? Fancy! And what do we know of the other one?'

I frowned. 'Not much, actually. The guy was very quiet when he looked round. But there is a bit of a problem with this one, I suspect.'

'Oh?' Mrs Ferguson looked up at me.

I pursed my lips and nodded. 'Well, I do remember this chap talking about siting static caravans on the site, unfortunately – he said something about some sort of "retreat" . . .'

'Oh yes, I remember him,' James Ferguson muttered. 'Scruffy chap, not in the least interested in what I had to tell him, just kept going on about the "vibe" or something – quite unsuitable – probably on drugs, I shouldn't wonder.'

'OK!' I said, brightly. 'What do you think, then, Mrs Ferguson? Better the devil we know, wouldn't you say? Iris and Pete have got the cash in the bank already – of course, it's entirely up to you, though.'

She appeared to be trying to recall something.

Eventually she spoke. 'This scruffy chap, his name's not . . . *Edmund*, is it?'

I checked the offer. 'Could be – Mr E. Leaf, it says here. You don't know him, do you?'

'Hasn't been bothering you, has he, mother?' her son asked, bravely.

'No, no, not at all! He's been up to the house several times since it went on the market! Lovely chap, gave me a hand pulling up some ground elder the other week!'

'Mother! Don't tell me you've been speaking with this . . . this *druggie*!'

'Oh, wheesht, James! He's very nice!'

'But, but, *caravans*, mother! Honestly! He'll be wanting to start a commune in the house before you know it!'

'No he won't! He was telling me over a scone and a pancake the other day that his plan is to set up a study centre for young botanists, that's why he's going to be needing the caravans, you see – to put all the young folks in who come up to stay.'

'Botanists?' her son echoed. 'Wasn't that . . .'

'Your dad's great passion, that's right.' She looked away, misty-eyed. 'He would have been a botanist, if the money had been there to send him to the university, you know, Anna.'

'Really?' I knew, from that moment, that Iris and Pete were going to have to look elsewhere for their holiday do-up idyll. 'I never knew that.'

'Me neither,' James Ferguson said in a small voice.

'Do I take it, then, that Edmund Leaf is the successful bidder?' I asked, slowly, and Mrs Ferguson nodded, and closed her eyes.

Chapter Nineteen

I thought it would be a chance to show Omar a bit of the fun that could be had within the Inverness business community. I thought he'd get a chance to see me in full swing, working the room, double kissing everyone, in my element and shining with supreme confidence – it'd make up for the fiasco when I'd answered the phone to him and tried to convince him I wasn't the receptionist, that was for sure. I knew that Ronald Young, the Young's Insurance Services boss and founder, had a bit of a soft spot for me so there was already a built-in bit of flirting in the bag. Oh yes, and we'd be on *my* rock, this time, not Eliza Doolittling away in London where the atmosphere always made me struggle to feel good enough . . . but anyway, the Young's Insurance bods were a nice bunch. For one thing, they've devised a killer of a contents policy for new tenants involving compulsory accidental damage cover which we tack on to our rental agreements and out of which we receive quite a tidy commission . . . but anyway, boring, snoring – they're a decent enough crowd and I was looking forward to their party. A second glance at the invitation, which was stuck on to Geraldine's pinboard, told me that they were proudly celebrating twenty-five years of being in business, covering the Highlands far and near against catastrophes great and small.

'Geraldine, could you get some champagne sent round?'

314

I asked, still scanning the invitation.

'What, round here?' she replied. 'Great!'

'No, madam, get it sent to Young's direct. And get something appropriate written on the card.'

'Like what?'

'Oh, I don't know. Think of something.'

'How about, "*Down the hatch, from Blakemore*"?'

'Something classy, Geraldine.'

'Ah. OK.'

Omar was to meet me at the party. He was going to meet Miranda when she finished school, and then the plan was he'd walk with her to my parents' house, Miranda would introduce them, and later he'd take a cab down town to Young's office before heading for the airport and his flight back to London.

The idea of me not being around when mum and dad met Omar had seemed preposterous at first, but the more I thought about it the more sensible, *appropriate*, even, it became, as it meant mum and dad would get their first impression of Omar laced with Miranda's enthusiasm, rather than my blustering anxiety. I had clued mum and dad up to within an inch of their lives about the situation, to the extent that I think they were quite looking forward to meeting him at last. Miranda was excited to have the responsibility of introducing her father to her grandparents and – perhaps most importantly, I wouldn't have to be there when she and Omar said their goodbyes.

Truth be known I was utterly, totally, hollowed out. The last couple of days had been too much to take in one large dose. The drama of Ben View was hitting home. Omar was here, and Jack wasn't. Rod, when I thought about him, was making my tummy feel funny and there was no one I could analyse the whole situation with. I couldn't confide in Iris – she'd been gutted when I rang her to let her know she hadn't got the house, although she was coming along to the Young's Insurance party later on so maybe I'd get a chance to speak to her then. Lisa was away on a hen weekend in New York. Omar was going away tonight, Rod wasn't going anywhere, and Jack? Perhaps he was already out of reach, wafted away by my complicated baggage. Now, which of these was the root cause of my melancholy?

So, back to work. It was a bit of a heartsink to note from the reference at the top of his offer that Edmund Leaf's solicitor was Gloria McNaughton from Humphreys & Co, a sharp, whippet-thin little woman who'd never been much of a one for chit-chat. After I'd said goodbye to the Fergusons, sending them off to spend the afternoon picking out carpet and ironmongery samples at the Cedar Park showhome, I pondered the paradox – Edmund Leaf, eco-hero, plantsman and all-round Good Guy, instructing one of the most pernickety clothes-horses Inverness could throw up to do his legal work – it just seemed a bit odd, that's all. After all, there were numerous laid-back young environmentally sound lawyers in town – why didn't he go for one of those? Anyway, I had to hold the line for my allotted penance before Gloria McNaughton took the call and I was able to pass on the good news.

'I see,' she barked. 'Fine. Well, now that you have let me know I shall expect the offer to be passed from you to the seller's solicitor for *formal* written acceptance at the earliest possible opportunity.'

OK, fine. In her eyes, no doubt, I was a measly commercial parasite, whereas she got to handle the important stuff, the meaty end of the drumstick, once I'd creamed off my ill-gotten cut. Or maybe that was just my own insecurity bubbling to the surface, coupled with my misery at not having got Ben View for myself? No, that didn't ring quite true, somehow.

Misery? *What* misery? Throughout the afternoon I

hadn't sunk even slightly into despondency at missing out on Ben View and as the clock heaved its way past four I came to realise, at last, that I hadn't after all *truly* wanted to own the house. What I *had* wanted was for things not to change; for there always to be a welcome for us at the end of the glen, an old lady with endless time for me, a scone and a pancake, a foothold in an era which was gradually, inexorably, slipping away.

'Very well, I'll have it sent round to my client's solicitor within the hour. Your client . . .'

'Ed?'

'Y . . . yes, Mr Leaf . . .'

'Pah!' she snorted. 'I do wish he wouldn't use that silly name. It started out as a bit of a joke, but unfortunately it appears to have stuck. Honestly, that boy!'

'What, you mean that's not his real name?'

'Didn't you know?' she appeared startled. 'He's my son!'

'Really?' It was all I could do not to bark with laughter.

'Yes, really,' she said, curtly. 'And he's frittering away his father's money on a rundown cottage in the middle of nowhere – honestly! He'll get bored of this eco-thing soon enough, though, believe me. Get himself a *real* job.'

My insides lurched. 'What, do you mean you don't think he'll go through with the purchase?' I squeaked.

'Of course he'll go through with it!' she snapped back. 'You don't think I would put in an offer in bad faith, do you? Because if that's what you're insinuating . . .'

'Of course it wasn't!' I said, hurriedly, feeling a whoosh of panic as I realised that I had succeeded in accusing her of being unethical and for God's sake, if I had one more ethical dilemma about Ben View to contend with then I'd drive up there and kick the walls down with my bare feet. Now *that* would be unethical.

'Even if he sells on straight away he will most definitely

go through with the purchase – not that it's any concern of yours, but he and I are both pretty sure there's still a bit of profit to be made from that one – now, I look forward to receiving the acceptance from your client's solicitor by Monday. Good day.'

Poor old Mrs Ferguson. However smart she had turned out to be, however clued-up about the market, she was still a little old lady whose function in the eyes of some of the world was to be worked over for profit. Was the whole world on the make? Actually, I knew the answer to that one. Yes, it probably was.

Dejectedly, I sent Rod off to hand-deliver Edmund Leaf's offer to Mrs Ferguson's solicitor. It was only round the corner but he was gone for a good fifteen minutes, returning, pink-cheeked, with a bag containing four fudge doughnuts and a nice bit of Bakewell slice.

At last, sluggish from fatigue and fudge doughnut, I shepherded Rod, Katy, Geraldine and the Lizard out of the Blakemore front door at twenty to five. Monica's hair didn't flinch at the blasts of unseasonably icy wind which tore down the street, but the rest of us let out numerous expletives of the blue variety as the wind whistled up skirt and down blouse. Geraldine had nipped through the back and changed into a grungy denim skirt which hung in handkerchief points around her ankles, and she had knotted her white broderie anglaise shirt above her waist so that it revealed glimpses of downy, concave tummy and an aggressive steel navel stud. She had poured a slick of gloss on her lips, and added another coat or ten to her electric blue mascara. The effect ought to have been dreadful but it was devastating. Katy had pinned her pale brown hair back with a diamante kirby grip, revealing pretty brown eyes and a broad, clear forehead and Rod had thrown caution to the cold, cold wind and taken off his tie.

'Lookin' good, kiddies,' I said, trying to lighten everyone up, as Monica ignored me and we strode the short distance to the Young's Insurance door where a wild party was foretold by the presence of three phallic white balloons tied to the door handle.

Oh. My. God. The only things that marked the interior out from a normal afternoon in an insurance office were the presence of two wine boxes and a single cheese and glacé cherry hedgehog, sitting on top of the photocopier at the back of the office beside a stack of plastic cups. Everywhere else, the Young's staff were still at their desks, on the phone, or shuffling papers around. We blundered uncertainly in, took our eager, party smiles off our mortified faces and stopped just inside the doorway, staring at the scene. Instinctively we bunched up closer together for mutual support and I knew, somewhere deep down, far beyond the realms of social horror, that I probably ought to say something. But I couldn't. For a few horrendous seconds nobody moved until Rod cleared his throat, stepped in front of me, produced a single party popper from his pocket, and, without smiling, raised it above his head and let it off.

'Hadn't you better get this party started?' he deadpanned. 'Or have we got the wrong day?' Pretty girls began to shut down their computers and re-shuffle their paper into different heaps. Ronald Young, previously engaged on a call, slammed down the receiver and barrelled towards me.

'Anna! How lovely! And the champagne – so generous!' He grasped my shoulders and kissed me enthusiastically. The Lizard sniffed, behind me.

'Are we early?' I asked, as he drew back.

'Early? Good grief, no! Told the chaps to keep working until we saw the whites of the first guest's eyes – and may I say that your whites are looking particularly sparkly and fragrant tonight! Now, would you care for a drink?'

Fragrant whites? 'Lovely – what's on offer?'

He gestured expansively towards the photocopier, the two wine boxes, and the cheese and cherry hedgehog. 'Oh, but my manners!' he burst out, clapping his hand over his mouth. Thank God, he'd remembered the champagne – I'd get some of that. 'Are you driving?' he beamed. 'I've got some lemon squash through the back!'

Frigging heck. Instantly, my next overriding thought was that I had to get through to Omar, to tell him the party had been cancelled and we had to meet at Cino's wine bar in the High Street. Or Beauvins, down East Alley, anywhere, ANYWHERE, but here! I began rummaging inelegantly through my bag for my mobile, until Rod, sensing and possibly sharing my flight instinct, laid a restraining hand on my arm, whispering, 'Come on, Anna – just stay for half an hour!'

Geraldine had stalked over to the photocopier and got to work bustin' open the two wine boxes, aided by one of the insurance girls, who appeared to be a friend of hers. A third produced a polythene bag from under her desk which, from the day-glo colours which peered through, seemed to be bulging with alcopops. Katy and the Lizard stayed resolutely by the door, looking for all the world as though they were thinking along the same lines as me and were about to turn tail and make a break for it.

Fortunately an older woman and two men had ducked off through the back and began re-emerging with trays of what looked like bought-in catering, covered with tinfoil. The two reception desks were hastily shoved together and the foil ripped off to reveal anaemic sausage rolls and triangular sandwiches, dried-up carrot batons, curly chunks of celery and magnolia dip. Mini quiches, shrunken like archaeological relics, vol-au-vents avec pas de vent et beaucoup de tristesse were half-filled with peach-coloured prawn cocktail which had a skin on it and hollered, *E-COLI! Run! Run while you still can!*

'Rod?' I whispered.

'Yes, boss?'

'I'm going to kill myself.'

He turned to face me. 'I'd hate you to do that, Anna.' He had a lovely low voice, actually, and he was standing very close to me, far closer than he ever did in *our* office. I felt a surge of affection towards him, and wanted to link my arm through his, but my party manners held me back. It was far too early in the evening to start making passes at the staff.

Gingerly, he picked up a prawn vol-au-vent and waved it at me. 'Have one of those – it should do the job nicely for you.'

I grimaced, but accepted the offering, and in a burst of what-the-hell bravado, took a bite.

'Not sure about this one, Rod, it's still frozen in the middle.'

A few more people had begun to arrive and maybe, just maybe, the room was beginning to look fractionally more like it had intended to hold a party. I recognised a couple of bankers from up the road, the crowd from Ormerod's, the stockbrokers, who had a dangerous *'We're always up for a party, we are!'* sort of look about them (no bad thing, under the circumstances) – two were wearing bow ties and one was brandishing a magnum of Moët.

Ronald Young surged towards me with a plastic cup of either white wine or lemon squash, who knew – but hang on! What had I just seen? A *magnum of Moët!*

Rod and I, estate agents possessed, made for the man like dogs on heat, swerving past Ronald Young and almost knocking Champagne Boy over as we descended excitedly upon him.

'Anna Morris – Blakemore Properties! I've just come to compliment you on your accessories. And you are?'

The chap must only have been about twenty-five, but he seemed delighted by the blast of attention. 'Hugo Bugo' (or something like that, I was too perked up by his magnificent magnum to pay any attention) '– Ormerod's – a pleasure!'

'May I help you open that?' asked Rod, shaking Hugo Bugo by the hand. 'My boss – Anna, here – doesn't drink anything else and I'm getting jolly worried about her as it's over an hour since her last bottle – Rod Dunsley, by the way. Now, why haven't our paths crossed before? Are you in the market for a new house?'

Two plastic cupfuls of Moët later and it was the best party I'd been to for *years – bloody fantastic!* And after the clock inched past five o'clock the place was suddenly packed with old friends, new friends, acquaintances and general nice folk and I began to actually look forward to Omar's arrival, which was scheduled to be at any moment. Cordelia Young, Ronald Young's twenty-something third wife, arrived looking devastating in a royal blue silk cocktail dress, slashed to the waist, a diamond necklace and blonde hair that didn't even need dyeing to be fabulous, shook her head in disbelief when she saw the food and drink her husband had seen fit to lay on, and instantly sent two of the staff out to Oddbins for some cases of champagne, and to M&S for new nibbles which hadn't been kept in the freezer since their Christmas dance, as the current ones apparently had.

Keeping half an eye trained towards the door, I chatted to the Ormerod's people for a while, moving on when things got a bit golfy to Cordelia Young, who was stroking Rod's arm as they talked about swivel chairs.

'It's all about lumbar support,' she was explaining, moving her hand to the small of Rod's back and beginning to slide it up and down. 'You're very tall, aren't you? Got to watch your coccyx, I shouldn't doubt.'

'Hear that, boss? You've got to watch my coccyx.'

'Do I, now? Lucky me – great party, Cordelia! Oh!'

Jack Anderson had just walked in. Now, why had it not occurred to me that he was going to be there? What was an engineer doing at an insurance party? I watched as his cool eyes swept the room, and flushed dark pink when he noticed me, and smiled. I lifted a shaking hand to wave, and began drifting away from Rod and Cordelia, who had moved on to examining the pressure points of the neck.

How had the room filled up so quickly? Within the space of only about half an hour, we had gone from being a quintet of over-eager planks standing in the doorway, to just a small part of a heaving ball of wool suits and shiny shoes. I prised my way through towards Jack, as diagonally opposite, he began to do the same to get to me. It seemed as though nothing would stop us; our eyes had locked and now was our moment to reconnect . . . until some stupid boy with crap timing offered him a glass of champagne and led him by the arm off towards the Ormerod chappies, who, despite their excellent start in bringing bubbly to the party, had now sprung back into a team knot and were talking loudly amongst themselves. Honestly, isn't networking on their syllabuses, these days? Hugo Bugo stretched out his hand and Jack shook it – not even a glance over his shoulder did he fling towards me – our slow-motion, romantic reunion was apparently all but forgotten – and he was sucked into the Ormerod Pod. I could see the last traces of him disappear behind a wall of designer suits, and unwittingly, I yelped in annoyance.

'Anna! I am sorry to be late.'

Omar looked strained and for once, I was lost for words.

'It took longer than I thought to leave Miranda. Your parents could not have been more charming.'

'I . . . I'm glad.'

'Are you all right? You seem a little tense.'

Well, given that the three men in my life were all under the same roof for the first, and possibly last time ever, that was hardly surprising, was it? I forced a smile and tried to pull myself together.

'How was Miranda when you left?' I asked.

He sighed. 'She was beautiful. She . . . she hugged me, and asked when she would see me again. She cried as I left, as did I.'

I could picture the scene, and it damn near finished me off – oh, God, I should have been there – Miranda would need me to reassure her . . .

'Your parents – they were going to take her for a walk with her dog, and to the ice-cream shop – she was fine, really,' he added, reassuringly, as though reading my mind. 'Such a wonderful child, Anna.'

I nodded at the one certainty of the afternoon.

'How was your day?' he asked, peering into my eyes. 'These people – they seem nice.'

'They are, yes,' I agreed. 'Oh, it was fine, really. A bit eventful – one of my closing dates kept me going for most of the day, but everything's sorted out now.' At least, I hoped so. 'Let me introduce . . .'

But my voice was suddenly almost drowned out by a frantic and insistent blaring of a car horn outside. I craned my neck to try to see what was going on but there were too many people in my way. All around me, people were tutting and frowning – I saw the Lizard hissing, 'Blasted car alarms!' and after the blaring had gone on for about thirty seconds, becoming increasingly loud as it drew near, one or two of the braver Ormerod lads made for the door to investigate.

The blaring became deafening as they opened the door, and as we all craned our necks to see what was going on, there were a few murmured gasps as an enormous, shiny white stretch limousine drew up outside and came to a halt at the door.

And then silence. The horn was finally hushed, and nobody moved a muscle as we waited to see who, or what, lurked within. A few late shoppers paused in their travels and watched the scene and after what seemed like ages but was probably only thirty seconds or so, the driver, splendidly uniformed in full chauffeur's rig-out complete with handlebar moustache and peaked cap, got out of the driver's door, puffed out his chest, marched round the car and opened the back door.

We held our breath. Omar, beside me, was smiling calmly and it crossed my mind that he might have something to do with this but no, he wouldn't be so tacky, would he?

Then, a movement from inside the limo. A white, lace-up shoe. White tights. More uniform? A white, cardboard hat poked itself out next, and a young, fair-haired woman in full nurse's uniform, cape included, uncurled herself from the leather banquette within and jumped out, smoothing herself down when she straightened up on the pavement.

'Wa-hay!' Hugo Bugo was the first to crack. 'Full marks, Ronald! Or was it someone else who ordered her?'

'It bloody better not have been you, Ronald,' Cordelia hissed, looking furious. Her husband just shrugged in bafflement.

'Whose birthday is it?' came a voice.

'Oh!' The Lizard had turned ghostly white. 'No!'

'*Come on, come on, come on, come on!*' the chant began to rise up from the Ormerod corner, as a slow hand-clap, mooted dramatically by Hugo Bugo, was gradually being picked up by some of the lads around the room. I looked at Omar, stricken with horror, but he had his eyes fixed on the scene outside, and his face now wore a look of puzzlement.

Sure enough, when my gaze returned outside, the nurse/stripper had turned back towards the limo and was busily trying to extract what appeared to be a complex piece of equipment.

'Has she brought her snake?' came a voice.

Not a single, bloody soul of them moved a muscle to help as she eventually extracted a shiny zimmer frame from the back of the car.

'Ah.'

The slow clapping trickled to a halt. Mortified hands slid heavily to sides as the chauffeur leaned in to help the nurse assist a very old and decrepit man out of the back of the limo, and to hook him on to his zimmer. The Ormerods, who had let the office door bang shut in their excitement, shrank back as the old man and his nurse made their way across the pavement. It was Jack who leaped across and opened the door, offering his spare arm to the man as he made his rickety entrance.

'*Dusty*,' Monica breathed, stepping forward through the silent crowd.

He smiled a papery smile when he saw her.

'*Peachyschnapps*,' he replied in a quivering, *darned old*, voice.

'What on earth are you doing here?' she hissed, her eyes darting about at everyone, before she moved up to him and clasped her hands on the top of his zimmer frame.

'Fenton?' the old man summoned the chauffeur, who was holding a large polythene bag.

'And who's Fenton?' she went on. 'Dusty, what is this?' She glared at the nurse. 'Ursula, you know it's not good for Dusty . . .'

The chauffeur, who may or may not have *really* been called Fenton, drew out a large tapestry cushion from the bag and stepped forward. 'Just here, sir?' he asked, respectfully, dropping the cushion at the old man's feet as he nodded.

It was the most bizarre sight. A nurse and a chauffeur, each grasping an arm of a man who was eighty-five if he was a day, and propelling him on to his knees on the cushion, where, clasping the zimmer with one hand and laying the other across his chest, he looked up at the Lizard, who for her part, was entirely unable to say or do anything.

'Peachyschnapps,' he repeated, 'will you, at long last, and once and for all and for however long I've got left, stop your silly nonsense and agree, before all these lovely young people, to do me the honour of becoming my wife?'

'Dustybags, *your knees!*' Monica squeaked.

'*Damn* my knees!' he shouted with brio. 'Well, old girl? What do you say?'

'Say yes!' came a voice from the crowd, which sounded awfully like Rod.

'Say yes!' an Ormerod lad repeated, and began an attempt at reviving his slow handclap.

'Say yes!'

'Just do it!'

'Say yes!' The clapping grew louder.

'*Yes!*'

The entire room erupted. Cheers, and whoops filled every corner, and about five people rushed forward to help Dusty unsteadily to his feet. He leaned across the top of his zimmer frame and kissed Monica on the cheek and Monica, quite overcome, buried her face in her hands.

'You old rogue!' she exclaimed from behind her fingers.

Omar leaned in and whispered, 'There is no rogue like an old rogue, is that not correct?'

'Pretty much,' I smiled, taking a deep breath and stepping forward to give Monica a first-ever hug.

'Congratulations,' I whispered.

'Why, thank you!' she replied, tears smudging her heavy eye make-up behind the silly specs. 'I, I never thought he really meant it!'

'Seemed pretty earnest to me,' I said.

'Come on, old gel, let's go dancing!'

'You're on!' she honked back, finding her old voice again, before tearing her boxy lime jacket off, quite provocatively, actually, and thrusting it into my arms. 'Here,' she barked at me. 'I won't be needing this! Not ever again, in fact – whoopee!'

We formed an applauding alleyway for their exit, cheering, and slapping Dusty, ever so gently in case he snapped, on the back. Omar seemed to be enjoying every minute of the spectacle, clapping along with the best of us. Monica hopped girlishly into the back of the limo and Nursula helped her ancient charge in beside her, then with much more tooting, hooting and cheering, they drove away.

I gazed down in astonishment at the warm, lime jacket which the Lizard had bequeathed me.

She had shed her skin.

Chapter Twenty

Omar went off to find a drink and as soon as he left Rod sidled up to me, clamping himself close to my side again and breathing heavily like a long, hot shadow.

'That's quite a tough act to follow, isn't it?' he said after a second or two, nodding towards the door. 'Who'd have thought the old boy had it in him? Or the old girl, come to that?'

I nodded. 'But didn't they look happy? It's so hard to believe that was our old Monica back there. I never really thought she had, well . . .'

'A life?' Rod suggested.

'Mmm, perhaps – no, not that, I knew she was shacked up with an old boy – there's a word, Rod, I'll get to it, just give me a minute . . .'

'Passion?'

The word made me jump, but Rod had hit the nail on the head. 'That's it! Exactly! Who'd have thought she had *passion* in her life?'

'Not me, that's for sure.' Rod was shaking his head. 'Still, just goes to show, there's hope for us all if that old geezer . . . mind you, come to think of it, if the likes of the Lizard's all that's on offer I'll probably be sticking to Internet porn at that age – too scary by half.'

'You're such a charmer.'

'Sorry.'

'S'OK. You're right about the passion, though.'

'Am I?' he murmured. I felt odd, again. Where had this sexy voice of his come from, all of a sudden?

'Everyone needs it in their lives, in some form or another, don't they? Even Mrs Ferguson . . .' I had veered off on an abrupt tangent which ripped through the moment like a bolt from a crossbow.

'Sorry?' Rod had recoiled a little, clearly not expecting the conversation to turn down the Mrs Ferguson road.

'*Passion*, Rod!' I exclaimed, with passion. 'It's not all about . . .' I jerked my head towards his crotch area and raised my eyebrows. 'I know you youngsters.'

'Careful,' he warned, in a low whisper.

'Mrs Ferguson's passion was her home, and it kept her going for years and years, didn't it? And her son's passion is money – I guess it's whatever turns you on, isn't it?'

'So what turns you on then, Anna?' Rod asked. 'That is, if it's not . . .' he returned the glance I had just thrown at his trousers, right down the length of my body. It was nice, but, well . . .

I laid my hand on his arm. 'Rod, I'm sorry, but this is getting a bit, well . . .'

'Sorry. I know.' He took a step away from my side. 'So, well, let me think – do you come here often?'

I smiled at him and we stood in silence for a few seconds until Rod nodded towards Omar. 'That Miranda's father? Not that I need to ask, they're so alike.'

I peered across the room at Omar, who had been intercepted by Cordelia Young and appeared to be at the start of a fairly major interrogation. Cordelia's body language told of a real pro when it came to getting what she wanted out of handsome men; she was leaning in close to him to catch what he was saying whilst he, with practised good manners, kept his eyes attentively upon her face rather than succumbing to the magnetic pull of her cleavage and letting his eyes plunge down her front. 'Do you really think they're alike?'

'Totally, don't you? Erm, he looks like a nice sort of bloke, I guess. So, um, are you two . . .' He was making odd circular motions with the hand that wasn't holding his drink.

'What?' I prodded, although I knew fine what he wanted to say.

'Well, are you going to be *together*, now?' His voice had a strange, tinny edge to it and from my angle he looked a little bit like a big soft puppy who was pleading not to be hit. 'Now that he's come back?'

'Rod, it's been a hell of a day. I . . .'

He backed off for a second time. 'It's OK, Anna, you don't need to tell me anything. Sorry.'

'No, no, don't be! It's just that, well, it's so weird, that's all, having all three men in my life under one roof, that's all.'

'Three?' Rod quizzed. 'What, you mean Miranda's father – Omar, isn't that his name – and Jack Anderson, and . . .'

I looked into his eyes and opened my mouth to speak.

'Ladies and gentlemen!' Ronald Young had climbed on to a chair and was about to make a speech. I was saved, by an insurance salesman. 'Thank you all so much for coming to join us in our little celebration – who would have thought I'd still be in business after all these years?'

'Not us, anyway!' yelled Hugo Bugo. Cordelia Young glowered at him as the men around him laughed corporately.

'But anyway, I'm very proud of what I've achieved here at Young's, and it has been a pleasure and a privilege to have provided so many of you with quality insurance products for so many, happy years. So, if you'd like to raise your glasses . . .'

'Ahem!' Cordelia let out a warning cough. 'Darling, the staff?'

'Sorry?'

She jerked her head crossly in the direction of the Youngs people, who were largely crowded around the drinks table, bent on sinking the equivalent of a couple of years' worth of disappointing pay-rises in the space of two hours.

'Don't you want to . . .'

He twigged. 'Oh! Of course! Just about to say, none of this would have been possible without the help and support of my marvellous staff – past, present and future! Julie, Edwin, Michael, Sara and Dominic! Thank you, chaps!'

'What about Yvonne, Rosemary and Gillian?' his wife prompted.

'Of course! Them too! Cheers, one and all!'

The applause was warm and heartfelt. I could see Jack, momentarily standing alone in front of the floor-length front window, half-silhouetted by the weak early evening sunlight which was worming its way into the room from outside. And then I thought of him, folded almost in half on the floor of the London sleeper, the heat of his body, our stifled giggles, and I felt a surge of possession, a thrill of knowing, which made me want to march over to him and *demand* his attention, given that he hadn't marched over and demanded mine. The silhouette trick made him appear preposterously tall; a busty young Youngs woman who couldn't have been much more than five feet high had just walked over and was trying to attract his attention by flicking her head upwards and taking deep breaths as if to begin speaking; I felt a twinge of awkwardness on her behalf as Jack appeared not to have noticed that she was there at all – she stood a full foot-and-a-bit below his airspace and all her deep breaths were deflected off the lapels of his – rather smart – grey suit. Then as the crowd thinned for a second or two as people repositioned themselves to head for home or to get more to drink, my eyes travelled south and I caught a flash of yellow poking out from the hem of his trousers. Hmm, something distinctly dodgy was happening in his sock department. I smiled, at no one, and shook my head.

'Anna, it is almost time for me to go to the airport.'

'Oh!' I jumped, startled to find Omar at one side and Rod, melting away into the thinning crowd, with a ruefeul little 'catch you later' glance.

'I should have thought,' I said, 'and stuck to the lemon squash, then I could have driven you there,' I mumbled, my cheeks hot at the lack of elegance involved in admitting to being over the drink-drive limit. 'Sorry, Omar, how inhospitable of me.'

He waved my apology away. 'No, no! Your father has kindly offered to take me there – I tried to refuse, but he insisted.'

Something inside me wanted to giggle. *Way to go, dad!* I knew instantly that however well he and my folks had got on, dad would be driving Omar to the airport to make bloody sure he got on that plane and left the district, as planned, without trying on any dodgy kidnapping stunts – I could understand in a way, because although I now trusted Omar absolutely, well, what on earth was a girl's daddy for? 'Oh, that's dad for you,' I said, lightly. 'Always keen to help out.'

'Besides, I would not hear of you leaving your party on my account, you have been more than kind.'

Had I? Had I *really*? I hadn't exactly shown full-on Highland hospitality of Mrs Ferguson quality, but yes I *had*, actually, come to think of it. All around us, throughout his visit and the run-up to it, people had made allowances for him and for the two of us, on sole account of our status as parents of Miranda. Quite right, too, but then . . . maybe enough was enough? Highland hospitality in the Mrs Ferguson tradition might well come heaped up with home-made jam but did it also involve churning up an entire series of relationships to make room for a new element in my life?

Hmm, I sensed the crux of the matter, as I regained my composure and smiled at Omar. He was lovely. Delicious, even, and Miranda was the happiest girl alive for having her father in her life for the first time. Unquestioningly, without bitterness or reproach, she had allowed him to be her father – her *daddy*, no less, but did that mean that I had to make room for him as well? Of course it did in many ways, our lives would now involve trips to London, shared decisions, a whole new sharing in the girl we'd made together, but surely my heart and soul were my own affair?

Or were they? Omar had given Miranda and me a million pounds and a London flat! Not to mention Miranda – he'd given me *her*! Everything I did, and was, and had achieved, could I honestly have done it without Omar? Omar had given me the life which I was now leading; there was little point in denying that. And it wasn't just the money; who knew how much determination to succeed I had derived from the fact of having my daughter? Oh, I could have ended up here, running Blakemore, living in a fancy flat, if I hadn't ever met him, but the stark fact was that my life was where it was because of him. My own efforts aside, had he given me – *everything?*

'I am so glad that you are going ahead with the London flat,' he said. 'I so look forward to spending time with you both in London. There will be so much to show Miranda!'

The surge of gratitude I felt towards him for not pushing things any further between the two of us went beyond words.

Then, just as I was mentally attempting to haul my head together and go and have a word with Jack I realised that I was accidentally thinking about Rod. Rod had given me, oh, what was the best word – *light* – into my working life – fun, friendship and the sort of moral support which went far beyond professional loyalty. Oh, he could be a real wuss, sometimes, his behaviour over the Leversedges being a prime example, but that was only because his heart was so solidly in the right place that it didn't have the sort of room for manoeuvre necessary to get himself safely out of difficult work situations without becoming seriously over-involved. Paradoxically, he just needed to toughen up a bit, in order to let his softer side shine through and to smooth his working path towards the resounding success he was just waiting to be. It was going to be an exciting time for all of us when that boy realised his full potential, and I wanted to be there when he achieved it.

But anyway, back to the business in hand. 'Omar?'
'Yes?'

I had to say it. 'Thank you for coming to find us.'

'Anna?' At last, it was Jack, arriving at my side and introducing himself to Omar, impeccably polite, although a little tense, and distancing his body a little by holding his glass by his side, between us.

I watched as they exchanged polite party chat.

And what of Jack? What had *he* given me? A whole new slant on it all, I guess. The element of choice, some insight into the fact that there were people out there who could challenge you in lots of ways and yet still make you want to hold them in your arms. I mean, work-wise, for heaven's sake, he had almost nicked Ben View from under my nose, and he'd almost certainly had a hand in whipping the Maclarens from Waterbank away, just after sending them to me – because his business interests suddenly made that his best option. He knew I'd survive that one – knew I'd

335

understand, too, after a bit, and the bonkers thing was that I *did* understand – I totally got it. Work is work and anyone who says otherwise has got their work–life balance wrong. Maybe it's a bloke thing, this separating out, but I knew it too. Professionally, I had met my match.

Yet, lest it should be forgotten, Jack had a silly car and a bad flat. Those socks *had* to be investigated. And yet, and yet. Despite almost opening my heart to Rod, and despite Omar being right here in the room, Jack was the one I wanted to have standing beside me. That passion thing. Maybe I had fibbed to Rod. Maybe passion *was* all about . . . I jerked my head discreetly to examine Jack's trouser area and was immediately unsettled once again by that glimpse of yellow at his ankles.

The party was as good as over. Shy Katy was being led away towards Abrams Vodka Bar by a jubilant Hugo Bugo, who gave a less-than-discreet thumbs-up to his mates as he opened the door for her. No way! I began to storm towards them to warn Katy not to be so bloody silly, until I noticed her giving an equally triumphant thumbs-up to Geraldine, who was tucked under the arm of Jeremy fforsythe, on her way out to dinner, and beaming back at her.

And then I was left, stranded, in the middle of the room, opening and closing my mouth like a fish. Omar and Jack had drifted into a small group in the far corner, which, I noticed, included a very animated Iris and a pink-faced Rod, and to my horror I realised that I might be about to cry. The room was swirling and for a few moments it seemed that I was a spectre, a fallen angel, unnoticed in the middle of the room as the party revolved around me. But I wasn't even that drunk! Shit! I was standing in the middle of a metaphor – something deep in my subconscious was telling me that I expected the world to revolve around me when in fact, weren't there other perspectives to take into account? Miranda?

And then, like a message, or a promise, there she was. Bounding in to the room, baseball capped and sneakered, dad's car parked on the kerb outside. It was so good to see her!

'What are you doing here, missy?' I asked, forcing my voice to sound as normal as possible.

'Grampa let me come with him to take daddy to the airport. I wanted to say goodbye again.'

'Did he, now?' I glanced outside and waved at dad, parked on the double yellow, solid, reassuring, and ready to knock the block off anyone who dared to hurt his girls – it was like having full-body armour, or a guardian angel that waved back.

'Mum?'

'Yes, poppet?'

'I asked daddy if you and him were going to get married.'

'You what?' I gasped. 'Miranda – you can't . . .'

'Well, I just wanted to make sure he wouldn't be too upset when he got to know that you had a boyfriend, that's all.'

'Ah,' was all I managed.

'I was scared he'd never come and see us again if you had a boyfriend.' She must have seen the stricken expression on my face because she looked up at me in alarm. 'Mum, I'm really sorry, did I do the wrong thing?'

The tears which had been threatening began to spill from the corners of my eyes. I snatched a serviette from one of the desks, wiped them away, and blew my nose. Bloody hell, almost anyone in the room must have been a more enticing prospect for a man than the churned-up pulp I was turning into. Catching my reflection in a stainless steel tray which was propped up to drain on the sink provided a timely reminder that the men, or boys, who would leave this party without me as their girlfriend may very well be the ones who had had the lucky escape. And Miranda, bless her little pink and white cotton socks with silver lurex threads that unravelled in the wash, had paved the way for my decision.

'No, love, you didn't do the wrong thing at all. You did absolutely the right thing.'

'Well,' shrieked a very familiar female voice from the man-huddle at the window. 'Anna Morris, talk about bloody buses!'

Iris was drunk.

Omar looked in my direction at the sound of Iris's screech, spotted Miranda, and his entire face split into a huge smile as he surged over to envelop her in his arms again.

'Lisa and I spend all this time trying to find *one* man for you, and now here you are with *two* to choose from! Isn't that just a lirrullbit greedy?'

The room fell silent and the remaining guests fell away to the sides as though they were the chorus in a musical and I had some sort of lung-busting aria to unload.

'*Ahem.*' Rod cleared his throat. 'Three, actually. I think she's got three to choose from and if I don't throw my hat into the ring now I may never get another chance. Anna?'

I wanted to be sick. Any teen fantasies I might ever have harboured about having tons of men lusting after me were blown out of the water by the reality of standing in the middle of Young's Insurance Services being asked by a drunk friend to pick a man, in front of half the (admittedly tipsy, most of them) Inverness business community. It was a nightmare. No, it wasn't – I wasn't naked as well, so it had to be really happening, which made it even worse than a nightmare.

'Miranda,' I croaked, 'please go and sit in the car with grampa.' I glanced around the room. Polite people were beginning to restart their conversations, the less polite were still staring but whatever, every sodding one of them had at least one eye on my face. 'In fact, I'll come with you.'

I stalked over to the pile of coats, recognising mine instantly because of its russet silk lining, barked a hoarse thank you to Cordelia Young, who nodded understandingly, and legged it out the door.

'It's OK,' I gasped to dad, who had shot out of his car when he saw my clattery approach. Glancing over my shoulder I saw that Iris, Rod and Omar were in hot pursuit. 'Miranda, can you sit in the car with grampa for a minute? I just have to have a word with the grown-ups.'

'I *hate* the word "grown-ups", it's so babyish!' Miranda threw herself crossly into the back seat of the car and stared straight ahead.

'Sorry.'

Dad tapped his watch. 'Omar has a plane to catch, Anna.'

'I know, dad.'

'Sure you'll be OK?'

'I think so. Just give me five minutes.'

'Four, then I'm coming in.'

I managed a smile. Then I realised it was freezing. 'Come on, let's go into Blakemore for a minute.'

'Fantastic idea – shall we photocopy our bottoms?' suggested Iris.

'Why not?' Rod agreed, although sounding distracted.

Like a teenage gang nipping somewhere quiet for a fag, we hurried along the pavement and as I unlocked the office door and pushed my way into the familiar atmosphere, something about entering my workplace, where I was the one in control, had a profoundly calming effect. I switched the lights on, turned round to face the others, and laughed. Not only because they all looked so out of sorts – Omar, utterly out of his element in the midst of the shambles, Iris, drunk, and Rod, nervously jumpy, but because just behind them, not only was I faced with the sight of Jack slipping in from the pavement as well, but also, sliding up the kerbside like a swan on a pond, dad's car eased into view and dad and Miranda could both be seen peering anxiously in at us.

'This is a bit mad,' I began.

'Too right!' Iris honked. 'Come on, Rob . . .'

'It's *Rod*, actually.'

'Rod! Yes, of course! Come on, Rod, lead me to the photocopier!'

'In a moment,' he replied. 'First, well, I need to know where I stand.'

'You don't stand, that's the whole point! You sit, or squat . . . oh, whatever.' Iris piped down, and shrugged.

'Anna?'

'Yes, Rod, I know.'

'This is really embarrassing, but . . .'

'Rod,' I cut in, taking a deep breath or two, and giving dad a reassuring thumbs-up through the window, all at the same time. 'You're any girl's dream come true, in my opinion.'

'You noticed,' Rod broke in.

'You're generous, thoughtful, caring and hardworking. Do you know, I've just thought – these words are trotted out so often, in reference letters and suchlike, that they almost sound meaningless, don't they? Well, I mean every one of them. But Rod?'

'Yup?' Rod replied, in a low voice – he knew.

'I value you as a friend and colleague more than anyone else in my entire working life, and I hope that, on Monday, you'll be in the office, bright and early for your first day as my assistant manager, but you know what?'

'Yes, I think so, but go on.'

We smiled at each other.

'You're too good for me, Rod.'

'No, I'm . . .'

'. . . and too young for me. Or I'm too old for you, whichever way you want to look at it.'

Iris lurched forwards. 'Are you trying to tell us, Goldilocks, that this man's porridge is too hot for you? My, my, what's your name again? Bob, isn't it? C'm'ere 'til I gerraproperlookatya, baby! Let's go dancing – try to find that old geezer and your friend Monica for a conga, howaboutit?' She made a show of dragging Rod away towards the door, but I caught the knowing, loving wink she gave me as she passed. Rod saw it too, and grinned.

'It's OK, you two, you don't need to worry about me – I can handle rejection. 'Specially when it's comes along in the same sentence as promotion – not confusing at all, that.'

Wow, *that's* how to take it on the chin. Rod had officially grown up. I was so grateful I could have kissed him, but the complications which that would have thrown up were far too hilarious to contemplate. 'Anyway,' he went on, 'after I've spent the weekend drowning my sorrows there's a rather tasty morsel working at the baker's who's been slipping me extra éclairs for weeks, now . . . I'll leave you to it, Anna. Good luck! Bye, Iris, and . . . thanks for the offer to go dancing – raincheck?'

'You're on!' Iris smiled.

We stood in silence, after Rod had gone, until dad, still staring in at us, beeped the horn.

'Anna, I must go,' said Omar.

'But . . .' At last I knew what I wanted to say to him. 'Those nine years took a long time to pass, Omar. And somehow knowing that you didn't completely cut all your ties with us made your absence harder to bear rather than easier, does that make sense?'

He nodded.

'But I will see you and Miranda when you come to London?' he asked, softly.

341

'Of course!' I replied with fervour. 'I'll ring you soon . . . next week, maybe?'

'That would be fine.'

'Anyway, something tells me there's somebody you need to speak to, isn't that right? In Amman?'

He smiled again. 'Perhaps. No, not perhaps – yes, Anna, there is. Thank you.' He picked up his overcoat, walked over and kissed me lightly on both cheeks, glanced over at Jack, inclined his head a little, and walked out of my office, towards the car where dad and Miranda were waiting. I blew them all a kiss and, smilingly, dad pulled away.

Once again I caught Iris's eye. I could see she was absolutely dying to carry on her Goldilocks theme now that she'd started it but if the words 'cold' and 'porridge' were so much as *whispered* from her lips, I would have flown over to her and knocked her block off.

'Which leaves?' came a low voice from the edge of the room. I turned round slowly.

'Which leaves *you*, I guess,' I said, looking into his eyes. He said nothing, but flicked the teensiest glance in Iris's direction before looking back at me.

Iris grinned.

I caught her eye and jerked my head towards the pavement.

She kept grinning.

'Do you need a taxi?' Jack asked her. 'I can call one for you . . .'

'Iris?' I said, gently.

'Yup?' she smirked.

'Thank you for everything you've done, my love, but could you please clear off now?'

She looked puzzled for a moment, before gasping loudly, understanding sweeping over her. 'Good grief, is that the time?' she honked, making for the door. 'I'll go and haul Pete out of Beauvins to take me home, then. You all right, then, Anna? You seem pretty sorted to me, I must say – good choice, too! Jack, you behave yourself, now – you know what they say about engineers!'

'Um, and what would that be?' quizzed Jack.

'Oh, I haven't the faintest idea – I'm just over-excited! Bye, kiddies! Be good!'

'Thanks, Iris, for everything,' I said with fervour.

'Are you kidding? I wouldn't have missed any of this for the world!' she retorted, swishing out of the door and across the street – she was a whole lot less drunk than she'd been making out.

I managed to wave feebly, before letting my hands fall inelegantly into the pockets of my russet silk-lined jacket. There, nestling at the bottom of one of them, I felt the unmistakable contours of a wine gum, and smiled.

'Are you all right?' he asked.

'I . . . I think so,' I replied, shakily. 'Jack, I'm sorry if that was embarrassing . . . I just needed to clear the air . . .'

'Don't worry,' he grinned. 'I got the result I'd been hoping for out of it, didn't I?'

I looked up at him. 'Really?'

He caught hold of my shoulders, gently. 'Oh yes, Anna. I've really missed you! It's been torture for me, leaving you alone to work through all this stuff.'

'Has it? I wondered whether you might have appreciated the space.'

'Not a bit of it. God, the number of times I've half-dialled your number, driven past your flat . . .'

'You haven't!' I said in surprise. 'I'm sure I'd have recognised the roar of your car engine, for one thing!'

He looked down at his feet. 'Um, I've changed the car, actually. You shamed me into it.'

'No!'

'Bought a Porsche.'

343

'What?' I was aghast. 'You haven't!'

He smiled, very, very sexily. 'Nah, I haven't – just wanted to see your face – I've gone for something that doesn't need a tin opener to get in and out of – very boring, if you ask me, but there you go – the things you do for . . .' he stopped short. *Just* short.

'Well, that's nice,' I said, after a pause.

Silence.

'Anna?'

'Yes, Jack?'

'Um, given that Miranda's being looked after for the time being – would you like to go somewhere a little more . . . comfortable? Dinner at my place? I've been working on my *restaurateur* skills since your last visit – or at least, I can order up the best Thai food you've ever had . . . ? Go on, please?'

He was leaning towards me. I could *smell* him.

I had to stand on tiptoes to whisper in his ear, 'Lift up your trouser leg.'

'Sorry?'

'You heard.'

He did.

Confirmation. Horrible, hideous . . . but not entirely unreconstructable, Homer Simpson socks.

'I can see that being with you is not going to be without its challenges,' I murmured, as I switched off the light, locked the office door and we left to go somewhere a little more . . . comfortable.